To Jean,
with
best wishes,
Helen
Spring

Strands
of
Gold

Helen Spring

PublishAmerica

Baltimore

First printing

ISBN: 1-4137-0453-0
PUBLISHED BY PUBLISHAMERICA, LLLP
www.publishamerica.com
Baltimore

Printed in the United States of America

For

Bob and Chris

With Love

PRELUDE

Western Australia, 1871

The first hint of trouble was the cold touch of the shotgun muzzle behind Jarvis Mottram's left ear.

"Who are you?" The voice was rasping, breathless, and yet oddly familiar. Jarvis gulped in air. His heart thumped wildly as he tried to blot out the insistent pressure of the gun.

"Mottram. Jarvis Mottram. I'm a stockman here."

"Why visit a barn at this time of night?"

"Came to check on a heifer…that one over there, she's due to calve."

The gun pressure increased, forcing Jarvis's head sideways.

"I don't believe you. Since when did the Lamont station play midwife to its heifers?"

The tone was sarcastic, prompting Jarvis to burst out defiantly, "It's one of the new pedigree herd, they calve here in the barn so we can keep an eye on them."

There was a soft exhalation of breath, and then a noticeable relaxation of tone as the gunman said quietly, "Alright Jarvis. Didn't mean to startle you. Just stand there while I think. Don't move."

I couldn't if I tried, Jarvis thought, still trembling with shock.

It has been said that when calamity threatens, when imminent disaster is about to change ones life forever, a sixth sense emerges to warn the unlucky recipient of Fate's caprice, and give a premonition of danger.

Jarvis Mottram regarded such intuitive insights as nothing but old wives tales, and he certainly had sensed no such warning as he squelched his way through the driving rain and thick, ankle clogging mud to the barn. Rather, he had been cursing his own over developed sense of responsibility, for who else would have ventured out in the worst wet in living memory, just to check that the heifer would be comfortable until next day.

"I must see my brother."

The gunman spoke suddenly, and at his words Jarvis could not resist the temptation to turn his head.

"Jack!" he burst out angrily. "What on Earth…?"

"I knew you'd remember me, damn it!"

The speaker pushed his sodden bush hat to the back of his head with the shotgun. He looked all in, a small, wiry man, unkempt and unshaven, but his black eyes held a slight smile, and a curious alertness.

"Of course I remember you!" Jarvis's sense of shock gave way to anger. "What do you think you're doin' out here in the barn skulkin' about…and pointin' guns at people! A fine way to come home after all this time…"

Jack Lamont raised both arms in a gesture of surrender.

"Alright Jarvis, calm down. I'm sorry, but I didn't want anyone to know I was here…"

"But why on earth not…?"

"Never mind why." Jack's tone was peremptory. "I must see my brother…"

"Well come up to the house, Mr. Henry's gone to bed but we can soon wake him…"

"No! I told you. No one is to know I am here…"

Jarvis decided enough was enough.

"Now look here Mr. Jack, I don't know what your problem is or why you don't want to be seen, but if you think I'm goin' to get Mr. Henry out of a warm bed, and down here on a night like this, you're surely mistaken!" Once started, Jarvis warmed to his theme, his Devon accent becoming more pronounced, as it always did when he became roused.

"You'll come up to the house with me," he continued, taking charge of the situation. "To the kitchen, you look as if you can do with a meal. Everyone is in bed so you'll not be seen. I'll fetch Mr. Henry and then you can do as you like, but let's have no more nonsense!"

Jack looked at him darkly, but he followed Jarvis through the drenching rain up to the house and made no further comment. At the back door however, he stopped.

"No one is to know I'm here, apart from Henry."

"I heard you first time…" Jarvis grumbled.

"Jarvis, I mean it. Not tonight, or tomorrow after I've gone. No one must know I've been home…"

"Tomorrow? You don't mean you've come home after all this time to be off again right away?"

"Promise Jarvis. You were always an honest man. Give me your word you'll tell no one."

Jarvis sighed. "Alright, I promise. You're obviously in trouble of some kind..." he said as they entered the warm kitchen.

Jack smiled broadly. "Don't you worry about me Jarvis; I'm not in any trouble."

Jarvis fetched a loaf of bread and some cold meat from the larder. "Help yourself," he said shortly. "I'll get Mr. Henry."

Henry Lamont was both surprised and annoyed to be awakened so soon after retiring, and Jarvis saw his mouth tighten at the news he brought. He hurried into his dressing gown however, and strode off to the kitchen.

Jarvis left the house, recollecting that he still had not checked on the heifer, and slowly made his way back through the thick mud to the barn. However, Fate still declined to send a warning, and he had no premonition that his life would never be the same again.

Chapter One

Singapore - 25 years later

"Well young lady, is Singapore as you remembered?"

Lucy Rowlands turned with pleasure at the sound of the gentle Scottish lilt. It belonged to Margot Graham, with whom she had shared a cabin on the steamship *Aurora* during the cramped but uneventful journey from England, and the two had become firm friends.

Lucy laughed and took Margot's arm. "Oh Margot, it's even more colourful, and certainly noisier than I recall it." She looked around excitedly, transported back six years, to the sights and sounds of her childhood. The bustle and clamour of the harbour at Tanjong Pagar fascinated her as it had always done, but it was the smell, redolent of exotic spices and heavily scented flowers, which let her know she really had come home to Singapore.

Lucy drank in the scene with obvious pleasure, her blue eyes sparkling with excitement and anticipation. "Of course, there are changes," she informed Margot, walking her along the deck to obtain a better vantage point. "So many steamboats in the harbour, apart from the *Aurora*. When I left here six years ago I had never even seen a steam engine of any kind, and when I arrived in England and had to board the train to London I remember I was terrified of the big monster!"

Margot laughed. "Yes, it's a wonderful invention, and has shortened our journey from England a great deal, but Lucy dear, please put up your parasol, you must be careful to protect your complexion here."

Lucy gave a sigh, but quickly opened the cream parasol, which she had trimmed herself with braid chosen to exactly match the cornflower blue walking suit she wore for her arrival. Leaning over the ship's rail however, she caught the edge of the parasol in her tiny hat, a ridiculous confection of pale straw and cream silk roses, almost dislodging it from its carefully angled perch on her thick chestnut hair. "Oh dear!" she giggled, "I do so hate wearing these newfangled things, a bonnet is so much simpler!"

"Come here child," said Margot indulgently, "I never knew a bairn so likely to get into mischief!"

She re-arranged the hat carefully, marvelling for the hundredth time at the purity of Lucy's complexion, and the chiselled grace of the high cheekbones and pert nose above her generous mouth. *How wonderful to be eighteen years old*, Margot reflected, *with a face and figure beautiful beyond imagining, and yet to be totally unaware of the fact!*

"There. A pretty picture for your father to meet," Margot fussed, adding "Do be careful," as Lucy returned to the ship's rail.

But Lucy could not bear to miss anything, and laughed delightedly as she called, "Oh, Margot, look!"

A small boat squeezing alongside almost capsized as the boatman, a painfully thin Malay with a huge grin but missing teeth, balanced cleverly in the prow, holding aloft trays of coconut cakes and bananas for sale.

Lucy's eager gaze took it all in. Home at last! Although she had enjoyed England, and would miss her school friends, and of course dear Uncle Matthew, it was Singapore she thought of as home. Her eyes scanned the crowds waiting on the quayside. Her father would surely be here to meet her. Even though his last letters were full of discouragement, to the point of suggesting she might be better to stay in England, she knew that in his heart he would be overjoyed to see her again.

Margot gave a shriek, "William! William dear!" She nudged Lucy, and her florid face assumed an even deeper hue. "There's my husband."

Lucy saw a tall, grey haired man in a top hat and frock coat making his way up the gangway. He waved his hand and called as he approached them.

"My dear, oh! but it's good to have you home!"

He kissed his wife gently on the cheek, and Lucy was touched to see their affection portrayed so openly. Introductions were quickly made, and Lucy did not miss the look of surprise on William Graham's face when Margot explained who she was.

"James Rowlands daughter you say?" He seemed disconcerted. "I can't say I've seen James here, was he coming to meet you?"

Lucy flushed. "There was no arrangement as such, but he knew I would be on the *Aurora*, and I imagined he would be here."

William Graham took her arm. "Then you shall come with us my dear. Don't worry; I think your father goes out very little these days. He's probably sent a driver for you."

Lucy felt a painful lump in her chest. After all these years, not to bother to meet her! She followed William and Margot as they left the ship, only half hearing Margot's nonstop flow of chatter.

During the journey Lucy had become accustomed to listening to Margot with only one ear. William was a bank manager in Singapore, and in consequence, Margot knew almost everyone who either lived there, or passed through. Apparently all the 'best people' on the fashionable globe-trotting Eastern circuit stayed at Government House, and Margot had an endless supply of titbits of useless information on all these notable folk. She knew their faults and foibles, their taste in clothes, and their family antecedents, and expanded on these at length. There had been, Lucy gathered, an increasing supply of new colonial subjects for Margot's scrutiny, with the adoption of Singapore as a new Crown Colony the year before, just prior to her trip to visit her family in England.

As they came ashore, Lucy managed to put on a composed and even happy performance. She sensed, knowing Margot, that her arrival would be fully discussed at the afternoon teas and sewing circles of European Singapore. The fact that she had not been met, whilst not being unkindly reported, would engender the sad upward look of Margot's eyes, and the sigh of "Poor wee bairn!" a phrase she continually used with reference to Lucy.

William left them to look for a driver, and Margot took Lucy's arm, and said with her faint Scottish burr, "My dear, you must promise to let me know if there is anything you need, or if you have any problems."

Margot smiled nervously as she said this, and not for the first time Lucy felt that Margot was privy to knowledge, which she did not share. She returned the smile however, and said happily, "I certainly hope we shall keep in touch."

At that moment William returned, and to Lucy's relief said reassuringly, "Don't worry; there is a driver here for you. It's rather an old cart, but it will take your luggage easily."

He gestured to the driver, a disreputable looking Malay in filthy cotton drawers. The man stared at Lucy, and muttered something unintelligible. He buckled to however, and Lucy's luggage was quickly stowed on the cart. Lucy turned to her companion.

"Thank you for your company Margot. I have appreciated it so much." She climbed up into the front of the cart, gathering her skirts into the small space. Margot hovered uncertainly.

"Are you sure you will be all right?"

"Of course. Move on please driver." Lucy turned and waved. "And thank you once again for your help Mr. Graham."

The cart drove away, and William and Margot Graham watched it weave through the crowded harbour traffic towards the Jahore road.

"Oh William," Margot sighed, "She doesn't know. She thinks everything is the same as when she went away."

"Didn't you tell her?"

"I couldn't. I did try to tell her there were problems at Winchester Station, but she said she would help her father to sort them out."

William took his wife's arm. "Lucy Rowlands isn't your responsibility my dear."

"I know that William, but she's such a sweet girl, and those looks, I never saw a prettier creature. That lovely chestnut hair, and the eyes William! A real sapphire blue, just like her mother's. Do you remember her mother?"

William sighed. "Yes of course, and Lucy is certainly a beauty. It was a tragedy she was sent away to school when her mother died. But my dear, it's not your concern…"

"But she's only eighteen William, she needs friends, someone to turn to…you recall William, that our dear Morag would have been about Lucy's age by now."

"Of course." William regarded his wife fondly. "As soon as I saw Miss Rowlands I realised that would have been on your mind, and no doubt you have become very fond of Lucy during the journey. But our darling Morag was taken from us at six, and if she had lived she may have been quite unlike Lucy Rowlands. Lucy is not our daughter my love, and you must remember it." The hint of admonition in his tone softened as he smiled and added, "I can see by your face you will take no notice of anything I say, and will be mothering Lucy in no time at all."

Margot smiled happily. "I certainly shall," she agreed, "If she'll let me. She has a very independent spirit that one. Anyway, with those looks I expect she'll be married in no time, poor wee bairn."

As Margot climbed into the elegant carriage which was to take them into town, her pleasure at seeing William again gave way to a more subdued mood. As usual, the mention of their much loved daughter's death had cast its long shadow, and William reached for her hand in quick understanding. Margot smiled up at him and gave his hand a squeeze. "Oh William," she sighed, "It is so good to be home."

As the cart trundled slowly along the streets of Singapore, Lucy marvelled at the changes which had been wrought since she last saw the town. She noticed immediately the elegance of the wide streets, and the large white bungalows surrounded by well kept green lawns and exotic borders. There was an air of languid well being about the place, as if the jungle had at long last been banished forever. As they left the poorer, built up suburbs however, it became apparent that this was not the case. The dense, green wall of jungle still waited on either side of the narrow road, and in the wood and thatch kampongs visible in the clearings, Lucy recognized the age old patterns of planting and gathering she remembered from her youth.

Lucy was not entirely sure what her welcome would be, and the fact that her father had not been at the harbour to meet her intensified her unease. Again, she wondered vaguely what Margot had meant when she had hinted that all was not well at Winchester station. Yet when Lucy had wanted to talk about her father, Margot had always changed the subject, and there had been an implied criticism, which Lucy had quickly suppressed. She reasoned that if her father had let things go a little, then it was a good thing she had returned home.

Lucy's heart began to pound with excitement as the rickety cart drew nearer to Winchester station, and she craned forward, eager for the first sight of her old home, certain that they were now traveling through the Winchester plantation. To her astonishment she saw that the coffee crop was fully ripe, indeed, the beautiful red berries were dropping. She turned to the driver.

"You speak English?"

The man nodded assent.

"Is today a holiday? Festival? Why no work?"

The man grinned. "No work on Winchester station now Miss. No work. Not for long time."

"But of course there is work. The coffee is rotting! Why is it not being picked?"

The man shrugged. "Coffee not picked long time now. Mr. James not pay. Men not work if Mr. James not pay."

For the first time Lucy felt real apprehension. Things must be much worse than she had thought. *Even if her father was short of money, surely the bank would lend him sufficient to pay the pickers until the crop was in and sold?* As she reflected on these matters, her concern grew, and as the cart turned into the entrance she leaned anxiously forward, only to draw in her breath sharply at the sight of the house.

The small Georgian style manor had been newly built when Lucy's parents had arrived in Singapore in 1875, but now Winchester Station, named for Alice Rowlands home in England and once so proud, white and elegant, was a ramshackle monument to neglect and ruin. Paint had peeled to the point of non-existence, windows were filthy and many were broken. A side door to the verandah hung drunkenly off its hinges, and everywhere the once beautiful gardens were a rampant jungle of invasive weeds.

The sight of the dereliction was like a physical blow. Lucy had nurtured the remembrance of her home for so long, and had looked forward to her return as a time for joy, celebration, and happy reunion. Her dream of an idyllic future crumbled, as she realized why Margot had been so reticent to discuss Winchester station. What had happened here? And why had Margot not warned her? Lucy realized belatedly that of course Margot had tried to do just that. *Only I wasn't listening,* she reflected bitterly. She became aware of the driver, who was waiting to help her down from the cart. He smiled up at her happily.

"Miss happy to be home! Soon be fix now like before! English ladies always fix good!"

Lucy got down from the cart slowly. She looked carefully at the driver, but did not recognise him.

"You were here before? In the old days? When—when—"

Her voice faltered. The driver, busily unloading her trunk, grinned cheerfully.

"Oh yes Miss. I am worker on coffee then. My name Liam. I remember your mama, very pretty lady. When I see you at ship,I think it is your mama again! You soon fix! You bring much money from England!" He gestured fiercely, and continued in his staccato manner, "Come in Miss! Come in! Mr. James through here!" He grinned again. "I get food, and good tea! And good gin sling!"

Lucy stared at his filthy hands. "Food?"

"Yes, Liam get food. No servants now. Me top boy now!" He hurried through the dingy hallway, pushing aside scattered copies of *The Straits Times* which littered the floor, calling, "Mr. James, Miss here! Miss come after all!"

Lucy tried to collect her wits. Her father must be ill, that was the only explanation for this dreadful state of affairs. She must be calm, and take care of him, and never let him see her disappointment. She took a deep breath, and then realized she was not alone.

In the far doorway stood her father, older, greyer and smaller somehow, but still, unmistakably, her dear father. His clothes, shabby and creased, hung on his frame loosely, and his eyes were tired and vacant. He stared at her a long time, and looked confused.

"Lucy? So you came after all? I thought perhaps you wouldn't, after my last letter."

"Of course I came. Where else should I go when I finished school, but here with you?" She approached him gently. "Oh father! It is so good to see you, to be home at last."

James Rowlands embraced her gently. "I couldn't believe it child. Just couldn't believe it, you are so beautiful, just like your mother…" His voice was hoarse with emotion.

Lucy took his arm and they went through to the drawing room. She was shocked at the neglected state of the once elegant room, but she sat down and smiled up at her father.

"Matthew sends his love."

"Ah, yes. How is my dear brother? Although I really feel you should call him Uncle Matthew, you sound rather disrespectful."

Lucy laughed. "I do call him uncle, sometimes, but Matthew and I are friends, true friends. You cannot imagine how good he has been to me. Always came to the Founders Day ceremony at school, and to see me in the tennis finals last term…"

"Been more of a father to you than I have. That's what you mean isn't it?" His tone was defensive.

"Of course not, father. You were here, so how could you look after me in England? All I meant was that I have become very close to Matthew."

Lucy leaned towards her father and kissed his cheek. "And now we shall become close again too, just like we were before I went away." She hesitated. "Why didn't you want me to come home father?"

"I should have thought that was obvious," he replied bitterly. "Don't patronize me Lucy. or try to treat me like a fool, just because you've had an expensive education."

Lucy blenched. "I'm sorry father. It's been a bit of a shock that's all. I can't understand how things got into this state. But we'll have our tea, and you can tell me about it, and I'll do what I can to help."

Suddenly an awful thought struck her.

"Father, was it my education, my school fees? I know they were expensive, and you've been having such a dreadful time."

"Ha! No such thing. Haven't paid school fees for four years or more." His tone became sarcastic. "No my dear, your conscience can be clear. You were not a contributor to my downfall."

Lucy was bemused. "Not paid my fees? Then how…?"

"Your Uncle Matthew, of course." Her father had the grace to appear slightly shamefaced. "Decent old stick Matthew. A dry old stick certainly, but also a decent old stick!"

He swayed slightly as he made his little joke, and Lucy suddenly realized he was drunk. *So this was her father's problem! It would also explain why friends in Singapore had dropped him, as it certainly appeared they had.*

Lucy felt a rising panic. She hadn't banked on this. Suddenly she seemed to hear the voice of Miss Collins, her old headmistress, addressing her class on the subject of "life skills."

"When you are faced with a difficulty, and don't know what to do, take action. It doesn't really matter what you do, as long as you do something. The action itself will give you time to think."

Lucy swallowed. "Father, I intend to find my room and attempt to make it habitable, which I'm sure it is not at present. I shall see myself installed, and try to ensure that our food is prepared in a hygienic manner. That's all I can hope to do for today. However, tomorrow I shall start to organize things on a better footing. In the meantime, may I request that you drink nothing further, so that you have a clear head tomorrow?"

She turned and went out, meeting Liam with a tray of tea.

"I'll have my tea upstairs in my room Liam, please. And then bring me a bucket of water, soap if we have some, and a scrubbing brush."

Liam stared at her receding back as she mounted the stairs. He looked at James Rowlands, who had a slight smile of wonder on his face. "A chip off the old block Liam!" he said slowly. "Yes, surely a chip off the old block!"

That evening, Lucy lay in bed and listened to the faint but unmistakable jungle sounds which penetrated the warm evening air. The chatter of a disturbed grey monkey, the sudden squeal of a wild pig, and near at hand the buzz of a hornet which had entered when she threw open the windows to freshen the room, and which now found itself singed by her candle. The exertions of cleaning her bedroom had tired her, but the physical exhaustion was as nothing compared to the confused tangle in her mind. Amidst the incoherent jumble of her reflections, one thought, of sweetest comfort, sustained her. *Dear Matthew! How like him to pay her school fees all those years and never even mention it. It wasn't as if he was wealthy, in fact quite the reverse.* She suddenly realized how much she would miss the quiet strength of her dear uncle and friend, and she felt utterly alone. She resolved to write to Matthew next day, to give him news of her safe arrival and to express her thanks. But this decision brought scant consolation, and with her thoughts still in turmoil, Lucy fell into a fretful sleep.

Chapter Two

"Miss— why we not have new cart?" Liam grumbled. He was immensely proud of his new cotton shirt and shorts, and worried about risking his finery in the rickety old contraption which was still the only means of transport at Winchester station.

"All in good time Liam" Lucy murmured, watching her father as he climbed into the cart. "Now take good care of Mr. Rowlands, and I'll see you both tomorrow." She waved as the cart trundled away, and her father responded with a cheerful grin.

Lucy sighed. She was tired, as she was most days now. Still, things were improving slowly, and she had learned a great deal in the last three months. She looked out over the garden to where Jarvis Mottram was pruning a straggling frangipani. Lucy regarded his grey hair and grizzled beard, and thanked God again for his strength. The old gardener had been willing to come and work for her for a while, without pay.

"For old time's sake Miss Lucy", was how he had put it, "and in memory of your dear mother, who was a true lady if ever I met one."

Lucy was painfully aware of what it must have meant to the old man to see the gradual decline of the garden he had tended with such care for so many years. She descended the verandah steps and walked down the reclaimed path towards him, noting every new flower bed or shrub which had been rescued from the wilderness. The garden was at last beginning to have some order. Like the house, it was responding to the consistent and painstaking daily routine of reclamation and refurbishment. Lucy looked down at her hands and sighed. Miss Collins would have prescribed immediate rosewater treatment and the compulsory wearing of gloves for at least a month. She let her mind dwell for a moment on sweet memories of cheerful school friends, and tennis matches under grey rumbling skies. In retrospect, she realised that the real luxury of her school life had been time itself. Moments of privacy and relaxation had been sadly lacking since she came home to Singapore.

Suddenly a few raindrops splashed her, foretelling one of the short heavy downpours which came every day in season.

"Jarvis!" she called, "Come into the house for a break, quickly!" She turned and ran, reaching the verandah well ahead of Jarvis, and laughing as she watched him fling himself into the shelter of the steps, rain streaming down his face and dripping from his beard.

"Oh lawks Miss! 'Tis all right for you to laugh! I'm soaked!" Despite forty years away from his native land, he still retained a lilt of Devon. He began to chuckle. "If the truth's told, I just can't move fast enough any more!"

"Come into the kitchen," Lucy led the way. "We'll have some lemonade." She handed Jarvis a towel and fetched the large glass jug from the larder, setting it down on the scrubbed table. "I wanted us to talk, Jarvis, if you don't mind. You are one of the few people who will remember how it was at Winchester Station before my mother died. I've been away so long, and so much seems to have changed…" She stopped, and a slight blush came to her cheeks as she poured the lemonade.

"Bless you, Miss, you don't have to worry about old Jarvis. I've known your family a long time, any secrets are safe with me. I'm not one for gossipin', never have been."

"I know that, Jarvis, and I can't understand what happened here. I've tried to talk to father, but he just tells me 'things became difficult' and changes the subject."

Jarvis took a swig of his lemonade.

"Yes," he sighed deeply. "He had a bad time of it, after your mother died. Perhaps it was because she was such a well-organized person, I don't really know. Took it real hard, your pa did. Didn't seem to be able to pull himself together. Lost interest for a bit, so to speak. After all, 'twas only natural. Lost his lovely young wife, and his little girl gone away to England; he seemed lost, somehow. And then…well…" he hesitated.

"I know about the drinking Jarvis, if that's what you were about to say."

"Well, yes, Miss Lucy, it did become a problem. At first people were sympathetic, said he was drownin' his sorrows, like. But it got worse. Caused a few problems at the British Club, at least so I understand. Of course I saw none of that myself, my not being a member, or in that class, so to speak."

Lucy thought she detected a hint of irony in the last words. She refilled his glass. "Please go on, Jarvis."

"Well, Miss, I could well believe the things that were bein' said about him, for the simple reason that I saw him comin' home most mornin's, just as I was arrivin' for work. Always the worse for drink he was…I'm sorry, Miss Lucy."

"That's alright Jarvis. I must know everything if I am to help him. Just pretend you're speaking to a stranger, not his daughter."

"All right, Miss. Well, he'd be sleepin' it off most of the day, and then when he woke up he'd be off again, on the same old round of drinkin' and gamblin'. It went on for months. Some of his friends tried to help. One chap, an officer in the army, lieutenant I think, even came to stay with him, to try and dry him out. 'Twern't no use. They all gave up eventually. He was so rude to them see? At first the staff tried their best to cope, to do what they had always done in the past, and keep things goin'. But it became impossible for them. No one gave any directions, and after a while no one even got paid. A few of the best staff got other jobs, they were well trained by your mama so they had no difficulty. The rot really set in after that. The coffee pickers thought they wouldn't get paid so the crop wasn't gathered. I stayed on as long as I could. I worked for nearly nine months without pay, then I decided I would have to stop, as I was eatin' into my little bit of capital. I had been savin' for years to buy a boat to live on when I retired. If I'd stayed any longer I should never have had the *Selangor Lady*."

Lucy pressed the old man's hand. "Thank you Jarvis. Thank you for doing what you could. As you know, we have very little money but perhaps one day I shall be able to make it up to you."

"Bless you Miss Lucy, you've done that already! Just to see you come home, and start to get things shipshape again, it's been a tonic to me!" he laughed. "To be honest Miss Lucy, although I'm satisfied with my old boat, I was well pleased to have a change from fishin'!"

"Do you catch much fish?"

"Oh, I don't do too badly. *Selangor Lady* is my home, and I catch enough fish for myself and some over to sell, so I get by. It's about five years now since I left, and I haven't seen much of your father since then. I gather that after a time there was no one left here at all except Liam, who agreed to stay, just for his food and lodgin'. He was not trained, and I think he had nowhere else to go." He smiled broadly. "Your coming home was a godsend for your father, Miss Lucy. He is lookin' like a new man already. When I saw him climbin' into the cart this mornin' to go into town, he looked so spruce, it was quite like old times."

"Yes, but I'm not sure about him being a new man. He still seems very anxious, and tries to avoid telling me anything. Today, for instance, I have no idea where he has gone. He received a note yesterday, apparently from a business acquaintance, who asked that father meet him in town today.

19

Although it's rather mysterious, I can't help feeling it must be good for father to take an interest in business again at last."

"Of course, so what still worries you? Do you fear Mr. Rowlands will be persuaded to indulge himself too much at the Tiffin rooms?"

"Oh no. There have been a few lapses of course, but not for some weeks. Father is looking so much happier now, and more confident. I do not believe he will need to drink, at least not overmuch."

Lucy walked to the window. The rain had just stopped, and she watched for the familiar steaming of the undergrowth as the hot sun reappeared.

"I don't know why I feel worried," she said finally, "Except that I don't see how father can have gone to see anyone on business, because we have none left. We do not even have a bank account any longer. I have been through all the papers and we are penniless, Jarvis. We have no crop to sell, so how can father be doing any business? The little money I brought with me from England is gone long since. It is only because I sold a brooch of my mother's that we have managed thus far."

A fleeting image crossed her mind, and she winced as she saw again the cold appraising stare of the Chinese trader who had turned the brooch over and over in his stubby fingers. *What it had cost her to part with it!*…and how bitter her anger as she blindly drove the cart back to the house, clutching her meagre profit, far less than the brooch was worth. She turned to Jarvis.

"I have very little money now," she said, "and nothing else to sell. The best of the furniture was already gone when I came home, and what is left would bring very little. Somehow we have to last out until I can get a coffee crop in. If we can hold on until then at least we shall have something to build on."

Jarvis sighed. "You mustn't bank too much on that Miss Lucy. Even if the crop is good and you can get it picked, the coffee prices have hit rock bottom. Last season all the growers were complainin' that the coffee wasn't worth pickin'."

"That all depends on how much you have to start with," replied Lucy grimly. "When you have nothing at all, even a pittance is an improvement. I'll get a crop in, even if I have to pick it myself."

Jarvis looked at the determined tilt of her chin and smiled. He had seen that look before, on her mother's face, when she had been put out, or suffered some small annoyance. He smiled at Lucy affectionately.

"You won't have to pick it all yourself," he countered. "There'll be the two of us at least, and we can rope Liam in."

20

He was rewarded by a dazzling smile.

James Rowlands arrived home next day about noon, and to Lucy's relief bore no sign of the after effects of drink. However, as Lucy went to greet him, she noticed that his new found confidence seemed to have deserted him, and as he climbed down from the cart he seemed unable to meet her eyes. Lucy enquired about his trip, but he made no reply until he was inside the house. Then he instructed Liam to bring tea right away, and turned to Lucy.

"Please come into the drawing room dear, I have to talk to you."

His tone was peremptory, and Lucy experienced a slight sense of foreboding as she noticed his agitation. She followed her father into the drawing room, and waited as he went over to the window and stood looking out, his back to her. As he seemed unwilling to speak, after a few moments Lucy ventured quietly, "Does what you have to say bear on our financial situation father?"

"Indeed it does my dear."

Suddenly Lucy was certain she had it. Her father had been to town to obtain a position for her, a governess perhaps, or a companion to an elderly lady. Such employment would at least keep her, but what would happen to Winchester Station in her absence? Lucy's mind probed the possibilities, fluctuating between hope and despair, as her father continued his contemplation of the garden. At length however, he turned to face her.

"My dear daughter, I have to tell you that you are to return to England right away, back to your Uncle Matthew. I'm afraid I do not have the fare, but I thought that perhaps your friend Mrs. Margot Graham might advance you the necessary amount…"

"Back to England?" Lucy's mouth dropped open.

"Yes Lucy."

"But father, why? Are you coming too?"

"No, I shall stay here."

"But I should much prefer…"

"It is not a question of preference Lucy, but one of necessity. There is no point in arguing, the decision is made."

At that moment Liam entered with the tea tray, and they fell silent until he had left the room. James Rowlands crossed from the window and took a seat in the armchair facing Lucy. He indicated that she should pour the tea, and in spite of her apprehension she did this calmly enough, trying to quell her rebellious feelings. She handed her father his cup and saucer and asked quietly, "Am I to receive an explanation?"

Her father put down his cup. "Of course. I should have told you long ago, as soon as you came home, but I wanted to spare you if I could..." His voice faltered, but he recovered himself and said shortly. "Everything is to be sold. We have no money and no hope of any. You must go to England right away, to your Uncle Matthew..."

"But our problems won't last forever father. As soon as we can get a crop in we shall be able to start again. It will be difficult, but after a couple of years..."

"No!" he interrupted sharply. "There is no chance of our being able to survive, believe me Lucy."

"But we can't sell Winchester Station, it's our home! Don't be downhearted father, together we can find a way, I will help you..." Lucy entreated.

James Rowlands turned away with a strange cry, and flung himself into the window seat.

"Oh Lucy, Lucy! If you love me, obey me in this! You must do so! You must!"

His agitation was extreme. He wrung his hands and Lucy was shocked and moved at the extent of his distress.

She took his arm and asked gently, "What is it father? Whatever it is we can face it. It doesn't matter if we are poor as long as we are together. I want to stay here with you, to take care of you."

"You don't understand Lucy, you don't understand..." he gasped, crying now.

"Then make me understand," she said gently, pulling his hands from his face and forcing him to meet her eyes. "Please tell me."

Slowly he controlled himself. He looked at her anxious face and his eyes fell. "There are debts," he said shortly. "It isn't a matter of getting a crop in. The house itself, and the whole estate is mortgaged to the hilt. We can never, never hope to repay the interest, and even less the capital."

He raised his hand in protest as Lucy made to speak.

"No Lucy, hear me out, you have to know. I owe a large amount in addition to all that...to someone else..."

"The man you went to see today?" Lucy asked faintly.

"Yes, Sir Gilbert Howell. He's a local man, very wealthy, owns a big estate, and tin mines. I thought I could persuade him to wait longer but he's insisting on payment right away."

"How much do you owe him?"

James Rowlands hung his head, and his voice was hardly audible. "Five thousand pounds."

"But how? So much?" Lucy wavered.

"Gambling." He made an effort to control his trembling hands. "I mortgaged the estate to the bank, and then the house and I lost it all. The bank is going to foreclose on the mortgage...yes Lucy, your friend Margot Graham's husband is going to sell us up!"

"Mr. Graham? Oh father I'm sure he won't! I'll go to see him..."

"It won't do any good Lucy. To be fair, he has held off foreclosure for a long time already, but now he is under pressure from his Head Office for the debt to be cleared."

"And the money, you lost it all?" Lucy's voice was incredulous.

"Yes, God forgive me Lucy, every penny. I realised I was getting into difficulties, and I thought I could win it back, that my luck was sure to change...so I kept trying. And then...when I had nothing left to mortgage or sell...I gave I O U 's."

Lucy was aghast. "To this Sir...Sir Gilbert...?"

"Yes. Sir Gilbert Howell. I have been promising him payment for ages, but of course I just don't have it." He glanced at Lucy's stricken face, and turning away mumbled, "I may as well tell you all, there may be...there could be a prison sentence, a question of fraud I'm afraid..."

"Father! Oh my Lord..."

"I'm sorry Lucy, so sorry..." James Rowlands gave a piteous sob. Lucy sat transfixed, unable to believe what she heard, as her father raised his haggard face and begged, "so you see Lucy, there is no alternative. You must go back to England, you must not be...be tainted by my disgrace..."

Lucy knelt down by his side.

"Father, you said fraud, how can this be? What did you do?"

"I don't want to tell you...it makes no difference..."

"Please father, I must know everything. Tell me the truth now, and we shall never speak of it again after today."

Her father sighed deeply, but then he said haltingly, "The I O U's...when Sir Gilbert asked for payment I wrote him cheques. I managed to persuade him to allow me to post date them, you see I thought my luck would change. I thought I would have the money..."

"Yes, yes father," Lucy responded impatiently, "but how is this fraud?"

"I had no bank account when I wrote the cheques; it had already been closed by Mr. Graham."

Lucy's face was white with tension. She looked at her father's fearful trembling, and her anger grew. His weakness had ruined them, and she felt a momentary loathing for the shambling figure that cringed before her, mumbling his pathetic excuses. It was monstrous, and so unfair! She strove to control her feelings, and after a few moments turned to him again.

"I cannot understand your behaviour father," she said, attempting an even tone. "But it all happened before I came home, and who am I to judge? I will think about it overnight. Yes, I need some time to think." She strode to the door and then stopped. "This man...Sir Gilbert Howell. Where does he live?"

"His estate is about ten miles inland, it is called *Straits House*, but it's no use Lucy, he's a very hard man."

But she had already gone.

Chapter Three

Danny hobbled across the mission compound as fast as his small stature and heavy leg brace would allow. As always when school was let out, he had waited as the other boys made their noisy exit, whooping with glee at the scent of freedom. Only then could he leave without being knocked over.

He wished with all his heart that he could go straight home, for his mother would be waiting and there would be much excitement. Today was the feast of Hari Raya Puasa, and there would be open house for visitors, and his sister Lela, would come home, perhaps with a present for him. Danny groaned as he came in sight of the small open-fronted surgery, for there were five people already waiting for the doctor, one of them a very large lady who would surely take much time.

Danny climbed with some difficulty up the wooden steps to the surgery and sat down on the end of a long bench. The large lady smiled at him kindly, and after a moment he smiled back, guilty at his thoughts of a moment ago. If it had not been for Hari Raya Puasa, Danny would not have minded waiting, for he was fond of Doctor Hunt, in spite of the leg brace. The doctor had explained that the brace would make his leg almost straight by the time he grew up, but Danny did not believe this, for had not his mother told him that the twisted leg was the will of Allah? And there was no arguing with that.

Danny started slightly as the inner door to the clinic opened and the object of his thoughts emerged.

"Good evening, doctor," the patients chorused, almost in unison.

"Good evening," Dr Hunt answered. "I am sorry to keep you all waiting…" His faded blue eyes scanned the queue, and as he spied Danny he added with a smile, "Ah, Danny, of course, it's Friday." Turning to the others he said, "This small boy will only take a few moments, perhaps he could come in first?" The other patients readily acquiesced, with the easygoing good nature which never failed to surprise Europeans, and Danny followed the doctor into the clinic.

Dr. Hunt lifted the small boy up and sat him on the edge of the examination couch. He inspected the brace and the leg carefully.

"Thank you sir," said Danny dutifully. In answer to the doctor's questioning gaze he added, "For letting me come in first."

"Well, I thought you might be anxious to get away," the doctor answered dryly. "It might be a special day and you want to be home early."

His eyes twinkled and Danny blushed. He had thought the doctor saw him first because he was a boy, and the other patients were all women. "No," he countered, "nothing special."

"But isn't it the feast of Hari Raya Puasa?"

Danny was scandalized. "How do you know about that Dr Hunt? You are Methodist, aren't you, like Reverend Jackson?"

The doctor laughed. "Yes, I suppose so, if I'm anything at all, I suppose it's Methodist." He released Danny's leg and lifted him down from the couch. "And you Danny? Are you a good Methodist?"

Danny blushed again, he had the feeling the doctor was making a joke, and he did not understand it.

"Yes" he responded. "I know nearly all the prayers by heart; I am a good Methodist, when I am at school."

"And a good Muslim at home?" the doctor teased; then seeing the boy's embarrassment he relented.

"Don't worry son," he said kindly. "It doesn't matter to me what religion you are, as long as you look after that leg. Come and see me again next week."

"Yes, I will sir," Danny promised. As he reached the door he suddenly burst out, "I am a good Methodist and I love Jesus. My mother she still loves Allah, but she loves Jesus as well."

The doctor smiled and ruffled Danny's hair. "As long as you both love rather than hate, everything will be all right Danny. Has it ever occurred to you that God and Allah might be one and the same?"

"No," said Danny, surprised.

"Well, think about it," said Dr Hunt as he opened the door. "But not tonight. Tonight, have a good feast of Hari Raya Puasa."

Danny scrambled down the wooden steps on his bottom; it was easier to get down steps that way. Then he got to his feet with difficulty and started down the slope from the mission, reflecting on the doctor's strange words.

Born with the grandiose name of Hoo Kuan Kay, Danny had received his Christian name from the Reverend Jackson, who had watched the two year old fight his corner with other children at the mission, despite his twisted leg.

"We have a Daniel here!" the minister had announced proudly, as he watched the small child's refusal to be bullied. "A veritable Daniel in the lion's den! I shall call him Danny," and so Danny he had become.

It had taken the same kind of fighting spirit for Juminah, Danny's mother, to approach the mission after her husband's premature death. Although she was not a devout Muslim, the teachings of many years were embedded deep in Juminah's consciousness, and it was dire necessity which drove her to the mission for help, having been told by a well wisher that no one was turned away if they were willing to attend the mission church. There had been a short wrestling match between Juminah's own pangs of conscience and her three children's pangs of hunger, and hunger had won an easy victory.

Later, when Reverend Jackson gave her cleaning work and offered to feed and educate the children in payment, Juminah's gratitude knew no bounds. She was to suffer the grief of losing her elder son from malaria at the age of ten, but was inordinately proud that she had lived to see her firstborn child, her daughter Lela, obtain a position at *Straits House,* one of the grandest European houses in Singapore, after being commended by the Reverend Jackson. It was Lela's wages which had allowed them to leave the mission and make a home once again in a small wooden house in the city. Once there, Juminah had felt free of the constraints of the mission, and although she still attended service on Sundays, she did this more in payment of a debt of gratitude than real belief. Gradually her cultural background reasserted itself, and her children were somewhat surprised to find some Muslim customs appearing in what had been for years, a very Christian household. Fortunately, it suited Juminah to recall only the nicest things about her Muslim childhood, one of these being the feast of Hari Raya Puasa.

Now, as she watched for Danny's arrival from school, Juminah anticipated the evening ahead with real joy. As was the custom, she had cleaned the small house from top to bottom and hung new curtains.

"I don't think it is necessary, mother," Lela had remonstrated mildly when Juminah had requested the material, "But if it will make you happy I will try to save the money."

Now Juminah regarded her new curtains with pride. At last it was the feast of Hari Raya Puasa and soon Lela and her darling Danny would be home. She had already said the special prayers for the feast, and as she was aware that Danny and Lela would not approve, she resolved guiltily to say extra prayers at the mission church as well next Sunday. *After all,* Juminah reasoned, *there was but one God, and that was Allah, everyone knew that. But it could surely do no harm to say 'thank you' to the God who had provided for her children in their hour of need?*

Suddenly, she caught sight of Danny hobbling towards the house, and her eyes misted as she watched his ungainly progress. He wore a shirt and a *kain* around his waist as most Malays did. Juminah knew Danny wanted desperately to wear the European style shorts which many of the mission boys now wore, but it would be difficult to put them on over his leg brace and the *kain* was simple. Juminah watched for a moment, feeling the effort which the boy made with every step, and then she quickly prepared the fruit cordial for his arrival.

"Hello, my mother," his face was flushed with exertion.

"Greetings, my son."

Juminah placed the cordial before him and he drank with pleasure. His mother waited a moment and then asked: "Did you see the doctor?"

"Yes, all is well." The boy frowned and then added, "I think Dr Hunt knows we celebrate Hari Raya Puasa."

Juminah smiled. "Perhaps he does, but it does not matter, he will not tell Reverend Jackson."

"No, but mother, I don't know that we should do it. When I am a man, I shall forbid it and…"

He broke off as his mother gave a cry of joy. "Lela, oh my darling girl…"

There was excitement as Lela entered and embraced them both. She was a slender girl, with large expressive brown eyes and long dark hair. She put her shopping bag down on the small table, and accepted some cordial from her mother, before sinking down onto a box which served as a seat.

"Oh, it is so good to be home," she said happily. "And look Mother, I have extra food for the feast which the cook gave me." She opened her small shopping bag and took out a paper parcel. "The cook is very fair," she added, "When there is food left over she gives it to the servants, each one in turn. Today it was my turn. Look…some chicken and some rice."

"Goodness! What luck, I think your master lives very well," said Juminah, surveying the food.

"Oh no, this is not from Sir Gilbert's table, this is from the servants dinner. Sir Gilbert eats very peculiar food which his English cook prepares for him. You have no idea of the strange things Europeans eat."

Lela stopped and gave her mother a conspiratorial look,

"Now?" she asked, and Juminah nodded happily.

Lela opened her shopping bag again and brought out a parcel. She turned to Danny. "On this, the feast of Hari Raya Puasa, a present for the man of the house."

Danny thrilled with excitement, knowing what it must be, for it was the custom in even the poorest families to have new shoes for the feast day. He undid the parcel and gazed at the shoes.

"They're new!" he gasped. "Really new, not worn at all!"

"Yes," Lela agreed proudly. "I had them made at the market. The old man made them to fit your good leg, and I explained to him that your other foot is smaller. He said if you go to see him, he will alter the left shoe to fit, and will not charge us."

Danny already had the right shoe on, and it fitted perfectly. "No," he said. "I will wear the left shoe as it is, and I will stuff it with paper to make it fit. Then when my leg is straight and my foot grows bigger I can take the paper out."

"Are you sure?" Lela said doubtfully.

"Oh yes," Danny said confidently. "Dr Hunt says my leg will be straight one day, and I expect he's right. Oh Lela, thank you for my lovely shoes, what a feast day this is!"

"Yes, and thank you for my new curtains," said Juminah, giving Lela a kiss.

It was only as she was serving up their meal that Juminah realized that Lela had bought no present for herself.

Straits House was a substantial, but rather ugly red brick mansion surrounded by well manicured gardens, and approached by a formal drive. Evidence of the owner's wealth was apparent, from the carefully positioned statuary which graced the approach, to the gleaming carriage standing outside the stable block. Lucy was conscious that very few of Sir Gilbert's callers would arrive in such a disreputable old cart, but nevertheless she clicked her tongue to her father's broken down old stallion Rory, and urged him to a reluctant trot up to the entrance.

The heavy oak door was opened by a grey haired native woman; who smiled sweetly as Lucy gave her name and asked to see Sir Gilbert.

"He not here, Miss," came the polite reply, "But please come in."

Lucy entered the enormous hallway, and waited as the woman scuttled away. The interior of the house was even more opulent than she expected, with rich hangings, pictures, and high quality furniture and carpets, but the overall effect was gloomy, and Lucy decided she did not like it. She had just reached this conclusion when the native woman returned, followed by a very fat Englishman wearing an ill fitting tropical suit.

"My dear Miss Rowlands, how nice." His tone belied his words, making it clear he resented the intrusion. He passed his fingers through his oily hair and extended his hand briefly. "William Cranston, I am Sir Gilbert's estate manager, how can I help you?"

"It is Sir Gilbert I wish to see, please." Lucy replied.

"He is not here, and I am privy to all his affairs, indeed I have a good idea as to why you have come."

"I prefer to wait for Sir Gilbert if I may, but thank you for your offer of help," Lucy replied crisply, and William Cranston bridled.

"Up to you dear lady, up to you." He strode back down the hallway without a backward glance, but the moment he had passed through the far door the native woman reappeared, and gave Lucy her sweet smile.

"You come Miss, wait in here, be comfortable." Lucy followed her into a luxurious drawing room, and sank down gratefully onto a large couch. The little woman insisted on taking Lucy's bonnet and gloves, and said confidentially: "I am Minna, I bring refreshment. You not worry, Sir Gilbert here soon, not long I think."

Lucy smiled her thanks, and contemplated the room, trying to imagine what kind of man was master here. During the drive to *Straits House* she had repeatedly rehearsed what she intended to say to Sir Gilbert, but now, a little intimidated by her prosperous surroundings, she became increasingly nervous.

What could she say? What could persuade Sir Gilbert not to prosecute her father through the courts, when he had a clear right to do so? She knew that probably only the immediate payment of the debt would suffice, and that was out of the question. *Perhaps her best course was to throw herself on his mercy...*

Lucy continued to worry at the problem for almost an hour, as she sipped the fruit cordial brought by the attentive servant woman. She had still reached no conclusion when the door suddenly opened and Minna reappeared, and a moment later Sir Gilbert Howell entered the room.

He was not tall, but had a stocky, well built physique which gave him a powerful and rather ebullient appearance. His features were heavily fleshed, but regular and not unpleasant, with darting black eyes below beetling brows. His dark hair was thick and well cut, if a little windswept. He was wearing jodhpurs, and a black riding jacket with white stock, and he threw his whip onto a chair as he came towards Lucy, holding out his hand and smiling as if delighted.

"My dear Miss Rowlands, my apologies, Minna tells me you have been waiting some time."

"It is my fault, Sir Gilbert; I came without invitation and must thank you for seeing me." Lucy stammered.

"Not at all, not at all." He took her hand and held on to it, adding, "It is not often I have the opportunity to entertain such an attractive young lady." He released her hand and smiled again. "We must have some tea." He went to the door and called a few words to Minna, then returned to seat himself opposite.

"Now, Miss Rowlands, how may I be of assistance?"

Lucy looked across into the smiling black eyes, which seemed to regard her with an open and friendly interest, and her mouth went dry. It was an impossible question; *surely he knew how he could be of assistance? He knew who she was, and it did not take much to guess why she had come.* She swallowed, and then said firmly, "We have not met before Sir Gilbert, but I am James Rowlands daughter."

"Yes, I know."

Lucy looked up and met his look of frank admiration. She blushed slightly and Sir Gilbert said evenly. "I agree we have not met Miss Rowlands, but I have seen you before."

"Indeed, Sir Gilbert?"

"Yes. Two weeks ago, when you were in town for your stores. You were pointed out to me." He grinned, a little sheepishly, and added, "That's not strictly true. I asked who you were and someone told me."

"Oh. I'm sorry, I didn't see you."

"I know."

There was a short silence, and as Lucy groped desperately for the words she needed, the door opened, and Minna brought in a perfect tea tray.

As she left the room, Sir Gilbert leaned towards Lucy and said quietly, "shall we get the business over and then we shall enjoy our tea the more?"

"Well...er...yes Sir Gilbert. I hoped..."

"You hoped to persuade me not to take action against your father?"

"Yes, you see Sir Gilbert; this behaviour is not like him. When my mother died..."

"No more!" Sir Gilbert interrupted quickly. "Your father has behaved very badly Miss Rowlands, and I am over five thousand the poorer for it. But that is no matter, I will not have you troubled for a moment longer." He rose and crossed the room, and opened a drawer in a large writing desk, returning with a small bundle of papers.

"These are your father's cheques, Miss Rowlands. Each drawn on a non-existent bank account." He held them out to her. "Please look, just to verify them."

Lucy looked at the cheques briefly before handing them back, and as she did so he tore them up, one by one. Lucy started forward in surprise, but Sir Gilbert put the torn pieces in a waste paper basket and returned to his seat.

"Now, that's done with, Miss Rowlands, we can enjoy our tea. Do try one of Minna's muffins…"

Chapter Four

By eleven o'clock the following morning Lucy was at the bank. She still could hardly believe the extraordinary outcome of her visit to *Straits House*, and her spirits were high, with the knowledge that whatever the future held, at least her father would be spared the ignominy of an appearance in court, and a possible prison sentence. Lucy smiled to herself as she recalled her father's delight when she had told him his debts to Sir Gilbert were cancelled.

"But why?" he had repeated again and again. "Why would Sir Gilbert do such a thing when I found him immoveable only the day before?"

"Whatever his motives father, let us not question them, but simply be grateful," Lucy had responded. "He refused to discuss it, and insisted on giving me tea! Then he showed me around the gardens and asked for my advice on some new shrubs!"

Now, as Lucy waited in an ante-room at the bank, she pondered again on Sir Gilbert's motives. She knew he found her attractive, and a slight blush coloured her cheeks as she recalled Sir Gilbert's gallantry, worthy of the pages of a cheap novelette, the kind the girls had passed round at school in England, and which were quickly confiscated if found by a teacher.

She dragged her mind back to the morning's business, and sighed. She was certain William Graham would give her a fair hearing, but she could hardly expect an outcome similar to yesterday. The amounts outstanding to the bank were considerable, and she doubted that even if he wished, Margot's husband had the authority to help her. At least he would give her advice, and Lucy was desperate to find out whether the sale of Winchester Station would bring sufficient to cover what was owed. Her father had explained that when the mortgages were taken out, the property was in good condition and the plantation productive. A current valuation was sure to be much reduced, especially as the coffee prices were so depressed. The spectre which haunted Lucy was that even after everything was sold, they would still owe a residual debt to the bank.

She was so lost in contemplation of this gloomy prospect that she failed to notice the entry of a clerk, and gave a start as he touched her sleeve lightly.

"Miss Rowlands, Mr. Graham will see you now," he said, and within moments she was in William Graham's office.

She was surprised at his demeanour, which she had expected to be grave. Instead, he smiled and told her that Margot sent her love, and wanted to know when Lucy would visit them. Lucy muttered a few non-committal replies, and then said guardedly: "William, I really came to see about the debt to the bank."

"Yes," he interrupted with a smile. "You don't know how pleased I am not to have to proceed with the sale. I confess that I hated the idea, but I was in a most difficult position..."

"What do you mean?" Lucy asked.

"Well, because Margot is so fond of you of course. But I couldn't..."

"No...not that." Lucy interrupted sharply. "What you said before, about not going ahead with the sale."

"Oh, I see." William said cheerfully. "You are perhaps concerned about the details of the transaction? You needn't be, at least as far as the bank is concerned. You now owe us absolutely nothing, not a penny. I must admit I was a little apprehensive as to your private arrangement with Sir Gilbert, but if you need advice you only have to ask."

"Sir Gilbert?" Lucy echoed faintly, "Sir Gilbert Howell?"

"Yes, of course." William's tone changed, and his brow knitted in consternation. "My dear Lucy, we are at cross purposes. Can it be that you do not know?"

"Know what?" Lucy was bemused.

"Why...that Sir Gilbert Howell was here first thing this morning. He bought up your mortgages, which of course the bank was only too pleased to sell. You are now in debt to Sir Gilbert Howell my dear, not the bank."

By the time Lucy arrived within sight of Winchester Station she had made only one decision, and that was to stop thinking about their predicament for the rest of the day. The situation was so ridiculous that trying to apply logic to it would surely drive her mad with frustration. If Sir Gilbert wanted to add Winchester Station to his own estate he could surely have bought it more cheaply by waiting for the bank sale.

Despite her decision not to tussle with the mystery further, questions continued to torment her during the drive home, and when she entered the gates and saw the elegant carriage outside the house, she had little doubt as to the identity of their visitor.

Liam came bounding down the verandah steps to meet her.

"Miss Lucy, come quick. Mr. James waiting for you, important man here."

"Yes Liam, I know."

A little weary now, Lucy went into the drawing room, where she found her father and Sir Gilbert Howell deep in conversation. Both stood as she entered, and her father came forward to meet her, clearly delighted.

"My dear, you are here at last, your trip to the bank was unnecessary…"

Lucy took off her bonnet. "Yes, I know father. What I am anxious for is an explanation." She looked across at Sir Gilbert, who came forward and smiled apologetically.

"I am so sorry Miss Rowlands; I should have come here first, before I went to the bank. I could have saved you the journey." His smile was so solicitous that Lucy's feelings of antagonism towards him melted. She sat down wearily on the sofa.

"Sir Gilbert, my journey is not the question. What I want to know is why you bought up our debts?"

Sir Gilbert seemed a little taken aback by her tone.

"I…er…thought it would help," he responded simply. "After your visit yesterday, I gave much thought to your situation; indeed, I had little sleep, and awoke determined to assist if I could. You see, although you did not mention it, I was aware that your father had heavy debts to the bank, er…forgive me, but it has been common knowledge for some time. I thought you would prefer the mortgage to be held by a person sympathetic to your problems."

"But why should you be sympathetic to us?" Lucy cried in some exasperation.

Sir Gilbert appeared a little shamefaced. "I have been discussing that with your father," he said quietly. "Of course, I cannot afford to tear up the mortgages as I did the cheques, much as I should like to." He smiled, and then continued enthusiastically, "My plan is to restore the house and put the estate back into production as quickly as possible. It will cost a fair amount, but I am sure it will be a good investment. I have put the suggestion to James that in view of today's coffee prices, it might be worth restocking half the estate with the new rubber plants. Of course, it's still an experimental crop, but the Governor is very keen, he expects the demand for rubber to increase considerably."

"I see," said Lucy miserably, "And how long before we have to leave?"

"Leave? But why should you leave?" Sir Gilbert asked. He seemed genuinely puzzled, and James Rowlands interjected: "No Lucy, you don't understand, Sir Gilbert wants us to stay here. He wants you to supervise the decoration and repair of the house, and myself the plantation. Think of it Lucy, we shall be back to rights in no time."

"But why?" Lucy quavered. It seemed too good to be true. "Why should you be so kind to us? We cannot hope to pay…"

"There is no need to pay anything," said Sir Gilbert. "On the contrary, I could pay a small salary for your help in the reorganization…"

"But why?" Lucy cried again. "Sir Gilbert, do not misunderstand me. All these plans seem wonderful, but you still have not answered my question. Why are you doing this for us?"

"I have reasons," he replied, as if slightly embarrassed. "I have explained them to your father, but I did not really wish to discuss them with you as yet…"

"I'm afraid you must!" Lucy's tone was sharp, and she rose from the sofa to confront him. "Sir Gilbert, you must forgive my directness, but until yesterday I knew nothing of the extent of our difficulties, and it has been a great shock. Everything was kept secret from me, and I will not have it happen again! I must know what your motive is in all this."

"In that case, Miss Rowlands, you force me to be bolder than I would have wished," Sir Gilbert replied quietly. "You see, it is my most ardent wish that we be married."

There was a sudden silence, and Lucy sank back onto the sofa in surprise. James Rowlands patted her arm and said, "You will insist on pushing things, won't you my dear?" He turned to Sir Gilbert. "No doubt you wish to have a private word with Lucy; I shall leave you alone."

He left the room, and Lucy tried to recover her composure. She felt quite unable to deal with this turn of events.

"Sir Gilbert, this is a great compliment of course," she heard herself murmur, "but we only met yesterday."

"I know." He sat down opposite and spoke earnestly. "I realise this may seem very sudden, but as I told you, I saw you in town two weeks ago, and since then I have been unable to think of anything else. Of course, I had no intention of speaking to you until we had come to know each other better. Perhaps I was wrong, but I imagined that working closely together on the house would assist our friendship. I hoped…I hoped the time would come when you would feel able to accept my proposal."

Lucy swallowed. "Marriage…I suppose I thought I would marry some day, but I have never considered it seriously."

"And you are not to think of it now," Gilbert said quickly, and then he continued: "Please put this conversation out of your mind. I had to make my interest known to your father, to set his mind at rest about the future, but I would never have spoken to you so soon." He laughed. "You did insist," he said pointedly.

"Yes, I did," Lucy agreed, and smiled back at him. Sir Gilbert took her hand and said gently, "Do not be concerned, I will never put you under any pressure. All I ask for now is that you regard me as a friend, and allow me to call you Lucy."

She smiled. "I do not think that will tax me overmuch. However, I cannot help but ask what our situation will be if I decide against marrying you?"

Sir Gilbert grimaced. "I don't wish to contemplate such a disaster."

"No, but if it happens?" Lucy insisted gently.

"Well in that case," Gilbert replied ruefully, "I shall still need an estate manager here, and I suppose your father will need a position…in fact I don't suppose things would change much, apart from me having a broken heart of course…"

"Winchester Station, why is it so important to you?" Sir Gilbert Howell raised his silver topped cane to move an invading branch from Lucy's path.

"I have always thought of it as home," Lucy replied. "When I was at school in England, I used to dream of the day I would return home to father, and my other friends."

"Other friends?" He seemed surprised.

"Yes, the servants. They were my true childhood friends. My amah, Kwim Lee, is no longer alive, but I was lucky to find our gardener, Jarvis Mottram. I have wonderful memories of him. He used to keep the best pieces of fruit for me, and I would sit on his wheelbarrow to eat them. I used to think I was helping, and he always pretended I was, but I realise now I must have been an awful nuisance."

"Ah! But a delightful child could never be a nuisance surely?" He turned and regarded her gravely. "And you, Miss Lucy Rowlands, were most assuredly a truly delightful child, judging by the truly delightful adult you have become."

Lucy blushed. It was the first time Sir Gilbert had paid her a lover's compliment, and she was flattered. Since the day he had made his feelings known, his manners and consideration for her position had been exemplary. He was aware of her misgivings, and had responded by making it clear he did not intend to hurry her for an answer. Lucy was grateful, and over the passing weeks had become accustomed to his company, as they discussed plans for the refurbishment of the house or took a walk through the estate, or a drive to the coast a mile away.

Already Winchester Station was responding to the efforts of painters, plasterers and glaziers, and Lucy threw herself into the work with delight, marvelling at the skill of the craftsmen Gilbert had engaged. As she watched her mother's much loved home gradually reappear she felt a glow of happiness, and knew it was Gilbert she had to thank for it.

Was gratitude enough? For weeks she had agonised over the prospect of marriage to Sir Gilbert. Her instinct was to refuse, but her reason argued with cold logic that she should accept. All the years of her English private school teaching had bred in her a recognition of the path of duty, of self denial and respect for family, and these traits were so deeply woven into the very fibre of her personality that they coloured her every thought and action. She chastised herself therefore, when personal inclinations were all she could find to counter the very obvious advantages.

She had to face the fact that there were no real arguments against the marriage, and almost everything in its favour. Already her father was a new man, as he watched Winchester Station return to life, and he was enthusiastic at the prospect of Sir Gilbert as a son-in-law.

"One of the wealthiest men in Singapore, Lucy," he told her repeatedly. "You will never have another offer like this, what a catch!"

In vain Lucy responded that she had no wish to catch anyone, but she recognized the reality of the situation. A major consideration was that if she became Sir Gilbert's wife, her father's future security was assured, and that alone, she reasoned, was worth some self denial.

She also realized that her father spoke the truth. Sir Gilbert Howell was undoubtedly a catch. Many young women would think it no hardship to become Lady Howell, mistress of one of the great houses in Singapore, and enjoy the style of life Sir Gilbert's wealth and position implied. She could find no valid argument against this, but only a vague feeling that she would perhaps miss something, but she could not have said exactly what. Romance? She hardly understood what the word meant. Her only romantic experience had been a sense of slight excitement when reading some of the little novelettes her friends had smuggled into school. Such stories were not like real life, as Miss Collins had often explained. Lucy had also heard that one learned to love one's husband after marriage, and the whole strange subject seemed to be surrounded by a conspiracy of silence. She recalled Miss Collins kindly but embarrassed explanation of what she called 'the ladies monthly problem,' and when the dismayed thirteen year old Lucy had asked why this had to happen, Miss Collins had mumbled that "it was to do with having babies and she would understand when she got married." There had been a giggling discussion with some of her equally ignorant school friends, when one of them had proclaimed loudly that she knew all about it, because people were only the same as animals, and she had often observed "goings on' in the stables at home. As Lucy had no access to stables other than her weekly riding lesson, she was none the wiser for this revelation. It seemed that when one was married, love arrived in some magical way, but she could not begin to imagine how.

Now, as she walked with Sir Gilbert along the path which skirted the shore, these reflections were uppermost in Lucy's mind, and she started slightly as she realized Sir Gilbert was speaking to her.

"I'm sorry Gilbert, what did you say?"

"My dear, where were you? You look troubled."

"No, not really, I was just thinking. What were you saying?"

"Only that we should perhaps go back to the carriage now?"

"Yes, of course."

She took Gilbert's arm as they strolled back towards the carriage, which had been left with the driver half a mile away. Lucy surveyed the long stretch of sand, as yellow as a buttercup, and fringed by graceful casuarina trees, and smiled happily.

"I love it here," she said. "Thank you for bringing me, Gilbert." She gazed out to sea, where clusters of thickly wooded islands shimmered in the heat haze. "I'd love to visit those islands; do you think they are inhabited?"

"Most of them are, but I don't think you'll get your wish. There isn't a steamer as far as I know."

"That's no problem. Jarvis will take me in his boat, I'm sure."

Gilbert laughed. "You and your old gardener, you are such friends, I almost feel jealous!"

They reached the waiting carriage and within a few minutes were driving along the dirt road back to Winchester Station. After a moment Gilbert took her hand and said, "My dear, I have a favour to ask."

Lucy's heart missed a beat, but he continued evenly;

"The Governor is giving a ball next Friday evening, in honour of Queen Victoria's birthday. Would you allow me to escort you? I have mentioned it to your father, and he has given permission if you are so inclined."

"A ball! Oh yes, I should be delighted to come. Oh..." Lucy's face changed.

"What is it?" Gilbert asked.

"I have not received an invitation."

Gilbert laughed. "I think that may be rectified." To make his point he smiled again and said, "Probably tomorrow."

Lucy was entranced, impressed in spite of herself. It was flattering to have a beau who could gain access to just about anything. She still felt slightly uneasy however, and a frown flitted across her face.

"What is it now?" Gilbert was still jocular.

"I was wondering what kind of reception I may receive," Lucy confessed. "You must be aware Gilbert, that my father's problems have led to a certain amount of talk."

"Stuff and nonsense! If there is any talk it will be as to the identity of the beautiful stranger. I hope that all your financial problems will be ended soon Lucy, but in the meantime you must begin to take your proper place in society. The Governor's ball is the ideal starting place."

He was clearly referring to their possible marriage, but it was so tactfully done that Lucy could not feel resentful. She took his arm. "Thank you, Gilbert, for your kindness and your consideration."

He gave an almost imperceptible smile. "I'm sure you will enjoy the ball. I shall call for you at eight."

As they drove back to the house they continued to chat in a desultory fashion, but Lucy's thoughts were preoccupied. She had suddenly realized she had nothing to wear.

Lucy's doubts were premature. Her father turned to her as soon as they had waved Gilbert's carriage away.

"Are you going my dear?"

"To the Governor's ball? Yes, if my invitation arrives."

"Of course it will, of course." He seemed delighted.

"I have only one problem," Lucy explained, taking his arm as they walked back to the house. "What am I going to...?"

"You have no problem, no problem. I know what you were going to say! Come with me."

Lucy followed him into the large kitchen, where she saw a huge brassbound trunk in the middle of the floor.

"I had Liam bring it down from the attic," her father explained. "It's your mother's things, her best things." He looked a little apologetic. "I couldn't bear to throw them away. They may be a little out of date but I'm sure you will find something you can make over." He smiled like a schoolboy at mischief, pleased with Lucy's expressions of delight. "Your mother had perfect taste you know, my dear..."

But Lucy already had the chest open, and was taking out the elegant contents. Dresses, skirts, blouses and walking suits, all perfect and still wrapped in the fine cotton muslin Kwim Lee had used when she had packed them. There was even a faint lingering perfume in the air. Lucy held the dresses to her, overcome by emotion.

"Mother's things," she whispered, "Mother's things." She did not understand her feelings. How strange to be both sad and happy at the same time.

Lela put the heavy bag of fruit and vegetables down onto the small wooden table with relief. It was good to have a few hours away from work, but it was very hot, and the walk home through the open market had seemed longer than usual. Her tiredness soon evaporated as she watched Juminah take out the contents of the bag, smiling with delight and approval.

"You have done well, my daughter, these are very good..."

"Yes, I have learned to bargain well. The cook at *Straits House* is a good teacher."

Juminah frowned. "But surely you are not employed in the kitchens? We were assured you were to be a housemaid, and if you do well, you may be a parlourmaid..."

Lela laughed. "I asked the cook to advise me mother, and already I am almost a parlourmaid. The housekeeper told me yesterday that because of my good English and my education at the mission, I shall be allowed to assist when there are visitors."

"Oh, my daughter! How our lives are changed now because of your position! You are so lucky to be at *Straits House*, the wages are much higher than at other European houses."

Lela frowned. "Yes, they are," she agreed. "And that is why the staff stay there, even though they may be unhappy."

"Unhappy?" Juminah repeated, genuinely puzzled. "How could they be unhappy to work in such a great house, with good wages and grand surroundings?"

"Perhaps 'unhappy' is not the right word," said Lela. "Perhaps 'uneasy' would be better. Now I have been there a while, I have come to realize that all is not as it seems. I think the estate manager Mr. Cranston is a bad man, everyone is afraid of him."

"But why?"

"Well, I don't have too much to do with him but..." Lela caught the look of concern in Juminah's eyes and stopped. She would not worry her mother by repeating gossip from *Straits House*. The housekeeper had already made it clear that those who kept their positions also kept their heads down and their mouths shut. She laughed easily and said, "I expect there are always ups and downs in houses with so many staff. I am lucky, I do my work and no one bothers me." Anxious to change the subject she added, "Where's Danny? Surely he should be home by now?"

As if in answer to her question, Danny arrived at that moment, and from his quiet entrance and muted greeting Lela surmised right away that something was amiss. Juminah appeared not to notice however, and bustled away to prepare cordial. Lela went over to Danny, and at her insistence he eventually turned to meet her gaze. His left eye was heavily swollen in his grubby, tearstained face, and a large bruise on his cheek was already turning black.

"Oh Danny, what happened? Who did this?"

Danny let out a half stifled sob and then countered aggressively, "I hit him first, I hit him hard!"

"But why Danny? It's not like you to fight! Why did you hit someone?"

Juminah had now joined them, and after a short display of what he hoped was manly defiance, Danny broke down and it all came out. Some of the bigger boys had been calling him names, picking on him because of his leg brace. It happened quite often, but today had been worse than usual.

"When I told them to stop it...they wouldn't!" He blurted out between sobs. "They kept calling me Iron peg and Cripple...and they said when I grow up I'll have to beg in the streets."

Lela hugged the thin little body close and reassured him: "But you know that's not true, don't you? You will have a good education at the mission so you will be sure to find work, just like me! And Dr. Hunt says your leg will be almost well."

"I know!" Danny agreed tearfully. "But they kept shouting 'Beggar boy!

Beggar boy!' and so I hit the big one..."

Juminah broke in angrily "Well done! I hope you hurt him!"

"Mother!" Lela remonstrated, "I don't think..."

"Yes, I did hurt him!" Danny said, his sobs lessening a little. "I must have done because he started to cry and said I had loosened a tooth, and then two of them started to fight me at once." His sobs began again and Juminah comforted him, as Lela fetched water and a cloth to bathe his face.

"You know Danny," Lela said as she applied a compress, "The other boys only pick on you because they are jealous. They know you are getting good marks at your lessons, and that Dr Hunt is taking a special interest in you."

"Do you think so? Really?" Danny asked tearfully.

"Of course," Lela soothed.

A few hours later as she walked back to *Straits House*, Lela reflected on her own words. She knew she was right about the doctor's special interest in Danny's leg, and only hoped this would continue as the boy grew older. If it didn't, and anything happened to her, the bullies could well be proved right, and Danny could end up begging for his living on the streets of Singapore.

Chapter Five

The gown Lucy had chosen for the ball was of pale blue satin, with a corsage of jewelled flowers in a deeper blue. When Gilbert arrived to collect her he congratulated her on her appearance, and in the carriage he took her hand.

"You are, of course, aware of my feeling toward you, and my deep regard."

Lucy was touched. "Yes Gilbert, and you have been most kind and considerate."

"Then my dear, although of course I have no wish to rush you, perhaps you would consent that at least we have an understanding?"

Lucy smiled, she could hardly object to so gentle a request.

"Of course Gilbert, we have…an understanding."

Gilbert squeezed her hand and they continued their journey in silence, Lucy contemplating the evening ahead with a mixture of delight and dread.

The Governor's mansion was ablaze with light, and they joined a queue of carriages as they approached. Alighting at last, they entered the huge foyer and were relieved of their cloaks. Lucy took Gilbert's arm as they entered the ballroom, and Margot Graham, who had seated herself within spotting distance of the arriving guests, hardly recognized Lucy as the usher announced: "Miss Lucy Graham and Sir Gilbert Howell."

"William, do look!" Margot grabbed at her husband's arm. "It's Lucy, little Lucy Rowlands! Doesn't she look wonderful? I knew she was a beauty, but…oh! William…"

Margot was not alone in her surprise. There was a short silence as Singapore high society took in the newcomer in their midst. The pale blue of Lucy's gown showed off her creamy young shoulders to perfection, and was a foil to her rich chestnut hair, which she had dressed into a becoming chignon. As Lucy turned from her reception by the Governor and his wife, she became aware of the eyes on her, and hesitated slightly.

"Oh my dear, how good to see you again!" Margot Graham rushed forward to her rescue, and took Lucy's hand warmly. "How lovely you look!

Don't you think so, Sir Gilbert? Do come and meet William, I really didn't expect to see you here, what a wonderful evening we shall have…"

For once Lucy blessed the idle prattle, sensing that Margot was making their friendship obvious to everyone. Her attitude said louder than words, "Whatever her father may be, this young lady is my friend."

What a kindhearted soul she was, underneath all that silly chatter, Lucy thought as she was whirled through a welter of introductions. An hour later she was feeling perfectly at ease, and enjoying herself immensely.

"My dance at last, I think?" Gilbert said in her ear.

"No, mine I believe!"

Lucy turned and looked into the intense grey eyes of a tall stranger, who turned to Gilbert with a slight bow.

"I had just been introduced, and Miss Rowlands had accepted my invitation to dance."

He offered his arm, and Lucy, surprised into submission by the grey eyes, took it. They walked to the floor, and Lucy, with a backward glance at Gilbert, was whisked into a waltz.

After a moment she recovered her composure sufficiently to remark: "Perhaps my hearing is at fault. I do not recall your introduction, and consequently sir, I have no idea who you are."

The grey eyes smiled. "In that case I must do it all over again."

Lucy found herself being waltzed to the terrace, where several couples were strolling and chatting around the potted palms, and admiring the garden view. In a moment the stranger had hurried her away, his hand under her elbow, down the terrace steps to the lawn, and into a formal arbour. To Lucy's surprise he then turned, and with his hands on her waist, lifted her swiftly and set her down upon a large stone mushroom.

He stepped back and surveyed her, and she stared back at the long lean figure and the magnetizing grey eyes.

"Yes." He appraised her again. "A princess! A fairy princess, sitting on a mushroom!"

Lucy became tongue tied. "What…I do not know…"

Grey eyes gave a deep bow.

"Gregory Lamont." It was a statement, delivered with some arrogance and a slight intonation in the voice which Lucy did not recognize. "At your service, Miss Rowlands."

"Well, Mr. Lamont, perhaps you can account for your strange behaviour!"

In spite of her annoyance, Lucy was enjoying herself.

"Strange behaviour? And what is strange about rescuing a young lady?"

"Rescuing me sir? I think I was in no danger until now!"

"Oh, but you were! The princess was in danger of being bored to death by high society flunkeys, whereas she would surely prefer to be amused by her devoted frog."

"And you sir, are the frog?"

"But of course!" he made a croaking sound, and Lucy laughed in spite of herself. He bowed again.

"I may be a frog at this moment Miss Rowlands, but surely you remember what happened to the frog when he was kissed by the beautiful princess?"

Lucy felt her colour rise, and in her confusion replied more sharply than she had intended: "You are impertinent Mr. Lamont. I should like to be taken back to the dancing, please. You see you were mistaken. I was enjoying the ball very much."

He had the grace to appear chastened.

"Then I apologise ma'am." He lifted her down from the mushroom, and Lucy felt a strange thrill at the pressure of his hands on her waist. He released her however, and gave her his arm as they began to walk back to the house. Lucy glanced sideways and noticed that his thick brown hair, worn slightly longer than was currently fashionable, curled a little at his temples and the nape of his neck. Suddenly she wanted to reassure him, to return the conversation to the lighthearted nonsense of a moment ago. She turned and smiled into the devastating grey eyes.

"Mr. Lamont," she began, but was interrupted by the sight of Gilbert hurrying down the terrace steps towards them.

"Lucy! I wondered where you were." He glared angrily at Gregory Lamont. "What were you doing?" he enquired suspiciously.

"Oh, I was a little overcome by the heat," Lucy explained sweetly. "Mr. Lamont was kind enough to escort me for some air in the garden."

Ignoring the amused question in the grey eyes, she took Gilbert's arm, and started up the steps. She turned her head. "Goodbye Mr. Lamont. And thank you for your concern. I could not have been better treated had I been a princess."

She saw the answering flash of humour in the grey eyes, before Gilbert hurried her away.

"What was that? What nonsense was that?" he queried.

"Oh, nothing at all. As I said, I felt the need for some air."

"And are you quite recovered now?"

"Oh yes, I am fine now, Gilbert."

"Good. I came to find you so we can hear the Governor's speech together. He usually says a few words about now. I think you will be interested." Gilbert looked at her meaningly, and Lucy was intrigued, unable to imagine how the Governor's remarks could be of such interest.

She did not have to wait long for enlightenment. The speech was short and to the point, dealing with the growing economy of Singapore, and the changes since its transfer to Colonial rule. The Governor emphasized the encouraging prospects for the experimental rubber crop, which it was hoped would in time offset the heavy losses now being sustained by the coffee growers. Then he delighted his audience by informing them that plans were well advanced for the celebration of the Queen's Diamond Jubilee next year. After the loyal toast, the Governor called again for silence.

"And now, to another reason for celebration. It gives me great pleasure to announce an engagement, ladies and gentlemen."

There was an audible gasp of delight from the assembled guests, and a few 'Oh!'s and Ooh!s' from the ladies.

"Yes, an engagement, between one of our most illustrious residents, Sir Gilbert Howell, and a truly lovely newcomer in our midst, Miss Lucy Rowlands."

The colour drained from Lucy's face. People thronged around them, shaking Gilbert's hand and laughing. She felt slightly sick, detached from her surroundings. She suddenly realized Gilbert must have asked the Governor to make the announcement. *How could he have done so without her agreement?* She smiled shakily at Margot, who was embracing her with glee.

"My dear! What a wonderful match! Sir Gilbert is the most eligible man in Singapore. I'm so delighted for you. Will you allow me to help you choose your trousseau?"

Lucy agreed that of course she would, and smilingly accepted the compliments and good wishes which were offered on all sides. As soon as she was able, she made her escape into a small ante-room, to recover her composure. She had not told Sir Gilbert she would marry him, although of course she had almost decided that she must. She recalled his words as they had left Winchester Station. "Then at least you will consent we have an understanding?" *And she had said yes! He had obviously taken that for her acceptance. Of course, she probably would have said yes, but it was too soon, too soon...*She leaned wearily against the mantelpiece, and felt the hot tears spring to her eyes.

"I beg your pardon Miss Rowlands." She turned swiftly to find Gregory Lamont standing a few feet away.

"My apologies for disturbing you, but I felt I wished to see you alone to express my deep regret for my behaviour this evening. If I had realized you were affianced to Sir Gilbert, of course I should not have been so forward." He bowed slightly. "It seems I have many apologies to make this evening."

Lucy smiled. "Please think nothing of it Mr. Lamont. You were not to know." *And neither was I,* she thought bitterly.

"No, I was not to know. How indeed could I have guessed?" The grey eyes were not laughing now, the handsome face was grave, and the eyes cold, like a grey, ice cold sea.

"No, I could not have guessed, or even imagined..." he continued. He seemed angry about something. He walked to the door, and then suddenly returned, as if remembering the civilities.

"May I offer you and Sir Gilbert my very best wishes for your future happiness?"

Was it her imagination, or were the grey eyes tortured? No, they had turned cold, that ice grey sea was there in the depths, boring into her...

"Thank you Mr. Lamont. I am sure with everyone's good wishes we shall indeed be blessed."

"Indeed Miss Rowlands. From what I have heard, Sir Gilbert is very well blessed already." And with that parting shot he left the room. Lucy watched him go with some sadness. *Now what had he meant by that?*

The excitement of the ball had tired her, and Lucy was quiet and non-committal as she and Gilbert drove back to Winchester Station. At the door Gilbert said quietly; "You're annoyed? That the engagement was announced?"

Lucy sighed, "It's done now."

"It was just that you looked so lovely, and I was so proud of you. I wanted to let everyone know."

Wanted to make sure of me, she thought. Aloud she said, "Don't worry Gilbert, it's all right. Good night."

"Good night Lucy." He bent his head and kissed her gently on the lips. It was her first romantic kiss, but as Lucy tossed in bed that night she did not remember it. Her mind wandered restlessly through a dancing, laughing court, where she was a princess in her mother's blue satin dress, and a frog prince with grey eyes was waltzing her away...

Margot Graham swallowed the remains of her coffee. *She must hurry; there was so much to do. Dear Lucy, with no mother to advise her, and probably no money. And even if Sir Gilbert was intending to pay for the wedding, what did he know? A single man, his family in England, now— there's a thought!*

"William dear."

William had his nose in the *Straits Times*.

"William!"

Her husband looked up enquiringly.

"Do you think Sir Gilbert's family will come out from England? For the wedding I mean?"

"Shouldn't think so."

"Why not? It's a very old family and the only son getting married…"

"He's not the only son for one thing, and for another, I doubt they will wish to be present."

"Why ever not?"

"I have no idea."

Margot bridled. William could be infuriating at times.

"William! You can't say things like that without explaining yourself."

William gave up the struggle and laid down his newspaper.

"Listen, my dear. I know you are pleased for Lucy, and think this marriage to Sir Gilbert will solve all her problems, but you really should know a little more about him before you give your seal of approval."

"What can you mean? Surely you do not know of anything to his detriment?" Margot was alarmed, and William smiled.

"Now don't go jumping to conclusions again. I know of nothing specific, at least not since he has been in Singapore. When he arrived here ten years ago, his father wrote to the bank from England, and sent money to open his bank account."

"What's wrong with that?"

"Nothing at all. But from the letter, and the way the money was to be administered by a very strict monthly allowance, I gained the impression that young Sir Gilbert had blotted his copybook in England, and had been sent away to Singapore as some sort of punishment."

"Never!" Margot was horrified. "Oh William, do you think Lucy will be all right? What can he have done?"

"I really don't know my dear, perhaps nothing very much. The only person I have met who knew the family was Andrew Williamson, do you

49

remember him? Only here a few months, went back to England a couple of years ago?"

"Yes, of course, a charming man." Margot responded. "What did he say?"

"Not much, but he was in the office one day when Sir Gilbert passed by the window. Andrew recognized him and was most interested to know how he was getting on in Singapore. I told him Sir Gilbert was doing extremely well and was one of the bank's customers, and Andrew seemed pleased. I recall he told me Sir Gilbert had a very unhappy childhood."

"Really? In what way?" Margot asked.

"Apparently he was brought up very strictly, not like a child at all. His mother was a rather strange woman and Gilbert and his younger brother were never allowed to play with other children or have a normal childhood. I remember I asked Andrew if Sir Gilbert had been sent to Singapore because of problems at home, but he didn't answer me directly. He just said that if Gilbert's mother had problems with the boy it was probably her own fault."

"Oh. Is that all?" Margot sounded slightly disappointed.

"Yes, I think so, but I remember something that struck me as a little odd. I had already asked Andrew to dinner the following week, and so I suggested I should invite Sir Gilbert as well, so they could renew their acquaintance. I thought he would be pleased, but Andrew would have none of it. I recall he said it would be 'better to let sleeping dogs lie', which I thought was a rather odd phrase to use. I suppose that added to my conviction that there was something unpleasant in Sir Gilbert's past."

"Oh William, I do hope not. But he has been most successful since he came here surely? He is very rich isn't he?"

Margot knew better than to expect William to answer such a question, as he had always laid great emphasis on the confidentiality of his work at the bank. To her surprise however, he confirmed her view.

"Oh yes, he's certainly rich. The problem is, where does his money come from?"

"From his estate, surely, and I understand he has tin mines."

William gave a long suffering sigh. Sometimes Margot took a while to see the point. He explained: "He has an income from his estate, now certainly, a large one. But where did he find the capital to buy it in the first place? Not from his monthly allowance I assure you. From the time he arrived here, he has had large sums paid into his account regularly, in cash, and there have been rumours..." William checked himself. His tongue was running away with him, and his thoughts too. He turned to his wife.

50

"Now Margot," he said carefully, "you must forget what I have said. I should not have mentioned it, and please pretend I did not."

"Of course William." But a worried frown still played across Margot's face. William leaned towards her and said kindly; "My dear, I'm only saying that you must look before you leap where Lucy's marriage is concerned. I do not know anything to Sir Gilbert's detriment; it's just that there are some unanswered questions. Those questions may have perfectly simple answers. In the meantime we know nothing, and have no suspicions of any kind. Is that understood?"

"Yes, of course my dear." Margot knew when William was serious, and in spite of her inclination to gossip, she knew when it was in her interest to keep her mouth firmly shut. "I was only thinking, William," she added hesitantly, "It could have been our dear Morag getting married…"

"Oh, my dear," William said with immediate understanding, "you really must not allow yourself these thoughts. Lucy Rowlands is not our daughter." He leaned over and kissed Margot's cheek. "Don't worry," he said. "I must go or I'll be late." At the door he turned.

"Don't worry," he said again. "I'll make it my business to make some discreet enquiries, although what use they will be I don't know. It isn't really any of our business."

After William had gone, Margot sat for at least ten minutes, gazing at the coffee pot. The excitement had gone out of the wedding plans. Although she was a respectable Scottish lady with limited social contacts, Margot Graham was no fool. She had lived in Singapore long enough to understand only too well the meaning behind her husband's words. She was aware that gaming, opium, and brothels were very big money earners in the colony, in spite of the British attempts to hide the flourishing low life economy from the well-heeled society in which Margot and her friends moved. The British seemed able to ignore anything they preferred not to see, and Margot was aware that darker currents flowed beneath her own somewhat superficial lifestyle.

She poured herself another cup of coffee, which was now cold, and as usual when she thought of Lucy the same words came to her lips.

"Poor wee bairn," she murmured to herself. "Poor wee bairn."

Chapter Six

Lucy had none of Margot's apprehensions as she walked to the shore. Since the ball two weeks ago, she had become accustomed to the idea of marrying Gilbert, and very soon. After some discussion with her father, Lucy had agreed that the marriage would take place in four weeks time, and now the decision was made, Lucy would not be sorry when her status changed. Gilbert had been as charming as ever, and Lucy had to admit that with his dark good looks and perfect manners she had little to complain of. In particular, Lucy was heartened to see how her father had responded to the challenge of the restoration of the house and estate. He was now actively seeking men to restart production on the plantation, and Gilbert had already invested money for work to begin.

Lucy had remonstrated that perhaps it was a little early for Gilbert to provide such money, but he was of a different opinion.

"The work needs to be done as quickly as possible," he explained, "to get in an early crop. In any case," he added, smiling at her, "One day the estate will be yours, and what is yours is also mine, so we can look upon it as an investment in our future."

Put like that, Lucy could hardly disagree, and she could see for herself the beneficial effect on her father, as he had not had a drink for several weeks. Nevertheless, Lucy did have an uneasy feeling that the investment put her under even more obligation to Gilbert, there could be no changing her mind now, things had gone too far.

Lucy tried to put this thought out of her mind. *Change her mind? Why should she want to change her mind?* She recognised she was not in love with Gilbert, but as she did not know what it was to be in love, how could she be certain? She found Gilbert attractive, and a pleasant enough companion, but in the back of her mind she was haunted by a pair of disturbing grey eyes...

She almost stumbled on the path, and suddenly the grey eyes were there, their look of concern changing to delight as Gregory Lamont leaned down from his horse and enquired gently if she was all right?

"Yes of course, I just stumbled." A tumultuous panic seized her. *Where on earth had he sprung from?*

"How delightful to meet you again Miss Rowlands," He looked down at her with obvious pleasure. "When I met you at the ball, I thought you were a princess, but now I see you really were a gypsy in disguise!"

Lucy blushed. Her hair had become wet from the morning rain, and she had loosed it to dry as she walked to the shore. It now cascaded down her back in tangled chestnut curls, and she was wearing her old flowered dimity dress. *What a fright she must look.* She stared up at him. "But what are you doing here, Mr Lamont?"

"I was on my way down to the beach. I am looking for a man named Jarvis Mottram. I don't suppose you know where the scoundrel lives? I was told he had a boat and a hut down here somewhere."

Lucy hesitated. She was on her way to visit Jarvis herself.

"Why do you call him a scoundrel, Mr Lamont? I have never found him to be so."

Gregory Lamont raised an eyebrow, and the grey eyes became wary. "You know him then?" He dismounted. "Miss Rowlands, I shall be most grateful for any information you can give me as to his whereabouts." When Lucy hesitated, he added testily, "It is a most important matter."

"To whom?" Lucy responded coldly. "Perhaps what is important to you Mr Lamont, is not of the same import to me, or indeed to Jarvis."

"Jarvis! You do know him then?"

"Yes I do. He was our gardener for many years."

"But I understood you had only recently arrived in Singapore, like myself."

"A few months ago. But I remember Jarvis from my childhood. He was always a good friend to me, and when I returned here he agreed to help to restore our garden…"

"From childhood!" Gregory Lamont intervened, "Ah yes indeed. It seems we share this paragon of virtue Miss Rowlands. I too remember Jarvis Mottram from my childhood, but not perhaps with the same devotion. Where is he?" His tone had become savage, and the ice grey eyes glinted coldly.

Lucy was taken aback. "But how could you know him? I don't understand."

"No, I'm sure you don't. Well, I am a little older than you Miss Rowlands, and before Jarvis Mottram came here and worked for you, he worked for my family in Australia. It was many years ago, and I was a very young child. I will not trouble you with the details, but suffice it to say that when I became of age

I determined to trace him, to see he pays for his mischief!"

He made an effort to control his anger. "Now Miss Rowlands, are you going to give me directions or not?" He leaned towards her, and Lucy took an involuntary step back. Then she looked up into the menace of the sea grey stare, and gathered her courage.

"Not, I think, as you are obviously in such a foul temper," she said tartly. "Except to inform you that you are in the wrong place. Jarvis lives about three miles further up the coast, towards the Chinese village."

Gregory Lamont looked at her suspiciously. "Three miles? But I thought…"

"About that." She turned away, unused to lying. However, he seemed to believe her, and remounted his horse.

"In that case I will say goodbye, Miss Rowlands," He turned his horse, but then hesitated.

"The happy day? When is it to be?"

Lucy thought she detected a trace of sarcasm in his tone.

"Four weeks time. On the twelfth."

He made no comment, but on impulse Lucy stepped forward and took hold of the rein, detaining him.

"Mr Lamont, please tell me, you surely do not intend Jarvis Mottram any harm?"

Gregory Lamont looked down into Lucy's anxious face. *A gypsy*, he thought, *or a princess, or an angel…No! not an angel, to be marrying that man for his title and his money. Why, she had only known him a few weeks…*

He gathered up the reins shortly.

"Do Mottram harm? Not if he has the answers I want. If he hasn't, I shall probably kill him! Good day Miss Rowlands."

Lucy watched him gallop away. Then, her heart beating fast with trepidation, she raced on down to the shore to warn Jarvis.

Jarvis had a wooden shack at the edge of the beach where he kept his tools and various bits and pieces of tackle from the boat, but when Lucy reached the shack there was no sign of him. She ran along the beach, praying he had not gone into town. As she skirted the small promontory beyond the shack, she was relieved to see Jarvis's boat, the *Selangor Lady*, riding at anchor in the bay some one hundred yards away. Originally a three masted topsail schooner of some one hundred tons, *Selangor Lady* had been converted to a fore and aft rig some years before, and now had the appearance of a ketch. As

Lucy started towards the boat she caught sight of Jarvis, stowing nets at the stern.

Within minutes Jarvis was pulling at the oars of the *Selangor Lady's* dinghy, which he used to transfer himself and his catch to shore. As the dinghy came ashore he beamed at Lucy.

"Ahoy there, Miss Lucy!" He was pleased to see her. Often she came down to see him at the boat these days, now they had servants again at Winchester Station and she had more time. She would come aboard the *Selangor Lady* and Jarvis would make tea, and they would talk about the old days...He noticed her agitation. "Miss Lucy. What is it?"

"Oh Jarvis, there's a man, he might kill you, please get away, you must go, quickly!"

Jarvis looked nonplussed. "Now wait a minute, calm down Miss Lucy, nobody's goin' to kill me. Whatever next!" He gave his slow smile, and extended his leathery hand. "Come aboard my dear, and tell me what's botherin' you."

Lucy grabbed his hand and almost tumbled into the dinghy.

"Quickly Jarvis, let's go back to the boat, and you can get out of sight, in case he comes back."

Jarvis stared at her with concern. *Whatever ailed the lass?* He turned the dinghy and started to pull out. Then he gave Lucy his full attention.

"Now tell me what this is all about. This man, does he have a name?"

"Of course. It's Gregory Lamont, Mr Gregory Lamont."

The big hands paused on the oars for a moment. "Lamont, you say?"

"Yes. He says you used to work for his family in Australia. Do you know him Jarvis? He says he wants some answers, and if you don't have the right ones he will kill you!"

The old man let out a slow whistle. He looked grave. "Young Gregory, it must be. Last time I saw him he would be about seven years old. Good heavens! After all these years!"

Lucy was almost beside herself. "Then it's true? You do know him?"

"Oh yes." Jarvis looked as if he were in shock. "I never thought...."

They were alongside the boat. Jarvis tied up the dinghy and then climbed the small wooden access ladder, turning to help Lucy as she clambered up behind him. They went below to the small cabin, Jarvis silent and thoughtful, and Lucy too troubled to know what to say.

Jarvis took down a billycan from a hook on the wall and filled it from the water barrel.

"I'll make some tea as usual, Miss Lucy, and tell you all about it. It's not a nice story, but you know part of it already."

Lucy frowned. "Jarvis, I'm dying to know the details, but do you have time? Shouldn't you be getting away? I sent him in the wrong direction but it won't take him long to find his way back here."

"Bless you child, no! I'm not goin' to run away, not from Gregory Lamont. He was a lovely child..."

"Well he's not a child now, and he seems very angry with you!"

The old man sighed. "Yes, of course, I can understand that. But Miss Lucy, I did nothin' wrong."

Lucy felt a little better. The billycan began to sing on the small wood burning stove, and Jarvis reached down the tea caddy.

"I was a stockman for the Lamont family in Australia. They had a spread north of Perth, not as big as some, but very well established. Several thousand cattle, and they were buildin' up a prize herd as well, when I was there. It was a raw new country you know, Miss Lucy, and Gregory Lamont's grandfather had been one of the real pioneers. Of course, they got huge tracts of land for next to nothin' in his day, but it took sheer grit and endurance to make that land into somethin' worthwhile. Anyway, when I came out from England, there was no free land any more, but earlier settlers like the Lamonts were well established by then."

Jarvis threw a large spoonful of tea into the bubbling billycan and took it from the stove. He stirred thoughtfully.

"When I joined the Lamont spread the old man was already dead, and his two sons were runnin' it. Well that is, the elder son Henry, (that's Greg Lamont's father by the way) was in charge, and the younger brother Jack, was doin' a bit here and there, but mainly playin' around. They had a few stockmen of course, and a girl who helped in the house, but there was always too much to do. There were constant rows between the brothers, because Henry felt he was doin' all the work. At the time I joined them, Henry was married to a lovely girl, Eleanor, her name was, and my— she was bonny. They already had a son called Samuel, and about two years later Gregory was born."

Jarvis paused. He poured the tea into two enamel mugs and handed one to Lucy. "I think Greg was about five years old when Mr Jack went away. The constant bickerin' was still goin' on between the brothers. It wasn't that Jack was bad, he just didn't care for life on the farm. Even in those days, when the spread was well established, it was still damned hard work, beggin' your pardon Miss Lucy. When we heard about gold bein' found in Western Australia, that did it for Jack. Honest, I don't think anyone who wasn't there can imagine what it was like, I can understand why they call it gold fever! Of course, everyone knew about the fortunes that had been made in Victoria and New South Wales in the forties and fifties, and when strikes were made in Queensland and Western Australia it was just one stampede after another." He gave a grim smile. "It was understandable I suppose. Most of the men were worn out scratchin' to make a bare livin', and suddenly there's the chance to make a fortune, just for diggin' it out of the ground! Well, at least that's what they thought. They went out in droves to the goldfields, and Jack was one of them. There was an almighty row. Henry didn't want him to go, said it was his duty to stay with the spread, thought Jack was just pleasin' himself, and leavin' him with all the work as usual. Jack wouldn't listen. He said he was goin' to find gold, and when he did, he'd come back rich and they could afford to hire all the help they'd ever need."

Jarvis took a swig from his mug. He paused in reflection for a moment, and then he continued:

"After Jack left, Mr Henry became very bitter. It was not surprisin'. It was a big spread and too much to cope with. Things started to go wrong, and when they did he always blamed it on the fact that Jack had gone away and left him to it. It wasn't true, Jack wasn't a lot of help even when he was there. Then Eleanor died, in childbirth, a little girl it was, Mary. It was a dreadful time, a dreadful time. After that, Mr Henry was a broken man."

Lucy was moved. It was plain Jarvis still felt the sorrow of those tragic events of so long ago. She attempted to lighten the mood.

"And what happened to Jack? Did he ever find gold?"

Jarvis shrugged. "Not as far as I know. When he came back I hardly spoke to him, everythin' happened so fast." He sighed, "You know Lucy, I've thought about that night so often over the years, every last detail, wonderin' what really happened between the two brothers, I suppose I'll never know."

Jarvis drew in a long breath, as if summoning his courage, and Lucy sensed that the next part of the story was difficult for him to relate.

"It was about ten in the evenin'. I went over to the big barn, to check on a prize heifer that was about to calve. It was in the wet, and I remember it was pourin' down. I heard a noise, and the next thing I knew a shotgun was at my head. It was Jack, he'd been hidin' in the hay. He looked like a dead man, and gave me quite a turn. He wouldn't hear of me fetchin' anyone, said he wanted to keep it a secret that he'd come home, and wanted to see no one but his brother. Acted like a wild man at first, pointin' the gun at me and makin' me promise I wouldn't tell a soul I'd seen him. Well, I promised, thinkin' he was probably in trouble with the law or somethin'. Then he calmed down a bit, and eventually I got him up to the house. We went into the kitchen and I got him some food, he looked as if he needed a good meal. Then I went and woke Henry and left them to it. I went and checked on the heifer."

Jarvis took another swig from his mug. "When I came back to the house about ten minutes later I heard them shoutin'. I went in to the kitchen mainly to remind Jack that everyone would know he was there if he didn't stop makin' such a noise. They were fightin'—a real struggle. I tried to stop them, and they fell towards the doorway, and there was a shot. Jack had put his shotgun against the wall by the door and when they knocked it over it went off. Henry just slumped down. He was shot right through the head, it was clear he was dead. I'll never forget the look on Jack's face. He didn't mean it to happen, it was an accident. We just looked at each other for a few seconds, then he backed away, and turned and ran."

"Oh Jarvis, what a dreadful thing. What did you do?"

I think I was paralysed for a few seconds. I looked closely at Mr Henry to see if anything could be done. It couldn't. I was angry then, and I went after Jack. I was goin' to bring him back, he had to face it. I knew it was an accident, but Mr Henry was dead and I was angry, really angry. It wouldn't have happened if they hadn't been fightin'. As I ran out of the house I heard one of the stockmen shout 'It's Jarvis! He's runnin' away!' I had no time to stop, I had to catch Jack."

"I caught him up at the river bank. The river was in full flood. We struggled. I was tryin' to get him to come back with me but he wouldn't listen. He broke away from me and ran, but he slipped in the mud, and suddenly he was in the water, upstream of me. He went under. I tried to wade in towards him but I couldn't get a foothold, the current was so strong. A big log came down and he caught hold of it and was swept past me. He shouted to me but I couldn't hear what he said. The log rolled over and he was gone."

Jarvis's shoulders slumped. He made an effort.

"After that I panicked, and that's the truth," he said. "I've thought about it since, and realised I did the wrong thing, but I heard the others comin' towards me from the house, they were shoutin'. They had found Mr Henry's body and they were after my blood. Nobody had seen Jack, or even knew he was in the area. Henry was dead, and I was seen runnin' from the house. I couldn't produce Jack, and his body would be miles downstream by mornin'.

It might never be found. Anyway, I hid, and all these thoughts were goin' through my mind. When I got the chance, I ran. I can't tell you the hardships I endured, tryin' to dodge the law, that's another long story. It took me over a year to get to Singapore, and you know the rest."

"Oh Jarvis, what a dreadful experience, and you've lived with it ever since." Lucy put a comforting hand on his arm, and Jarvis smiled at her. "It's been good to tell someone at last," he said. "I've never told a livin' soul about that night." ·

"More's the pity!" They both whirled to face the sharp voice. Gregory Lamont stood there, his tall angular frame filling the cabin doorway. "Yes, more's the pity Jarvis Mottram! Your silence has cost many dearly! Did you never think what you left behind? Did you never think of my brother and my sister and myself, growing up knowing nothing but that their father was dead, murdered by a stockman for no apparent reason?"

The grey eyes flashed bitterness and anger, but Jarvis held his look.

"Of course I have," he returned. "Many, many times. But you were very young at the time and would not have understood anyway. And the others, I was sure they would not believe me." He paused, then; "How much did you hear?"

"Enough." Lamont replied shortly.

"Enough for you to believe me?" asked Jarvis. "I swear every word is true. It is important to me to know you believe me."

"I care little for what is important to you, Mr Mottram. I have spent most of my life waiting to confront you." Gregory Lamont paused, then continued in a slightly softer tone, "I cannot stop hating you in a matter of moments, but yes, I do believe you."

He turned to Lucy: "Although I shall think twice before I believe you again madam."

Lucy avoided his gaze. "I apologise for sending you the wrong way Mr Lamont, but from the way you spoke, I felt I had to warn Jarvis."

"Such loyalty is touching, I wonder, will you be as loyal to your new husband?" Gregory Lamont responded. "He will be a lucky man indeed if you are, for loyalty is a precious commodity these days, so often it can be bought."

Lucy was stung at the sarcastic tone of his voice, but before she could reply, Gregory Lamont turned to Jarvis again.

"Mr Mottram, you will understand I am a little upset. I have just ended a quest that has been part of my life for many years. I need some time to reflect, and when I have done so, I would like to see you again, to clear up any remaining doubts in my mind. That is, if you agree?"

"With great pleasure sir, it is the least I can do," Jarvis replied warmly.

"Then perhaps tomorrow? At about this time?"

"Most certainly, I'll be here."

"Then I'll bid you good day. And good day to you, Miss Rowlands."

A slight bow, and he was gone.

Lucy went on deck and watched as Gregory Lamont climbed down into the small dugout he had hired to bring him out to the boat. He sat in the prow with his head bent as the skinny Malay paddled back to the s hore. Despite his rudeness, Lucy felt for him. *How dreadful to have grown up with such unanswered questions.* She wondered about his thoughts, and watched him climb from the dugout and walk slowly towards his tethered horse. With his head bent and his shoulders slumped, he did not look like the frog prince at all.

William Cranston tapped on the office door and opened it carefully. Seeing Sir Gilbert at his desk he sidled in, trying to give the impression he was anxious not to disturb his employer. Sir Gilbert knew him well however, and said shortly: "Well, what is it now?"

"Nothing of great import really…only if you have the time sir…"

Sir Gilbert sighed and laid down his pen. He did not know which aspect of Cranston he disliked most, his obsequious fawning, or his conniving self interest. However, he was useful, and Sir Gilbert waited for the estate manager to continue.

"It was only that…this morning…I thought you would wish to know…" He stopped, but receiving no sign from Sir Gilbert he continued in his oily tone, "When I went to the bank…the manager…William Graham you know…"

"Yes, I know William Graham, come to the point man, if there is one!" Sir Gilbert was becoming irritated.

Cranston bridled. "He was asking questions, rather pointed questions if I may say so…"

"Asking who questions?"

"Why me! Me of course."

"About what?" Sir Gilbert asked patiently.

"About you, about you sir. That's why I thought you'd want to know."

Sir Gilbert looked puzzled. "About the business you mean? The bank handle all my affairs and there's nothing untoward."

"Not about the business sir, about your personal life...how you spend your spare time...and which clubs..." Cranston stopped, taken aback by Sir Gilbert's expression.

"My personal life? How dare he? What else did he want to know?"

"Well, he was fishing really...about when you were in England, why you came out...whether there was any trouble."

Cranston wavered, he had seen that look on the master's face before. He attempted to avert the storm. "Of course I said there was nothing at all, I was certain." He looked up, and as he met Sir Gilbert's penetrating gaze he flinched slightly.

"And? What else?" Sir Gilbert snapped.

"He was asking about rumours he had heard...but I told him it was all nonsense...to my certain knowledge..."

Sir Gilbert swung on his heel and paced the room. Then suddenly his face changed and he smiled a little. "Of course," he said softly, as if speaking to himself. "William Graham and his wife are good friends of Miss Rowlands. It is only natural they should wish to check up on me. After all, her father is in no position to do so." He smiled again and turned to Cranston.

"I trust you gave me a good reference?"

Cranston started slightly before he saw the joke. "Oh yes sir, of course," he said happily, pleased that the conversation had taken this turn. "I told him you were so busy with the business you had little time for relaxation, and often did not stir from *Straits House* in the evening."

They both smiled a little at this, and Sir Gilbert walked across to the sideboard, his mood completely changed. "A drink? I think the sun is over the yardarm."

"Thank you sir."

Sir Gilbert handed Cranston his glass and poured another for himself. He sipped thoughtfully, and then observed, "Yes, that's all it will be. William and Margot Graham doing their duty as they see it by their little motherless friend."

"Yes, I expect so sir." Cranston hesitated, and then ventured, "I must say sir, I was a little surprised myself, about your getting married I mean. It had never occurred to me that you would want...Of course, it's nothing to do with me sir," he added hastily, but Sir Gilbert was smiling.

"Everyone has to settle down sooner or later," he said cheerfully. "And you haven't seen her Cranston, she's a real beauty."

"I did meet Miss Rowlands briefly, on the day she called to see you,"

Cranston rejoined. "I agree she is all you say, but all the same, marriage may be something of a restriction for you…"

"Not at all. I have decided it is time I took a more prominent place in society. Wealth is not enough to obtain real influence. I am of course of good family, but since I came to Singapore I have neglected to cultivate the best society, and Miss Rowlands will be of great assistance to me. I made enquiries about her. She had an excellent education in England, but just as importantly she knows Singapore and chose to live here. She loves it, Cranston, she is not one of those lily-livered English misses who arrive here and faint at the first sight of a lizard!"

Cranston nodded in agreement; he was gratified to be taken into Sir Gilbert's confidence about such a matter. "I understand now sir, and I'm sure you have made a good choice. But as to your other requirements, will you continue to need me to supply you…"

Sir Gilbert laughed out loud. "But of course…no doubt a few weeks after the wedding we shall all be back to normal. Miss Rowlands coming to *Straits House* can surely not make very much difference?"

Chapter Seven

The morning of Lucy's wedding day dawned bright and clear, with an early shower which refreshed Margot's garden for the festivities to come. The four weeks following Gregory Lamont's visit to Jarvis had passed by in a flurry of dressmakers, shopping and arrangements. Margot had been in her element, and Lucy was aware it would have been difficult to cope without her. A large wedding was not intended, but Sir Gilbert Howell was so well known in Singapore that his business acquaintances alone mounted to a formidable number. Some of them were traveling to the wedding from the Malay peninsula, from as far away as Langat and Kuala Lumpur. Lucy had insisted the arrangements should be simple, and was to wear one of her mother's dresses for the ceremony. It was of heavy cream shantung, with a lace insert for the high yoke, and had been simply altered for a perfect fit. Margot had been a little put out not to have the pleasure of escorting Lucy to order a new wedding dress, but when she saw the finished result she was overjoyed.

"What a picture you will be my dear," she enthused happily, "You will be the most beautiful bride Singapore has ever seen!"

In spite of her garrulous tongue and fussy ways, Lucy was grateful to Margot, who was well versed in the etiquette of Singaporean life, and advised her on everything from invitations to flower arrangements. To Lucy's alarm, the number of expected guests seemed to increase every day.

"Where shall we put them all?" she opined to Margot. "We have only one room at Winchester Station which is ready to receive guests, and that is far too small for so many!"

"In that case the answer is simple." Margot replied smoothly. "It will give William and I the opportunity to do what we hoped. We shall give the reception for you. We have plenty of room, and as we are nearer town it will be much more convenient for the guests. No, not another word young lady," she admonished, seeing Lucy's face. "It's all settled, provided your father agrees of course. William and I will love it, we haven't had so much fun for years!"

So Lucy was swept along in a tide of preparations which seemed never ending. She had visited *Straits House* again in the company of her father, and he had been visibly impressed by the grandeur of the building and the large number of servants, who greeted them shyly but spoke little. Lucy thought she detected a slight undercurrent of tension in the house, as anyone she tried to engage in conversation, seemed anxious to find other duties. She surmised this was due to speculation about her arrival, as the house had been without a mistress for many years.

Gilbert was tact itself. "They don't know what to expect," he explained. "Don't worry my dear. As soon as they get to know your sweet nature they'll be trying all sorts of dodges to get round you, and they'll probably succeed!"

Lucy laughed, but could not help feeling that for all its opulence, *Straits House* did not have the comfortable atmosphere of a genuine home, which Winchester Station still offered despite the years of neglect. She decided Straits House needed a woman's touch, and was sure Gilbert would agree to its redecoration. He had shown her round with obvious pleasure, and had assured her that she would want for nothing in her new life.

Lucy was left with only one vague worry, and once again it was Margot who came to her aid. Lucy, embarrassed and nervous, stammered her way incoherently through a few sentences before Margot, unable to comprehend the tongue tied murmurings, turned in exasperation.

"Lucy, for goodness sake! I don't know what you're talking about!"

Lucy blushed. "Neither do I, and that's the problem. You see, I don't understand what is expected, and you have been married a long time so I thought..." She trailed off lamely, and the penny suddenly dropped.

"Oh Lucy, my dear child," Margot, slightly embarrassed but with a kind smile, came over to where Lucy sat sewing some new underwear, and took her hand. "My dear, I apologise. I should have understood your innocence. After all you don't have a mother to explain things to you."

She sat down. "Some ladies believe these things should never be discussed, but I am not one of them. Married life can come as something of a shock if you are unaware what to expect."

She smiled encouragingly, and then spent the next half hour gently probing the limited extent of Lucy's knowledge, largely gleaned from her school biology class and the furtive gigglings of the fifth form. Margot was touched at Lucy's wide eyed astonishment as she gave careful explanations and answered the hesitant questions. Lucy was unable to understand why people should want to behave in such a strange fashion.

"Don't worry," Margot told her. "If you have a gentle and considerate husband you will soon find out the reason, and will develop a wonderful and loving relationship."

And that was that. Lucy, still bewildered but a little more at ease, put the matter out of her mind. After all, almost everyone got married, and Margot and William seemed happy enough, so no doubt it would be alright.

Now, as she dressed carefully for the wedding, she thought briefly of Margot's words with some apprehension, but told herself her fears were certainly groundless. *After all, Gilbert had always behaved as a perfect gentleman, and was extremely considerate in all things.* They were to spend their first few days at Straits House, before leaving on an extended honeymoon tour to the mainland, where they were to visit Gilbert's other properties, including tin mines, coffee plantations and the newer rubber plantings which were expected to become increasingly important.

Lucy smiled to herself as she slipped into her wedding dress. She was looking forward to the trip. En route they were to stay with Gilbert's managers in Malacca, Langat, Kuala Lumpur and Taiping, and Lucy happily contemplated the pleasure of meeting Gilbert's colleagues and their wives and families.

She surveyed herself in Margot's long dressing mirror. Yes, the dress fitted very well, but perhaps it needed something at the neck...her face clouded, as Margot entered the room.

"What's this now? Frowns on your wedding day?"

"No, but I was just thinking that mother's brooch would have looked just right here, at the neck. I had to sell it a few months ago."

"Well, borrow one of mine. Here—" Margot picked up her jewel box, "Have a look through these and see what you would like."

Lucy smiled her thanks gratefully. "Margot, you have been so kind to me, I really don't know how to begin to thank you. I mean it," she reiterated. "But I don't really need a brooch, the dress looks just as well without it. It's only my mother's brooch which would have seemed right somehow."

"Of course Lucy." Margot was sympathetic. "I understand. And you look simply beautiful. Let me help you with your flowers, and then it will be time to go."

The church was packed for the simple service, the European community delighting in the rare opportunity to display their finest clothes and meet with friends and acquaintances rarely in town. Everyone seemed happy and relaxed, not least James Rowlands, who was secretly delighted to have the worry of the reception taken from him and Winchester Station.

After the service, as Lucy came down the aisle on Gilbert's arm, she felt a calm serenity, as if the anxieties of the last months were now soothed away. Suddenly she felt her heart lurch as she met the eyes of Gregory Lamont in the congregation. His look held her in a moment of deep unity, before the grey eyes clouded and he gave a formal bow. Lucy felt slightly faint.

Outside the church, she recovered her composure in the round of congratulations, kissing and hand shaking. Just as they were about to leave for the reception, she felt a light pressure on her elbow. Turning, she met the grey eyes again, and felt the now familiar churning.

"May I offer you my sincere congratulations?" His tone was formal.

"Thank you Mr. Lamont." Lucy extended her hand. As Gregory Lamont took it, she felt a small, hard, pressure.

"A wedding gift, but for you only." He explained in a low voice. He held her hand a little longer than necessary. "Perhaps to be opened when you are alone."

"Oh!" Lucy was nonplussed, but closed her fingers around the object. "Thank you Mr. Lamont."

In a second he was gone. Lucy was ushered into the carriage amid a welter of laughing people.

"Your bouquet! Lucy! Your bouquet!"

Lucy dimly recognised Margot's voice, and dragged her thoughts away from Gregory Lamont. She leaned from the carriage window.

"Sorry, I almost forgot!" she laughed, and threw the posy of flowers into the crowd.

Within seconds she and Gilbert were alone, as the carriage sped its way to Margot's house. As Gilbert reached for her right hand, Lucy quickly switched the small parcel into her left.

"Well, there we are then," Gilbert smiled at her. "Married at last."

"Yes."

"You could look a little more pleased about it!" Gilbert remonstrated mildly.

"Oh Gilbert, I'm sorry! It's just that it's been quite a morning, and I still don't really know why...."

"Why what?"

"Why you picked me, I suppose," Lucy smiled at him. "You must have been able to choose, and I'm certainly not bringing you a great fortune!"

Gilbert smiled, he was mollified. "Well, as to that," he said seriously, "I didn't need a fortune, but what I did need was someone who would be an asset in other ways."

"What ways?"

"Well, in my circle, it is important to marry a lady who is well educated, and can run my house efficiently. It is also important that her manners and behaviour are beyond reproach. It is not inconceivable that one day I might wish to return to England, and of course my wife has to be acceptable there also."

"Oh. You make me feel like a package."

Gilbert laughed. "Well it also helps that the package is a very attractive one. Everything I have has to be the best. You will find that out in future. I assure you Lucy, you shall not go short of anything that money can provide." Lucy squeezed his hand. "Thank you Gilbert, you have been so kind already. But I do not need riches to make me happy. I have watched my father regain his self respect these last few weeks, and that has given me all the happiness I could wish for."

Gilbert did not respond to this, and within a few minutes they arrived at Margot's home for the reception. Lucy made her way to a bedroom, to refresh herself before the guests arrived. Within a few moments she was unwrapping the small object secreted in her hand. She stared at it dumbfounded, and a glow of sweetest pleasure engulfed her.

It was her mother's brooch.

By the time the reception was over and they had arrived at Gilbert's home, Lucy was exhausted. To her dismay they were met by a welcoming group of all the servants, who were gathered in the hall at *Straits House*. Lucy dutifully went down the line, shaking each hand and murmuring her thanks. It was a surprisingly subdued welcome, she thought. Gilbert gave a short speech of thanks and then told the housekeeper to dismiss the staff. They all disappeared quickly and quietly, and Lucy realised that the welcoming display had simply been a matter of form, what was expected in the circumstances.

She made her way up to a large bedroom, following a tall Malayan girl, who beckoned her with a shy smile. Upstairs, she found a bath prepared for her in the adjoining bathroom, and relaxed gratefully as the girl, who was called Lela, and said she was assigned to Lucy, busied herself putting away clothes and laying out Lucy's nightdress.

Having finished her bath, Lucy was attempting to engage the girl in conversation when the door opened, and Gilbert entered in his dressing gown. He gave a curt movement of his head, and the girl went out hastily. Gilbert followed her to the door, and then to Lucy's surprise, he turned the key and removed it, putting it in the pocket of his dressing gown. He came towards Lucy.

"Well now, Lady Howell," he said softly.

As he came towards her Lucy smiled, expecting his kiss. Gilbert made no attempt to kiss her however, but simply stared for a long moment, and then put out his hand and took hold of the flimsy lace which decorated the top of her nightgown and commanded, "Off."

Lucy hesitated a moment, "Oh Gilbert...I am a little shy...could we..."

Gilbert's hand struck her hard across the face. It was a heavy blow, and Lucy staggered a few feet before she whimpered "Gilbert...what...?"

He struck her again and the pain was terrifying. Lucy had never been physically assaulted in her life, and her reaction was as much surprise as fear. Transfixed by the look on Gilbert's face, she shrank visibly as he said harshly, "Lesson number one. In the bedroom, don't talk. Obey!" He twitched at the nightgown again. Lucy's trembling fingers struggled pathetically with the silk covered buttons, and in a few moments she stood shakily before him, as his eyes slowly devoured her body.

Shocked and trembling, Lucy suddenly realised that all her fond ideas of tender love and affection had been a drastic mistake. Gilbert did not want her love, he wanted something else, but she did not understand what. Then as she lifted her head and met his ecstatic gaze, it came upon her with a rush of horror. Gilbert was enjoying her helplessness, her fear, the sound of her shallow breathing and her distress. He smiled now, as if satisfied, and then he ordered brusquely: "Now Lucy, kneel down!"

And so began the long nightmare, the time of terror, rape and pain, the time of cruelty and sadistic torture which Lucy was to recall with horror for the rest of her life.

From the huge verandah of *Straits House,* Lucy could see in the distance the neat Chinese villages which had been claimed from the jungle by the workers at the nearby tin mines. The villages were clustered around the hillocks of disused tin workings, and Lucy gazed at the far side of the hill, where Gilbert's senior staff lived in their white painted bungalows.

"Did they know?" she wondered to herself. *"Did anyone who worked for Gilbert know the monster that lurked beneath that polished exterior?"*

"Only Cranston!" she answered herself bitterly.

During the three months since the wedding, Lucy had come to understand William Cranston's evil influence only too well. He had accompanied them on their so-called honeymoon trip to the mainland, and Lucy had found he did not improve with acquaintance. He was an obese man, with protruding eyes and a greasy smirk, like a repulsive toad. His lascivious manner, and sly, leering innuendo left Lucy in no doubt that he was fully aware of Gilbert's abnormal sexual appetites, indeed, she suspected Cranston encouraged them. His lecherous stares left Lucy feeling soiled and humiliated, but Gilbert seemed to find his offensive manner amusing. Cranston was careful to keep his distasteful manners hidden from other staff, and Gilbert's public attitude showed complete solicitude and care for his wife. In private however, each night he subjected Lucy to the most depraved cruelty.

At first she could not believe it. On that first night, bruised and bleeding, with tears of pain and humiliation coursing down her cheeks, she had begged Gilbert for mercy. His response had been gleeful laughter, and she had realized again and with ever mounting horror that this was what he sought, her degradation provided his enjoyment. Since then, Lucy had endured three months of physical and mental torture. During the day, she kept up the required restrained and polite behaviour, visiting mines and plantations, shaking hands and taking tea with the wives of Gilbert's senior managers. At night, she became the object of her husband's sadistic cruelty.

During the day, Gilbert seemed quite normal. He spoke to her in the same courteous manner he had used before the wedding, and no one observing him would have guessed the truth. On one occasion since their return to *Straits House*, when he seemed so sane, kind, and approachable, Lucy had made the mistake of trying to talk to him about her misery, telling him she felt she could no longer bear his brutality. His immediate white-lipped fury had been terrible to see.

"How dare you madam?" he had retorted angrily. "How dare you attempt to discuss matters of the bedroom in the middle of the day! Have you no shame? No sense of decorum?"

Lucy, astonished and sickened by Gilbert's double standards, determined not to accept them, and pressed on.

"But Gilbert, I cannot speak to you in the bedroom, you are like another person…"

"Hold your tongue madam!" His tone was so threatening that Lucy drew back, and shivered. His eyes held a snakelike menace. "I shall give you my reply this evening Lucy," he said softly.

And that night he beat her within an inch of her life.

Now, as she gazed at the view from the verandah, Lucy was in turmoil. Since they had returned to *Straits House* she rarely saw Gilbert during the day, and in trying to busy herself with the affairs of the house, she had come to realize that the servants were aware of her predicament. Occasionally she had caught a look of pity on a smooth Malayan face before the eyes were averted, and duties were resumed with the usual quiet efficiency. Her personal maid Lela, the shy girl who had welcomed her on her wedding day, certainly knew. The morning after Gilbert's ferocious beating, when Lucy was hardly able to get out of bed, Lela had helped her to the bath, and had gently sponged her down, all the while making soft murmuring sounds of sympathy. She had patted Lucy dry, like a baby, and had left her lying face down on the bed, returning shortly with some sweet smelling ointment which she had applied gently to the still bleeding cuts on her back. Lucy's pain and exhaustion were such that she was unable to demur, and she lay on her stomach, whilst Lela administered to her needs with quiet sympathetic care. That evening, Lucy had attempted to get out of bed, but Lela had stopped her.

"You will not move madam, you will stay here." Her voice, usually so soft, was firm.

"But I must go down to dinner. Sir Gilbert insists upon it, he will be angry if I do not…"

"Not tonight," Lela said shortly. "I will explain to Sir Gilbert that you are not well, and will not leave your room for a few days."

"Oh, but Lela…"

"That is final madam. Lie and rest, I will bring you supper on a tray."

Lucy watched as the calm young face relaxed into a smile. "Don't worry madam, Sir Gilbert will not harm me. I will explain that you have a stomach upset."

An hour later Lela returned with a tray, and a small arrangement of flowers in a vase.

"From Sir Gilbert," she announced without comment. "He hopes you will soon be recovered, and will see you when he returns from Johore, he will be away for a few days." She put down the tray. "Try to eat a little supper," she encouraged, "then I will apply more ointment. Tomorrow you will feel better."

Now, recalling those few days, when there had been a brief respite from

Gilbert's attentions, Lucy realized that the staff understood only too well the double standards which existed in *Straits House*. Gilbert paid his staff well, better than other employers in the area, and his high wages bought their silence. Lucy knew she could rely on their quiet co-operation, but on the matter which concerned her most she had nowhere to turn. The only person she could really talk to was Jarvis. She had been to visit him at his boat several times, and Gilbert seemed to have no objection. She resolved to call and see him again, but was still reluctant to confide in him. *How could she confide in anyone, least of all a man? Tell of her fear and humiliation, and the degrading misery her life had become?*

She turned resolutely and walked to the stables. *She would not endure it, she would not! If she lived under these conditions much longer she would have no energy to fight back, and Gilbert would have won.*

"Jackson, saddle Brandy, please. I am going to visit Jarvis Mottram, I will leave in ten minutes."

Yes, Jarvis would give her sound advice about the garden, but could he advise her about this sham of a marriage, this living hell she had been forced into? Perhaps "forced" was not quite correct. After her initial misgivings, she had not fought very hard against marrying Gilbert, so was it not her own fault? If only her father had not...But thinking that way could lead to madness, and already she sometimes felt she was losing her reason.

Lucy went upstairs to change into her riding habit. Even if she did not confide in Jarvis, a visit and a mug of tea in the homely surroundings of the *Selangor Lady's* cabin, would at least give her a feeling of temporary security, and help her keep her tenuous hold on reality.

Juminah walked slowly up the incline towards the surgery. She was getting older and a little overweight, and could not hurry uphill. Lela, several yards ahead, turned and waited for her mother to catch up.

"Come on mother, Dr Hunt will be waiting."

"I cannot hurry Lela, my body does not obey me as it used to."

Lela took her mother's arm and a few minutes later they reached the surgery. They need not have hurried, for it was another ten minutes before Dr Hunt showed them into the small clinic, greeting them warmly. He motioned them to sit down and then opened a cupboard. "It's about this," he said, "I've had it made for Danny."

It took a few moments before Juminah realised Dr Hunt was showing them a leg brace, as it was very different one to the one which Danny wore.

"It's a new type," the doctor explained. "But I wanted to tell you about it so you will understand what I'm trying to do."

"But Danny already has a leg brace," said Juminah, "And you have said it will make his leg almost straight. Why does he need another?"

"The one he has is doing its work, certainly," the doctor agreed. "But it is an old fashioned type and rather heavy. It is straightening the leg, but as it takes a lot of the weight, Danny's wasted leg muscles don't have to work too hard, and they need to do that if they are to improve. Come and look."

He spent about five minutes explaining how the brace was worn, and reiterated that the lighter brace meant Danny's leg muscles would be exercised more fully.

"You see, I'm not trying to simply straighten his leg, I want it to hold his weight, so that as he walks his leg grows stronger. The more work we can do now the better, while his bones are still young and malleable."

"Yes, I see," said Lela. "We must of course take your advice on the matter Dr Hunt."

"Well I do need your help," the doctor explained. "There is a disadvantage to this treatment, and that is pain. Danny's leg muscles are very weak, and when he first wears this new brace he will find it hard work and very painful. Of course I shall explain this to him, but I need to know that you understand the treatment and will be encouraging him to walk every day. Slowly to begin with, and not too far. Then gradually a little further each day. I am confident it will work if we all help him."

Juminah and Lela exchanged glances.

"We'll help him doctor, you can rely on us." Juminah spoke for both of them. They left the surgery and discussed Danny's leg as they walked back to the house.

"Dr Hunt is a very kind man," Juminah observed.

"Perhaps he is, but until Danny is older, we shall not know if he is right," Lela said. Her voice was slightly cynical as she added, "Like all our dealings with the Europeans, we take what Dr Hunt says on trust, because we have no choice, but they are not all what they seem to be."

Juminah glanced at her. "You are talking about *Straits House* are you not? I think you are upset my daughter. Do you have trouble with the new mistress? You said she was very kind."

"She is. I suppose that is why I am upset. I cannot tell you all, my mother, it would be wrong and a disgrace to the mistress. But she has married a bad man, an evil man…"

Juminah started. "Lela! Do not speak so of the man who pays your wages and allows us to keep our dignity in the world. We must be grateful to Sir Gilbert Howell!"

"I know mother, and I shall never speak of it to anyone else. But it is true, and I am sorry for the mistress…"

"Sorry? I am amazed. How can you be sorry for a great lady, who lives in a mansion with many servants?"

"But mother, you don't understand. He…he beats her…"

Juminah snorted. "Then she probably deserved it, and what man does not beat his wife occasionally?" She realized it was time to be firm with her daughter.

"Lela, listen to me. The affairs of the Europeans are not your concern, they are well able to take care of themselves. Your mistress has many friends of great wealth who can help her if she needs it. Do your job and keep your distance, remember if you should be sacked we shall probably starve."

"Yes mother. I am sorry for my mistress but I know you are right. I will do as you say."

Jarvis glanced again at Lucy as she carefully steered *Selangor Lady* out to sea. It was the first time he had allowed her to take the wheel and she was obviously enjoying it. He regarded her closely, and noticed that a little colour was returning to her cheeks. He had been shocked when he saw her. She looked tired and drawn, but it was more than that. There was a hunted look, a nervous apprehension that had been entirely absent when she had returned from England. Even when she had been working so hard to clean up Winchester Station she had not looked as she did now. *It was since her marriage*, Jarvis thought, *and it was obvious things were not right.* He took a pull on his pipe.

"Steady as she goes, Miss Lucy. Just aim for the headland, and I'll take over when we need to turn back."

"Oh Jarvis, she's a good boat isn't she? I've never taken the wheel of a boat before."

"Oh yes, she's a good boat all right. Built in Brixham, see? Originally she had three square rigged topsails, and spent the first part of her life in the Azores trade. Oranges," he explained, seeing Lucy's quizzical expression. "Of course, she's gettin' on a bit now."

"But how did a schooner from Brixham come to be in these waters?" Lucy asked, frowning with concentration.

73

"Not so tight, Miss Lucy! Relax a little, nice and easy, that's better. Well, the *Selangor Lady* was called the *Emma's Pride* when she was in Devon, after the owner's first wife. He told me he had always wanted to travel, and when his wife died, he took off to foreign parts, and ended up in Malaya, which was where I met him. He was quite old then, and had altered the rig to make the boat easier to handle. He changed the name of the boat as well, to *Selangor Lady* after the Malayan girl he married. He had spent twenty years plying up and down the river Klang, ferrying goods from Langat round the coast and up to Kuala Lumpur and back. When I met him his health was failin' and he was pleased I bought the boat, me bein' a Devon man." He grinned, "'Course, she's past her best, but she's still fine for these waters, and I keep her well maintained. Mind, I'd think twice before I'd take her out in a squall."

It was a long speech for Jarvis, and Lucy smiled happily. *If only she could stay here, safe on the Selangor Lady, going somewhere, anywhere, away from Gilbert.* Her face clouded as she realised the futility of her thoughts, and Jarvis looked at her keenly.

"I'll take the wheel now, Miss Lucy, and we'll head back. Perhaps you'd like to put the tea on."

Half an hour later, with the *Selangor Lady* at anchor, they sat in the small cabin sipping their tea. Jarvis was still troubled. *She was so quiet, it was as if she was somewhere else.* He tried a gentle enquiry.

"How is it up at *Straits House*? Wonderful fine house it seems to me, must take a lot of lookin' after?"

"Yes, but there are plenty of servants," Lucy replied. She seemed to be making an effort. "More servants than I have been used to, anyway." She turned and smiled at him, "It's quite grand in fact, being Lady Howell."

"Then why are you unhappy, my dear?"

Lucy started. "Why do you think...?"

"Plain as a pikestaff, Miss Lucy. Not that I'm meanin' to intrude like..."

To his horror huge tears welled up in Lucy's eyes. "Oh Jarvis, you are right, I am so terribly unhappy! But I find it very difficult to talk about, even to you."

The old man's big hands fumbled with the tea mug. *Here was a pretty kettle of fish!* He felt ill equipped to deal with a woman's tears. He had never seen Miss Lucy like this before, and she was not the sort to cry about nothing.

"Now, if it's difficult, my dear, a woman's thing like, perhaps your friend Mrs Graham could help, you said she's been like a mother to you."

"No!" Lucy's vehemence surprised him. "I can't...er...I mean it's not the

74

sort of thing I want anyone to know."

Jarvis frowned, "Then there's only one thing to do Miss Lucy. When things is private, and difficult, there's only the family should be involved. Yes, that's it, family only. Blood's thicker than water, as they say. You must talk it over with your father."

Lucy sighed, "You're right of course Jarvis, as usual. I think I knew this all along. I've been putting it off for weeks, but I won't any longer. I'll make an opportunity to visit Winchester Station next week and confide in my father."

Jarvis grunted, "Seems to me you'm doin' it again."

"Doing what?"

"Puttin' it off. Since when did you have to make an opportunity to visit Winchester Station? Trouble never goes away if you keep pretendin' it's not there, Miss Lucy!" he smiled at her and took her hand. "Come my dear, I'll row you back to shore. That beautiful horse of yours has been tethered up long enough, I'm sure he'd love a canter across to Winchester Station. Don't run away from it my dear, whatever it is. Tell your father about it now, and get it over, you'll feel all the better for it."

Lucy found it less difficult than she had thought to broach the subject with her father. Knowing she could never divulge the extent of Gilbert's excesses to anyone, least of all a man, she decided as she rode to Winchester Station that she would confide to James Rowlands only a part of the abuse she suffered at Gilbert's hands, the continual beatings. She was sure that her father would be horrified to hear of her situation, even if he understood it only partially, and would be able to advise her. What she expected him to do she was not certain, but she knew she was unable to continue to bear her burden alone.

After his delighted response to her unexpected appearance, James Rowlands looked at her anxiously, and asked Liam to bring tea to the verandah. Once seated, he turned to Lucy with concern.

"My dear, are you all right? You look so pale and thin, have you been ill?"

"No father, not ill exactly, but…"

"Of course, of course! What an old duffer I am! A child is expected! What good news…but my dear, I really don't think you should be riding…"

"No father!" The words came out sharply, and James Rowlands paused, aware now of her anxiety.

"I'm sorry father, it's just that I wish to speak to you about something, to ask your advice about a great trouble, and I shall find it hard to explain."

Her father's face changed.

"Then compose yourself my dear, and be assured I shall listen with interest to all you say, and shall be as much help as I can. Ah! here's tea."

He busied himself with milk and sugar, and when Liam had gone he continued: "Start at the beginning, leave nothing out, and go on to the end. All the best explanations are thus!"

Lucy was unable to follow this advice completely, but began to speak quietly, and over the next half hour her father, with mounting concern, came to understand at least part of the anguish which had been her daily lot since she married. Several times he drew in his breath sharply, or asked a question, but for most of the time he just listened to the low tremulous voice, as it described some of the callous and pitiless brutalities Gilbert had inflicted, those which Lucy felt able to repeat. Lucy spoke in a matter of fact tone, born of habitual ill usage, and as he listened, James Rowland's blood ran cold. Eventually the low voice stopped, and then Lucy added quietly, "You told me to leave nothing out father, but I have been obliged to do so. I have only told you those things I am able to. There are others which I cannot relate, for the sake of my modesty and your peace of mind."

There was a silence. Then: "My dear child, oh! My dearest child, this is all my fault, I have brought you to this terrible situation!"

"No father. You were not to know he was such a monster. He hides it so well from everyone, he certainly hid it from me."

"But, I encouraged you to marry Gilbert, more than that; I put pressure on you to do so. If I had not been in such financial straits you would never have considered it. Yes, it is I who am to blame." His voice dropped to a whisper. "Oh my dear child, what would your mother think of this dreadful affair, and of my hellish part in it?"

He put his head in his hands, and Lucy gazed at him in dismay. This was no use. She had come to her father for advice and help, not to add to his feelings of guilt and self reproach. For the first time she raised her voice.

"Father, this will not help. It does not matter where the fault lies, and it is Gilbert, not you or I, who is at fault. Reproaching yourself does not help me, and I need help, I need to know what to do!"

Her outburst ended on a note of panic, and this seemed to rouse James Rowlands at last. He gazed at Lucy for a moment, and then stood up.

"You are quite right my dear. You will not go back to *Straits House*." He rang the bell for Liam, who appeared with alacrity.

"Liam, ask the new maid to prepare Miss Lucy's room. She is going to stay with us for a few days."

Liam's face broke into a huge smile, and he bustled away, full of self importance. With a sigh of relief, Lucy turned to her father.

"But what about Gilbert? How can I leave?" She shuddered. "He will be sure to come here to take me back. He will never allow me to leave. He thinks of me as a possession, some sort of asset to his business and social life."

"I shall go to see Gilbert, and make it clear you will not return," her father responded. "Just let him dare, let him *dare* to try and take you back! I will threaten to divulge his monstrous behaviour to his business associates, and he will not risk that!"

James Rowlands rang for Liam again. He was full of self confidence now, and for the first time since she had come home, Lucy saw the father she remembered from childhood, firm, decisive, and in command of events.

"Liam, please saddle Rory, I am going to ride over to *Straits House*."

Liam was horrified. "But Mr. James, you not ride for years! I will get cart ready."

"No! Please do as you are told and saddle Rory. I shall be there much more quickly across country." He turned to Lucy.

"Settle yourself here, my dear. Whatever your future problems, the cruelty of that man will not be one of them."

Lucy started forward. "Father, you don't know how much your help means to me. Nevertheless, I must warn you to be careful; you don't know Gilbert as I do."

Her father snorted contemptuously. "*Me* be careful? I think it is Sir Gilbert Howell who needs to take care. To take a man's home and estates by ruthless gambling is one thing— yes Lucy, I realize now that he divested me of my home by a careful and sustained plan. He would ply me with drink and then encourage me to gamble, and I was unhappy enough, and fool enough, to allow it to happen. But this—ah! this is different entirely. Any man who treats a woman as he has treated you deserves nothing but contempt. He will be lucky if I don't kill him!"

He turned to go.

"But father, don't go in haste like this! There is so much to be considered."

"On the contrary, my dear, there is nothing to be considered but your happiness. When I return we shall sit down and discuss our future. Of course I shall have to agree to Sir Gilbert taking Winchester Station, but we can still return to England and go to your Uncle Matthew, I'm sure we shall find the fares somehow. Now settle yourself, and leave it to me."

At the door he was stopped yet again by Lucy's soft voice.

"Father…"

"What now?"

"Thank you. And father…"

"Well?"

"I love you very much."

James Rowlands strode out with even more confidence. It was strange how this most dreadful of calamities should bring his daughter closer to him than at any time since she had returned from England. *She was a wonderful girl*, he thought, *and he was proud of her, although he had not told her so. He would make that bastard Howell smart! If he tried any nonsense all Singapore would soon know that his wife had left him because of his behaviour. No details, nothing to sully Lucy's reputation, but enough to make Gilbert squirm. Margot Graham would help in that quarter he was sure.* He felt suddenly secure, and confident of his own ability, in a way he had not felt for years. *It was Lucy who had made him feel thus, it was she who had restored his life to him, given him something worth living for. He would get her through this dreadful time, and they would build a future together…*

He mounted Rory and galloped away, deaf to the pleading of Liam, who scurried after him like a mother hen, entreating him to be careful.

But James Rowlands was young again, and inspired with chivalry. Still smarting from the terrible tale he had heard from his daughter's lips, he was nevertheless filled with a fierce joy, for he was the one who would save her. Like a knight in armour he rode fast and free, invincible in defence of his daughter.

But poor old Rory was not inspired by any thoughts of chivalry. He had not been ridden cross country for years, and at the first boundary fence he stopped dead, sending James Rowlands catapulting over his head. Liam, still watching from the yard, had started to run even before the fence was reached, and was there in minutes. But there was nothing to be done, for James Rowlands neck was broken.

Chapter Eight

It was a lovely morning, sunny and clear, but with freshness fairly unusual in Singapore, and Margot Graham contemplated her garden with satisfaction. The heavy overnight rain had left a dewy softness over plants and lawn, and she turned to Lucy with a smile.

"The rain has refreshed the garden; it looks so pretty this morning."

Lucy did not reply. She was still sitting at the breakfast table, and did not appear to have heard. Margot left the French windows and crossed her elegant dining room. Her brows knitted with concern as she regarded her young friend; Lucy seemed so remote and withdrawn. Margot understood grief from personal experience, and she swallowed as she wondered fleetingly how she would cope if she ever lost William. She put her hand on Lucy's shoulder.

"My dear..."

To Margot's consternation Lucy gave a start, as if she had been frightened out of her skin. "Oh!"

For just a second Margot caught that hunted look again, the look she had noticed several times. Then it was gone and Lucy smiled apologetically.

"I'm sorry Margot. I must have been dreaming. Did you say something?"

"Nothing important. Only how nice the garden looked after the rain. Come and look, it's a lovely day."

"Nice day for a funeral you mean?"

The sarcasm hung in the air. Lucy was immediately contrite, and said sadly, "I'm sorry Margot. I'm behaving very badly aren't I? I don't know what's come over me, I know I have to pull myself together, but I can't seem to do it."

"I understand dear. After the funeral is over, and you are back at *Straits House* with Gilbert, you will begin to feel better."

The hunted look returned.

"Oh, do I have to go back today? I thought perhaps I could stay for a few more days..."

"But my dear, of course you may stay if you wish, as long as you like. But

I am not so sure Sir Gilbert would be pleased. He dotes on you my dear, and if you recall he was not keen on your coming here after the accident."

Lucy gave a nervous laugh. "Oh yes, of course. Gilbert will need me at home and you've been so kind. It's just that time has gone so quickly."

"Funerals are held very quickly out here my dear, they have to be. And as far as kindness is concerned, I came over as soon as I heard the news, because at times like this we girls need a woman friend."

Lucy smiled gratefully. "That's true. I shall never forget your friendship."

"I shall always be your friend, Lucy, always. But to return to present matters, I suggest that immediately after the funeral, you return to *Straits House* with Gilbert. He is bound to be missing you and your place is with him. I will come over and see you at the weekend, and you know I am always here if you need me."

"But…"

"I understand how you feel my dear, it must be daunting to face the responsibility of that great house so soon after your father's death, it has all been a great shock to you. But I am sure you will find that once you are home, you will be able to come to terms more easily with your loss. Life goes on my dear, and your husband must come first now."

There it was again, that hunted look. If Margot didn't know better, she could have sworn that Lucy actually didn't want to go home. However, as she gazed at her with concern, the look cleared, and Lucy smiled brightly.

"Yes, of course, you are right as always Margot. After today things will be easier, and there will be lots to decide. What is to happen to Winchester Station for one thing?"

She got up from the table. She had suddenly become brisk and businesslike. "This will never do, I must go and get ready, it wouldn't do to be late."

She hurried from the room, and Margot was left with the uneasy feeling that Lucy was concealing something. There was a remoteness about her behaviour that was entirely foreign to her usual sunny, open nature. Of course she was grieving for her father, but it was more than that. *Could it be that her marriage to Gilbert was a disappointment to her? She certainly didn't seem happy to be going home. But how could that be, married to the most eligible man in Singapore? So rich, and quite handsome into the bargain. Still, men were odd creatures, and it could be that Gilbert was a little strict, and Lucy was a very independent spirit.* Margot sighed, remembering the times in her early married life when William had scolded her, usually for prying into other people's affairs, some of them customers at the bank. He had been quite scathing, and there had been tears and recriminations before they finally made it up. Well, Margot had learned her lesson. She was not going to pry into Lucy's affairs, and no doubt she and Gilbert were better left to sort out their own troubles, as she and William had.

As Lucy entered the huge hallway at *Straits House* with Gilbert, she was met by Lela, who hurried forward to murmur her condolences.

"There is some mail for you in the study madam, and Jarvis Mottram brought these flowers a few minutes ago."

"Oh, how lovely," Lucy buried her face in the sweet scented posy, touched at the kindness of the old gardener. A half formed idea flitted through her mind, and she added for Gilbert's benefit, "I must go and see him, to thank him. He knew my father very well."

"I hardly think it necessary, but if you wish I have no objection my dear." Gilbert's tone was solicitous. "Have some tea sent to the study please, Lela, Lady Howell has had a trying time, and we must all take good care of her."

Lela's face was impassive. "Of course, Sir." She took Lucy's black silk jacket and scurried away. Lucy made her way to the study, and Gilbert followed.

"Now my dear, you must try to pick up the threads again, and not allow your loss to affect your health." He cupped her face in his hand and turned her towards him. "Yes, you are looking decidedly peaky. I do not like to see you looking like this. I am giving a dinner next week for some business associates, and I cannot have you looking like death. Rest, and a little fresh air will do the trick, make sure you heed me now."

Lucy knew better than to demur, and answered quietly, "Yes, very well Gilbert." She turned to her desk and began to look at the mail. There were a few formal letters of condolence, and she could not help but reflect that these were sent because she was now Lady Howell. She wondered how many of the correspondents would have bothered to write to her if she had not been married to Gilbert, and she knew the answer was none. *There were few real friends,* she reflected, *just Margot and William, and of course Jarvis.* At the bottom of the pile was an envelope with an English postmark, and the familiar sloping handwriting, and immediately her mood lifted. *Dear Matthew! She would keep that letter to read later, savour it in privacy. Strange to think he did not know even now, that his brother was dead.* Lucy had written right away, to catch the first ship, but he could not yet have received the news.

"Lucy, come and sit down." Gilbert's voice startled her from her reverie. "Here's tea."

But it was not tea. Instead, the tap on the door was followed by the entrance of William Cranston, who sidled in with obsequious murmurs of regret and sympathy. Lucy responded quietly, chilled by the sidelong leering glances which darted, with astounding effrontery, from the heavily lidded eyes.

A further tap on the door admitted the maid with the trolley, and Gilbert exuded bonhomie.

"Ah, at last. Sit down Cranston and take tea with us. These are indeed sad times, but life will go on."

"Oh, how kind. No wish to intrude, but as you say life does indeed go on…"

Lucy closed her mind to the servile flattery of the estate manager. *She must hold on at all costs and keep her options open. She must let Gilbert think she had accepted her fate, until the time was right to escape.*

"You won't be needing the packages then? Those you ordered?" The low muttering tone of Cranston's enquiry caught Lucy's attention.

"No, not now." Gilbert resumed a normal tone. "Lady Howell is home now; we shall not need the extra help I asked for."

"Of course, of course…" Cranston's tone was smooth, but Lucy caught a half smothered grimace, a leering smirk which was momentarily answered by Gilbert's raised eyebrows and half smile. *What was that about? Certainly something they did not want her to know.* She declined to rise to the bait.

"If you don't mind Gilbert, I will rest a little before dinner; it has been a long day."

"But of course my dear." The tone as usual in daytime was solicitous. "You know I am very anxious for your quick return to good health and vigour."

Lucy nodded briefly to Cranston and left the room. *How she hated that man, almost as much as Gilbert.* In her room she fell into the arms of Lela, who welcomed her with tears in her eyes.

"Oh madam, I was so sad when I heard. I was worried about you. There are bad things…"

She stopped, her beautiful eyes clouded with pain.

"Yes Lela, there are bad things." Lucy hesitated, not sure how to go on, but Lela needed no explanations.

"I understand madam. You do not need to tell me anything." She lowered her voice. "I only wish you to know that I wish to help in any way I can."

Lucy was touched, and took Lela's hand affectionately. She realised how the girl's simple statement laid her open to tremendous risk, the prospect of Gilbert's anger and the loss of her precious means of support.

"Don't worry," she smiled a little. "I'll be all right."

Lela looked dubious. "But if there is anything I can do madam…?"

Lucy smiled again. "I'll let you know," she promised. She might indeed need Lela's help soon, for she had decided what she was going to do.

Lucy stared miserably out of the study window, watching the waving palms, bent almost double by the lashing wind and rain. Singapore was always hot and wet, but this year the rainy season seemed to have gone on forever. She longed for the end of October, anticipating that once November arrived, the rain would magically stop, the heat would become less intense, and life more pleasant. Which is what it usually did. She reflected grimly that it would take more than the seasonal weather changes to make life pleasant at *Straits House*, and a shudder went through her, as the thought of the evening ahead filled her with disgust. There had been a brief respite from Gilbert's perversions for the last two weeks, during his visit to the tin mines in the north, but he was expected home today. Perhaps he would be delayed; perhaps the rains would be so bad he would not return until tomorrow.

Her mood lightened a little, it surely could not be long now. She craned forward, to ensure she got the first glimpse of the postman as he delivered the afternoon mail. Watching for the post had become a daily ritual during the two long months since Jarvis had taken her letter to the England bound ship, the letter beseeching Matthew's help. *Surely the reply must come any day now*. She considered the delay for the hundredth time. She was certain she could rely on Matthew, but perhaps he had found it difficult to raise the sum of money she had asked for. His only income was his small pension from the bank, and Lucy frowned as she recalled her letter thanking him for paying her school fees. Matthew had replied with the admission that he had paid only half, as he was unable to find the full amount. The balance had been made up by the headmistress, Miss Collins.

Lucy smiled briefly as she thought of the sacrifice of these dear people, who had scrimped and pinched in their old age to ensure her education was completed. She felt a pang of remorse at once more putting a burden on her uncle, but she had nowhere else to turn, apart from Jarvis. The old gardener had been a true friend. Lucy had confided her unhappiness to him the day after her father's funeral, and he had been horrified and sickened by her plight. He had immediately volunteered all his savings, but it was very little, insufficient for the fare to England. When he had offered to sell his boat Lucy had steadfastly refused, explaining that she might well need the boat to get away, and this reasoning he had eventually accepted. Lucy had insisted the best way he could help was to act as a contact between herself and Matthew, in strict secrecy. Jarvis readily agreed, and had taken Matthew's letter to the ship by hand, but Lucy found it necessary to forbid him to call at *Straits House*, as he found it impossible to behave as if nothing was amiss. It was vital that Gilbert's suspicions were not aroused, but Jarvis's fierce anger could not be contained. Lucy wondered how he would have reacted if she had told him the true extent of Gilbert's brutality, for out of respect for Jarvis's age and her own modesty, she had not divulged all the details of her daily abuse.

Money for her escape was the paramount problem, and until it was solved there was no point in planning further. Hopes that she might gain financial independence from her father's will were soon dashed. Winchester Station and everything connected with the estate had been willed to Gilbert, "in grateful and just recompense for his financial help and investment in the estate, and the knowledge of his sure provision for my dear daughter." Gilbert had informed her of this phrase with ill-concealed relish, and outlined his plan to absorb Winchester Station into his growing empire. Although Lucy lived in style at *Straits House*, Gilbert was very careful to ensure she had no access to cash. She could buy anything she wished, but all purchases were charged to the many and varied accounts which Gilbert held in Singapore. He had even insisted that Lucy's jewellery was locked away safely in the office strong box, to which he held the key. He explained this was for greater security, but Lucy realised the true intention was to deny her access to any means of raising money. The only exception to this rule was her mother's brooch. It would not have raised a great deal, and Gilbert knew Lucy would never part with it, as she wore it every day. He still did not trust her, despite her attempts to give the impression that she had accepted her lot.

At least the beatings had stopped. Gilbert had become aware that his wife was losing her looks due to tiredness and exhaustion, and that did not please him. Now, after two weeks respite, Lucy had lost the yellowish pallor which had so annoyed Gilbert before he left, and a slight colour had returned to her cheeks.

Several times Lucy had been on the point of confiding in Margot, but always at the last moment she said nothing, preferring to wait for help to arrive from Matthew, and for only Jarvis to be privy to her plans. In this way secrecy was assured, and her friends would be spared Gilbert's inevitable anger once she had made her escape. For escape she would, on that she was determined. *But when...oh when...?*

Lucy bit her lip in disappointment as she saw the postman arrive.

There were only two letters, and the footman took them both through to the office. *Surely there must be a reply by now?* She had directed Matthew to reply to Jarvis, poste restante at the Chinese village, so it was not likely that he would write to her at *Straits House*. But it had been so long, and Jarvis had heard nothing, and she had started the daily ritual of watching for the postman more in desperation than real hope of news. Even bad news would be better than this interminable waiting.

A dreadful thought struck her. *Perhaps Matthew was ill, dead even. When her father died it was weeks before Matthew got to know of it, and if anything had happened to Matthew there would be a similar delay before she had news.*

She turned from the window. Gilbert would soon be home. Beads of cold sweat formed on her brow and she felt the familiar lurching sickness in her stomach. *She must try to hide her revulsion tonight. Her terror would show, but that was no matter, in fact, Gilbert would enjoy it. However, when he saw the revulsion he would lose control completely, and then it was always much worse.* She put her fingers to her mother's brooch in the agitated gesture which had lately become a habit; just touching it seemed to help her gather courage. As her fingers smoothed the polished stone, once again came the sweet memory of a pair of intent grey eyes, recalling the moment at her wedding when Gregory Lamont had pressed the brooch into her hand. She caressed the brooch lightly, wondering if she would ever see him again. According to Jarvis he was due to leave for India soon, perhaps he had gone already. It was Jarvis she really had to thank for the brooch, as he had told Gregory Lamont about it the day after their altercation on the *Selangor Lady*.

"I thought he was coming to see you about his problems, not mine!" Lucy had remonstrated to Jarvis.

"But he asked me, Miss Lucy," the old man had replied. "He wanted to know why you were marryin' Sir Gilbert, and said he thought you hadn't known him very long. I said it was your own affair like, and I did say you had financial troubles. I'm sorry about that Miss Lucy but I was angry at the way he spoke, it sounded as if he was criticisin' you. I soon put him straight. I told him about all you had done up at Winchester Station, I told him how hard you worked, but there just wasn't enough money. I told him you had even sold your mother's brooch, and how much it had meant to you. He looked all thoughtful then, and said it might be possible to get it back, although I'm sure I don't know how he managed it."

Now Lucy's eyes misted, thinking of the kindness of a relative stranger, though oddly, she could never think of Gregory Lamont that way. Since the moment he had lifted her up on to the stone mushroom at the Governor's ball, she had known there was a close bond between them. Not that there was any surface attachment of course, and she had only seen him twice since then. It was something deeper, an unspoken unity which would always be there, whether or not she ever met him again. The brooch seemed to be her contact with him, with Gregory Lamont and her mother.

What fanciful notions! she scolded herself. *They are both gone forever, and can't help you now. These troubles you have to solve yourself, my girl!* And having administered this self reprimand, she went upstairs to change.

"I'm sorry madam, Sir Gilbert has asked for you to go to his room." Lela's tone was desperate, and on her face was a look of pitying despair.

"What? Now? Oh dear God help me!" Lucy could not stop the whispered prayer which escaped from her lips.

"Don't go madam, don't go!"

"I'll have to, or it will be worse." Lucy dragged herself out of bed and reached for her wrap.

"But madam…"

"Please Lela, I…I'll be all right."

Would she? Would she be all right? Lucy was sick with fear as she tidied her hair. Gilbert never asked for her to go to his room, he always came to hers. *What was this new departure? Perhaps he would kill her this time, he had threatened it often enough. Perhaps he would really do it this time, and then it would all be over.*

Less than an hour ago he had left her room in a filthy temper, furious at what he called her lack of response. Tonight she had refused to beg, to kneel and pray for him to stop, to debase herself by further pleading. She did not do it tonight because she knew it was no use. He wanted her to beg and plead with him, so that he might take even more delight in further torture. So she had stood, in dumb acceptance, refusing to fight him, refusing to take any part in the nightly ritual of horror. Gilbert was beside himself at her sullen acquiescence; it was opposition he wanted, so that he might enjoy the subjugation. Lucy's dogged endurance infuriated him, and eventually he flung her violently from him.

"Get away you bitch! What use are you to me? You have no spirit, you mawkish doll!"

And now what did he want? What new cruelties had he devised to test her spirit? For a moment Lucy was tempted to take Lela's advice and run, anywhere, just to get away. She pulled herself together, and trembling violently, she tapped on Gilbert's door and entered.

For a moment she could not take it in.

Gilbert lay sprawled in the huge bed, between two naked Chinese girls, who were cavorting and giggling. As they became aware of Lucy, they stopped, pulling the heavy silk bedspread towards themselves, sulky and bemused. Gilbert, very drunk, struggled up on to his elbows.

"Oh there you are my dear! Girls, I want you to meet Lady Howell! Come and join us my dear, there's room for one more, just about!"

He roared with laughter at his little joke, and at Lucy's stricken face, as she stood, rooted to the spot. Gilbert struggled out of bed and lurched towards her. Lucy regained her wits and turned to fly, but not before Gilbert had grabbed her wrist.

"Don't go Lady Howell, come and join in…" he slurred. He staggered back towards the bed, pulling her along with him.

Lucy found a new strength. She wrenched and twisted her arm, struggling for all she was worth. Gilbert relished her humiliation.

"I thought that would revive your spirits!" he chortled, "knew that would get you going!"

He made to heave her onto the bed, but in his drunken state he slipped. Sliding down to the floor, still laughing, he reached out to save himself and Lucy was free. Within seconds she was out of the door, with his gleeful voice still ringing in her ears.

"Go then! Go you bitch! You can't come to our party…"

When she reached her room Lucy was still trembling. Lela awaited her anxiously.

"Are you all right madam? You were not long…"

"No." Lucy breathed, leaning for support against the door jamb. She had no idea what to do. Although she had been shocked, her main feeling was of relief. Gilbert was too drunk to trouble her again, at least for tonight. She saw the pity in Lela's eyes.

"Oh madam, come and sit down. I must tell you something…"

"Lela, did you know? He has girls in his room…"

"Yes madam, I know, I know," she soothed, "It is not new here."

"It has happened before? He has had women here before?"

"Many times madam, before you were married. Mr Cranston arranges it for him."

"And since we have been married?" She could not look Lela in the face.

Lela spoke quietly. "A few times perhaps. When you were away staying with Mrs Graham, and…one or two other times."

Lucy's shoulders drooped, and she put her hands over her face in abject misery.

"Now madam, don't worry about it. I have something…"

"Do all the servants know?" Lucy interrupted harshly.

Lela stared at the blank face.

"Well do they?"

"Well…"

"Of course they do! Oh dear God!" Lucy began to pace the room.

Lela took her arm gently. "Sit down madam, and listen to me. Listen!"

Lucy raised her head, and the blue tear dimmed eyes looked helplessly into the dark brown pools. The long lashes blinked, and Lela began in a soft but firm voice.

"There is no shame for you to feel. The shame is only Sir Gilbert's. All the servants love and respect you. You are not aware of it, but things are much better for us at *Straits House* since you came. Yes really!" she reiterated in response to Lucy's questioning look. "It is just the way you do things, the way you treat people. Do you think we did not know about Sir Gilbert before you came? Of course we did. There were the women Cranston arranged, and other things…" She faltered for a moment, and then went on steadily.

"There were rumours, mainly from downtown and the Chinese villages. Stories of beatings and ill treatment of some of the women. One girl died, a whore from one of the opium houses. Of course there was never any proof, money takes care of everything in Singapore, and Sir Gilbert is a very rich man!" Lela's tone was heavy with sarcasm, but softened as she spoke again.

"I only tell you these things now, madam, so that you know how we feel. Everyone here admires and respects you. When we heard Sir Gilbert was to be married we were amazed, and then when we saw you we understood. You are very lovely, and he wanted this beautiful decoration for his house, and to show his rich friends." Lucy dropped her head at these words, and Lela took it in her hands and lifted Lucy's eyes again to hers.

"But you are more than a beautiful decoration, madam. You have beauty inside you; nothing Sir Gilbert can do will ever change that."

"Oh Lela…"

"Madam that is all I have to say, but it needed to be said. Now I will help you get dressed to go out."

"Go out? But it's after twelve…"

"I know madam, but you will want to go. I have been trying to tell you since you came back, there is a message from Jarvis Mottram. He wants to see you at his shack as soon as possible, and he warned me to keep it secret. As Sir Gilbert will be busy all night, now seems like a good opportunity doesn't it?"

The next half hour passed in a flurry of quiet excitement. By the time she had dressed and stolen down the stairs to the kitchen door, Lucy had almost forgotten the demoralising incident in Gilbert's room. Lela, fearful but determined, came down to lock the door behind her.

"Don't forget madam; just tap lightly when you come back. I shall be waiting to let you in."

Lucy pressed her hand in gratitude. "Take care Lela. If anything should go wrong and my absence is noticed, just say you heard a noise and came downstairs to investigate. Say you have no idea where I could be."

"Yes, madam. Now go, quickly."

Lucy made her way to the stables and quietly saddled her chestnut mare, Brandy. The poor beast was surprised at being needed at this unusual hour, but was docile enough as Lucy led her softly down the long drive. She had decided to walk the mare until they were out of earshot of the house. Everything was quiet. At the entrance gates, Lucy mounted, and it took her less than half an hour to reach Jarvis's shack. All was in darkness, but after knocking twice, a dim light appeared and the old man answered, opening the flimsy wooden door.

"Good Lord Miss Lucy! I didn't expect you in the middle of the night!"

"I couldn't wait. And things are difficult and I wasn't sure I could get away tomorrow." Lucy could not keep the eagerness from her voice as she asked, "You've heard? You've heard from Matthew?"

"Yes, at last. Come in child, come in, you mustn't be seen."

Lucy entered the dim cabin, and started as she heard a sound behind the door. Whirling quickly, her fearful look changed to open mouthed incredulity as she scanned the familiar and much loved features. Overwhelmed with relief and delight, she flung herself into Matthew's arms.

Chapter Nine

It was several minutes before Lucy could be persuaded to let Matthew go. She clung to him, crying and laughing at the same time, and could not stop herself from repeating, "Oh Matthew! Oh Matthew!" Her uncle was similarly affected, and at length Jarvis intervened, with the admonition that if they did not stop dancing about and calm down, it would be dawn and nothing would be solved. "Now you sit quietly," he ordered, pleased but anxious. "You have a lot to say to each other. I'll make some cocoa, I'm sure we could all do with a cup."

And so, while Jarvis busied himself round the tiny hut, Lucy and her uncle talked in low monotones, bringing each other up to date. Lucy was horrified to hear that Matthew had sold his small house in Maida Vale, to come out to Singapore. Appalled, Lucy remonstrated, but Matthew was not apologetic.

"Listen my dear, and try to understand. When I received your letters I was heartbroken. Not so much about James, for although I remember him with great affection, we had little contact over these last years. But to find that you were in such a situation, married to a man who seems little short of a monster; and with your father gone..." Matthew hesitated, his aquiline features twisted into an expression which bordered on despair. He continued purposefully: "It seemed to me you were very alone, and needed my companionship and advice more than a ticket to England. The more I thought about it, the more I realised that it would be better for me to come here, rather than for you to return to England. After all, what is there for you? I was managing on my pension from the bank, but it would not have kept us both."

"But I could have found work."

"Could you? I doubt it very much. As a married lady who had left her husband in Singapore, life would not have been easy for you, the scandalmongers would see to that. Sir Gilbert's is an important family, and he could make things difficult. There is very little work for women apart from perhaps a position in a shop, which would be poorly paid even if you could get it. No my dear, there is nothing for you in England."

"But Uncle Matthew, the taunts of the scandalmongers would be nothing to what I suffer now! If only you knew..."

"Don't worry my dear; I have thought it all out. As we have so little money, we are rather vulnerable, but I have a plan. If I arrive at *Straits House*, Gilbert will be obliged to offer me hospitality until I can buy myself a small place near to you. My money will go a little further out here, and I have arranged for my pension to be transferred. Whilst I am in your house, I can make it clear to Sir Gilbert that you have someone to assist you. Once Gilbert gets used to the idea that I intend to take a close interest in my niece's affairs, perhaps he will begin to change his behaviour, and even if he is not pleasant, at least things may become bearable."

Lucy sighed. It was impossible for a scholarly gentleman like Matthew to understand that people like Gilbert existed. She regarded the patrician face of her uncle with affection, and noticed now that the fine boned features were perhaps a little thinner, the lines a little deeper. His old fashioned values of fair play would make him a poor adversary for Gilbert. With an affectionate eye she watched as Matthew ran bony fingers through his grey hair, and recalling the habitual gesture, she knew it meant that her uncle was worried. She had to make him understand, and Jarvis too. It was time for the truth.

Jarvis offered her a large mug filled with steaming cocoa. She took it and beckoned him to sit beside them. "I have something more to tell you both, my dear friends. But first, before anything else, I must thank you for your help and support. What I would do without you..."

A tear tried to escape but she brushed it away. Matthew began to speak but she stopped him, putting her fingers to his lips in gentle reproof.

"I must try to make you understand, both of you, for I have told you the truth, but not the whole truth. I know of your concern for me, and I had no wish to worry you more than necessary. Matthew, your plan will not work. My husband is not merely unpleasant, he is vicious and cruel. My treatment at his hands has been indescribable. I cannot for shame's sake tell you all the details, but I assure you mine are not the fears of a silly young girl. I am not talking about matters that are merely unpleasant, but about real torture and beatings, and perversions of every kind. I must tell you I fear for my life, indeed, for the life of anyone who opposes him."

There was a shocked silence, and then a gradual dawning of comprehension on the faces of the two older men, as they listened to the small voice.

"At this moment he is in bed, in a drunken stupor, with two Chinese whores brought in from the village."

Matthew started. He had no idea his niece even knew such a word. "Not in your house? Under your roof?"

Lucy's heart ached for the old man, but she responded firmly, "Not only in my house, but I was invited to join them. Uncle, you must understand for your own sake as well as mine, Gilbert is an evil man. If you cross him, if he even suspects that I have an ally, it is likely he will have you killed. Our estate manager, William Cranston, can arrange anything for him."

Jarvis broke in. "Oh Miss Lucy, you should have told me all this. I thought it was just that you didn't get on, that he had a bit of a temper and was unkind to you…" He pounded his fist on the rickety table, which sagged in a lopsided manner, threatening to collapse. "If I get hold of that bastard…beggin' your pardon Miss Lucy!"

Lucy put a restraining hand on his arm. "But don't you see Jarvis? It is just because I knew you would respond like this that I didn't tell you how bad it really is. You cannot take on Gilbert, either of you. He is too powerful. He has money, and there are plenty of people willing to do anything he wants for payment. He holds all the cards."

"No, he doesn't." Matthew's face was taut, but his voice was firm and controlled. "We go over to my second plan, that is all."

"You have a second plan?"

"Yes. I knew from your letter that it might be really serious; I knew you would not have written for help to escape what you call 'the fears of a silly young girl,' although I hardly expected it to be as bad as this. I have thought about the fact that you might want to leave him completely, to get right away." He turned to Jarvis. "It involves you Jarvis, and I hope we can count on your help."

"Goes without sayin'," Jarvis regarded Matthew expectantly.

"My second plan is the reason I came here in such secrecy, and why I came to Jarvis, and not to *Straits House*. I imagined that if you wanted to escape, you would not want Sir Gilbert to be able to find you. Not ever. So I booked my passage under an assumed name, and traveled here incognito. Only my bank knew the true facts, and my letters of credit can be drawn here in my new name, Matthew Marshall." He grinned. "I thought I might get mixed up if I changed my Christian name as well." He smiled at Lucy, "Or you might let it out in public."

"But I still don't understand," Lucy said. "How will this help me get away?"

"Gilbert knows you have an uncle in England. If you disappear, he will conclude you have returned to me, your only relative. He will not know that I have already come to Singapore, and if he should check there is no record of my arrival. While he is trying to get in touch with me in England, we shall be well on our way."

"But where?"

Matthew looked at them both in turn. Then, as if trying to weigh the effect of his words, he announced peremptorily, "Australia."

"Australia?" Jarvis and Lucy spoke in concert.

"Yes. It sounds strange at first, but think about it. Gilbert will never guess you would think of going in that direction. He will be checking the ships to England, but in the meantime Jarvis will take us away from Singapore, any port will do, as long as we can pick up a ship for Australia. Mr. Marshall and his companion, embarking from a port far from here, and en route to Australia, will hardly arouse Sir Gilbert's suspicions." He turned to Jarvis, "That is where we need your help. Not only helping us get away, but advice as to where and how we join an Australia bound ship. I do not know the shipping services, but I expect you do. I thought we could go from Kuala Lumpur, or even from Sumatra, or as far away as Borneo, that is if your boat would carry us so far."

Jarvis frowned, "She might, but Kuala Lumpur would not be good. Sir Gilbert has many business interests there, and some of his people have met Miss Lucy. It could be a risk. I will have to think about it, but it can be done, certainly."

"There is a bigger problem," Lucy spoke quietly. "If I suddenly disappear, one of the first people Gilbert will look for will be Jarvis. If Jarvis and the boat are gone, he will realise that is how I have escaped, even if he does not know you are with me, Uncle. Jarvis would be in real trouble when he returned. I can't allow that."

Before Jarvis could intervene, Matthew responded, "I have already thought of that. I suggest Jarvis lets it be known locally that he is off on a trip, perhaps fishing or a little freight transport, and that he sets off at least a week before we make our escape. Of course, Jarvis diverts and picks us up at a prearranged point. That way, when Gilbert makes his enquiries, he will be told Jarvis left the area well before you left, so he cannot have been involved. When Jarvis returns, he will be astounded to hear you have disappeared. He could even call at *Straits House* to find out what has happened, as he is so concerned about you."

Jarvis laughed, "I'd enjoy that! It could certainly work."

Lucy was still bemused, "Well, I can see that perhaps it might. But Australia! I have never even thought…and what about you Uncle, from all accounts there are many privations for some of the settlers there…"

"And many opportunities too," her uncle cut in. "That, my dear, is the main reason for this plan. I see that you must certainly get away from Gilbert, but you must not jump from the frying pan into the fire. In Australia we can find a new life, under our new names, and we are more likely to be able to obtain work, or perhaps a little place of our own. Land there is cheap, and I have the money from the sale of my house to begin again. "

Lucy smiled at her uncle's enthusiasm, "But Matthew, are you sure? How can you think of starting again at your age?"

Matthew laughed, "I'm not in my dotage yet Lucy. To be honest, after you left, life in England became rather boring. If it wasn't for your dreadful situation I'd say I'm feeling more alive than I have for years." He became serious, "Well, are you with me? Shall we try the unknown, Australia?"

Lucy could not hide a smile as she caught Matthew's eye . *The old dear was positively enjoying himself. In the face of such an adventurous spirit, how could she oppose the plan? And truth to tell, it did seem to be the best option, and had the best chance of secrecy.* She took a deep breath, and held out her hands to Jarvis and Matthew. "Australia it is then!"

The days following their momentous decision flew by for Lucy. Although they all hated the idea of her returning to *Straits House*, all recognised the necessity of at least a few days for preparation. They were fortunate that *Selangor Lady* was in good repair. Jarvis had recently spent several weeks re-caulking the hull, and this now proved to be time well spent. Nevertheless, there were stores to buy, and fuel and fresh water to bring aboard.

For his part, Matthew was to visit the bank to make his financial arrangements, and then take a room in town, where he would stay as inconspicuously as possible until he met Lucy at the entrance to *Straits House* on the night of the escape, arranged for the following Friday. In case of trouble, Jarvis had insisted on providing Matthew with an old shotgun which had been hanging on the wall of his shack for some years. This was now taken down and cleaned carefully, and its mechanism and operation explained to the protesting Matthew.

"But I've never shot at anything in my life," he complained. "I just couldn't use it."

"I know that, and you know that," said Jarvis firmly, "But Sir Gilbert and his cronies, they don't know nothin' of the kind. This gun is for pointin' at and for frightenin' with, not for shootin'."

With that, Matthew had to be content, and eventually he even agreed to a little target practice on the shore near the hut.

As any communication was a risk, they agreed not to meet again until the night of the escape, any vital message being relayed by Lela. Matthew was concerned that Lucy would be at *Straits House* for a few more days, but as it happened he need not have worried.

On the day after the incident with the Chinese girls, Gilbert appeared at breakfast, showing no signs of the previous evening's debauchery. Although she was well used to his amazing ability to switch from one personality to another, Lucy watched in disbelief as he approached the breakfast side table with obvious relish.

"Good morning my dear, lovely morning. Well, this certainly looks good!" he helped himself to kidneys and bacon. "Mm! Some eggs too, I think. You know Lucy, when I first came here I thought I'd never eat a decent breakfast again. All that fruit! It's taken years for the servants to understand what I wanted, and to get it right," he beamed. "Well, nearly right anyway."

He brought his plate to the table and sat down. "You're not having any kidneys?"

"I'm not very hungry this morning."

Gilbert frowned. "You must eat my dear. I must say you're looking a little peaky again today. Didn't you sleep well?"

Lucy swallowed and reminded herself this hypocrisy would not last much longer. In the meantime she must be amiable and not risk his temper.

"No, I didn't sleep too well, that's probably it. But you are right; I think I will have a little breakfast." She moved to the side table and lingered over filling her plate. The less time she had to spend sitting opposite him, watching that calm and urbane facade, the better. Eventually she moved back to the table.

"That's better," Gilbert nodded at her plate approvingly. "What are you going to do today my dear?"

Lucy started momentarily, her thoughts had been full of what she planned to do. "Oh, I...I thought I might go into town, to see the dressmaker. She said she was expecting some patterns in from London. I...I shall need a new gown for our next dinner party Gilbert, if you think it proper for me to be out of mourning by then. Most of your friends have seen the dinner gowns I already have, and I don't want to let you down."

Gilbert shot her a cold look. *Was this a little sarcasm?* He studied her face carefully. Lucy, tucking in to her scrambled eggs, looked up and gave a slight smile. He relaxed; perhaps she had learned how to behave after all. He leaned across the table and patted her hand gently.

"Do that my dear. Have two gowns if you like."

To Lucy, frozen at his touch, the tap on the door was a godsend. William Cranston came in, his pudgy fingers stroking the gold watch chain stretched across his protruding stomach. He grinned greasily at Lucy.

"Morning ma'am, morning sir," his glance slid over them appraisingly.

"Morning," Gilbert grunted. He was not pleased at the interruption of his breakfast. "What the hell do you want at this hour?"

"Sorry sir, I'm afraid there's been an accident in the mine at Langat."

"There's always an accident. Why bother me with it?"

"You said to always let you know if production was interrupted..."

Gilbert rose angrily, "Production stopped? Has production stopped?"

"Well, yes sir, I'm afraid so," Cranston's fat face sweated more profusely than usual. "Temporarily of course..."

"Well? Out with it man!"

Cranston licked his lips, "They've...they have refused to go back to work. The coolies. They say there's too much gas..."

Gilbert was outraged, "They say? Who are they to venture opinions, on gas or anything else? We'll see what opinion they have about starving." He turned to Lucy, "You see my dear; you see what I have to put up with?"

Lucy, following the conversation, turned to Cranston, "Mr. Cranston, how bad an accident was it?"

"Quite bad ma'am, six killed, more injured, twenty or so. A few more are expected to die. It was an explosion, see?"

"Six dead! But that's dreadful!" Lucy could not help the outcry. Immediately Gilbert turned to her with concern.

"Don't worry my dear, nothing for you to bother your pretty head about," he turned on Cranston. "What do you mean by it Cranston, upsetting Lady Howell? She does not understand business." He frowned, "I suppose I shall have to go up there, or it will take months to sort out. We can't afford to have Langat idle." He turned again to Cranston, "Make the arrangements, I'll leave immediately."

"Of course sir, do you wish me to accompany you?"

"I think not. I will need you here to look after the estate." He gave Cranston a meaning look, and then his eyes flickered to Lucy, "I need someone to make sure everyone behaves themselves."

A slow smirk crept across the fat jowls, "Of course sir, I understand. Everything will be kept in order sir..."

Gilbert swallowed the last of his coffee and turned to Lucy.

"I'm afraid I shall be away for at least a week my dear." He bent and gave her a quick peck on the cheek, "Don't worry, the mine will soon be working again." He left the room. Lucy could hardly believe it. *What luck! Gilbert would be away, giving her ample opportunity to escape! How strange that this dreadful accident should be the means of her own happy release. Six men had lost their lives, and twenty more were maimed and injured, and yet their tragedy and pain had caused her own task to be made easier.* She felt guilty, in spite of her lack of fault.

"Penny for them, ma'am," Lucy started, to see Cranston leering at her with undisguised contempt. "Lost to the world you were then ma'am. Whatever were you dreaming of? How much you'll miss Sir Gilbert when he's away I shouldn't wonder."

Lucy returned his look with disdain, "I believe my thoughts are my own, Mr. Cranston." Her voice was icy.

"Of course ma'am, of course. Just thinking how you might be lonely that's all, especially with Sir Gilbert being such a fine husband to you, and you so fond of him." He roared with laughter and then leaned forward, his voice a suggestive whisper: "If you do get lonely, I'll be glad to come along for a game of cards or whatever..."

With the knowledge of her imminent escape burning her soul, Lucy lashed out.

"One more word and I will inform Sir Gilbert..."

"You can't do anything to me. Sir Gilbert relies on me..."

"Not when I tell him you came into my bedroom and attacked me!" Lucy almost laughed out loud at Cranston's look of astonishment.

"But I wouldn't...and Sir Gilbert knows I wouldn't..." he blustered.

Lucy's composure was impressive. "He would believe me. He knows I do not lie. Your character also is well known to him," she said pointedly as she walked to the door. She turned, her hand on the doorknob.

"Remember your place here Cranston. If I do have cause to complain to Sir Gilbert, he will probably kill you."

And with this sally she left the room, leaving William Cranston with his mouth sagging open.

As Lucy was having her altercation with William Cranston, Jarvis was entering the store in the Chinese village. The storekeeper, an ancient Chinese who knew Jarvis well, welcomed him with his usual courtesy.

"Ah Mr. Mottram, welcome, welcome. Not see you long time."

It was the perfect opening. Jarvis took the wizened hand and replied, "No old friend. I have been working hard on the *Selangor Lady*. I have re-caulked her, and overhauled the rigging, but the old stove still eats too much wood!"

The old man's laughter cackled merrily, "Your *Selangor Lady* is an expensive mistress Mr. Mottram! You will have no money left to spend with me!"

"More than I wish to spend, that is certain," Jarvis smiled. "I have put the *Selangor Lady* in good order to take her on a trip to Kuala Lumpur, to see an old friend who was also her previous owner. I did not want him to see her not looking her best."

The old man cackled again. "No, that is true," he wheezed, pleased with the humour. "But if you wish to go on such a long trip, you will need many stores?"

"Yes, old man. That is, if your prices are keen. I will also stock up for my return journey, as I am sure you will be cheaper than those robbers in Kuala Lumpur."

The old man chuckled with delight, "Good prices for you, old friend! Very best!" He busied about, fetching flour, oatmeal, tea and coffee without being asked. "How long you away?"

"I'm going tomorrow," Jarvis said carefully, "At first light, and I shall be away for three weeks or so." He drew out a piece of paper, "I've made out a list, I think we should use it, or you'll surely bankrupt me."

Matthew's preparations did not meet with such singular success as those of Lucy and Jarvis. He was tired and uncomfortable from the unaccustomed loss of sleep and the hard narrow bunk in Jarvis's hut. Even worse was the knowledge that he had allowed his niece to go back to *Straits House* to face he hardly knew what. Despite his delight at seeing Lucy he had been shocked at her appearance. He sat a long time in the cramped little room considering this. It was not so much that she had become thin and pale, although that was certainly the case. There was something more, something missing, a perplexing difference he could not put his finger on. He tried to imagine Lucy as he had last seen her, leaning over the rail of the *Aurora* as she left Southampton, and then it came to him. It was Lucy's spirit which had changed, that impish, bubbling certainty which had spilled over into everything she did, and which at times had tested even his indulgent nature. He remembered Lucy a few years ago; dancing with delight at the Zoo, pulling him along with an excited, "Can we see the elephants? Oh Matthew *please!*" He recalled her exuberant play on the tennis courts, her impatience with what she called 'boring old needlework', and sighed. Now, he thought, she could probably sit quietly and sew industriously all afternoon. It did not seem right somehow for his darling Lucy, who could never sit still for two minutes together.

Matthew sighed again as he realized that Lucy had changed, and perhaps the Lucy he knew was gone forever, beyond recall. The experiences she had undergone since coming to Singapore had transformed her from a sensitive, vibrant and confident young girl, to a withdrawn and impassive woman. She had been brutalized by that callous monster until her spirit was numbed, cowed into apathetic indifference. And yet there had been a moment, when she had taken their hands and talked of Australia, when he had seen a flash, a momentary hint of her former sparkle. *Perhaps it was not too late, in Australia it was possible to bury the past, indeed, many others had done it.*

Matthew's depression deepened as he prepared for his trip to the bank. *If only he was younger, and could be of more help in the future they faced in Australia.* His mood darkened further as he recalled the words of the serious faced young doctor in London. *This was a problem he must keep from Lucy at all costs.* When he had heard the dreaded news he had been stunned for a few days. Then Lucy's letter had arrived, and the slow realization that the only person she could rely on was himself, a poor dried up old relic with a few years to live at most. He thanked God that Jarvis Mottram had agreed to help them. Although Jarvis was almost as old as himself, he was in sturdy health and it was plain he was a sure and reliable friend.

Matthew pulled on his jacket and opened the door of the shack. Outside, the day was already steaming and hot, much better for his chest than the cold raw air and thick fogs of London. Cheering himself with this thought, he made his way slowly along the shore, and set about finding a driver and cart to take him to the bank.

With Gilbert absent, Lucy's escape plans went unhindered. When Friday came at last, and she was secure in the knowledge that her preparations were complete down to the last detail, she sat down to compose a note to Margot:

My dear friend,

By the time you read this letter I shall have left Singapore. I cannot give you my reasons, but ask you to believe that I had no other option, and that my decision was taken after the most careful thought. If I may still count you my friend, (for that is the way I shall always think of you) would you please do what you can to help the bearer of this letter, my maid Lela? She is excellent in every way, and with your recommendation will find it easier to find a new employer. I am also worried that Liam, my father's servant for so long at Winchester Station, may be in need of assistance, and beg you to use your best efforts on his behalf.

It is unlikely we shall meet again. I cannot go without letting you know how much I have appreciated the care, and indeed love, which you and William have given me. I shall always remember you with the fondest affection and most grateful thanks, and hope that despite my problems I may still sign myself,

Your sincere friend,
Lucy.

This letter Lucy entrusted to Lela, with instructions that it should be taken to Margot the following day, in complete secrecy.

Lucy had packed carefully, as she could take little. Apart from steamship regulations, she might well be on the *Selangor Lady* for as long as two weeks, and space would be limited. Jarvis had rigged temporary hammocks in the hold for himself and Matthew to sleep, so that Lucy could have the tiny cabin to herself, but even so it would not be easy. She made a quick mental check of her packing. One best dress, (one of her mother's, as she intended to take nothing which Gilbert had bought for her), her two old dimity dresses, which she had carefully washed and mended, and a selection of undergarments and stockings. She would wear her riding habit when she left, as she intended to ride Brandy and release the mare when they met up with Jarvis, knowing she would find her way home. Lucy had also packed her precious personal possessions, mementos and letters from England, and a few books. To these she added a small pack of medicines, ointments, bandages and herbs, calculating that they might be useful in Australia, and possibly difficult to obtain.

With only a few hours to wait, Lucy crossed to the study window, and gazed out along the drive, mentally checking her plan of escape for the hundredth time. *Steal downstairs about ten minutes before midnight, having made sure that all the servants were asleep. Make sure you re-lock the kitchen door behind you; and that you have the rope to tie your bag to Brandy, then quietly walk the horse down the drive...* She froze, rooted to the spot. "Gilbert—oh God!" Even as she spoke the carriage loomed larger as it careered up the drive.

Lucy's hand flew to her throat, and fastened onto her mother's brooch, as panic engulfed her. *What was he doing back so soon?* She had an impulse to run, not to have to face him. The feeling was so strong that she obeyed instinctively, and hurried upstairs to her room, where she attempted to control her trembling limbs and chaotic thoughts.

Slowly she made herself cross to the window, in time to see Gilbert alight from the carriage and enter the house. *She must think, she must calm down and think, this must not be allowed to ruin all her plans. In the meantime Gilbert must not guess anything was wrong.* There was a tap at the door, and the downstairs maid entered.

"Excuse me madam, but Sir Gilbert has just arrived home." Lucy gave her usual smile, "Oh, what a nice surprise, I'll come down right away."

Gilbert lay sprawled in the largest armchair. His face was suffused with colour and his cravat was awry. He leaned toward Lucy and belched loudly. "Oops! sorry my dear, it musht be this won-wonderful claret! Musht remember my manners with Lady Howell!" He looked askance at Lucy, and leered evilly. "Time for bed, Lady Howell! Time for a real," he gulped and drained his glass, "a real homecoming! Yes, thatsh what it is. A home...a homecoming." He reached out for her, and Lucy slid out from his grasp just in time.

"Of course Gilbert, a real homecoming! But there's some claret left, we must finish it. You are quite right, it is very good claret!"

Lucy filled his glass again, emptying the second bottle. She had contrived to take only one glass herself, and to ensure that Gilbert enjoyed several pre-dinner drinks. *It was working, he was certainly very drunk, but would he be drunk enough?*

As if in answer to her thoughts, Gilbert's head suddenly lolled back, and he collapsed, sack like, into the recesses of the armchair. Lucy gazed at him intently, her revulsion masked by a kind of disinterested scrutiny, which enabled her to control what was happening. She was filled with a cold sense of purpose. *Nothing, no nothing, would stop her from meeting Matthew as arranged, and nothing would stop her escape.* She leaned over Gilbert and touched him gently, but there was no response. She shook his arm and he gave a stentorian snort, but merely shifted position a little and settled back into a deep sleep. Lucy walked over to the bell pull, and summoned Gilbert's valet.

"Will you help Sir Gilbert to bed please?" she said sweetly when the man eventually appeared. He was dishevelled and had obviously been asleep. "But of course Lady Howell." The valet grabbed Gilbert's arm and put it round his own neck, hauling the recumbent figure to something approximating upright. He was embarrassed to see his master in this state in the presence of Lady Howell. He knew Gilbert's habits well, and had put him to bed many times, but these ministrations were usually hidden from the mistress. Now however, Lucy opened the door wide, and followed anxiously as the valet dragged the prostrate Gilbert into the hall and toward the stairs.

"I'm afraid Sir Gilbert had a little too much wine," she fussed, "It must have affected him after his long journey."

The valet did not turn a hair, "Of course madam."

"You will make sure he gets to bed? And has a good night's sleep?"

"Leave it to me madam. He'll sleep like a baby, never fear."

I hope so, oh! Dear Lord, I hope so, Lucy prayed as she watched the valet struggle upstairs. *By the time Gilbert woke she would be miles away, aboard the Selangor Lady.* She carefully turned out the lamp and made her way to her room. She had just over an hour to wait before it would be time to change.

When Gilbert awoke he had no idea where he was. His mind struggling into comprehension, he made for his bathroom. *At home, of course. Strike almost settled when he got there, long journey for no reason. That fool Cranston, no judgment at all...* His mouth was foul, must have been asleep with his mouth open, and he was wearing his dressing gown. But how...?

A sudden picture flashed across his muddled brain. *Lucy...Lucy by God!...With the claret bottle!* He forced his brain to function. *The little baggage...she had got him drunk!* He gave a great belly laugh and, having relieved himself, staggered back towards the bed. *Whoops! Certainly was drunk...more drunk than he could remember. Baggage! Little baggage!...* He giggled a little at her audacity. *Thought she could get rid of him by making him drunk did she? Well, she would soon find out otherwise.* He lurched towards the door, knocking over a small table as he did so, and sending a carefully arranged flower display crashing to the floor. *Drunk...yes, really was drunk, perhaps go to bed after all, settle with Lucy tomorrow...* He sank back onto the bed, but the phrase 'settle with Lucy' stayed in his mind, and he began to play with the idea. He contemplated what he would do, how he would make her pay. His lascivious thoughts acted on him like an aphrodisiac, and he rolled to the edge of the bed and stood up shakily. *Cold water, that was it. Dunk his head so he could walk straight, at least as far as Lucy's room. Then...ah then, the little baggage would pay...she certainly deserved a beating...*

A few minutes later he was in Lucy's bedroom, finding it difficult to comprehend the fact that she was not there. After taking his time to look around the room and into her bathroom, his fuddled brain refused to cope and he decided to go back to bed. It was only when he was back on the landing that he heard the noise below. *Sounded like the back door...now who could be messing around at this time? Everyone was in bed and...*The answer suddenly crashed into his mind like a thunderbolt. *She was running away! His wife was running away!*

Gilbert frowned. *No, she couldn't be, he'd got it wrong. She wouldn't dare, and anyway if she wanted to run away she could have done it days ago, when he was away. But where was she?* He crept downstairs, taking care with his footing as he found himself liable to sway and miss the tread. He peered from the kitchen window...*yes...there was a light flickering...someone had lit a lantern in the stables*! Gilbert tried hard to concentrate, and was just in time to see Lucy silhouetted against the light, as she led Brandy out into the yard. Then the light was extinguished, and he could see nothing.

Gilbert's main problem was that he couldn't get the back door open. With mounting anger he struggled with the handle until he almost ripped it off, and then got down on his knees to fumble with the big bottom bolt. At least two minutes elapsed before he realised that the bolt was already drawn and the door was locked from the outside. *She had locked it behind her.* Fury engulfed Gilbert as he struggled to his feet. He yelled aloud for help, and having climbed onto a cupboard with some difficulty, he opened the kitchen window and flung himself after her.

The shock of his fall sobered Gilbert somewhat. He gathered himself up and stumbled towards the stables. *He must get a light, couldn't see a damn thing*! The lantern Lucy had lit in order to saddle Brandy was still warm. Gilbert relit it with trembling fingers and staggered outside. He was beside himself with fury. *Leave?...How did she dare?* He stumbled down the drive, peering drunkenly ahead, straining for a sight of her. *Where were the damned servants? He must hurry; once she was on the horse he would never catch her. But he'd hunt her down, and when he caught up with her she'd wish she* *had never been born…*There…a movement caught his eye, and he discerned Brandy's rump swaying rhythmically ahead. He stopped, breathing hard; *she must not hear him and get away. He would follow her, catch her by surprise.* He sheltered the lantern under his dressing gown and lurched after the horse, and it suddenly came to him that she must have an accomplice, she would hardly go riding off in the middle of the night alone. Gilbert's mind raced, *that Graham woman perhaps…or more likely that old gardener fellow…*

Whether it was a sixth sense, or a slight noise which made Lucy suddenly turn and glance behind, she could not tell. All she could recall later was that horrifying moment when she saw Gilbert, his face diffused with hate, bearing down on her from a few yards away. As she struggled to mount Brandy, Gilbert grabbed her arm and swung her fiercely backwards. "Think yourself very clever madam, don't you? Think you can get away from me, do you? You bitch; you'll pay for this…" He lurched towards Lucy, who was now struggling to mount Brandy from the other side. His violent swipe missed her by inches, but a second punch caught the side of her head and knocked her to the ground. As the horse whinnied and pranced, Gilbert swayed over her.

"Yes madam, you'll pay." His voice was still slurred but held such deadly menace that Lucy was frozen with fear. As she stared up in terror, she saw such evil reflected in Gilbert's eyes that she knew beyond a shadow of doubt that he intended to kill her. "I'll beat you to death, you bitch! Starting now…" He raised the lantern high above his head, and brought it crashing down to brain her. Lucy was hardly aware of her own reflex twisting action, as her ears seemed to explode from the deafening report behind her. Gilbert jerked upwards, and then he stood, looking down at her stupidly, blood pouring between his fingers, as he clutched at his chest. Then he seemed to crumple, and as Lucy struggled to rise she saw a dark trickle of blood ooze from the corner of his mouth. His face had a surprised look, and he gasped, "What?…Who?"

He fell heavily to the ground, but Lucy did not go to his aid. She simply stared at the grotesque figure of her husband, too numbed with shock and terror to approach him. Gradually, as Gilbert failed to stir, her senses returned and she eventually understood that he was dead. She turned, white-faced, and there stood Matthew, the old shotgun still in his hands, as if he would fire it again into Gilbert's body. Slowly, confusion came upon him, and he knelt down beside Gilbert, his voice incoherent.

"I shot him! I shot him…I thought he was going to kill you."

"He was…oh Matthew, he was!"

A shaft of light appeared near the rear of the house, and the sound of raised voices reached them. "Oh Matthew, we must go...we must go. Come quickly..."

The old man did not respond. He looked at the gun and then at Lucy. "But I killed him...I really killed him!"

Lucy grabbed his arm. "Don't talk now, come on, we must go to meet Jarvis, we must get away. Come on Uncle, *come on!*" And almost pushing the old man to his horse, she bullied and badgered him until they were well away from the house.

Chapter Ten

Danny stared doubtfully along the huge drive to *Straits House*. It was the biggest house he had ever seen and it frightened him, all the blinds were drawn and it seemed as if the great mansion was staring at him from its many sightless eyes. Even more frightening than the house and the grand people who lived there, was the thought that he might be chased away before he saw Lela. There was a carriage waiting near the porch, and much as Danny wanted to look at the horses, he was aware that someone might appear at any moment.

Danny hesitated, resting his left leg by transferring his weight, as he had learned to do in the weeks since Dr. Hunt had put on his new brace. *The fish seller had told him to go round to the green door at the back, but how did you get to the back without walking up the long drive, where anyone could see you and chase you away?* For the tenth time since he left home, he wondered why Lela needed to see him so urgently. When the fish seller had come to Juminah with the message that Danny must go to *Straits House* right away, they had both been surprised and worried. The fish seller had explained that after he had made his usual delivery to *Straits House* that morning, Lela had followed him and begged him to carry her message, and had paid him a good coin for his trouble.

"Lots of people there and everyone in a state," the fish seller had told them. "I asked what the matter was but they just told me to go away, so I did."

Danny sighed anxiously. In spite of his apprehension he started down the drive, hobbling as fast as he could. It still hurt him to walk and he was tired, he had never walked so far before. As he neared the house he was horrified to see the front door open and two European men emerge. For a second Danny was tempted to try and hide among the shrubs which bordered the drive, but it was too late. One of the Europeans, a fat man who looked as if he had been up all night, called out imperiously: "You there…boy…what do you want?"

Danny hobbled forward, quaking in his shoes.

"Excuse me sir, I wanted to go round to the back door…"

"What for?"

"To see my sister, sir…" Danny replied. "But only for a moment," he added anxiously, aware that servants were probably not allowed visitors.

"Your sister?"

"Yes sir, her name is Lela, she works here."

The fat man scowled. "If you can call it work, waiting on that trollop! Your sister won't work here much longer…"

"Come now Cranston," the other man interrupted. "I know you are upset, but all this is hardly the servants fault."

"Perhaps not." The fat man wiped his face with his handkerchief, "However, I remain unconvinced about Lela. She may well be implicated." He turned to Danny. "What do you want to see your sister about?" he demanded suspiciously.

Danny quailed; he did not understand what the fat man said, but a sixth sense told him that Lela was in trouble. He swallowed and then said cheerfully, "My mother sent me to ask Lela for a little money, to go to market." He smiled, and added, "Lela takes care of us with the wages she has from her kind master here." He assumed the fat man was the master, and hoped this would go down well. It didn't. The fat man seemed angry and shook his fist at him. "Be off you little brat…be off with you…"

The other man came to the rescue. "Now Cranston, don't be so hasty. You're upset and have had no sleep. Get some rest, I'll take care of the boy and see to things. You need sleep before the police come back this afternoon."

The fat man still looked sulky, and Danny, listening with round eyes, was relieved when he nodded and went back inside the house. The other man turned to Danny and said, "Come on then, let's find your sister shall we?"

He held out his hand with a smile, and Danny, conscious that he had found a friend, took it and asked, "That man said the police were coming. Are there robbers about?"

The old man smiled grimly. "No my boy, not robbers, I'm afraid it's worse than that, but nothing for you to worry over."

He led Danny round to the rear of the house, and they entered the kitchen, where the man told him to rest his leg, and a small elderly woman said she would find Lela. When she returned she gave Danny a glass of cordial, and the man departed, saying he had stayed too long already.

Danny drank the cordial gratefully, and a moment later Lela arrived. It was immediately obvious to Danny that his sister had been crying, and he became even more certain she was in dreadful trouble, for had not the fat man talked of police, and said she was to lose her job?

Danny took the initiative, and said immediately: "Mother sent me to ask you for a little money for the market."

Lela looked stunned for a moment, then smiled tremulously and answered, "I only have a little until I am paid, but I will give you what I can. It is in my room; I will go and get it."

She went out, and a moment later Danny heard angry voices, and the fat man entered the kitchen. Immediately he turned on Danny. "What are you doing here? I thought I told you to go?"

"The doctor thought he needed to rest his leg and take some refreshment," answered Minna. "He wishes to see Lela…"

"And I have said he cannot," answered the fat man. "Lela is confined to her room, until the police have seen her again this afternoon." He turned to Danny. "After that, young man, you can see her all you want, because she will no longer be part of this household."

"Oh, Mr. Cranston!" Minna remonstrated, "I'm sure Lela had nothing to do with it…"

"Hold your tongue Minna, unless you wish to join her. In any case, Lela was Lady Howell's personal maid, and as there is no Lady Howell, no maid is needed." He opened the kitchen door. "Boy, out!" he commanded, holding the door open. Danny got down from his seat. His leg still hurt and Lela hadn't told him what she wanted.

"Please sir, couldn't I just…"

"You heard me! Out!" The fat man roared, and Danny limped out quickly, hearing the kitchen door slam behind him.

At the corner of the house he stopped, his eyes full of tears. *Lela had lost her job! He did not know why, but she was in dreadful trouble and he could not help her.* He crouched down and stared at the big unfriendly house, wondering which room was Lela's. As if in answer to his prayers, a window at the top of the house opened, and he heard Lela call softly, "Danny!"

Danny hobbled beneath the window, keeping as quiet as he could as he passed the kitchen door.

"Here I am Lela! What has happened? Why…?"

"I can't explain now. Take this…" A white envelope fluttered down from the window and Danny picked it up.

"Hide it Danny, quickly…" Lela instructed. "I want you to take it to Mrs. Graham; the address is on the envelope."

"Alright Lela, but can I have some money for a rickshaw? My leg is hurting…"

The kitchen door opened and the fat man emerged, his face purple with rage.

"Trying to talk to your precious sister are you?" He took hold of Danny by an ear and pulled the squirming boy round to face him, shouting as he did so, "Shut that window girl! You damn yourself more every moment!"

The window shut quickly, and the fat man shook Danny hard. "Well young man, what were you up to? Stealing I shouldn't wonder…"

"No sir…I wasn't…"

The fat man shook him again. "Throwing something down to you was she, now she knows she's lost her job…? Turn out your pockets boy!"

The fat man pushed Danny against the wall, and pinned him with one hand. Danny, the tears now coursing freely down his face, emptied his pockets. A grubby scrap of handkerchief, a small spinning top, and a mango stone he was going to plant to see if he could grow a tree.

"Turn them inside out!"

Danny obeyed, still sniffing, and then the fat man felt under his shirt and *kain* to make sure he was not hiding anything. Eventually, he let Danny go, with dire warnings of what would happen to him if he ever found him in the vicinity of *Straits House* again. Danny, sobbing with indignity and frustration, hobbled away along the drive, promising himself that such a day would never come.

When he reached the road he looked around to make sure he was not being followed. Then he limped into the undergrowth at the side of the road and tried to retrieve the letter, but it had worked down underneath the leather and he couldn't reach it. Sighing, Danny positioned himself near a tree trunk so he would be able to get up again, lowered himself to the ground, and began to unfasten his leg brace.

The letter was a little crumpled, and Danny read the address on it with mounting dismay. *It was such a long way, and he had no money for a rickshaw.* Carefully he put the letter in the pocket of his shirt and began to re-fasten the leg brace. He had some difficulty in getting back to his feet, but eventually he managed it, and panting a little with exertion, he regained the road and began to walk.

It was early evening, but her shirt and drawers clung to Lucy like wet rags. They had been at sea for two weeks, and she had quickly realized that her long skirts were totally impractical for life on the *Selangor Lady*. With intuitive foresight Jarvis had purchased for her two pairs of long cotton drawers of the type worn by the local men, reasoning that it might be necessary at some time in the future for Lucy to disguise herself as a boy. Now, wearing the drawers combined with one of Matthew's shirts and a tattered broad brimmed straw hat, Lucy did indeed look more like a young native boy than a girl, especially as her hair was pushed up under the hat in a forlorn attempt to keep cool.

She stood, lost in thought as she watched the huge red globe of the sun sink into the sea. *It was such a vibrant colour, a real red, a colour you never saw in England...blood red...blood...*

She turned impatiently, wiping away beads of sweat from her brow with the back of her hand. It was sickening how it always came back. Gilbert was dead, and the terrible memories of that night kept returning to torment her. No amount of logical reasoning could dispel the certainty that if she had not tried to leave, Gilbert would still be alive. *Still be alive, to torture and humiliate her, and how could she have continued to stand it? Perhaps it would have been better if she had been the one who died. If she had found the courage to take her own life, her dear Uncle Matthew would still be safe in his little villa in Maida Vale, living out his retirement in quiet contemplation with his books. Lucy imagined him for a moment, returning from his afternoon walk in the park to tea in the small cosy sitting room she knew so well. And now? He had been uprooted from all he knew, had sold up everything to travel half across the world for her sake, and how had she repaid him? It was her fault he had become embroiled in this sordid mess, and was now cursed with the name of murderer in the eyes of the world, and what was worse, in his own eyes.*

She looked across to where Matthew sat, head bowed, trailing a fishing line in the water. After they had reached the shore on that dreadful night and had met up with Jarvis, Matthew had seemed unable to stop talking, so much so that she had feared for his reason. He had explained, over and over again, how he was sure Lucy was going to be killed. Jarvis had hoisted sail and had the *Selangor Lady* under way in record time, and since then Matthew had sunk into a quiet lethargy, speaking rarely, and then only in answer to questions. Lucy could almost read his tormented thoughts, and suffered with him. Now, she noticed his mechanical smile as Jarvis pointed out to him that there was a fish on the line. Matthew pulled in the fish slowly and carefully, and unhooked it. It was a sea bass, a good three pounder, and would make an excellent supper. Jarvis, who had been busy doing as much work as possible in the slightly cooler evening temperature, took the line and began to stow it as he shouted: "Look alive Miss Lucy. Supper's arrived!"

Lucy hurried over and began to gut the fish. In the last couple of weeks she had become adept at this, as the fish were plentiful and good eating in these waters, and Jarvis had insisted they did not use their stores before it was really necessary. After she had cleaned the fish and removed the backbone, she hauled up a bucket of sea water and washed the fish again, carefully removing the skin as Jarvis had showed her.

"It's a lovely fish, Uncle," she said smiling, in an attempt to cheer him. "It will be really good with some of the relish we have left."

Once again the mechanical smile, and then the vacant look returned as Jarvis joined them.

"Yes, a special supper tonight, Miss Lucy. Do your best if you will, and just to make it really grand, we shall have some of the dried peaches afterwards, just cook them for ten minutes."

"I know how to cook peaches Jarvis, but why the special supper?"

"Because," the old man replied, "I have somethin' important to talk to you about. A conference, or a meetin', or whatever you like to call it. There are things to be decided by both of you," he said pointedly, turning towards Matthew, who looked a little startled.

"Well, it must be important if we're allowed to eat some of the peaches," Lucy said lightly, in an attempt to break the slight tension. "But you don't know everything about cooking Jarvis, because before you use dried fruit it has to be soaked for several hours."

"Quite right, Miss Bossy," retorted Jarvis. "That's why I put 'em to soak this mornin'."

The *Selangor Lady* was a tidy little boat, and Jarvis worked hard to keep her up to scratch. Now he set the wheel in the beckets in order to join Lucy and Matthew in the small paneled cabin where they usually ate their evening meal. Normally they ate in turn, one always acting as helmsman, as Matthew had by now become almost as proficient as Lucy at the wheel. When they had finished their unexpected treat of the peaches, Jarvis pulled out his pipe and turned to Matthew. "Would you mind checkin' above to make sure all is well? Then we can start our meetin'."

As soon as Matthew left the cabin, Jarvis turned quickly to Lucy.

"Look, Miss Lucy, I don't want you to take offence at what I'm about to say, but we have to do somethin' about him. He's goin' to pieces sure enough, and we have to stop it, for his own sake."

"You've noticed it too?"

"Of course. We must try and get him back with us, takin' an interest like.

I intend to be a bit hard on him, and I shall be hard on you too. Trust me Miss Lucy, and try to go along with it, at least as far as you can." He sighed, "He's a wonderful gentleman, your uncle, and he's had a most horrible experience."

Jarvis was lighting his pipe as Matthew returned, affirming all was well.

"Well now", said Jarvis, drawing on his pipe, "It seems to me there are decisions that have to be made, and the first one is exactly where we are supposed to be goin'." He paused a moment, then: "The way we planned it, we were goin' to find an Australia bound ship for you, and you would join it in secrecy and I would go back to Singapore, all innocent like. We are now in the Java Sea, and you should be able to pick up a ship in Jakarta, and in any case we need stores. But if we're goin' in to Jakarta, we have to settle a few things first."

Matthew sighed. "What things? And does it matter?"

Jarvis looked at him sharply. "Does what matter?"

"Does it matter where we're going? Does it make any difference?"

Jarvis raised his voice a little. "You'll beg my pardon sir, but it makes a deal of difference! I'd ask you to remember you are not the only person on board this boat, and if you don't care, there are others who do."

Matthew coloured slightly. "Very well. Whatever you and Lucy decide will be all right with me."

"I'm afraid you don't understand, Matthew. I don't need your agreement, or your permission. As master of this boat I shall decide where she sails. However, I do need some co-operation, and a bit of hard work wouldn't go amiss, from both of you."

Lucy and Matthew both stared at him. They had never heard the old man speak so sharply. Lucy took a deep breath and leaned across the tiny table. "All right Jarvis, let's have all of it."

"The first thing is that the situation is completely changed now. Before, we needed secrecy to stop Sir Gilbert catching up with us, but now, we have to avoid a full scale murder hunt. Police all over the area will be on the alert." He turned to Matthew. "And have you realised Matthew, that it is not you who is being hunted for murder, but Miss Lucy?"

Matthew's face was a picture. "I...I don't understand. I..."

"No, of course you don't understand, either of you. You have both been so concerned with feelin' guilty and miserable that you have not been thinkin' at all. But I have been thinkin'. For this last two weeks, while you have both been enjoying your misery, I have been tryin' to sort our way out of this mess." He paused and regarded them sternly. "As well as doin' almost all the work around here."

Matthew and Lucy sat silent, recognizing the truth Jarvis spoke, but unable to respond.

Jarvis regarded them both in turn, and then his lined face broke into a rueful grin, and his voice softened. "Do you think I don't understand? Don't realize what you've been goin' through? Me, that spent half my life runnin' away from a murder that didn't even happen? I understand your feelin's, better than you know."

"Oh Jarvis, of course you do!" Tears sprang to Lucy's eyes as she recalled the death of Gregory Lamont's father. This was the second time that Jarvis had been in this dreadful situation. Quickly, she turned to Matthew and related the story of Henry and Jack Lamont, telling him of Gregory Lamont's arrival in Singapore, and how he had blamed Jarvis for his father's death for so many years.

Matthew was sufficiently concerned to respond with some interest and sympathy, but eventually he said, "The difference, Jarvis, is that you didn't do it. I did, I shot Sir Gilbert. All my life I have been under the delusion that I could never do anything violent. I have been thinking about it, and the awful thing is that I meant to do it. I did mean to stop him. It wasn't an accident; I can't say the gun went off suddenly or anything like that. I saw him, I knew he was going to kill Lucy, so I shot him, it's as simple as that. I did murder him."

"You saved Miss Lucy's life!" Jarvis spoke with exasperation. "You are both behavin' as if you are responsible for all this, as if it's your fault. It isn't. It was Sir Gilbert's fault, all of it. If you think about it clearly you'll see the truth of that. The man was a pig! Beggin' your pardon Miss Lucy, but he was...a lecher and a tyrant! That's where the fault lies, which you Matthew, seem to have forgotten."

Jarvis rose to his feet and regarded them gravely. "I just want you both to start thinkin' for yourselves," he said. "And thinkin' clearly. I must get back aloft." He left the cabin, and Lucy and Matthew looked at each other.

"He's very angry isn't he?" Matthew said.

"I don't think so, he's just trying to help us," Lucy responded. "But he's right about the chores, neither of us has been pulling our weight." She got to her feet. "Come along Uncle, we can at least help out. And perhaps as we work, we can think the whole thing through."

Matthew nodded and they made their way on deck.

"What do you want us to do Jarvis?" Lucy asked.

The old man smiled. "You take the wheel Miss Lucy if you will, you're quite capable, and I'll show Matthew how to take in sail with the hand winch."

The two men spent almost an hour together, but eventually Matthew mastered the procedure to Jarvis's satisfaction, and went below to make their evening cup of tea. Rejoining Jarvis and Lucy at the wheel Matthew handed out the steaming mugs and then said quietly, "What you said Jarvis...about my not being responsible for Sir Gilbert's death. I know you are right, but it doesn't seem to help. I can't forget it."

"Of course you can't, how could you?" Jarvis was emphatic. "I didn't forget Henry Lamont's death, still haven't if truth be told, although it happened so long ago. It's askin' too much of anyone to be able to forget it." He took a swig from his mug and then continued, "All I'm sayin' is, life has to go on. You have to live with it and do the best you can, for yourself, and for Miss Lucy."

Matthew looked at him guardedly. "What did you mean before? When you said they would be looking for Lucy?"

"Just what I say. Of course they will be lookin' for Miss Lucy. Who else would they be lookin' for? Nobody knows you were even in Singapore, we made sure nobody knew, didn't we? Sir Gilbert shot dead and his wife missin', that's all they will see, and that will be enough."

"But they won't believe it! No one who knows Lucy would believe her capable..."

"I think you're wrong there Matthew," Lucy interrupted quietly, as she realized for the first time the full enormity of her situation. "You see, I know the staff were aware of my problems, at least some of them were. My maid Lela, for example, she had tended my cuts and bruises on several occasions, they all knew I had every reason to hate Sir Gilbert."

"But even so, you would not have killed him."

"I'm not so sure of that, Uncle. When Gilbert attacked me that night, if I had been holding the gun in my hands instead of you, who knows if I would have used it for self preservation?"

"Whether you would or not butters no parsnips!" Jarvis broke in. "There you go again, both of you, feelin' guilty instead of decidin' what to do. You can take it from me; they'll be lookin' for Miss Lucy."

"Yes, and for another reason also," Lucy said. "You see, before I left I wrote a letter to Margot Graham."

"Oh Lucy, how could you?" Matthew was clearly annoyed. "You know we agreed on secrecy."

"I know, but I was concerned about Lela and Liam, and couldn't leave without thanking Margot, she had been so kind to me. I said nothing about where I was going."

"Nevertheless, it will be a further nail in your coffin," said Matthew. He suddenly seemed to come to a decision, smiling cheerfully at Jarvis and holding out his hand.

"Thanks, Jarvis, for jolting me out of my self pity, for that is what it was. It's clear what we must do."

"And what is that?" Lucy asked, with a growing fear of his reply.

"We go back, of course. I will give myself up to the police and we shall explain all. With your evidence Lucy, and hopefully that of Lela, you will be exonerated completely. It will be unpleasant, but eventually it will be over, and then you will be able to go back to England. Somewhere quiet, where you are not known. Bath would be nice, or Bristol. Or you could still go to Australia if you prefer…"

"And what about you, Uncle?" Lucy was horrified. "You will be arrested."

"Distasteful as it is my dear, I'm afraid you're right. But I did kill Sir Gilbert, and it's right I should pay for it…"

"Now hold on, both of you," Jarvis intervened. "You are at last beginnin' to face up to things, but as I told you, I've had two weeks to think about it. There are several choices we can look at, one of them is goin' back to Singapore and facin' the music, but I've considered it and I don't recommend it."

"Why not?" said Matthew. "You surely don't expect me to allow Lucy to be blamed?"

"Because," said Jarvis firmly. "They probably won't believe you."

Matthew was puzzled. "Why not?"

"Put yourself in their shoes. We have just agreed on all the reasons why they will be convinced Miss Lucy shot her husband and ran away. Over this last two weeks it will have become sensational news, and by now Miss Lucy will certainly have been branded as a fortune seeker, who married Sir Gilbert for his money, and then tried to run out on him. People will believe this, even if Lela tells them about Sir Gilbert's cruelty. In fact, that will make them even more certain she was trying to escape, perhaps with money or jewellery."

"But I…"

"Let me finish. What happens next? Miss Lucy turns up, with an elderly

115

relative in tow, who claims he did the shootin'. What will they think then? They will say what a decent gentleman he is to offer to take the blame, especially as he can say the shootin' happened tryin' to save his niece! Well, he would say that, wouldn't he?"

"But, I can prove I did it," Matthew protested.

"Can you? Think about it. You came to Singapore in secrecy and straight to my hut. You made sure you were not seen. Nobody saw the shootin' except you and Miss Lucy." Jarvis paused, and drew on his pipe thoughtfully before he spoke again. "You may be right Matthew, you may be able to make them believe you, but can you take the risk? Or more to the point, can you allow Miss Lucy to take it?"

There was a long silence. Eventually Matthew said, "I did stay in town, and go to the bank, to make my arrangements. That would prove I was in Singapore."

"Are you certain the clerk who saw you will be prepared to swear to your identity? Or did you see the manager perhaps? Or make an appointment?"

"No, I'm afraid not, I only saw a clerk," Matthew replied flatly. "Damn it all man! I was trying to be inconspicuous!"

"Exactly."

Silence fell again. The only sound was the slight slap of the sails and the creaking of timbers, and as Lucy sipped her tea she wished with all her heart that all these questions would go away. *If only they could sail away forever on the Selangor Lady and never have to arrive anywhere, never have to face other people.*

After a few moments Jarvis cleared his throat, he seemed slightly embarrassed. "There's another matter to consider, my own position."

"Of course Jarvis," Lucy was contrite. "We have been very selfish and we apologise, don't we Uncle?"

"Excuse me, Miss Lucy, but I don't mean it in that way. I mean how my position affects your own. After I had seen you safely to a ship, I was to return to Singapore and play the innocent, and I was quite happy to do that. Tellin' Sir Gilbert a few fibs wouldn't have bothered me a bit. But now it's different. Now, I'd go back to a murder investigation, and tellin' those same fibs to the police isn't quite the same thing. Don't think I could do it."

"Of course," Lucy said in consternation.

"There's another thing," Jarvis continued. "I had set up an alibi, by tellin' the storekeeper at the Chinese village that I was off to Kuala Lumpur to see an old friend, thinkin' he would pass that on to Sir Gilbert. If he now tells the same thing to the police they will probably check up on it, bein' a murder hunt, and by now they probably know I was never in Kuala Lumpur at all."

"Oh Jarvis, I'm sorry," Matthew cried. "It's my fault you have been dragged into this awful affair. If only I'd had the presence of mind to send for the police there and then."

"But we didn't, and that's as much my fault as yours," said Lucy. "I practically dragged you away, all I could think of was to get away."

"I'm blamin' nobody, so don't think it for a moment," said Jarvis. "It's just panic, that's what it is, just what I did myself, all those years ago."

"Well, I must say Jarvis, you are the only one of us that has been thinking clearly," said Matthew, "and I'm grateful." He looked up at Jarvis with a lopsided grin, "I don't suppose you have also thought of a solution? Other than going back to Singapore?"

"Well I may have," said Jarvis, drawing on his pipe, which seemed to have gone out.

Margot Graham started suddenly as the closing of the front door awakened her. She glanced at the clock, guilty at having succumbed to a nap in the middle of the afternoon. Then she rose quickly, as she heard William's voice in the hall. Of course, William had not been to the bank today.

The door opened and Lela came in, followed by William.

"Will you want tea Mrs. Graham?"

"Yes, please, Lela, but…just a moment dear…" She turned to William. "My dear, if you have anything to tell me, it's only right Lela should hear it as well."

"Of course, but I'm afraid there is nothing very much," William replied. He smiled, feeling a sudden sympathy for the two women. Both their lives had been changed by the scandal at *Straits House*, and through no fault of their own.

"There is no news of Lucy," he told them. "I had a word with the police inspector and she has completely disappeared. As for the funeral, I suppose the inquest verdict of unlawful killing was bound to attract a salacious element. The church was full, but there was hardly anyone I knew. Lots of Sir Gilbert's business colleagues, but none of our friends."

"What about the will? Was there any news from Sir Gilbert's family?" Margot asked.

"Only a telegraph wire asking me to keep them informed," said William, "The will only serves to make matters more complicated. When Sir Gilbert married, he revised his will. Most of his business interests are left to his family in England, but *Straits House* and estate, and of course Winchester Station, are willed to Lucy." William smiled ruefully, "That was at my suggestion," he added. "Gilbert seemed to want to make no provision for her, but I insisted this was the minimum he should do, and eventually he signed the codicil. Of course it is only a small part of Sir Gilbert's estate, but even so, it is a very valuable inheritance, if only Lucy would come back to claim it."

"I doubt she would want it," Margot said bitterly. "Now we know what kind of life the poor bairn was living!" She stopped and sighed deeply. "What happens now?" she queried.

"As Sir Gilbert's executor, the bank will carry out his wishes as far as we are able," said William. "I shall write to his family with the details and ask for instructions regarding the business, which will continue to trade as usual in the meantime. As far as Lucy's inheritance is concerned, it will be the bank's duty to see the estate is run profitably, and the house is kept up in her absence. That is all I can do until the police complete their enquiries."

"And when will that be?" asked Lela.

"Goodness only knows," William replied. "When they find her I suppose. As they seem to have made up their minds that Lucy is guilty, I suppose we should hope they never find her."

"Amen to that," agreed Margot. "Well Lela, I suppose you may serve the tea now please."

Lela rose, but hesitated a moment. "Mr. Graham, if you are to act as administrator for *Straits House* and the estate, I should like to mention something if I may."

"But of course, Lela."

"The estate manager, William Cranston, he is a bad man. He was always afraid of Sir Gilbert, and so could never go too far, but perhaps now..."

"Thank you, Lela," said William. "I have already heard a few rumours, and shall be going over everything with a fine-tooth-comb. I doubt Mr. Cranston will be bullying the staff much longer!"

Lela smiled briefly. "I will get the tea now," she said, " Thank you both, so much, for all you have done for me, and for Danny."

She left the room, and Margot sighed. "All we have done for her!" she repeated bitterly. "The poor girl works here as a parlourmaid for less money than she was paid at *Straits House,* and she thanks us!"

"Well, it would probably have been much harder for her if we had not received Lucy's letter," William responded.

"Yes, I suppose so, thanks to Danny!" Margot smiled.

"What a character the child is!" said William, "I shall make sure he has his opportunity!"

The door opened and Lela brought in the tray, and Margot waited until she had gone before saying quietly, "And Lucy? What kind of future does she have William?"

"Heaven knows, my dear." William regarded his wife with concern, "We can only pray for her. You must stop worrying so much. If she is with that old gardener fellow, we know he will take care of her."

"Oh, but William! Why didn't she come to me?" Margot burst out. "I would have helped her."

"I know my dear, of course you would."

"I let her down, she did not feel she could confide in me..."

"Margot, you must stop this, stop torturing yourself. Don't you realise why Lucy didn't come to you?"

Margot raised her head with a questioning look, and William took her hand and said fondly, "Don't you realise that Lucy wanted to confide in you? That she certainly considered it? Put yourself in Lucy's shoes and try to think as she did. If she had told you of her problems, it is certain you would have insisted she come here. That would have put you, and me, as Sir Gilbert's banker, in a very difficult position. Lucy knew that, and she would not do that to her friends."

Margot smiled uncertainly. "All the same I wish..."

"I know my dear, so do I."

Chapter Eleven

Lucy straightened up and rested for a moment. For the last hour she had been on her knees scrubbing the deck. She looked at her handiwork with satisfaction and then glanced behind her. Nearly done…she only had to scrub as far as the cabin door.

Scrubbing the deck was one of the many duties which had now been shared out between them. Once she and Matthew had come to understand what had to be done and why, the work was not too onerous, and at last Matthew seemed to be more his former self. Jarvis had divided the deck into four sections, fore and aft starboard, and fore and aft port. Matthew was responsible for the port side and Lucy the starboard. Each day they scrubbed one section and swabbed the other, which meant that the *Selangor Lady* had her deck completely scrubbed every other day. Today however, Lucy was required to carry out all Matthew's deck duties as well as her own, as Jarvis had stipulated Matthew must not leave the cabin whilst they were at anchor off Jakarta. Instead, Matthew toiled below at the tiny stove, concocting what he hoped would be a delicious sauce to accompany whatever Jarvis brought back for dinner, whilst Lucy, looking for all the world like a rather scruffy cabin boy, polished the brass and scrubbed two sections of deck.

As she finished her chores, Lucy heard Matthew call her for tea. Having emptied her bucket over the side and stowed her brushes, she climbed down to the cabin with relief.

"Oh wonderful!" Lucy sat down and reached for the mug. "Thank you Uncle, I'm exhausted."

Matthew looked at her anxiously. "You must be. I don't know that all this secrecy is really necessary."

"Well, I think Jarvis is probably right. If anyone should be interested in us, all they will see is Jarvis going ashore quite openly, having left his cabin boy on board. That will seem perfectly normal. If there should be any enquiries, Jarvis is entitled to be here, and should be able to fend off any questions."

"They might think it rather odd, a boat of this size with only two people aboard. Originally I think Jarvis said the *Selangor Lady* would have had a crew of five."

"Well, yes," Lucy responded, "that was when she had square topsail rigging. She needed a full crew then in order to make sail. Now, with only a fore and aft rig we should be able to manage her, although of course we shall make way much more slowly."

Matthew laughed. "Quite the sailor, aren't you? I must say you are better at the rigging and the knots than I am. I'm sorry you had to do my work today. Once we get under way I promise I'll do yours for a day. To be honest I think I'd prefer it, it's sweltering down here, and I'd love a breath of air."

"Oh, but think of it, Matthew! Jarvis is sure to bring back plenty of fresh fruit and vegetables, what a dinner you can serve up tonight."

"Yes, I've already made a sauce for the fish, and we shall have fresh food for at least a week. And then..." His tone became serious. "What do you really think Lucy? Do you think we can reach Australia in this old tub?"

"She's not an old tub!" Lucy responded fiercely, "And I'm becoming very fond of her. She is old I admit, but she's not a tub, and although her rig may make her look a little dumpy, it also makes her able to be handled by only three of us on such a long journey."

"But that's exactly what I mean," Matthew rejoined. "I know she has sailed long journeys and deep water before, but then she had much more sail and an experienced crew. Do you think she can make Australia?"

"I don't know, but Jarvis thinks she can, and he has much more knowledge than either of us. From what he says the biggest problems will be when we reach the long stretch across the Timor Sea, as the weather there can be so unpredictable. If we can overcome that and reach the Australian coast, we can rest on land, then sail on around the coast for as long and as far as we wish."

Lucy clasped her fingers around the tea mug and regarded Matthew gravely. "What is it, Uncle? Do you have doubts? We did discuss it all very thoroughly."

Matthew smiled. "My dear child, of course I have doubts. It would be a very foolhardy person who did not have doubts about such a journey, and in such circumstances. But you are right, we have planned it with great care, or at least Jarvis has. We shall be as well prepared as possible. It's only..."

"Only what?"

"Well..." Matthew was hesitant, "I'm sure we are doing the right thing, but have you thought how vulnerable we should be if anything happened to Jarvis?" Seeing Lucy's look of alarm he leaned forward and patted her arm. "Of course my dear nothing will, we shall take great care it doesn't, but we are very much reliant on his good seamanship. That is why it is so important we learn everything Jarvis has to teach us, not only in order to help during the journey, but to be prepared, in case he should ever be put out of action."

"Yes…yes I see," said Lucy thoughtfully. She looked up enquiringly at Matthew. "Is that why Jarvis has been working us so hard, and has been insisting we both do the navigation plotting with him?"

Matthew smiled grimly. "The more I see of Jarvis, the more I find to respect and admire. He is no fool, and he knows he is an old man. He is trying to make sure we can take care of ourselves if anything should happen to him. There is no need to dwell on this, or be dismal about it, but during the next few weeks we must both work really hard to learn everything we can from Jarvis, about the boat, the sea, and Australia. We owe him our best efforts; after all he's done for us."

Lucy agreed soberly, and with much to think about she clambered back on deck. Seconds later her head appeared once again, framed in the cabin doorway.

"Look alive Matthew. Jarvis is coming back in the dinghy, and trailing another, both fully loaded. And Matthew, guess what? Watermelons!"

During the next few weeks, the *Selangor Lady* and her unlikely crew sailed gently and quietly through the Java Sea, keeping about two miles out from the Indonesian islands. Gradually Lucy and Matthew found their strange life easier, as they became more proficient at handling the boat, and coping with the thousand and one small chores. Both found a strange kind of peace in the discipline of their new duties, and after a short while became fitter and stronger. Their diet was good, mainly fresh fish and vegetables until they ran out, and Jarvis planned to put into one of the islands for fresh supplies and water very soon. Jarvis had rigged up what he called a 'long bath,' similar to those used by the Europeans in the early days in Singapore. This was simply a large rainwater butt behind a tarpaulin screen, and to bathe they stood in a small tin bath and soaped themselves from a tin of soft soap, afterwards ladling the rainwater over themselves to rinse off. When she had become used to it, Lucy found the 'long bath' refreshing, and was able to wash her hair in the same way. A similar tarpaulin screen hid their latrine bucket, which Jarvis explained each person must empty immediately after use, by letting down the bucket into the sea on the attached rope and then hauling it up again and replacing it clean for the next user. Lucy thus found their hygiene standard better than she had expected, and the days dissolved into a routine of chores, cooking, meals and spells at the wheel, combined with regular lessons from Jarvis on navigation. These Lucy found quite difficult, but Matthew devoured the information eagerly, as a long lost boyhood interest which he had never before had the opportunity to indulge. Most of all, Lucy loved the warm evenings, when they would sit on deck in the fading light, one at the wheel and two off duty, and talk quietly of their hopes and fears for the future. Accompanied only by the slow steady creaking of the *Selangor Lady's* timbers and the slap of the sails, Jarvis would tell long tales in his low Devon drawl, aware that recent events were still too close for Matthew and Lucy to speak of them without distress.

Jarvis talked of his home in Devon, his parents and his long dead wife. He told them of the unspeakable journey when he had shipped steerage to Australia, and of the hardship he encountered when he first arrived. He told them of jobs on farms, in a tackle shop, and on a coastal vessel which plied from Fremantle down to Melbourne and Sydney, and often his Devon accent and down to earth wit had his listeners tearful with laughter. On one such evening he expanded, mainly for Matthew's benefit, on the story of his life on the Lamont cattle station, and Lucy wondered with sadness what the frog prince with the devastating grey eyes would think if he could see her now, a grubby deckhand with broken fingernails and a face tanned brown by the sun. She turned to Jarvis with interest: "What happened to Gregory Lamont? I never saw him again after my wedding. Did he return to Australia, or is he still in Singapore?"

"I don't know," said Jarvis thoughtfully, "I had a long conversation with him on the day after he came to see me at the boat, you remember Lucy..."

"Yes."

"He said then that he planned to go to India, and I didn't see him again. I wanted to see him once more, to give him somethin'."

"Give him what?"

"Oh, just a sort of map, or rather a plan really, which belonged to his Uncle Jack. You recall I told you of the awful night when Jack drowned, and when my life took such a terrible turn?"

"Of course," Lucy was intrigued.

"What I didn't tell you, is that as the water swept him away he threw somethin' on to the bank. He was shoutin' somethin', but I couldn't hear. It was a kind of pouch made of oilskin, and had just a very little money in it and a piece of paper, nothin' much, a sort of rough map, scribbled in pencil."

"But what was it? Is it important?" Lucy asked, a shiver of excitement running through her.

"I shouldn't think so. Not enough details on it to indicate where it is. There's a part marked 'Town' and a line to the east of it marked 'River'. Then to the north of the town there's a big circular shape, and a big letter 'M'. The trouble is there is nothin' at all to tell you which town and river it refers to, so it could be anywhere. There is a cross which presumably marks somethin', but what; there is no way of knowin'."

"But Jarvis, how exciting! It might be important. If it wasn't, why did he bother to throw it to you?"

"My feelin's exactly, which is why I kept it all these years. I suppose at first I had some idea that one day the whole story would come out, and I could return the paper to the family, but then I left Australia, and somehow over the years I forgot about it."

"But, you still have it?"

"I do indeed, but the more I look at it the more I'm convinced it means nothin'. It may have done once, but no longer. There is no way of pinpointin' the location."

Jarvis drew on his pipe and laughed out loud. "Look at her face Matthew! Lucy is convinced that it's a treasure map, that Jack really did find gold, marked it on the map, and came home to tell the family about it."

Lucy blushed. "Well, it's one explanation, at least an interesting one."

"Yes, I know my dear. I've thought about it often over the years, and have had the same idea myself. But it doesn't make sense. First of all, if Jack had found gold and came home to tell his brother, why did they fight? You would think they would be celebratin'. And anyway, even if the map was intended to mark a special place, for example a gold strike, it certainly doesn't now, because as I say it could be anywhere. The general location was in Jack's head, which means it's gone forever."

Lucy was disappointed, "I suppose we'll never know. But Jarvis, why didn't you give the paper to Mr. Lamont when he came to see you?"

"Well to be honest, Miss Lucy, I didn't even think about it the first time. If you remember he was a bit angry, and I was more concerned with gettin' him to believe me than anythin' else."

"Yes, I remember."

"Well, next day we had a long talk. That's when he asked me about you marryin' Sir Gilbert, and I told him about your mother's brooch. I still hadn't remembered about the map, and when I did I thought…well…I decided to ask you to give it to him."

"Why should I give it to him?" Lucy asked.

The old man shuffled a little with embarrassment.

"To be honest, Miss Lucy, I thought I'd do a little matchmakin' like. Oh, I know I shouldn't have, but I liked Mr. Gregory when I got to know him better, and he seemed so interested in you, I thought he might be keen on you, see?"

"Jarvis!"

"Yes, alright, I'm an interferin' old man! I knew you were already engaged to Sir Gilbert, but I wasn't that keen on him, mainly because you didn't seem to be. Anyway, to get back to the tale...I was goin' to give the map to you, but I didn't see you for a while, and there seemed to be no hurry after twenty odd years. By the time I did see you, the weddin' was very near, and you were so full of the arrangements I thought better of my silly matchmakin'."

"I wish you hadn't," Matthew spoke feelingly. "I don't know Mr. Lamont, but there surely is not another man in the world would have made as bad a husband as Sir Gilbert."

"Husband? What are you saying?" Lucy coloured furiously. "I hardly know Mr. Lamont. Why is it that the men I know, even those who have my best interests at heart, seem compelled to try to marry me off?" Warming to her theme, her voice rose. "My father kept insisting I should marry Gilbert, when all my instincts were against it. Why do men assume they know what is right for women? And why should women have to put up with their arrogance?"

"Calm down, I didn't mean it like that, and anyway, I happen to agree with you," Matthew consoled her. He turned to Jarvis.

"Do you think there is any chance of meeting Mr. Lamont again if he has returned to Australia?"

Jarvis smiled. "I very much doubt it. Australia is a very large continent. Coming from England it's impossible to imagine how large, until you have been there and experienced it for yourself. It's possible we could meet up I suppose, as I think it's best for us to settle somewhere near Perth, as I know that area, but we are unlikely to run into him unless we want to. All the same I should like to make sure Gregory Lamont gets the map, he might like to have it for sentimental reasons, I got the impression he was very fond of his Uncle Jack. Perhaps I can post it to him from Perth. We should perhaps try to stay near the coast."

"In case we have to run away again?" Lucy could not help but ask bitterly.

"We shall be prudent always to take care, and to have an avenue of escape available to us," replied Jarvis. "With the *Selangor Lady*, at least we have that escape route. It is always much harder to find someone at sea."

Lucy turned away, her heart like stone. Matthew's innocent remark had brought to the surface feelings, strong and tumultuous, which she had denied for too long, and she felt thoroughly shaken. Now, trembling slightly, she realised she had deliberately suppressed her thoughts concerning Gregory Lamont. *No...Not her thoughts, for she had thought of him often, on those warm balmy evenings when she was relaxed in contemplation of the tropical night. It was her feelings she had suppressed, because they were too difficult to cope with, too heartrending, when every dream she dreamed began with "If only..."*

Chapter Twelve

It was a big fish, so big that Matthew could hardly handle it. He shouted for help and ran along the edge of the deck, paying out the line. Suddenly the rod was almost wrenched from his hands as he was stopped by the sharp tug of the tie-line around his waist. The other end of the tie-line was securely fastened to the heavy anchor windlass, and Matthew struggled to hold on to the rod as he gasped out: "The tie-line! Undo the tie-line Lucy, I'm being cut in half!"

Lucy laughed as she undid the knot of rope at his waist. "You can always let go of the rod."

"Certainly not! Look at the size of it!" Free now from the constraints of the tie-line, Matthew leaned over the side, playing the fish expertly, until he hauled it in a few minutes later.

"What about that?" He grinned up at Lucy, his sun tanned face almost boyish with excitement.

"It's so big you should have let it go. It's far too much for one meal."

"Oh. Yes, I suppose so," Matthew sounded disappointed. He turned and retrieved the tie-line. "This damned thing nearly cut me in two. How much longer do we have to wear them?"

"Until we are safe in Australia I suppose."

"Well, they're a great nuisance!" Having retied the line, Matthew knelt down and gave the flapping fish a sharp knock on the head and removed the hook from its mouth.

"You won't think so if we strike bad weather and you go overboard to feed the sharks." Jarvis had joined them from the hold and regarded the fish gravely. "My that's a beauty, Matthew, we'll make a fisherman of you yet."

"He nearly lost it," Lucy said, "The tie-line pulled him up."

"Yes. I know they're a nuisance, but in these waters the storm can come up very suddenly, and I don't want anyone swept overboard."

"But Jarvis, how much longer?" Matthew asked. "It's over two weeks since we left Flores, surely we shall sight the Australian coast soon?"

"Within a week perhaps," Jarvis replied. "But it won't be the mainland, more likely one of the islands off the coast. I only hope this weather lasts, we have been lucky to get so far without more than a slight squall." He scanned the horizon keenly. "Keep alert to the riggin', Miss Lucy, the wind changes direction really fast. In the meantime," he added, "We'll make a good meal of that fish. If storms do come we may not have hot food for days."

His words were prophetic, for just after the evening meal the typhoon struck. It was so sudden that Jarvis only had time to point out the heavy black skyline, and within ten minutes the deluge of rain was upon them. Matthew was off watch, and was tipped from his hammock by the first huge wave which hit *Selangor Lady* broadside. Grabbing his tie-line, he attached it to his belt and clambered on deck, where he found Jarvis at the wheel, and Lucy struggling to take in the foresail by means of the hand winch. Having made sure Lucy was proving a match for the flapping canvas, Matthew quickly made his way to the hand pump. Thanks to the strict instructions Jarvis had given, he and Lucy knew the jobs assigned to them. For the duration of any storm, Jarvis would be at the wheel, Lucy was responsible for the rigging and Matthew was to man the pump, in order to prevent the bilges from overfilling. As Matthew began to pump, it seemed a matter of minutes before the seas began to wash aboard, and in no time the little ship was in the grip of the typhoon.

When Lucy had safely stowed the canvas, she hurried to the cabin and her next appointed task, to secure everything possible and put out the stove. It was a small wood burning range and was normally never allowed to go out, keeping them continually supplied with hot water, drinks, and meals, and Lucy had become adept at using the tiny oven to good effect. Now, as she poured seawater over the sputtering embers, she had misgivings that she would ever get it alight again. However, it was patently obvious that Jarvis was right, the stove would be a real hazard as the little ship pitched and rolled.

On deck, Matthew was almost bent double, aware that the water was coming in faster than he could pump it out. He recalled Jarvis's advice to try and keep a steady rhythm, and settled down to a slower but stronger action for maximum effect. However, every time the ship rolled he slid away from the pump and had to struggle back, so eventually he shortened his tie-line, attaching it with some difficulty to the pump housing. This improved matters a little, and he settled again to a steady pumping action.

For over four hours the *Selangor Lady* rode free with the wind directly abaft, but then the wind changed, and its constant gusting and shifting gave Jarvis a hard time at the wheel. As the wind rose in intensity he fought to keep the *Selangor Lady* on course, but the wheel jerked and lunged in his hands like a demented beast. Realising that as yet they had only penetrated the edge of the storm, he attempted to steer out of it, but *Selangor Lady* was caught in a maelstrom which tossed her like a floating cork, and Jarvis knew that all they could hope for was to ride it out. Visibility was down to a few yards, due to the drenching rain and a curious light which tinged the onset of darkness with a muddy yellowish hue.

Lucy found that her familiarity with the rigging, hard won after many hours of instruction and practice, suddenly deserted her in the face of the freakish wind and mountainous seas. It was not that she didn't know what was needed, but that her strength was unequal to the task. Having already taken in the foresail, it was soon apparent that every inch of canvas must be taken in, and by the time this was done, Lucy was exhausted. As soon as Jarvis saw the canvas was safely stowed, he shouted to her to go below and tie herself securely in the cabin and remain there. Her agonized "But Jarvis…" was met with such a fierce frown that she capitulated immediately and hastened to obey, desperately holding on to anything she could find, to stop herself from being flung across the deck. She struggled to the door of the cabin, but as she heaved it open and squeezed through gasping with relief, the wind slammed the door into her back with such ferocity that she was catapulted down the steps to the hard cabin floor. Thoroughly winded, it was a few minutes before she could raise herself, as the floor bucked and pitched beneath her. Gingerly feeling her bruises she surveyed the cabin, which despite her earlier efforts was littered with debris. Nevertheless it was a respite of some sort, an escape from that hideous shrieking wind, which had torn the breath from her lungs and tossed her across the ship like a rag doll.

She made her way to the porthole, where through the flying spray she could just make out the figure of Matthew, bent almost double over the hand pump. He was retching and was obviously very sick, but he kept on pumping, up, down…up, down…Lucy watched her uncle in agonized horror. Matthew, who had never known seasickness, and who had adapted to life aboard the *Selangor Lady* like a duck to water, was suffering badly. She gathered together some biscuits and a mug of water, and having eaten some herself, struggled back on board to take some to Jarvis. She took the wheel briefly, finding the only way to control it was to brace her back hard against the wheel shelter, digging her feet into the grating below. As Jarvis ate appreciatively and drained the half empty mug, she shouted in his ear, "Are we still on course?"

"Can't tell..." Jarvis shouted back, "Certainly south west. Doesn't matter...as long as we get through it." He gave her the mug and took the wheel, the rain streaming down his face, and dripping from his grizzled beard. He leaned down to Lucy with his head close to hers. "May lose the mast...be very careful..." he shouted.

"Yes, I will." Lucy glanced up at the mainmast as it creaked and groaned above her. "Can I take over the pump for a while? Matthew is sick."

Jarvis frowned heavily, but after a moment agreed. "Very well...an hour only."

Lucy clawed her way forward to where Matthew was hunched over the pump. His arm moved mechanically, and when Lucy touched his shoulder he did not respond. Lucy bent over and lifted his head, and encountered a vacant stare before recognition dawned.

"Lucy...what?...get below..." Matthew gasped, his arm still sawing as if frozen to the pump handle. Lucy put her hand over his and shouted in his ear, "I've come to relieve you, Uncle." She attempted to take the handle.

"No...go below..." He could not stop the sawing motion.

"Jarvis's orders," Lucy shouted, knowing this was the one thing which would move him. "Only for an hour...help tie me on."

After a moment's hesitation Matthew complied, but his fingers were so cold he could not tie the line, and so continued pumping while Lucy made herself fast and loosened Matthew's own tie-line from the pump housing. "Be careful..." she shouted, "Have some biscuits and water...and rest if you can..."

She watched as Matthew made his way slowly to the cabin door, her heart in her mouth as a sudden violent squall sent the frail old man careering across the deck. But the tie-line saved him and eventually he was able to clamber to the door, opening it with difficulty and disappearing inside.

Lucy lowered her head and bent to her task. Like Matthew, she doubled up against the storm, but after half an hour her back ached so much she found it easier to sit, her legs wrapped around the pump, her hands reaching high above her head as the pump handle raised, and then pulling it down hard. In this position she continued to pump, her breath coming in tortured gasps, until after a while she scarcely knew what she did or why she did it, only that she must not stop. *Must not stop...Up...down, must not stop. Up...down, up...down...*

It was several seconds before she realised Matthew was tugging at her shoulder.

"Go below..." he shouted. His face was white and drained. He stared at Lucy's streaming face, her hair plastered flat, and through her exhaustion read the question. He forced a smile.

"Go below..." he shouted again. "Don't worry, I'm alright now."

He untied her tie-line and knotted his own on again. "Be careful..." he shouted in her ear. Lucy tried to get to her feet. She ached in every bone and sinew, and could hardly keep her feet on the heaving deck. She was thrown wildly towards the rail, only being saved by her tie-line, which jerked at her waist as if to cut her in two. Giving up the struggle, she crawled towards the cabin door an inch at a time, wanting only to get behind the door, to find some relief from the screaming wind, which tore at her frozen body like a demon, deafening her with its violent howl. Somewhere in the back of her mind she knew she was going to die, *they were all going to die*...Struggling with the door handle she failed to open it, she did not have the strength...*the wind would not let her through...the wind wanted to kill her, as Gilbert had wanted to kill her...*

Suddenly she had the door open and was inside, but as before the door slammed violently, sending her flying down the steps. She saw the stove coming towards her face, and then the world shattered into fragments, and she knew sweet oblivion.

Years later, when she thought about that dreadful day, Lucy could never determine with any accuracy the length of time she spent unconscious on the floor of the cabin. It was a time which had no beginning and no end, a time when she drifted, floating in a sea of changing images, immersed in impressions and dreams. Her father was there, confident and assured as she remembered him when a girl. The mocking grey eyes of Gregory Lamont teased and delighted her, and Matthew struggled with a fish so large he could not pull it over the side. Then Jarvis and Gregory Lamont came to help him and together they hauled the huge fish safely on board. The image changed, and she fought to retreat, back to the dark corner she craved, away from Gilbert, who advanced towards her, his eyes boring into her soul with such a look of menace that she felt her heart stop, and knew that she was dead. But she was not dead, because Gilbert still advanced, intent on killing her. She screamed, but no sound came. She tried to retreat into the blackness but he caught her roughly and shook her hard. She looked up and saw the heavy lantern raised above his head, coming down to smash her skull...

She woke with a scream of horror, and stared in terror at the face above her.

"Take it easy, Miss Lucy. You'm all right, thank God."

Lucy stared at him, not comprehending. Then as her brain cleared she heard again with a thankful heart the familiar Devon brogue: "Frightened me to death you did. Come now, let me help you up."

"Matthew?"

"Yes. He'll be all right."

"Oh Jarvis…I don't know what happened."

Lucy managed to stand up and hold on to the table. Her head throbbed and she felt dreadful. The ship was still lurching and rolling, but less violently. Feeling slightly sick, she stared at Jarvis, horrified at his appearance. His black ringed haggard eyes met hers, and he made an attempt at a smile. The effort made him wince, as salt water rash had seared the skin from his cheeks, and his beard was encrusted with salt. Aware of her gaze he smiled crookedly and said, "You don't look so fine yourself this mornin'."

"No, I suppose not."

Bedraggled and exhausted, they stood together in the tiny cabin. There seemed nothing to say. Then, to Lucy's horror, Jarvis seemed to crumble. He lowered his big frame into a chair and put his head in his hands, in a vain attempt to hide the flow of tears, which ran through his fingers as he tried to control the great racking sobs which shook him. Lucy put her arms round him.

"Oh Jarvis, don't…please don't. The worst must surely be over now."

"Yes…oh yes, Miss Lucy." The old man made a supreme effort. "That's just it. We're through the worst of it and all alive, thank God. Thank God! But I didn't know…all that time. I couldn't leave the wheel, just had to leave you both to fend for yourselves."

Lucy bent to comfort him, understanding for the first time the depth of the old man's devotion, usually so well hidden under his stalwart and practical nature.

"We're all safe, thanks to you," she said, kissing the top of his head. "Without your guidance, and the orders you made us obey, we should never have stood a chance."

Jarvis wiped his face on his scarf. "Well, that's as may be," he said, reverting quickly to his normal tone. "But I'm afraid there's still much to do, and the first thing is to get Matthew down here. I know you're tired, but you'll have to help me, he can't stand. I've left the wheel in the beckets. I shouldn't have done really, there's still such a swell."

But Lucy was already on deck, and hurrying towards Matthew, who sat

132

hunched over the pump. His arm still moved mechanically, and he seemed to be asleep sitting up. Nevertheless, as she shook him gently, one eye opened and he murmured, "Hello my dear, I see we're all still here."

"Yes Uncle, all safe. Come down now, to the cabin."

"Easier said than done..." Matthew gasped. "Don't seem to be able to straighten up..."

"Come on old chap, arm round my neck..." Jarvis was back in charge. "Give him a shove Miss Lucy, to get him to his feet."

Together they carefully manoeuvred Matthew to the cabin. Once again, Lucy gave thanks for Jarvis's forethought as she sorted out their dry clothes, which had been stowed in a top locker with towels, for just such an emergency. They were all exhausted and needed sleep, but Jarvis insisted on a timetable.

"First, we must all bathe with fresh water from the rain butts to remove the salt, and then rub in coconut oil to calm the salt rash. Then we change into dry clothes. Matthew, you will sleep first. No arguments," he added as Matthew attempted a feeble protest. "You're half asleep already, and you deserve it, you kept us afloat. Four hours only. I shall go back on deck and take the helm, she's still laboring heavily. I shall be able to leave the wheel occasionally to man the pump, but the main problem is over." He turned to Lucy. "I know you're tired my dear, but after you are changed you must light the stove and make us all a hot drink, we can have biscuits with it."

"Wake me up to give me mine," said Matthew, who was shivering visibly.

"Right," Lucy agreed, wondering how she would get the stove alight. "And then I'll put something in the oven for a hot meal later."

Jarvis nodded. "Then come on deck to help me. We shall soon be able to make sail again, instead of being tossed around like a cork. After four hours you will wake Matthew, we shall have our meal and then you will sleep."

"But Jarvis, what about you?"

"I shall be all right, now let's get started."

Somehow over the next few hours the *Selangor Lady* reverted to some kind of normality. After they had each washed and changed behind the little curtain which normally afforded Lucy privacy, they set about their tasks, Matthew still having to be helped to the bunk, suffering from severe back strain. Despite her misgivings, Lucy managed to light the stove quite easily, having taken Jarvis's advice and dipped the kindling wood into the barrel of paraffin which they used to fill the lamps. It blazed away merrily, and very soon mugs of hot tea helped to revive their spirits, if not their aching bodies.

Getting the *Selangor Lady* under sail was not so easy. The storm had wreaked havoc with the standing rigging, and Lucy almost despaired to see how her painstaking maintenance work of the last few weeks had been thrown into chaos in just one night. It took almost two hours to rig the foresail, and by this time Lucy was near to tears. The swell had abated a little however, and the *Selangor Lady* rode proudly, responding to the helm as if the last twenty four hours had never been. Jarvis was both pleased and surprised. "To tell you the truth," he confided to Lucy. "I didn't think you would be able to manage it."

Lucy caught his look of affectionate pride, and in spite of her tiredness, she felt a sense of achievement. Later she woke Matthew, and together they ate some of the stew she had prepared. Then, as Matthew made his painful way on deck, she fell at last into the deep and heavy sleep of exhaustion.

The aftermath of the storm lasted for several days. The sea remained a glassy green, and the sky a yellow streaked silver grey, as the strange white sun strove to regain ascendance. Slowly they worked their way back to normality, between spells of thankful sleep, and gradually the *Selangor Lady* regained her pristine rig and gleaming brass, and her crew recovered their health and spirits. Matthew had been worst affected, and when it became clear that his back injury was not improving, Jarvis insisted he lie flat for three days, whilst he and Lucy shared the chores. This had the desired effect, and Matthew was able to resume some of the lighter tasks, Jarvis ensuring that the back injury did not recur. Lucy found herself doing the most demanding chores quite cheerfully, now realising the reasons for them. Even deck scrubbing was tackled with fortitude, as after the storm the deck had been so salt encrusted and slippery that Lucy had found it hard to keep a foothold.

As the weather improved, and the whiteness of the sun gradually became burnished gold and copper red, their flagging spirits rose with it, and their tired bodies responded to the increasing warmth. It seemed there was an unspoken agreement to avoid talk of the typhoon, and the ordeal which had almost cost them their lives. Instead, they spoke of the new life they would have in Australia, and Jarvis explained that their best opportunity for an unobtrusive life probably lay in the purchase of a small plot of land near the coast, in the area he knew. Here they could raise a few sheep, and feed themselves by keeping their own livestock and growing vegetables, as long as the plot had good water.

For her part, Lucy reflected sadly that her two dear friends were both embroiled in an adventure which was not of their choosing. *If it had not been for me, Matthew would be living quietly and happily at home in England, and Jarvis would be spending his old age fishing serenely from the Selangor Lady within sight of Singapore.* She felt a nagging sense of guilt as she went about her duties, and would have been surprised to know the true feelings of her companions.

Matthew was also feeling guilty. In his case, guilt sprang from the knowledge that if he had not shot Gilbert they would not have been exposed to such dangers. True, they would still be escaping, but the murder had put Lucy's whole future in jeopardy, and had involved Jarvis in aiding and abetting them. Gilbert's death still preyed on Matthew's mind, and there had been moments during the storm, as his brain became numb and his hand felt frozen to the pump, when he had seen the typhoon as some dreadful act of retribution, a punishment meted out to him by a vengeful God. Yet, when he thought about it clearly, he knew that given the same situation he would shoot Gilbert all over again. His instinct to protect Lucy remained paramount, and he worried that his failing health would prevent him from playing a full part in the building of their new life. His lungs had improved as soon as he had arrived in Singapore, but the stress of the storm had exposed his weakness, and he knew it could happen again.

In spite of these worries, which he kept exclusively to himself, Matthew drew a perverse pleasure from the daily grind of life on the boat, and took an obstinate pride in the chores allotted to him. In the evenings, as he watched the newly restored red orb of the sun sink over the horizon in a sky of vivid orange and yellow, he knew he would not have missed this for anything. *If he had to die soon, he would rather it was here, in this world of savage beauty, with people he loved and respected, than in some stuffy hospital room in London.* He breathed deeply as the doctor had showed him, and reveled in the beauty of the sunset.

In contrast to his companions, Jarvis had no guilt feelings. In his usual pragmatic fashion, he wasted no time in looking back, but accepted the situation as it developed, and applied to it his lifetime habit of taking one day at a time. He had been pleased and surprised at the extent of Lucy's fortitude. He had always known she had inherited her mother's strength of character, but now he had seen it tested to the full he was confident that she would make a success of her new life. He had also developed a grudging admiration for Matthew, and was aware of the effort he had made, and continued to make.

From what they had told him, it was clear that Matthew had saved Lucy's life, and in Jarvis's eyes this made him a bosom friend.

The storm had driven them well off course, and they were now far to the west of their planned route. Jarvis cursed inwardly that he had not taken the opportunity to obtain new charts for the Timor Sea and the Australian coast before he left Jakarta. At the time he had not wanted to draw attention to their eventual destination, a decision he now regretted. He explained to Matthew and Lucy that he had given up any hope of their making Darwin. They had been driven so far off course that he deemed it best to continue southwest, and once they had sighted land, to continue south within sight of the coast until they eventually reached Fremantle. This would take some weeks, and although they had plenty of fresh water, the heavy rain having replenished the water butts, they were running short of food. He set Matthew to fishing again, hoping they could last out until they reached the first of the small settlements along the coast, where there should be a store. He was not sorry to have missed Darwin, as he was aware that Lucy's appearance there would have attracted attention. There were still few white women in the Northern Territory, and the risk of discovery would be considerable. He had already decided on the strategy for landing. He intended to sail on past Fremantle, keeping well out to sea. Then he would turn the *Selangor Lady* due north and sail back into Fremantle harbour, so it would appear they were arriving from the south. Their story would be that they had sailed all the way across south Australia from Adelaide, to try their luck at a new life further north. Jarvis had a sketchy and outdated knowledge of Adelaide, and imparted as much as he could remember to Lucy and Matthew, hoping it would be enough to see them through any awkward questions.

Twelve days after the storm, as Lucy and Matthew laughingly competed to devise a fish recipe from the few spices and oddments they had left, a shout from Jarvis brought them both running to the helm. Jarvis waved expansively, and his lined face beamed with delight.

"Look! We've done it! Australia!"

Chapter Thirteen

For Lucy, the next two months were to prove one of the happiest periods of her life. The *Selangor Lady* made her way slowly and sedately southwest, stopping only when Jarvis decreed they should anchor off shore and take the dinghy to some secluded strand of golden beach. Here they would swim or fish, and occasionally Jarvis would take them on short forays into the dense vegetation of the interior to hunt. At these times he would tell them they were 'getting the lie of the land,' although Lucy and Matthew felt they were far from doing anything of the kind.

It was all so strange and different. The trees and plants were exotic and unknown, and although the glimpses of wildlife and colourful birds intrigued and delighted them, they began to recognise that they were out of their element. Jarvis attempted some lessons on the flora and fauna, but was seriously hampered by his own lack of knowledge, so much so that the instruction would end in helpless laughter, as his pupils asked yet another question he couldn't answer. However, in spite of his ignorance of botanical names, he was able to point out some plants and tubers which were edible, and also some best avoided, knowledge he had acquired from bitter experience. During his time on the run he had been befriended by an aborigine named Boo-on, who had shown him how to survive in the most inhospitable areas. Jarvis drew on this knowledge to show Lucy and Matthew how and where to dig with a chance of finding water, and if desperate, how to obtain water from water-frogs. When they had ventured further inland, they would camp overnight, making a fire as Jarvis showed them, and cooking whatever they had managed to catch. Usually this would be rabbit or some small animal or bird, and on rare occasions a delicious wild turkey or some kangaroo meat. They soon became proficient in skinning and preparing whatever they caught, and Lucy's initial distaste for this chore was quickly overcome when Jarvis ruled that anyone who didn't help, didn't eat. Very often their hunting efforts were unsuccessful, as Jarvis found his eyesight was failing and Matthew's hands were not sufficiently steady on the gun. After a little tuition Lucy proved she had a good eye and a steady hand, and their diet improved as a result. When they had caught nothing, they would make do with a few boiled tubers or perhaps some berries, and find their hungry way back to the *Selangor Lady* next day, where at least there was always fish.

The days were hard and tiring, but Lucy grew to love the quiet evenings when they sat around the camp fire, and usually she managed to persuade Jarvis to resume his storytelling. Now that they had reached Australia, she and Matthew were even more interested in the details of his former life, and realising that this knowledge would be useful to them, Jarvis obliged. He also told them everything he could remember about raising sheep, and gave them information on the kind of crops which could most easily be raised in the area north of Perth where they hoped to settle.

Occasionally Lucy would steer the conversation to the time Jarvis spent on the Lamont property, and she enjoyed hearing him talk of his life there, and Henry Lamont's struggle to maintain the cattle station after Jack left. She tried to imagine Gregory Lamont as a young boy, growing up in that well established but still savage territory. She imagined the child's anguish when, still suffering from the loss of his mother, he was rejected by an embittered father who, according to Jarvis, had little time for his children. She felt a strong bond between herself and this imaginary child, remembering her own misery when her mother died. As she came to understand more, she realised she had been unjust to Gregory Lamont at their last meeting, and regretted that she would never have the opportunity to put matters right. One evening, as they sat cooking their meal, they talked again of Jack Lamont's roughly penciled map, and after Jarvis had shown it to them, Matthew pronounced that he could not see any possible use for it.

"It has no starting point," he remonstrated, when Jarvis said he thought he should send the map to Gregory Lamont. "If for example, we knew which town was meant by the word "Town", written here, or even which river is indicated, there might be a chance, but this map was meant to be vague. It can only be understood by the man who made it, and as he is dead, I'm afraid the location is lost with him."

"All the same," said Jarvis stubbornly, "I think I'll send it to Greg Lamont when we get to a town. I'll send it by post, with a note to say I knew Jack, and he gave it to me. I can say I've only just found out where Jack's family lived, and sign it Bill Bloggs or somethin'. That way there'll be no connection with us."

"Well, if it makes you feel better," replied Matthew, "But, I still don't see what use it will be to him."

"Do you...do you think we shall ever run into him?" Lucy couldn't help asking. "I don't think he'd give me away."

"I hope not," said Jarvis. "But it's possible if we settle in the area I have in mind. I certainly think he was taken with you in Singapore, but that was before Sir Gilbert was killed, and killin' changes matters. We shall do well to stay out of his way if we can."

"Yes, of course you're right," said Lucy, and suddenly miserable, she turned away to gather more wood for the fire.

As the *Selangor Lady* continued her journey south, the first settlement they reached of any size was a place called Broome. In spite of Lucy's enthusiasm, Jarvis was adamant that she should not go ashore, but stay completely out of sight in the cabin, whilst he and Matthew attempted to buy stores. They were away a whole day and a night, and Lucy spent a lonely time wondering what they were doing. When they returned to the beach next day, they were accompanied by two shabby looking men, who helped them load the dinghy. Lucy breathed a sigh of relief and kept well out of sight. At least they had found some provisions, and Lucy's mind dwelled upon the delicacies she would produce if they had managed to obtain flour, and perhaps butter, and even fresh eggs and milk.

She watched from the cabin with impatience as the dinghy was unloaded, and Matthew and Jarvis got the *Selangor Lady* under way. The men waited on the beach and waved and shouted their farewells as Jarvis weighed anchor. They were the first people Lucy had seen since they left Flores, and she felt cheated not to have been allowed to speak to them, but it was another half hour before she was able to emerge from hiding and hear about the trip. Apparently Broome was a poor town, and they had not been able to buy all they needed, but they had been made very welcome by the local people, and had immediately been invited to stay the night with a family. There they had eaten a very good lamb stew, and had played with the children. They had adopted the identity of Darwin traders, who were investigating the possibility of starting a freight transport business between Darwin and Fremantle, calling at the settlements along the coast. This idea had been welcomed so heartily by their hosts that Jarvis and Matthew were consumed with guilt at their deceit, and had felt obliged to warn their new friends that the idea was by no means decided, and that the people of Broome should not assume that another regular supply line was certain.

This excursion was their only human contact during the journey along the coast. As the *Selangor Lady* sailed on, past Port Hedland and Onslow, and down towards Carnarvon, Jarvis insisted that if their story of having traveled up from Adelaide was to be believed, they must not take the risk of being seen north of Fremantle. Having stocked up with provisions and water at Broome, he felt sure that with care, and their occasional forays ashore to hunt, they could avoid any such risk, and could confidently arrive at Fremantle and adopt their new identities.

"You must give some thought to your new name, Lucy," Jarvis said one morning, as they prepared the dinghy for one of their short trips ashore. "There's not far to go now and we should begin to use our new names, so we don't forget and give ourselves away."

"Well mine's easy enough," said Matthew, "But if we are to remain as uncle and niece then your surname is Marshall, the same as mine."

"Not if I'm a widow," said Lucy laughing. "It's rather nice being able to choose who I am and what my name is to be. I would rather have never been married, so I will be Miss Marshall. It's probably better to keep as near to the truth as possible to avoid making mistakes. If we say we are uncle and niece and have no other family; that is the truth. As to my Christian name, I will think about it."

Later that morning as they made their laborious way up a dry sandstone ridge, Lucy signaled to her companions to stop for a moment, as she had sensed that Matthew was finding the climb rather difficult.

"I've decided on my name," she announced. "I'll be Catherine."

"I thought that's what you would choose" said Matthew, and he came over to Lucy and embraced her gently.

"It was my mother's name," Lucy reminded Jarvis, who smiled in quick response.

"Of course, and such a lady she was too. Well I'm goin' to be Sam Rogers. That's a real name too, he was a good friend of mine when I was a lad back in Devon. He wouldn't mind me usin' his name. I shall enjoy bein' Sam Rogers." But Jarvis never used his new name. Minutes later, as they started down the other side of the steep sandstone bluff, he cried out sharply, and staggered. Lucy turned just in time to see the long black snake sliding away into the undergrowth, as Matthew loosed off a shot. Jarvis was on the ground and had his boot off and his knife in his hand in seconds.

"Cut it, cut it," he commanded Matthew, who was already kneeling by his side. "Quickly, it's poisonous, I can feel it already. Two cuts, like a cross, right across the bite. You can see it..."

Matthew could indeed see it. The spot with the two telltale pinpricks was swelling visibly as Jarvis spoke. For once Matthew's hand was steady as he wasted no time in doing as he was bid. He cut, deep and sure, two cross cuts about an inch long. The wound bled copiously and Jarvis pummeled his ankle, trying to increase the blood flow.

"Aren't we supposed to suck the poison out?" asked Matthew.

"Bit of an old wives tale I think," said Jarvis, "But you can try it if you like."

Matthew tried. He sucked as hard as he could at the spot, spitting the venomous blood onto the ground, but Jarvis quickly lost consciousness. They carried him into the shade of a huge rock, knowing there was nothing else they could do but bind up the wound and wait.

All that afternoon and through the night they sat with him, as he veered wildly between delirious raving and lucidity. Matthew and Lucy tended him with sips of water and kept him as comfortable as possible. Several times they knelt down and Matthew prayed aloud. At about three in the morning Jarvis suddenly became lucid, and gasped out to Lucy, "Miss Lucy, do you have a pencil?"

"No Jarvis, not here. Don't worry..."

"A pencil...quick...a pencil..."

"I have one, in my pack." Matthew went to fetch it and returned quickly.

"Paper..." Jarvis sounded very weak.

"I don't have any..." Matthew was almost in tears. He rifled in his pack and found a small New Testament. "Will this do? You can write in the front of it."

"You write..."

"All right Jarvis. Tell me."

"I leave my boat, the *Selangor Lady*, and all my worldly possessions to my dear friend Lucy...no, Catherine Marshall," although his voice was little above a whisper, Jarvis managed a grin.

"Oh Jarvis, please don't..."

"You'll need it. I'll be better in the mornin', but just in case...indulge me Miss Lucy." His voice became even weaker. "Let me sign it..."

Matthew put the pencil into his hand and Jarvis signed shakily. He lay back and rested a moment, breathing in shallow gasps.

"Miss Lucy..."

Lucy bent her head to catch the whispered words. "Go to Fremantle, and sell the *Selangor Lady* there."

"Oh Jarvis, no…" Lucy's tears were falling unheeded.

"Promise me…you'll need the money…settle somewhere quiet, can't roam the seas all your life…promise me."

"Oh Jarvis…"

"Promise…" It was hardly more than a breath.

"Of course I promise."

"Matthew…?"

"I'm here Jarvis." Matthew kneeled down at his side as Lucy turned away, unable to hide the torrent of tears which now overwhelmed her.

"Matthew…good friend…take care of her…"

"Of course I will."

"And Matthew…at sea…you understand?"

It took a moment, and then Matthew replied quietly "Yes Jarvis, I understand. Nothing to worry about, just rest now."

Jarvis died an hour later, in Lucy's arms. Overcome by grief, she clung to Matthew and sobbed, great shuddering sobs which broke his heart. "There, Lucy, there now, take comfort my dear. Jarvis loved you, and you loved him, and he had a good life…"

"No! If it wasn't for me he'd still be alive." She almost spat out the words. "It's all my fault we're here, in this God forsaken place where snakes can kill you and there's no doctor for hundreds of miles…"

"Of course you are not to blame, it's bad luck that's all. You know Jarvis was always telling us to be careful in case of snakes, he just didn't see it in time. It was an accident that's all, a horrible accident."

Matthew comforted her and slowly the sobbing lessened. He insisted Lucy rest until dawn, which would not be long coming. "I'll sit with Jarvis," he told her. "In the morning we have to get him back to the boat. He wanted to be buried at sea, and we must do the best we can for him."

"Yes," Lucy whispered, and did as she was told. By the time the sun rose, a fiery orange ball accompanied by the clamour of screeching birds, Matthew had made a rough stretcher from poles cut from branches, held together with the rope they always carried with them. He laid Jarvis on it and picked up one end.

"We'll have to drag him," he said, "He's too heavy to carry all the way."

Slowly they made their way down the sandstone ridge. It was difficult where the gradient was steep, and after a time they stopped and tied the body to the stretcher so that it didn't fall.

Although they were only about a mile from the shore the journey took almost two hours. They took turns pulling the stretcher, about fifty yards at a time. When they reached the beach they were both exhausted, lack of sleep and sorrow adding to their physical discomfort. Gently, and with unstinting care, they transferred the body to the dinghy and cast off, and Jarvis began his last voyage back to the *Selangor Lady*.

The preparations were simple but harrowing. The biggest problem they had was to get Jarvis on deck, but by tying the rope tightly around him and using the hand winch to lift him gently over the side, slowly it was accomplished. Once on board Matthew took over, instructing Lucy to find canvas and needle whilst he prepared the body.

Having dressed Jarvis in his best garments, Matthew wrapped him carefully in the canvas Lucy had taken from the sail locker, and they stitched the canvas tightly together, securing it with heavy chain. The pathetic bundle seemed smaller now than the man it contained, and with mute accord they got the *Selangor Lady* under way. They had agreed to bury Jarvis at least five miles out, and with heavy hearts they sailed towards the horizon. By the time they were in place it was four in the afternoon. Matthew unscrewed the hinges from the cabin door and took it off, to make a bier for the body. They laid the door on water casks with one end on the ship's rail, and lifted Jarvis on top. Lucy fetched her prayer book and Matthew his New Testament, and they held the simple service. Matthew read the unfamiliar words in a subdued and shaky voice, and after the Lord's prayer and the prayer of committal all was done. Lucy's red rimmed eyes met Matthew's in tacit agreement, and together they lifted the end of the door so that the body slid gently down into the sea, where it immediately disappeared from sight.

Lucy and Matthew gazed over the rail for a while, still suffering from a sense of disbelief at the events of the last twenty four hours. It seemed impossible that Jarvis was dead, and both had the uncanny feeling that perhaps soon they would wake up, and he would be there with a mug of tea, and they would hear the strong Devon voice telling them to look lively. Eventually Lucy said, "I wish I had some flowers, to throw on the sea perhaps."

"Jarvis would understand, he knows we have no flowers," Matthew replied gently.

She remained silent a while, and then, as if considering carefully, she asked: "Matthew, do you think Jarvis can see us now?"

"I'm sure he can."

"And we have no flowers."

A moment after she said this Lucy turned and went to the cabin, returning a moment later with the large sail scissors. Before Matthew could stop her she was cutting off her hair in huge chunks and sprinkling it over the side, where it danced in chestnut curls on the surface, catching the light from the early evening sun.

"Lucy, your lovely hair! Jarvis wouldn't have wanted you to do that!" Matthew was distressed, feeling that perhaps she was losing control. However, she turned to him with a semblance of her normal smile.

"But I had no flowers, and he always liked my hair, said it was like my mothers. If he is watching, he'll understand."

And that was that. Matthew made an entry in the small log which Jarvis had always kept:

Captain Jarvis Mottram died from snake bite poisoning during a trip ashore. We buried him at sea this day May 6th ,1898.

They both signed the entry, Matthew re-hung the cabin door and then they made sail. They were aware that their plans had to be reviewed, but were too tired and sick at heart to begin to think about it. Anchoring once more in the same bay which had seen the start of their tribulations, they made a light meal, and sank into fitful sleep.

The journey south continued slowly, and for their peace of mind it was fortunate that Matthew and Lucy were kept so busy they had little time to dwell on recent events. The loss of Jarvis meant not only extra physical work, but that they were now obliged to think ahead, and make all the decisions which had normally been his province. They were conscious of his forethought in preparing them for just such an event, and found themselves coping very well, even though it seemed there were never enough hours in the day.

Jarvis had evolved a pattern of eight hours on duty, followed by eight hours off, and this had meant there were always two people on deck when they were in sail. Now it was more difficult, and after trying several methods without success, they decided that the best plan was to sail from early dawn to late evening, with both of them on call. During this time they each had occasional one hour rest periods. Late in the evening they weighed anchor offshore, and so were both able to get some sleep; the possibility of accidents due to tiredness also being reduced. They intended to make for Fremantle as fast as this arrangement allowed, hoping their dwindling stores would last out, rather than risk going ashore to hunt. In the back of both their minds was the dread that a similar accident could happen to either of them, and so as the journey progressed, each took care of the other, with a concern born not only of their long association, but a new realisation of the hazards of this dangerous country.

Matthew worried particularly for Lucy, and what kind of future awaited her. He was even more conscious now of his failing health, and although he was feeling remarkably well, he knew this was probably only a temporary remission of his lung disease. He had intended to confide his problem to Lucy once they were settled, but now decided against it. She was still very quiet and withdrawn, and he knew she was grieving for Jarvis, and blaming herself for his having ever left Singapore. One evening, almost three weeks after Jarvis's death, he decided it was time to broach the subject of their future.

"In a very few days now we should sight Fremantle. I think we should follow Jarvis's plan and go well out to sea, and then turn back as if we have come from the south."

"Yes, I suppose so."

"We must get used to using our new names, I shall start to call you Catherine from today."

"Yes, all right, Uncle."

"Lucy, I want you to give some thought to what kind of life you would like to make in Australia. For instance, are we going to stick to our original plan and try to buy a small place in the area Jarvis knew, or do you think we should try to stay in town? Or perhaps we could live in Fremantle, staying on the boat?"

"I don't mind, Uncle. You decide."

"No, you must decide for yourself." Matthew remonstrated. "Lucy, my dearest, you are very young, and still have the best part of your life to come. Many people have come to Australia to start anew, and that is what we must do. We must put the past behind us and start again."

"I suppose you're right Uncle, but it doesn't seem the same somehow, without Jarvis."

"No, of course it's not the same. It would be better if he was still with us, but he isn't, and so we have to do the best we can. We are fortunate to have received so much advice from him, and in that sense he will still be with us. Every time we remember something he showed us and act upon it, he will be there."

"I suppose so." Lucy sounded doubtful.

"There's no suppose about it." Matthew spoke sharply. "Lucy, I really cannot allow you to let Jarvis down, after all he did for us."

Her eyes opened wide in astonishment. "Let Jarvis down? Whatever do you mean?"

"Just what I say. Why do you think Jarvis helped us? Why do you think he helped you at Winchester Station when you came out from England, and then again when you needed to get away? He did it because he loved you, from the time you were a child sitting in his wheelbarrow in the garden. You should remember he never had children of his own."

Lucy stared at Matthew blankly, but he pressed on with increasing emphasis.

"If you give up now and stop trying, you're giving up all his hopes and dreams for you. He wanted to see you happily settled in a new life, that's why he didn't hesitate when you needed help. He gave up everything for your future, and I can't bear to hear you being so negative about it."

The shock showed clearly in her eyes, but she did not reply. She got up and walked slowly to the cabin, leaving Matthew at the helm. She did not re-appear, and after half an hour Matthew called out.

"Lucy...I mean Catherine..."

After a second or two she came on deck.

"Take in sail, the wind's freshening." She hastened to obey, and Matthew watched with affection as she worked quickly and expertly at the hand winch. He reflected that she looked even more like a boy than ever, with her bobbed hair and her long cotton drawers and shirt hanging loosely on her thin frame. She had lost weight since Jarvis's death, and he made a mental note to watch her diet more closely.

She came across to him and stood for a moment, watching the mainsail attentively. Satisfied, she turned to her uncle.

"Sorry Matthew."

He smiled back at her. "Got it straight now?"

"Yes." She put her arm around him and rested her head on his shoulder. "I've got quite a few things straight. You are right, I owe it to Jarvis to try my best to make a good life." She hesitated. "And to you too. Jarvis wasn't the only one to give up everything to help me."

"Nonsense, I've enjoyed every minute, until..."

They fell silent, watching the water begin to cream from the *Selangor Lady's* bow with the freshening wind, until Matthew broke their mood: "I keep thinking, if only I hadn't killed Gilbert…"

"Do you Uncle? Do you still think about it? I don't. It seems so long ago."

It was true. During the long voyage they had become so completely adapted to their new way of life that the world of manners, houses, commerce and indeed every kind of civilised activity had become like a vague dream, a place in the memory which had no real relevance for them.

"It certainly seems as if it happened in another world," Matthew admitted, "But we shall soon be back to it. Think of it, Lucy…I mean Catherine, streets of shops! I believe Perth is quite large and sophisticated. I shall go to the bank and hopefully all should be in order, and my money awaiting me. Then…a hotel, a hot bath and a well cooked meal with a little wine…Can you imagine such luxury?"

"Hardly," Lucy laughed, "And I must find a post office, I intend to post this…" She reached in the pocket of her drawers, drew out a rather grubby sheet of paper and handed it to Matthew.

"It was the only paper I could find," she explained.

Matthew motioned her to take the wheel and opened the paper, trying to shield it from the wind as he read:

Dear Mr Lamont,

This note is to let you know that an acquaintance of yours, Jarvis Mottram, has died in an accident. I was with him and he asked me to send you the enclosed, which he believed to be a map.

It was given to him by your Uncle Jack Lamont on the night he died. Although it seems of little use, Jarvis felt his family should have it.

Yours sincerely,

Bill Jones.

Matthew smiled. "Yes, Jarvis would have wanted you to send it, but how will you know where Lamont lives?"

"I thought you could perhaps ask at the bank. The family is prominent in the area, so I'm sure someone will know. If not, we could address it to 'The Lamont Station, somewhere north of Perth'. Jarvis said the Australian post is wonderful. It may take a time, but it always gets there, even in the most remote areas."

"Yes, all right. Have you decided on anything else?"

"Yes. Although it may break my heart, I think we should take Jarvis's advice and sell the *Selangor Lady*. We shall need the money and we shall have no further use for her. I also think we should buy some land as we planned, and try to be self sufficient. We can also raise a few sheep, to enable us to buy the extra things we shall need. It will not be much of a living, but enough to enable us to live quietly. That is all we need. I thought at first I could perhaps obtain work in Perth, but too many questions would be asked, and we can't risk it."

"I agree," said Matthew, "And I know that was Jarvis's intention. We must be careful where we choose to live, but provided we are not too near the Lamont station we are unlikely to meet anyone who could question our past."

"Yes. Perhaps when we have established ourselves for a few years so that we are known, we can move to a town without much risk."

Matthew smiled. "If of course we wish to. But by then you may be the proud owner of a huge cattle ranch, with a great house and hordes of servants. After all this is the land where fortunes are made."

"Yes, perhaps we shall find a seam of gold on our small plot of land!" Lucy responded, smiling. She became serious again. "No Uncle, if we can make enough to live on I shall be satisfied."

They sailed on quietly for some minutes, before she approached Matthew again.

"Uncle, at the moment we must be sailing near the coast of the area where Jarvis said we might settle. Shall we go ashore and have a look at the country? Jarvis said there was some good land around here."

Matthew agreed. He was not anxious to go ashore but felt thankful that Lucy was at last taking an interest in their future. An hour or so later they embarked from the dinghy and once more set off into the bush.

Matthew stirred the billycan thoughtfully. As they intended to camp for the night, he had jointed all of the rabbit Lucy had shot earlier, and had made a well-seasoned stew. He glanced up as Lucy returned with more sticks, which she began to break up and push into the glowing fire, saying "This is lovely country, but I've seen no water as yet."

About to reply, Matthew became aware of a rustling sound. He touched Lucy lightly on the shoulder and put his finger to his lips. They listened, and to their astonishment heard the whinny of a horse. The sounds continued, and they stared at each other in consternation. It was clear someone was making directly for them.

Chapter Fourteen

Seconds later, as they held their breath, a horse crashed through the undergrowth, ridden by a big red faced man with a well groomed moustache and beard.

"Whoa, whoa there! How d'ya like that! I saw ya smoke!"

He seemed delighted, and dismounting swiftly, stretched out a big calloused hand.

"Bob Middleton, crack shearer, though I say so! From Murchison district. Made a detour when I saw ya smoke."

"Marshall," said Matthew, rising and clasping the outstretched hand, "Matthew Marshall. This is my niece Catherine."

The big man looked disconcerted. "Well, excuse me ma'am, didn't realise it was a lady." He removed his bush hat and regarded them quizzically before bursting into a shout of laughter and slapping his thigh.

"Oh my! I never did see a lady dressed like that before!"

Lucy suddenly realised what kind of picture she presented. "Oh Mr. Middleton, please forgive me. I only have one good dress, and I was sure it would be spoiled in the bush, so I wore these old things to save it."

"Oh sure, Miss Catherine, I understand. Just took me by surprise that's all!" He gave another great hoot of laughter and walked his horse over to a clearing, leaving it to graze.

"Got coffee, Matt?" he asked, walking back to the fire.

"Er, no. I'm afraid we haven't had coffee for some time," said Matthew, still trying to recover his wits.

"I got some." He walked over to the swag tied to his saddle and took it down. After a moment he came back with a billycan, coffee and sugar. He filled the billy from a large water bottle and put it on the fire.

"We were just going to have some dinner," said Matthew. "You're more than welcome."

Bob Middleton peered into the pot. "Looks good, don't mind at all, done ya damper?"

"Er, no," said Matthew, feeling that discretion was his best bet.

Bob returned to his swag and came back with a bag of flour and a round pan. He gestured to Lucy. "You want to do it?" he asked. "No," said Lucy quickly. "I mean…I mean I always like to see other folks damper…compare it."

Bob took this as a serious and quite normal response. He nodded sagely. "Oh yes, there's some can do a good damper, and there's some as can't. Some blokes damper you can't hardly get your teeth into." He shook some flour into the pan and mixed it carefully with water, using a stick. He added a little more flour and mixed again, until it seemed it was to his satisfaction. He beamed at them and nodded towards the meat. "That'll go lovely on this, make it go round better. Some don't bother no more, but me, I like me damper." He inspected the billycan and nodded to Lucy. "Throw the coffee and sugar in Cath, it's coming to boil."

Lucy did as she was told with some inward amusement. While Bob cooked the damper, she fetched their tin plates, and when Bob had divided the damper into three, she spooned out the meat and they sat down to enjoy it, dipping the damper into the juice. It was a delightful change of food, especially when washed down with real hot coffee. The added luxury of someone new to converse with made Lucy feel she was at a party. Bob obviously felt the same.

"Well Matt, that was real good. Must say I didn't think I'd have company tonight. Great stroke of luck, meeting up with you folks." He drained his mug. "You on your way to the Kelly's place?"

"Er, yes. We lost our way I think." Matthew replied.

"Sure you did. Missed it three miles back. New out here aren't you?" He smiled knowingly, and tugged at the big moustache. "Not long from England I'll bet? I can tell by your accent."

"No, not long. Well, a couple of years actually but we're new to the area." Matthew was thinking fast. "We've been in Adelaide, but came up here to find a small plot to settle on." Matthew reasoned that the nearer he could stick to their planned story the better it would be, in case they ever ran into Bob Middleton again.

To his relief Bob gave his quick grin and responded, "Never been to Adelaide myself. Can tell you anything you want to know about this country though. If you're looking to buy the Kelly's place you'll not go wrong, that's if you're satisfied with a real small block. Only about five hundred acres, but might be enough for just the two of you. Depends what you want to do of course."

Matthew thanked his luck. It seemed the Kelly's place was for sale. "Well, we're just looking for a small plot...er...block, for us to live on quietly," he responded. "Five hundred acres sounds rather a lot."

Bob gave him a strange glance. "You really are townies, aren't you? That's about the smallest size block you can get." He gave his big laugh again. "Beats me how you got this far!" He looked around him, apparently mystified. "And come to that, where's your horses?" he asked, looking from one to the other. Matthew gulped the last of his coffee and appeared to have a coughing fit. Lucy patted his back and waited for him to recover, then turned to their new friend.

"I can see it is no use, we shall have to own up. Yes Uncle," she said turning to Matthew, "Mr. Middleton is no fool, he guessed our little secret right away." She stooped down by the fire and faced Bob.

"You see Mr. Middleton..."

"Bob."

"Yes, you see Bob, we truly are what you call townies, but we have some experience of sailing, and we made our way from Adelaide on a sailing ship. We called in at Fremantle and went to Perth looking for a small plot, er block, as my uncle said. We heard so much about the perils of the journey over land that we decided to sail up the coast and try to find the Kelly's block by anchoring off shore and trekking inland. That's why we have lost our way a little."

Bob's face was a picture, and Matthew's cough seemed troublesome again.

"You mean to say...you've got a ship around here somewhere?" Bob looked wary, and then broke into a big smile. "Go on, you're having me on!"

Lucy could hardly keep her face straight. "It's true alright," she said. "Of course the *Selangor Lady* is not really a ship, only a hundred tons or so. She was originally a topsail schooner, but she had her rig adapted to fore and aft, so she's more like a ketch now really..."

"Will you listen to that!" Bob let out the huge laugh with such gusto that it was almost a roar. He laughed so much that Lucy and Matthew began to laugh too, delighting in the infectious joy of this big happy man. Bob wiped his eyes with his neckerchief and chuckled again.

"Oh what a story, what a story," he said, still sniffing and wiping his eyes with the back of his hand. "Wait till I tell me mates at the sheds." He struck an attitude. "I was just riding over Kelly's block, and I come upon this gentleman and a boy. Bit scruffy they was, but nice folks, just out from

England, well at least sounded like it. Well, then what happens? First off, I discovers the boy isn't a boy at all but a girl, hair cut short and dressed in trousers, and then I discovers they've come to look at Kelly's place on a ship! Oh Lord, they'll love it, they'll love it!"

Matthew and Lucy joined in the laughter, and after a little more banter and posturing, Bob grew serious.

"You could easy have got here from Perth, up the Swan River a bit and then strike north west, it's not much more than two hundred miles." He frowned. "Where is this ship then?" he asked, as if he still doubted its existence. "Back there, about four miles," Matthew explained. "We brought a compass with us so we can find our way back."

Bob dissolved into laughter again, then leaned forward confidentially, "Wouldn't like to do me a great favour would ya?"

"If we can."

"Well, I've never been on a ship in me life. Seen a couple passing, when I've been at the coast, but never been on one. Don't suppose you could let me..."

"But of course!" Matthew responded eagerly, "And in return you can do something for us."

"Name it Matt, and you've got it."

"You take us to look at the Kelly's place and show us around, and then tomorrow we'll take you back with us to the ship, and you can join us for supper there. Fresh fish."

"Done. Whoever would have thought it? Was my lucky day when I met up with you folks, what a story, what a story!" And with another great laugh Bob began to gather his swag together.

Kelly's place proved to be a simple chock and log built cabin, with a thatched roof and dirt floor. It was elevated from the ground, with two steps and a wide boardwalk verandah all round it. Inside there were three rooms, a large main room which ran across the front of the building, and two smaller areas which had obviously been the sleeping quarters. The rooms were separated by wattle and daub walls, which had once been painted but which were now dingy and unkempt. However, there was a solid door, and the glass in the small windows was sound, apart from one broken pane.

"Good cabin this," was Bob's verdict, delivered with relish as they walked through the bedrooms. "This is the best bit, Cath," he added as they returned to the main room. "Come and look."

152

Lucy followed him to where a large cast iron range gleamed dully. Bob enjoyed demonstrating it, opening the doors of the two ovens and inviting Lucy to look inside, and to work the spit which swung out over the fire space.

"Molly Kelly's pride and joy this was," said Bob. "Brought it out with them all the way from Perth. Got a good chimney, too, hardly ever smokes. Yes, I've eaten many a good stew here, cooked on that range."

Suddenly the cabin took on a more human aspect, and Lucy asked, "What happened? Why are the Kelly's selling?"

Bob looked surprised. "Thought they'd have told you that in Perth." He poked around at the range, "Yes, this will clean up real good."

"I'm sure they did tell us," Matthew volunteered, "But we were asking about several blocks and I can't remember which was which."

"Sad, the Kelly's. Will Kelly died, and his wife has gone to live with her sister in Perth." Bob straightened up from the range and shook his head. "Lovely folks. Been here about eight years. I remember when they came, a young couple, just married and real daft they were. A hard worker was Will Kelly. He built this cabin and started a flock from almost nothing. Mainly sheep he had, because this is good land for sheep, and not enough of it for anything else."

"It must have been hard," Lucy said, trying to imagine the life of the young couple.

"Oh, they had a bad time of it at first, but after a few years of hard work they started to get on well. They had two children, a boy and then a girl. As they grew up Molly wanted a better house, I don't know why because I think this is fine myself, although it has flooded a few times in the wet. Anyway, they were getting on well, and had a bit of money in the bank, so Will said he would build a new house, on that rise behind the cabin, so it would be safe in the wet. It was going to be a real house, and he got proper plans done for it. He was going to build part of it himself and get tradesmen in to do the plastering and suchlike. He'd got all the timber and had made a start, and then he got the fever, very sudden like. He was dead in a week."

"Oh how dreadful," Lucy said, imagining the plight of the young wife, struggling to cope with a sick husband and two young children.

"Yes, it was. They had a black stockman here, and he went to Stannerton as fast as he could and brought the doctor, but by the time they got back it was too late."

Bob sighed. "Molly couldn't cope with the place and the children, so when her sister asked her to go to live with her in Perth she didn't have much choice really. All their plans come to nothing. Will was going to have proper running water, and had already got the pipes put in, and a pump to send the water up to the new house. Of course they have artesian water here, which means they never really run dry. That's why it's such a good block. Come on, I'll show you."

He led the way outdoors to the well, a deep hole cut into the stone, with a whip pole to raise the water. A bucket was still attached to the rope, and Bob let it down and worked the whip pole to raise it again, urging them to taste the water. It was fresh and sweet, and Bob grinned with satisfaction.

"Yes, a good block this. There's this well, and some of the year you got water from the creek as well, unless there's drought, like now. Come and see."

He led the way over a steep rise and they looked down on a large flat creek bed, its surface crazy paved by the cracked and sun baked sand.

"It's very dry. Is it usually like this?" Matthew sounded disappointed.

"Well we've had the mother and father of a drought for the last three years. Come the wet, that's if it's a good wet, it fills right up and floods as far as you can see there." Bob gestured across to where a few scrubby trees struggled for existence on the far side of the creek. "That's the boundary of the Kelly block," he explained, "And pretty useless land over there. But this side's good. You got the creek to water the sheep a fair part of the year, and it gives real good grazing after the wet." His arms swept wide. "All this just springs up green almost overnight. On the other side of the cabin you've got the best land, going towards the coast, and it's only a mile or so to a little beach, a real pretty spot. Will and Molly used to take the children there on Sundays, for picnics. Molly had a wonderful garden behind the cabin, used to grow good vegetables, and flowers too, when she could get the seed from Perth."

He led them round to the rear of the cabin, but Lucy could see no garden, or any sign of one.

"All dried out." Bob looked sadly around him. "Been empty almost a year now, but shouldn't take long to get it right again. Look, here's the pipes Will laid."

He showed them the system which had been installed to transfer water from the well, and they followed the pipes, climbing up about a hundred and fifty yards to the site of the new house. The foundations had been laid and the large floor joists were in place, but that was all, except for a very large pile of timber nearby, covered with tarpaulins. Bob nodded towards it.

"That's the timber for the walls," he said. "All well seasoned, real good stuff. Will said if he was going to build a house it had to be a good one. Anyone who buys this block, buys the main materials for a good house as well."

Lucy walked around the site and tried to imagine how Will had planned it, noting where the pipes ended and deciding where the kitchen would be, and the wash house. She turned and looked back towards the cabin and caught her breath.

"Oh Matthew, look…"

They stood together and contemplated the scene spread out below them, for the site of the house commanded a very beautiful and extensive view. To the west was a broad flat plain of scrubby grass, bordered by native cypress, black wattle and other shrubs. Ahead and to the east beyond the cabin, they could see the dry creek bed, distance giving it a smooth sandy look, and Lucy could imagine the beauty of the place when the creek was full. Beyond the far banks in the distance they could see the outline of a high red sandstone ridge, with purplish mountains beyond, as far as they could see.

"Will Kelly knew how to pick his spot," said Matthew. He put his arm around Lucy. "What do you think of it?"

"Oh Uncle, it's perfect. I'm sure it's exactly right for us. What luck to meet Bob and to find this…"

She stopped, recollection interrupting her moment of indiscretion. "I mean, who would have thought the Kelly place would have such a view? I don't think they mentioned that."

"No," murmured Matthew. "I'm surprised it hasn't been sold before now. You say it's been empty a year, Bob?"

"Almost. Mind you, that's no surprise, no surprise at all."

"Why not?"

"The price of course. Five pounds an acre is far too much."

Lucy's heart sank. "Five pounds? But we couldn't possibly find so much! That would be two thousand five hundred pounds!"

Bob looked surprised. "Well, surely you knew the price before you came to look at it? I thought probably Molly had offered you a lower price, something more realistic. She'll never get five pounds an acre, even counting the extra timber. Folks say Molly put a silly price on it because she couldn't bear to sell. You should be able to get the price down if she really wants to sell it, there's not many folks now would want a place as remote as this."

"We didn't see Mrs. Kelly," Matthew put in, "Just got details of a few blocks from the bank. We wanted to see it first, to decide whether we were interested."

"Makes sense." Bob led the way down the slope back to the small cabin, "Molly might take an offer, now it's been empty so long. Probably feeling a bit better about things now a year's gone by. Anyway, if you do see her, give her my best."

"Yes of course," Matthew agreed, "Bob, what do you think would be a fair price?"

"About three pounds an acre I should think. A bit more for the timber perhaps."

Matthew caught Lucy's anxious glance at him, and he smiled, trying to reassure her. *It was still an awful lot of money, and would take every penny he had in the bank. If they took the risk and bought it, what would happen if something went wrong, and they couldn't make a go of it? It was a perfect spot in many ways, but there would be a great deal of hard work, and what if he couldn't cope?*

These thoughts dominated Matthew's mind as they made their way slowly back to the *Selangor Lady*, Bob leading his horse, and telling them of his travels as a shearer. Apparently he could be hired in the season, and he joked that perhaps they would be hiring him to shear their flock next year, if they bought the Kelly place.

"How does the wool get to market?" Lucy asked, already working out the practical details.

"Oh, Carmody takes it." Bob replied. "At least, you get it to Stannerton, where he buys it from you, and then he sends it to the new railhead, and sells it there. Everyone round here sells their woolclip to Carmody."

"Who's Carmody?"

"The big wheel in Stannerton, that's George Carmody. Got his finger in lots of pies."

Lucy considered. "Presumably he gets a higher price for the wool when he sells it at the railhead?" she asked after a moment.

"Of course, a much higher price. It's daylight robbery in my view, the price Carmody pays to the farmers."

"Then why don't they take their wool to the railhead themselves and get the higher price?"

Bob laughed: "Ah, that's the question."

Lucy persisted. "Well, is there an answer?"

Bob became grim. "Well Cath, the stock answer is that it's too much time and trouble to transport. It's a hundred and fifty odd miles from Stannerton to the stock agents at the railhead, so it's better just to take it to Stannerton and sell to Carmody. Easier."

"Yes, easier, I can see that. But you said that's the stock answer, what's the real answer?"

Bob looked uncomfortable. "Most small farmers round here wouldn't give you the true answer. Afraid to, really. Carmody wouldn't like it if folks started cutting him out." Bobs voice became heavy with sarcasm. "He gets his cut on every fleece that goes out from Stannerton."

"Well, if we do move here he won't get a cut from our sheep," Lucy stated briskly. "I shall take our wool to the railhead myself and get the best price I can."

Bob looked askance at Lucy, and then at Matthew. "She's a bit of a firebrand our Cath, isn't she Matt? Like her hair, a bit of a hothead!" He laughed his big laugh and shook his head.

"Don't think it would work Cath, one chap tried it about four years ago. Refused to sell to Carmody, and took a big waggon of wool to sell at the railhead himself. At least, he tried to."

"What happened?"

"Who knows? They found him about twenty miles out of Stannerton lying on top of his woolclip. He was shot through the head." Lucy's eyes opened wide in astonishment.

"Shot? But what happened?"

"There was an enquiry, a constable came out from Perth, but they never found who did it. Some said it must have been Carmody, or one of his men. Some said it was a bush robber, although nothing was taken. The police never charged anyone, and Carmody pointed out to the farmers how fortunate they were to be able to sell to him, as the journey to the railhead was so dangerous. Nobody argued with him."

Lucy fell silent, reflecting on this matter. Apparently raising sheep was not so simple after all. The story remained with her as they carried on towards the beach, and she was only shaken from her reverie by Bob's uninhibited delight when he saw the *Selangor Lady*. Leaving his horse in the shade at the end of a long tether, he whooped up and down the beach, his exuberant laughter sending the sea birds wheeling and crying above them. He almost upset the dinghy as they pulled away, and his delight when they were aboard was infectious. He wanted to know what everything was for and how it worked, and seemed very impressed, not only by the boat but their knowledge. He was delighted when, coached by Matthew, he caught a big sea

157

bass for their dinner, and with much laughter he bedded down later in Jarvis's hammock. Still laughing, he declared next morning that once he stopped falling out of the damned thing, he never had a better nights sleep. After breakfast he packed his swag regretfully.

"Don't know when I enjoyed myself so much. What a story," he said as they climbed into the dinghy to take him back to shore. "Still, must get on me way, two days late already. Sam Lamont will have me guts for garters!"

"Who?" Matthew stopped rowing and leaned on the oars. "Did you say Lamont?"

"Yes, you know them? That's where I'm going. The Lamont spread. All cattle of course, but a real good place and nice folks too. Me and a couple of mates always meet up at the Lamont place every year after the shearing. Sam Lamont always gives us a couple of months work with the cattle. Of course I'm a sheep man myself, but there ain't enough work year round for shepherds."

Matthew began to row again.

"You know the Lamont folks?" Bob asked again.

"No, I don't think so," Lucy said faintly. "But I think we heard of them in Perth...how far away is their place?"

"Not far, about seventy miles I suppose."

Lucy sighed with relief, but Bob didn't notice.

"Yes, the Lamonts will be your neighbours if you buy the Kelly place. Not that you'll see them. They don't go your way when they go in to Stannerton, got a better road from their place, see?"

"You said Sam Lamont, is he the owner?" Lucy asked, having recovered a little.

"Yes, at least part owner. He and his brother run it between them, there's a sister too, about your age I should think."

"Oh? What are their names?" Lucy tried to express mild interest.

"Samuel and Gregory are the brothers, and their sister is Mary. Mind you, Sam looks after the place mostly. Greg is a bit of a wanderer, travels around looking for the best stock bulls and that sort of thing. Went on a big trip abroad last year, Singapore and India I think, he was away a long time."

"Oh really?"

"Yes, folks say he takes after his Uncle Jack, he had the wanderlust as well. Went off in the gold rush and never came back. Well folks," Bob gave his expansive grin as he climbed from the dinghy, "Looks like this is goodbye." He reached across and took their hands, shaking them vigorously

158

with many smiles and expressions of thanks. They watched as he waded up the beach, turning as he reached the waterline.

"If you buy the Kelly place I'll see you next year when I come across for the shearing," he called, waving his hand.

"How will you know?" Lucy shouted back, "If we've bought it? How will you know?"

They heard his big laugh as he strode up the beach. "Oh, I'll know. Sooner or later we get to know everything in the outback."

A week later Matthew and Lucy sailed the *Selangor Lady* into Fremantle. Following Jarvis's plan, they had made their way well out to sea to avoid being sighted sailing south, and then made a turning arc, approaching the harbour as if they had made the long journey from Adelaide.

They were confused by the sheer size and complexity of the harbour, and having at last berthed the *Selangor Lady* were not a little dismayed to find they had to be cleared by the harbour master. This proved to be a formality however, for after showing him the *Selangor Lady*'s papers and log, and the brief will signed by Jarvis, the harbour master went out of his way to be helpful.

Matthew explained that they had originally intended to operate as traders around the coast, but without Jarvis they felt less confident, and had therefore decided to sell the *Selangor Lady* and settle north of Perth. Did he by any chance know of a potential buyer?

The harbour master puffed with pride. If he could not find them a buyer, he announced, nobody could. He knew every captain, every seaman, indeed every fisherman around this coast. Just leave it to him, he intimated, and all would be well.

Taking him at his word, they left the sale of the *Selangor Lady* in his hands and traveled to Perth. Lucy found the city stimulating, but at times a little overpowering. She felt decidedly uncomfortable in the long skirts and restricting bodices she was now obliged to wear, and was conscious of a distinct loss of freedom. Nevertheless, soon she and Matthew settled into a small guest house, where they read and re-read the newspapers, eager for every snippet of news from the world so long denied them. They learned that during their trip Mr. Gladstone had died, and that many Australians were joining the rush to America, where the goldfields of the Klondike beckoned, with promise of easy riches.

They spent many mornings investigating the details of several small blocks of land which were for sale, including the Kelly block. Matthew expressed misgivings about buying a plot next to the Lamont ranch, but to his surprise Lucy was keener than ever.

"It's seventy miles away Uncle," she remonstrated. "You can hardly call that near. We are most unlikely to meet anyone from the Lamont station, and at least we've seen it and know it has good water."

The capital from the sale of Matthew's London home was awaiting him at the bank, and the soft voiced manager, Mr. Scott, proved helpful, putting in an offer of three pounds an acre for the Kelly block on Matthew's behalf. It was turned down the same day. The other blocks which were up for sale did not seem promising, and after some discussion they decided to wait until the *Selangor Lady* was sold before deciding if they could afford to increase their offer.

The decision to sell the *Selangor Lady* had been made after much heart searching by both Lucy and Matthew. The little boat had been home for so many months that they parted from her in Fremantle as if from an old friend. Only the knowledge that Jarvis had wished her to sell helped Lucy make up her mind. It was partly her wish to avoid seeing the brave little ship sold, that made Lucy decline to accompany Matthew, when after three weeks in Perth, he travelled back to Fremantle. He discovered that the harbour master had not only failed to find a buyer, but appeared to have completely forgotten about the matter. Annoyed, Matthew settled himself on the *Selangor Lady*, and advertised her for sale.

During the ensuing days Matthew occupied himself making the *Selangor Lady* as attractive as possible to prospective buyers. Her decks were scrubbed, brass polished, tack was overhauled and the little cabin gleamed. After two weeks without a single enquiry, by pure chance a buyer came his way. On the quay he entered into conversation with a man and his son who had recently arrived from England. Within an hour the *Selangor Lady* was sold to them for five hundred pounds. The new owner was an experienced sailor, and could see the possibility of a good profit in using the *Selangor Lady* as a coastal vessel, trading and transporting between the settlements along the coast. As Lucy had made arrangements for Matthew to act on her behalf, the ship's papers were assigned the same day, and Matthew, with a backward glance at the *Selangor Lady*, started on his journey back to Perth.

Lucy was overjoyed to see Matthew again, when he returned to the guest house in Perth. Complimenting him on the sale of the *Selangor Lady*, she could hardly contain her excitement at her own news.

"I have not been idle these ten days, Uncle," she said happily. "I have persuaded Molly Kelly to accept our offer."

"How on earth did you manage that?" Matthew could hardly believe it.

"I asked Mr. Scott at the bank for her address, and I went to see her," Lucy explained. "At first, she said very little, but when I mentioned we had met Bob Middleton that seemed to break the ice, and after a while we were talking like old friends. Bob was right, she knew our offer was fair, but just couldn't bring herself to let go of the place where she had been happy with her husband. I told her about us, as much as I could of course, and I promised her we would do our best for the place."

"But that's marvellous," Matthew said. "Well done! Perhaps our luck is changing at last."

"Oh, Uncle, I do hope so. I went to see Molly again a few days ago, and she gave me lots of advice on what vegetables will grow there, and the things we shall need to get started. You should see the size of the shopping list!"

Years later, Lucy was to look back on the move to Kelly's place with mixed feelings of horror and amusement. Nothing went right first time. Lucy ordered some simple furniture and the many varied household items and tools they would need, and most of these arrived before the covered wagon on which they were to be loaded, causing much confusion. The amusement began when the wagon was eventually loaded for the journey. "Like one of the lost tribes of Israel," was how Matthew described the chaotic little group which departed from Perth on the long journey north.

They had decided to take with them only those things they had to buy in Perth, as they would be able to stock up on basic food and stores when they reached Stannerton, the small settlement about forty miles from Kelly's place, and where they would also need to buy an extra cart. They left Perth with their huge covered wagon pulled by two horses, and an extra riding horse. Their furniture was carefully stacked in the wagon to preserve it from the weather, together with pans, crockery, fabrics, rugs and linen. A big tin bath was fastened along one side of the wagon, together with a large collection of tools, buckets and water butts, rolls of chicken wire and animal feeding troughs.

Mr. Scott had arranged for them to collect two hundred sheep from a farmer on one of the more northern Swan River settlements, and these were to form the basis of their stock. It was a good arrangement for both parties, as it meant the sheep did not have to be driven too far, and the farmer had the cash payment deposited in his account without the trouble of driving the sheep to be sold. Other livestock had to be taken with them however, and trailing along behind the wagon was a bullock and two cows, intended for domestic use only.

The journey to Kelly's place took three weeks, and during that time they often reflected that perhaps they would have done better to keep the *Selangor Lady* as their home, and to try making their living as the new owners intended. However, despite its attractions, this choice would have entailed many risks, with constant meeting of new people and the inevitable questions. The real attraction of Kelly's place was its isolation.

Although the trail north was well established the going proved to be very hard. This was not so much due to the journey itself, but the constant need to find feed and water for the stock, to ensure they survived the journey in good condition. When they collected the sheep they were lucky to obtain the services of a black stockman named Tomghin, and although he had few words of English, he and Matthew seemed to strike up an immediate friendship. Tomghin rode constantly at the fringes of the flock to make sure they didn't stray, Matthew drove the wagon, and Lucy kept an eye on the bullock and the two cows.

Stannerton proved to be a meager settlement, hardly a town at all, but it did have a small hotel and a good store, and the people seemed friendly and anxious to help. The word soon got around that the new owners of Kelly's place were in town, and Matthew had no difficulty in buying an extra cart, two piglets and a dozen hens, which were crated and put into the cart with a good supply of stores. As soon as this was accomplished, they set off again, Tomghin driving the sheep, Matthew the wagon with the bullock and cows attached on long tethers, and finally Lucy with the cart.

As they left Stannerton, a small middle aged woman crossed the dusty street and accosted the store keeper, who was watching the straggling procession depart.

"They the new folks bought Kelly's place?"

"Yes," the man answered, raising his hand in acknowledgment as Lucy turned to wave. "Name of Marshall, uncle and niece."

"Hmm." The woman stared at the back of the retreating cart. "You would have thought they could have stayed a night or two, after all, they could hardly have been warned off yet."

She stroked back the wisps of mousy hair which straggled down over her ears, and then smoothed down the front of her plain grey work dress, as if she was preparing to meet someone. The storekeeper smiled at her sympathetically, he was sorry for the widow Moore.

"No, nothing like that Jenny. They said they were anxious to be on their way because of the stock, and I expect they are used to camping out by now." He hesitated then added, "To be honest, I expect they couldn't afford the hotel. They seem to be doing things on a shoestring. Makes you wonder doesn't it?"

"Wonder what?"

"What a couple like that are doing buying a place as remote as Kelly's place. They'll never make a go of it."

"Will and Molly did," the woman answered after a moment.

"Well, yes, but Will was a real shepherd. Mr. Marshall is an old man, doesn't look too strong to me. Thank goodness they have Tomghin along with them, or I doubt they'd even get there." The man laughed, and then continued: "They are real townies, Jenny, at least according to Bob Middleton. Did I tell you Bob met them when they looked around the place? Nice folks though, so he said."

"If Bob says they're all right that's good enough for me," Jenny Moore responded firmly. "I should have liked to have met the young woman though, she looked nice."

"A real good looker, no doubt of that," the storekeeper rejoined. "But her looks won't help out there. They're in for a rough time those two. I give them six months."

"Oh, don't be such a pessimist, Jim! I wish them luck anyway," the woman said, watching as the back of the cart disappeared in a small dust trail. "Mind you," she continued with a sigh, "Even if they are able to get by, they'll be in trouble when they come to sell their wool."

"Surely Carmody won't trouble them," the storekeeper replied. "They won't have a woolclip worth the bother."

"No matter how small it is, Carmody will want his cut," Jenny Moore replied bitterly. "No family is too poor for him to make poorer." She gazed at the last of the small cloud as it disappeared from view, and added quietly, "Poor sods!"

"Yes," the storekeeper agreed sadly. "Poor sods!"

Two days later, bearing even more resemblance to one of the lost tribes of Israel; Matthew and Lucy, along with Tomghin and their exhausted animals, at last reached the little corner of Western Australia which was to become their home.

Chapter Fifteen

The heavy brass bell jangled loudly in the kitchen at *Straits House*. Minna hurriedly took off her white apron, and went to answer the front door. As she reached the hall she was joined by a middle aged Englishman, who grinned and said, "This will be Mr and Mrs Graham, don't worry Minna, I'll get the door."

"Certainly not Mr Blake," Minna said reprovingly, "It is my job to open door. You go into study and I will show them in. It is only proper."

Blake smiled and raised his hands in a gesture of surrender. He went into the study and Minna hurried to the door.

"Oh, Mr and Mrs Graham, how lovely to see you! Come in, come in."

"How are you Minna?" William asked, as she took Margot's hat and gloves.

"I am well sir, we are all well here." She smiled her sweet smile and then her eyes widened with pleasure as Margot gave her a small parcel.

"A gift for the staff," Margot said. "Just some sweetmeats to serve with tea. Lela made them specially."

"Oh Mrs. Graham, how kind! Please thank Lela for us." Carefully Minna put the parcel on the hall table and then asked, "How is Danny? I have not seen Lela recently to enquire."

Margot smiled. "He is becoming such a clever young man, Minna, you have no idea. He..."

"Nonsense!" William interjected. "He's a young rip!"

Margot laughed. "You must understand Minna, that my husband's opinion of Danny is coloured by the fact that he hit a cricket ball through our kitchen window last weekend."

"Oh dear..." Minna was apprehensive. She was about to say she was sure Danny didn't mean to break the window, when William Graham asked affably enough, "Is Mr Blake in the study?"

"Oh, yes, Mr Graham, please go through and I will bring refreshment."

As they entered the study Margot whispered, "You don't understand Minna, he's not so annoyed that Danny broke the window, but that he was the bowler!"

"Oh?" said Minna, none the wiser as she hurried off to the kitchen

William extended his hand. "My dear Edward, time passes so quickly, it hardly seems three months since our last visit."

"Indeed you are right," Edward Blake came forward to greet them. "And I am so glad to see you both," he added, smiling.

"No problems?" William asked as he saw Margot to a chair and then seated himself comfortably.

"Far from it," Edward Blake replied. "I am particularly pleased to see you this time because at last I can report that I am winning. I really feel we are making progress, not only financially but with the staff. *Straits House* is at last a happy place to live and work."

"That is good news Mr Blake," Margot responded warmly. "I know Lady Howell will be delighted if…when, she comes back."

William agreed. "The staff had a poor time of it until I dismissed Cranston," he said bitterly. "And if Lela had not alerted me as to his character, it may have been years before I discovered the thefts. He must have started milking the estate immediately after Sir Gilbert's death." He smiled ruefully, and then added; "You have done a good job here Edward, we are grateful to you and Mrs Blake for taking charge so efficiently."

"It is we who are grateful." Edward Blake said. "Running the estate is demanding work, and I enjoy the challenge. Ellen loves living here, especially since we made the changes you suggested, and the staff is excellent now we have won their confidence." He hesitated a moment, and then continued, "To be honest, when I was invalided out of the Army I thought my life was over. My career was ended and I was not sure I should be able to support us both. This position was a godsend, but when I took it I didn't realise how much I should come to enjoy it."

As Minna entered with a tray, Edward rose and took it from her. "Many thanks Minna, it looks delicious." He put the tray down on a small table and turned to William.

"We can go over the accounts as soon as we have had tea," he said cheerfully, "I have one or two new ideas and would like your opinion." He sat down and turned to Margot.

"Ellen will soon be back from the dressmaker to take you on your tour of the house, Margot," he said, "But in the meantime, would you like to pour?"

Lucy straightened up, stretching her arms and body in an attempt to relieve her aching back. She regarded the rows of cabbage plants with some satisfaction, with luck there should be a good crop again this year.

For the first two years after clearing Molly Kelly's garden patch, success had eluded her. The carefully planted seed had either failed to germinate, or produced weak scrubby plants which wilted and died with the first real heat. Last year she had finally got it right, and the long process of terracing had paid off. The problem had been the slope of the land. The water Lucy applied so assiduously drained down to the bottom, ensuring that only the plants at the edge survived. By dint of much hard work they had managed to change the slope into a series of flat terraces, each one shored up by stone brought up painstakingly in the bullock cart, and reinforced in place by a mixture of mud and cement. The two terraces completed last year had provided plentiful healthy crops, and this year they had added two more, which should mean a surplus to sell in Stannerton.

As Lucy thought of her plans, her sunburned face took on a look of resolve, an expression which Matthew had grown to know and understand well, during their first years at what was still known as Kelly's place. The look meant Lucy was determined not to be beaten, not by the heat, not by lack of money, not by the ever present ants and flies, or any other tribulation sent to test her. She looked around the garden now, pleased with what she saw, but reflecting ruefully on the tears and exhaustion that could have been saved if they had only had more experience.

It had been a time of trial and error. Even in the case of the cheese making, the first attempts had been disastrous. Now, following much discussion with Molly Kelly by post, and meticulous attention to her advice, the cheeses provided a small but increasing income, and were taken each month into Stannerton, from where most of them were sent to the store in Perth run by Molly Kelly's brother-in-law. Lucy was confident that this year she would have surplus vegetables to send along with the cheese, to be sold in Stannerton. She was sure of the market for them. Certain green vegetables were difficult to cultivate in the area, and Lucy had not forgotten Bob Middleton's amazement when he saw the cabbage she had served when he called to shear their sheep in November.

"Cabbage! Oh my Lord, it's cabbage! I haven't seen a cabbage for years, Cath!"

Matthew and Lucy had quickly realised that they could not afford to do what other settlers did, and concentrate on beef, lamb and wool. They simply did not have enough acreage. However, they did have good sweet water, and although this was not in sufficient quantity to water huge herds of beef or sheep, it was enough to produce smaller quantities of very high quality. They had started with two hundred sheep, a bullock and two cows, two piglets and a dozen hens. Although their sheep had done well, the seasons had been very dry, and they found they could not feed more than five hundred, so had been forced to keep their flock at that level. The wide variety of plants which made up the pasture near the creek ensured their cows gave a rich milk ideally suited to cheese making, and due to the success of the cheese venture they now had twelve good cows.

Tomghin, their aboriginal stockman, had worked on much larger sheep stations, and had given invaluable help in the early years, becoming very close to Matthew as they worked together each day. Lucy was continually surprised at the depth of understanding and respect which had grown between these two unlikely friends. They communicated by a combination of words, gestures and sometimes pictures, and often Lucy would observe them squatting on the ground, Matthew deep in contemplation of something Tomghin was explaining by drawing on the ground with a stick. The one disadvantage to Tomghin's help was that occasionally he would withdraw it, and disappear for two or three months to visit his tribe, and at these times they missed him sorely.

Now, Lucy made her way down the slope to the cabin, calling out to Matthew, who was on the way to the trench with the earth closet bucket.

"Tea in fifteen minutes, Uncle."

Matthew waved his hand in reply; a break for tea together was a daily ritual. Lucy entered the cabin and fetched the tea kettle. She took it out to the well and worked the whip pole to draw up fresh water. It was a small matter of pride to her that she always drew fresh water to make tea, rather than fill the kettle from the water barrel in the cabin. She hung the kettle on the large hook and swung it over the fire.

She checked her bread dough, and was pleased it had risen well. She took a handful of flour and scattered it on the marble topped cupboard next to the sink, and began to knead the dough with quick deft movements. She made a dozen rolls and a large round cob loaf. Then she changed her mind and remoulded the loaf into a thick plait. It looked nicer, she thought, and it was just possible Bob Middleton would arrive today. He was due any time, and was very fond of her home baked bread.

She had just brewed the tea when Matthew entered, going straight to the sink to wash.

"Just on time," Lucy said, as she did every afternoon.

He came to the table and they settled to enjoy their tea in companionable silence. Lucy often thought of this as the best part of the day, and she also enjoyed the time after the evening meal, when they would sit together near the fire if it was cool, or out on the verandah in summer, and she would sew whilst Matthew read aloud.

"What are the receipts like this month?" Matthew asked. He was aching in every limb, and sipped his tea gratefully.

"Same as last month for the cheese, may be less next month though, I think Gypsy's going dry."

"Oh." Matthew sounded disappointed.

"Anything you want in particular?"

"No. I only thought perhaps we could afford to hire some help before too long. Since Tomghin went walkabout it's difficult to keep up with everything."

"I wish we could, but it's out of the question. Even if Tomghin comes back I don't know if we can afford to pay him." Lucy regarded her uncle sympathetically. "I'm sure we shall do better this summer, if I really nurse the vegetables we shall have some to sell in Stannerton."

"I hope so." Matthew said dully. He did not say that he could not last until summer, that if he didn't rest soon he would surely die…

"Uncle, there's someone coming…" Lucy flew to the window, and then ducked back in sudden alarm.

"Is it Bob?" Matthew asked, staring at her. She was obviously distraught.

"No, it's Gregory Lamont! It is, it's him, I'd know him anywhere. What on earth is he doing here?"

Matthew came to the window quickly, sharing her alarm. He saw a tall bushman on a good horse, approaching at a measured pace.

"You must hide!" Matthew decided quickly. "He's never seen me, so he won't suspect. Go into your bedroom and stay there. If he asks where my niece is I'll say you've gone in to Stannerton with the cheese."

"But the cart is here!"

"Then I'll say you rode in on some business. Quickly now."

He bundled Lucy out of the room and went towards the door.

"Uncle!"

"What now?"

Lucy gestured to the table. "Get rid of my teacup."

Matthew hastened to put the cup in the sink and walked out to the verandah as the visitor alighted from his horse. Matthew saw a tall rangy man, his hair worn a little longer than usual under a broad brimmed bush hat. His regular features were strong and suntanned, and he turned towards Matthew a look so penetrating in its grey observation, that Matthew averted his eyes quickly.

"Good day. Lamont, Gregory Lamont."

Matthew took the outstretched hand and shook it warmly.

"Glad to see you Greg. I'm Matt Marshall. Come on in, I've just made tea, there's more water in the kettle."

As they went in, Matthew took the opportunity to examine his visitor more closely, and he suddenly knew beyond a shadow of doubt why Lucy had often seemed to become rather agitated at the mention of Gregory Lamont, and why she had agreed to making him their neighbour. The man was handsome certainly, but it was more than that. There was a presence about him which was almost overwhelming, especially when he looked you in the eye. Greg now did this, observing Matthew closely as he lifted the singing kettle and made fresh tea.

"Thought it was time I looked you up. You've been here, let's see, about three years now isn't it?"

"Yes, a bit more, but surely this is out of your way?"

"A little, but I heard some news in Stannerton I thought you would want to know, especially as you are from England…"

"Oh?" said Matthew warily.

"Yes, sad news I'm afraid, Queen Victoria has died."

Matthew sat down with a jolt. "Oh dear me…dear me…" he repeated, quite upset. "Of course she was an old lady and it was to be expected, but still…" he murmured "It's quite a shock." He smiled at Greg a little uncertainly. "You know Mr Lamont, the Queen has been on the throne for my entire life, I can't remember a time when she wasn't there. It's the end of an era certainly. First Mr Gladstone a few years back, and now the Queen…" He motioned Greg to the table and stirred the teapot thoughtfully. "I suppose being born here you don't feel the same, especially since Australia was proclaimed a Commonwealth so recently…"

Greg smiled. "Perhaps not quite the same, but like you I can't remember a time without her."

"Well it was kind of you to come so far out of your way to tell us," Matthew said warmly, pouring the tea.

"Not so far, only about thirty miles, not much to meet a neighbour who is so well spoken of." Greg smiled, an open infectious smile that lit the grey eyes with flecks of hazel light. Matthew thought of his dear Lucy and groaned inwardly. He gave Greg a querying look.

"We're talked of?"

"Oh yes, Bob Middleton always reports on you and your niece, and what a nice little place you are making here. It must be hard work, with just the two of you."

"Yes. It's not bad when Tomghin is here, but he's away at present." Matthew hesitated. "And my niece will be sorry to have missed you. What bad luck for you to come when she's away."

"Away?" The grey eyes were wary.

"Yes, she's gone to Stannerton. You probably know she makes cheese, and sells it to a store in Perth. She's hoping to sell vegetables this summer, and has gone to Stannerton to make an arrangement with the store there."

Greg frowned, and the grey eyes clouded, but he responded cheerfully enough, "Oh yes, I've heard about the cheese. Heard it's excellent."

"Then you must take some home with you. And in the meantime perhaps you'd like to see what we've done here?" Matthew said, hoping to get Greg out of the cabin.

Greg finished his tea and nodded agreement, and for the next hour Matthew showed him round, describing their problems and how they had been overcome. He welcomed the opportunity to talk about their block with this knowledgeable man, and Greg was particularly impressed with the terracing of the slope behind the cabin.

"Wouldn't have even thought of that myself," he said admiringly. "I suppose it's because there's so much space out here, if you can't grow something you just try somewhere else, or something else. It takes real dedication to persevere with vegetables like that."

"Oh, Catherine has dedication all right," Matthew agreed. "We knew we had to do something on a small scale, but something there was a demand for, hence the cheese and the vegetables."

They were now at the top of the slope and standing at the site of the Kelly's proposed new house. Greg nodded towards where a timber wall was partly constructed.

"I see you've made a start with the house at last," he said. "Is the timber still good?"

"Yes, it's excellent, but I doubt it will ever be finished. I have managed to build half way up one wall, but it nearly killed me. I thought that if I could just put in one piece of timber a day I would eventually get the house built, but it's defeated me. The planks are so heavy that we can only just about lift them, with one of us on each end. When we had built to about five feet high we just couldn't lift the timber to build any higher. It's a shame, because we have all the materials." Matthew smiled, and continued as they started to walk back to the cabin, "Molly Kelly let us have the plans for the house. She was a real brick, and has helped us a lot. It was at her suggestion that we started making the cheese."

"Yes, she is a good person, and so was her husband, I was fond of them both." Greg said with genuine sadness. He turned again and looked up at the house site. "But to return to your problem, it's nonsense to think you could build the house yourselves. You need to get some help."

"Help has to be paid for."

"Not necessarily. What you need is several men for a time, a concerted effort. I'll be glad to send you say, four or five men for a week or so, as long as it takes to get the frame completed and the roof on."

Matthew turned to him in surprise. "But we couldn't afford..."

"Nothing to pay. The men are on the payroll already. They are a good lot, and if you can manage to feed them, that will be enough. They'll do a good job for you, never fear. They'll enjoy getting away for a bit of a trip and a change of work."

Matthew was overwhelmed, and said slowly, "I hardly know how to thank you, it would be a wonderful help. I'm sure I can manage all the smaller work, if only we can get the frame up, I'd love Catherine to have a decent place to live."

"Yes," said Greg, "And I'd like to see Molly Kelly's dream house built at last. You can expect the men in about three weeks time if that's convenient."

They reached the cabin, and Matthew hurried to the cold pantry and brought out a cheese for Greg to take with him. He wrapped the muslin covered cheese carefully in brown paper, and Greg smiled his thanks and promised he would not forget to send the workmen.

"I can't thank you enough, Catherine will be so pleased," Matthew said gratefully. The grey eyes flitted around the room, and then Greg turned to the door. "I'm sure she will be pleased to move to more modern quarters, but no doubt she'll miss the magic of this old cabin."

"Magic?" said Matthew, mystified.

"Yes, didn't you notice? While we were outside, the bread that was proving over there in the corner put itself in the oven. It smells wonderful."

And with this sally he departed, and Lucy reappeared and watched from the window as Greg packed the cheese into his swag, then mounted his horse and rode away

Greg Lamont proved as good as his word. Three weeks later five men arrived, announcing their intention to "do a bit o' graft' for the Marshalls, and they seemed to welcome the change of scene and work. They cheerfully bunked down on the floor of the new house, and were apparently happy to put in long days of hard work. One of them, a heavy red-bearded Scot named Jim McLeish, seemed to be accepted by the others as the boss, and it was with Jim that Matthew discussed the plans. It seemed to Lucy that the house took shape almost by the minute, and every time she ventured into the garden or to milk the cows, she would stare up at the site, amazed at the progress. To Matthew's astonishment, it took the team less than four days to complete the timber walls, and he was kept busy mixing the cement infill, which was used to close any cracks and to ensure the walls were draught proof.

Then they started on the roof. They used a winch to raise the heavy joists one at a time, two men steadying it as a third pinned it into place. After only two days of heaving and hammering, they began the much lighter task of tiling the roof with the red baked clay tiles which had been Molly Kelly's pride, and the building began to look like a real house.

Since Greg Lamont's visit, Lucy had been uneasy. His final comment about the bread had made her feel guilty about deceiving him, especially in view of his kindness. She found that images of Greg impinged on her thoughts at unlikely moments, and sometimes she experienced a feeling of profound melancholy, although she could not have identified its cause.

The arrival of the workmen had soon dispelled this introspection however, as Lucy was run off her feet cooking and baking bread, and making never-ending pans of tea. The larder had been full when the men arrived, but was quickly becoming depleted, and to add to her difficulties Bob Middleton arrived to do the shearing. Lucy ran out to meet him.

"Bob, welcome, I'm so glad to see you. We expected you earlier than this."

"G'day, Cath, sorry I'm a bit late, stopped at one of the Swan River blocks to give a mate a hand."

Lucy smiled in quick understanding. That was Bob all over. *Probably some poor man who had lost his stockman or couldn't pay his bills.* Bob was a friend to so many, and she laughed happily as she beckoned him towards the cabin.

"Oh Bob, it's so exciting! We are getting the house built, come and look!"

Bob stood looking up at the hive of activity for a few moments, and his voice was soft as he murmured "How d'ya like that? Will and Molly's dream coming true. I've been waiting a few years to see this, Cath."

"Yes, and they're making a good job of it. I expect you know the men, Greg Lamont sent them over to help us. We should never have built it without them."

Bob nodded. "Oh yes, I know them all. Greg and Sam Lamont are both decent blokes and will always help a neighbour. Of course they can afford to, but it's not every rich man will help those less well off."

Lucy took his arm. "Come on Bob, come and have some tea and then we can take some up to the site, and you can see for yourself."

"Hang on a minute, I got something for you."

Bob returned to his horse and untied a large pack, which he carried across to the cabin and slung onto the scrubbed table.

"Flour and tea," he explained. "I heard the blokes were here house building and thought you might need some extra from Stannerton." He grinned. "Mighty big appetites."

"Bob, you are wonderful, I was getting a bit short. Add what I owe you to the shearing bill." She handed Bob a mug of steaming tea and looked at him closely.

"What is it Bob?" He had been with her at least ten minutes and she had not heard the big laugh once.

"What do you mean?"

"What is worrying you?"

Bob looked at her askance. "Nothing," he announced shortly. He looked at her again. "Damn it Cath, you could always read me like a book. How d'ya do that?"

Lucy sat down and regarded him across the table. "Well, what is it?"

"I thought you might have already heard the wool price."

"What about it?"

"The price has gone up in Perth and Adelaide. About time too, most farmers have been working for nothing the last few years."

"That's good news surely."

"Yes, for most folks, but not those who sell to Carmody."

Lucy's face tightened. "Tell me the worst."

"He says he can't pass on the higher price. He's only going to pay the same price as last year."

"But he's already robbing us!" Lucy cried angrily. George Carmody was a source of friction between herself and Bob, the only subject on which they disagreed. For the last two seasons Bob had persuaded her to go along with the other local settlers, and sell her woolclip to George Carmody in Stannerton. Lucy had done this with a bad grace, well aware that if she could sell her wool direct to the stock agent at the railhead, the price would be considerably higher.

"The price is up almost fifteen per cent," said Bob dully. He knew he would never stop her taking on Carmody now.

"Fifteen per cent, but that's wonderful." Lucy was enthusiastic. "Bob, you surely won't try to talk me out of selling my wool independently this time? We simply can't afford to sell to Carmody, he's getting rich on our hard work!"

"I know, I know, Cath. Lots of other farmers feel like you do. Wat Higgins for one, and Mick Taylor, and Clancy Bright as well. They're grumbling all right, but they'll sell to Carmody, and at his price."

"But they can't! We must stand up to him this time. If we all stick together we can take the wool to the railhead in a column, with guards."

"They won't Cath. I'm sure they won't." His tone was so decided that Lucy saw red.

"How can you be so sure?" she cried angrily. "You…"

"Because I already asked them!" Bob yelled back at her.

They looked at each other across the kitchen table. Bob reached across and took Lucy's hand. "I already asked them, Cath," he repeated quietly. "I asked them because I knew that is what you would want to do, same as you wanted last year. It's no go, Cath, really it isn't. If there was a chance of some support I'd say let's take him on, but you can't do it by yourself."

Lucy turned her head so that Bob should not see the hot tears which had sprung to her eyes. She thought a moment and then smiled briefly.

"It's all right, Bob," she said. "And thanks for trying. You know how I feel about this whole thing with Carmody. I just can't bear to be bullied." Her voice dropped to a whisper. "That's what he does Bob; he bullies us into accepting his terms."

"I know Cath, I know."

Lucy rose from the table and went over to the window. Bob watched her narrow shoulders droop in a deep sigh. She remained at the window and spoke in a low voice.

"Bob, you'll never know how much Uncle Matthew means to me. I've been watching him up at the house, mixing the cement for the men. He works so hard, and he's not strong enough to do it. In England he worked in a bank all his life, do you know that? In a bank..." her voice trailed off almost to a whisper, and Bob leaned forward to catch her words.

"He has given up so much for me, so much. He is my only relative and my truest friend, and if we made just a little more money we could afford a stockman, and life would be easier for him."

Lucy's voice broke, and Bob crossed to her quickly. It was not like Cath to go on like this. He'd never seen a tear, never seen her really down, not even that time when all her vegetables died. "Matt will be all right, Cath, he enjoys life here."

If he expected to see tears on the face she turned to him he was wrong. His heart sank, she was ready for battle, he knew that look. She smiled up at him brightly, a glint of pure steel in the blue eyes.

"Oh yes Bob," she said firmly. "Matthew will be all right. I intend to see to it."

Bob finished the shearing at about the same time the men completed the heavy work on the house, and so he decided to travel on to the Lamont station with them. Although the house had no glass in the windows and no furniture, Lucy and Matthew spent every spare moment there, just walking through the rooms, planning, deciding, and glorying in the space and comparative luxury that was to be their future home. Matthew made a long list of all that was required from the store in Stannerton, and measured carefully for the glass.

"It's easy making lists, let's hope we can pay for it all," said Lucy. "We shall have to buy the urgent things first and the others as we can afford them."

"Yes of course," said Matthew, a little testily. "But I like planning it."

Lucy looked at him affectionately. They were sitting quietly in the cabin, making last minute arrangements for Lucy's visit to Stannerton next day with the wool waggon.

"It was quite a party last night, wasn't it?" said Lucy, laughing at the memory.

"Yes, but I thought Jim McLeish would never stop singing!"

"I liked it," said Lucy, "He has a good voice and I love that Scottish sound he gets."

Matthew grinned. "He's never seen Scotland you know," he said. "He learned it from his father, the family were early settlers."

"Yes. It was grand having all that company, especially the get-together last night, but it's good to be on our own again."

They sat in silence, Lucy wondering how to broach the subject of her trip. At length Matthew solved her problem.

"You will be careful Lucy won't you? I really don't like you making the trip to Stannerton alone. I wish I was coming with you."

"But Uncle, someone has to care for the stock."

"I know, I know. But perhaps I should go, and leave you here."

"Uncle, we've already discussed that. Remember, that as well as the wool, I have to send the cheese, and I want to talk to the storekeeper about vegetables. If I start early tomorrow I shall only have to camp out one night."

Matthew sighed. "That's what I'm worried about. I never worried when Tomghin was with you, but if you are alone, and anything should happen..."

Lucy understood his thoughts. It was a memory which had never left them. "Don't worry Uncle; a snake is not going to get me. I shan't camp on the ground anyway; I shall sleep at the front of the wagon. There is one thing you should know however," she paused, and chose her words carefully. "In Stannerton I intend to see George Carmody."

Matthew looked up in alarm. "Whatever for?"

"The price of wool has gone up substantially, in Perth and Adelaide. It's probably due to so many sheep being lost with the drought, production has gone down. Bob told me about it, but Carmody is still paying the same price as last year."

Matthew understood immediately. "Lucy, I know how you feel about this, and you're right. But he's a big man, and very important in Stannerton, you can't stand up to him."

"I can Uncle, and I will. We have a good woolclip this year, almost six pounds a head, nearly two pounds more than our first, if you remember. After all the work you and Tomghin have put in to improve the yield and the quality, we deserve a fair deal." She swallowed. "I will not allow myself to be bullied, Uncle, not ever again."

Matthew fell silent, then: "What do you intend to do?"

Lucy gave a short laugh in an attempt to relieve the tension. "Oh, nothing heroic. I just want to talk to him, to see if I can persuade him to give me a better price."

"Are you sure that's all?"

"Of course. I'll take my best blue walking suit and put on my big hat, see if I can charm him."

"What if he won't give you a higher price?"

Then I'll have to think again. Uncle, please don't worry, I shan't do anything foolhardy. I only mention it in case I'm not home as soon as you expect."

"You intend to take the woolclip to the railhead yourself don't you?"

"Of course not, I told you, I'm happy to sell it to Carmody if he'll give me a fair price. But our order for the window glass may be ready fairly quickly, and if so, I may stay on and wait for it."

Matthew sighed. "We could go round in circles all night like this," he said. He got up and went to his bedroom, and Lucy frowned, perhaps he was more upset than she thought. A moment later Matthew was back, holding Jarvis's old shotgun.

"If you're determined on it, you had better take this," he said quietly.

"Oh Uncle, I don't think…"

"I know, I know. There won't be any trouble. But just in case, I'll feel happier if you have it."

Lucy crossed the room and took the gun. "Thank you Uncle," she said, and gave him a kiss on the cheek. "I'd better go to bed if I'm to make an early start."

"Just a moment Lucy."

She turned back with a questioning look, and waited until her uncle spoke again.

"Lamont, er…Gregory Lamont." Matthew said hesitantly, noting the way Lucy's hand flew to her mother's brooch.

"What about him, Uncle?"

"I like him; he's a good man I think."

"I'm sure he is, he was very helpful over the house."

"That's not what I meant."

"What did you mean?"

Matthew noticed the faint flush of colour suffuse her face. He crossed the room. "Lucy, my dear. I thought…I think there might have been something…something between the two of you."

A faint shock passed over her face, but then her head drooped and she said softly, "No, Uncle, there wasn't. I just met him at the Governor's ball in Singapore. We danced, and walked in the garden." She turned. "There was nothing more."

"But…?" Matthew persisted gently.

"But…" she answered, remembering. "There was something I suppose, a feeling, a sort of understanding, as if we had always known each other." Her face became animated. "You know, Uncle, he was so funny, a little forward perhaps, but he made me laugh..." Her face changed. "I was very young then, Uncle, very naïve and silly."

"Not silly, just young," Matthew smiled. "It's not surprising that you've changed."

"Yes, and he's changed too. I hardly recognised him when he came here. When I first saw him at the Governor's ball he was in evening dress, very elegant. The man who came here a few weeks ago was harder somehow, and it wasn't just the way he was dressed. Older of course, but somehow stronger too."

"Like you."

She smiled. "Perhaps. Yes, that's probably true. You don't think he suspected?"

"He certainly knew my niece was here, and not in Stannerton. But I honestly don't see how he could guess that my niece and the Lucy Rowlands he once knew are one and the same."

"I hope not. As far as he is concerned Lucy Rowlands is a murderess on the run from the police." There was a bitterness in her tone which hurt Matthew.

"I'm sure he would never believe that of you. My dear, what shall we do if he comes here again? You can't hide forever, and I honestly don't think he would give you away if we explained."

"No. He probably won't come again, having done his duty as a good neighbour. You may be right that he wouldn't give me away, but we can't take that chance unless it is forced on us." She turned to face Matthew. "Don't imagine, Uncle, that there can ever be anything between Gregory Lamont and me."

"But Lucy, why not? If he believes your story, he will accept your new identity."

"No!" Lucy became agitated. "Please, Uncle, put any such thing out of your mind." She made an obvious effort to control her trembling lower lip. "Uncle, it's not just what happened to Gilbert; it's that I was so...so stupid! The night I met Gregory Lamont I knew, yes, if I am truthful I must admit I knew, that I was attracted to him. That same evening Gilbert asked the Governor to announce our engagement, and what did I do? Nothing. I let myself be persuaded into something I really didn't want. I was so weak I allowed myself to be manipulated. I didn't even make a conscious decision,

I just sort of floated into marriage, because it had been announced and everyone expected it. All the troubles I had later, and the troubles other people had too, stemmed from that one thing. My weakness."

"My dear child, you were under great pressure, your father…"

"Yes, my father," she responded bitterly. "My poor father. Oh Matthew, I know he was weak and had got himself into all sorts of difficulties, but there were other ways out. I should have tried to find one of them, not just given in. If I had not married Gilbert father might still be alive, and Jarvis."

"Nonsense. You really must not punish yourself like this. Your father had a good life. He had a wonderful marriage and a lovely child, and that's more than many people have. As for Jarvis, he wouldn't have made different choices if he had his time over again, you know that. In any case, what does this have to do with Greg Lamont?"

"Nothing I suppose. Except I don't want anyone else to get into trouble because of me. Believe me Uncle; it's better for us not to have any contact with the Lamonts."

"I'm not so sure, my dear," Matthew said fondly. "If I've learned anything at all in my life, it is that the moments of love are the only moments which really matter. You will understand that when you are old, but by then it may be too late." He kissed her cheek gently. "Think about it," he said.

"All right, Uncle. Good night."

"Good night, Lucy."

Lucy stopped in the doorway and turned back. "Matthew? Were you ever in love with anyone?"

"Yes, once. Only once."

"But you never married?"

"No." He smiled easily. "She wouldn't have me. Now off to bed with you."

"Good night, Uncle."

"Good night."

Matthew stayed a few more minutes, laying the table for Lucy's early breakfast. *His niece was getting older,* he thought, *and although she was still beautiful, it was a stronger, more mature beauty, a natural fluid grace so different to the prettiness of the young girl who had left England.* It saddened him, even though he knew Lucy was a better person as a result of all she had endured. What she had said worried him, it was obvious she still carried a heavy burden of guilt, no matter how undeserved.

What was that she had said about finding a way out, and not just floating along with the tide? He reflected on this, and decided it applied to himself as well. *His niece was entitled to a proper life, a family life, if of course that was what she wanted. From her reaction when he spoke of Gregory Lamont he was sure she did. When the time came he would not make the mistake of floating along with the tide, he would do something positive.* A small smile played around his mouth as he extinguished the lamp and went to his room. As he prepared for bed he recalled Lucy's question about his own love life, and gentle memories came to him of the only woman he had ever loved, the woman who, in the end, had chosen to marry his brother.

Chapter Sixteen

Lucy made good time the following day, and camped for the night within fifteen miles of Stannerton. She had enjoyed the journey, and the ever changing prospects of the countryside. When they had first arrived in this strange and frightening land, she had been impressed by the landscape, but had seen it as entirely composed of large, bold effects. She had gazed with admiration at the purple mountains, huge red sandstone bluffs, and the silver and black stunted trees, etched in relief against monumental red and amber skies. It was as if some great primaeval artist had splashed all the boldest colours from his palette across the land, and the effect was at once awesome and humbling. With time however, Lucy had come to appreciate the smaller and more intimate flora and fauna, and as she drove the big wool waggon she was delighted on all sides by the beauty of the broad reaches of the river. Deep forest swept down to the curving bays, and on the banks she saw flocks of black swans, pelicans, shags and wild duck. Heavy creepers roamed over shrubs, gums and stringy bark trees, and there were wild flowers in abundance.

Lucy chose to camp out although she knew she would have been welcomed at any of the small homes spread along the river valley. She still preferred to keep her distance from friendly settlers who would undoubtedly enquire about her background. She chose a camp site beneath a solid canopy of eucalyptus trees, lit a fire and made coffee. She did not cook, as she had brought sufficient prepared food with her to last the journey.

The raucous screaming of butcher birds woke her at dawn next day, and by noon she was in Stannerton.

Her first call was to deliver her cheeses to the store, and then she booked into the hotel for one night, obtaining permission to leave the wool waggon in the hotel yard. She was fortunate to be able to obtain a bath almost immediately and dressed with care, putting on her blue skirt and the matching tightly fitted jacket. She examined her reflection in the mirror, plumping out the wide sleeves, and then she carefully pinned her one and only hat at a slight angle. It was a silly affair with the brim crammed with cream roses, and having smoothed down the flat front of her skirt and given a swirl to the fullness at the back, Lucy was satisfied with her reflection, and giggled a little, suddenly pleased to have an opportunity to wear her best things. She picked up her cream gloves and parasol and made her way downstairs and along the street to George Carmody's stock and station office, trying without much success to keep the heavy velvet trim of her skirt out of the dust. When she arrived she gave her name to the greasy haired clerk at the desk and prepared to wait, but almost immediately a door opened and George Carmody emerged, his rather chubby face breaking into a smile.

"Miss Marshall, what a surprise, and what an honour! Do please come in, how very nice to see you."

He offered his hand, and then bowed briefly as Lucy entered the office. She was surprised at the effusive welcome, as she had never spoken to him before. He had been pointed out to her on a previous visit to the town, and she now saw that he was smaller and stockier than she had imagined, a body rather like Gilbert's, she thought with sudden repugnance.

"We have not met before, Mr. Carmody," she began, "I have usually dealt with your Mr. Walsh."

"Ah yes, indeed Miss Marshall, but I know you, or at least I know of you and your uncle. We have had the pleasure of buying your woolclip for two seasons now. A very small wool transaction as far as we are concerned, of course, but I am always anxious to help our newer and poorer farmers."

Lucy ignored his patronising tone, and smiled sweetly.

"I am so pleased to hear that Mr. Carmody, for you can indeed help us a great deal. That is why I asked to see you personally, rather than approach Mr. Walsh."

Carmody leaned forward across his desk. "Be as personal as you like my dear," he said, his eyes appraising her with obvious lechery. "I'm sure I shall enjoy it."

Lucy felt a slight anger, but ignored the comment and continued evenly.

"It's about the wool price Mr. Carmody. I was very pleased to hear that prices have at last increased in Adelaide, and by as much as fifteen per cent. Of course, I do not expect to receive the same price from you; after all you have the transport costs to bear. I thought perhaps ten per cent less than the Adelaide price might be fair? That would allow you five per cent to cover transport, which should be more than enough as you take so much wool in bulk, and five per cent profit."

George Carmody looked at her in silence, he appeared to be thinking.

After a moment he said levelly, "I'm paying the other farmers the same price as last year, but then, you knew that already didn't you?"

"I had heard that was so, Mr. Carmody, but I could hardly credit it. I did not believe you could be so mean."

He flushed slightly. "Believe me, I would not wish to be mean with you Miss Marshall, in fact I am sure I could be more than generous."

"What price will you offer for our wool Mr. Carmody?"

"Well now, let's say I agree to your terms, provided you will agree with mine."

"And those are?"

"Come now, Miss Marshall, you are not a child. You know only too well what my terms are. You are a very beautiful woman, and must have been told so many times. If you would like to stay in Stannerton for a few days whenever you come in for stores, I'm sure we could become good friends." He leaned across the desk and fondled her arm. "I mean really close friends."

Lucy fought the impulse to snatch away her arm. Instead, she slowly removed it from his reach and spoke in a normal tone.

"I must apologise, Mr. Carmody, I forgot to congratulate you. I heard some time ago that you had another addition to your family, a little girl I believe? I must make the time to call on Mrs. Carmody and take the child a small gift. No doubt your wife will be most interested to hear that you wish to have such a close friendship with me." She glanced up at Carmody, whose face was becoming suffused with purple, and continued in the same tone, "But to return to business, what price will you offer for my wool?"

"Same as last year," he spat out the words.

"Then in that case, I regret we cannot do business, and I will waste no more of your valuable time. Good afternoon Mr. Carmody."

Lucy got to her feet, but Carmody was not finished.

"And what do you intend to do with your woolclip? You'll find no one else here willing to take it to the railhead for you."

Lucy turned in the doorway and gave him her sweetest smile.

"It is of course my wool, Mr. Carmody. So what I do with it is entirely up to me, is it not? Good afternoon."

As she left Carmody's office Lucy felt herself trembling with anger. She went to the store and collected payment for the cheeses, and arranged with the storekeeper for the surplus to be sent to Perth as usual. She also gave him the list of stores she needed, explaining that she would pick them up in a few days time, and requesting a price for the window glass. Then she went back to the hotel and took off her unaccustomed finery.

"So much for dressing to impress," she observed to herself, spinning the hat around idly in her hands. "It doesn't always have the effect you intend." She smiled wryly and lay down to rest until dinner, her mind in ferment.

For the first time since she had planned the trip, she felt a small niggle of fear. It seemed her bluff had been called, and she was faced with the reality of trying to take the woolclip to the railhead herself. She was not worried about the loneliness of the trip, aware that after about forty miles she would probably meet up with farmers joining the route from other directions, and so would be afforded some degree of protection. It was the first forty miles or so that was the problem, and she could not help recalling Bob Middleton's story about the fate of the Stannerton farmer who had tried to sell his own woolclip. Even if she got as far as the railhead, she would not know who to contact, how to go about selling the wool.

As she entered the hotel dining room that evening, prepared for a lonely meal, a blowsy looking woman with mouse coloured hair, came over to her table with two glasses of sherry.

"Thought you might like a bit of company, dear," she said, "and a glass of sherry won't go amiss before your steak." She smiled encouragingly, "Bottoms up."

Lucy accepted the glass. "Thank you, and bottoms up."

The woman drew out a chair and sat down opposite Lucy, smoothing out her faded plum taffeta gown. "I'm Jennie Moore," she said, "I own the hotel. I know who you are, Catherine Marshall from Kelly's place."

"You're well informed," Lucy said, "It's good to meet you."

"Well, I thought I'd come over for a chat," said Jennie, "There's not many of us left."

"Many of whom?"

"Those of us prepared to stand up to Carmody. I saw you go out earlier, you looked real smart. Then I heard you had refused to sell Carmody your woolclip. His clerk let it slip and it's all around town. What are you going to do now?"

Lucy hesitated. "I'm not really sure," she said slowly. "I'm still thinking about it."

"Hmm." Jennie sipped her sherry thoughtfully. "Don't suppose you've found anyone else to back you up?"

"No." Lucy admitted.

"Not surprised. Poor sods are frightened to death. Oh, beg your pardon for the language Miss Marshall, I heard you were something of a lady."

Lucy laughed, "No, certainly not. I'm just another of the poor sods who's frightened to death as well."

They both laughed, and Jennie said, "Well you can't blame them. Carmody is pretty ruthless, and he won't let his profits go without a fight. He's made an easy living for years, simply because of his reputation. I think some of the men round here would stand up to him, if they didn't have families to consider. I mean, if they were to get killed what would happen to the children?"

"You think it's true then? That Carmody had that man killed, the one who defied him?"

"Who knows? Probably it's true. The bloke was certainly shot dead. Carmody doesn't have to do things like that these days, people know his reputation, and take the easiest way out."

"But surely the law…"

"What law? We're too far out for it to reach us here. Or at least by the time it got here it would be too late, and nothing able to be proved, just like before." Jennie's tone was bitter, and after a moment Lucy commented, "You said there weren't many of us left. What did Carmody do to you?"

Jennie smiled ruefully. "Nothing too bad yet," she said, "But it's getting worse every day. He's trying to ruin me."

"How?"

Lucy's steak arrived, and Jennie waited until the bumbling old waiter was out of earshot before she replied. "Catherine, this hotel isn't much but it's all I've got. When my husband died a few years ago it was all he left, we had put everything into it when we came out here, and we hoped the hotel would grow with the town, so to speak. Well, after John died, Carmody offered to buy the hotel from me. I was tempted because I was a bit nervous of trying to run it on my own, but the price he offered was next to nothing. In the end I turned it down, although I knew it would be a long time before I got another offer. I thought I'd be letting John down to sell it for a pittance after all his work, and I decided to pull myself together and put all I could into making the hotel a success."

"Good for you," said Lucy warmly.

"It was for a while. I started to do quite well. As more people came to settle they all came in to Stannerton for stores and stayed here. Carmody was furious. He came to see me and offered again to buy the place, same price as before. When I refused he said he'd see me out of business, and he almost has."

"But how can he do that?"

"The same way he makes people sell him their wool. The same farmers who won't stand up to him on the wool price, won't stay here when they come into town. They'd like to, my prices are cheap and they are looking forward to a good bed and a bath after a few days on the road, but Carmody let it be known he wouldn't like it. It's as simple as that. You stayed here because you didn't know I'd been declared out of bounds, but most farmers camp out rather than stay here, so as not to offend Carmody."

"I thought the visitors were scarce," Lucy said. She thought a moment. "It's hard to know what you can do about it."

"Yes, trade is so bad now I can't keep the place up properly. Got nothing to spend on it see? Sooner or later I'll probably have to sell to Carmody and move out. I have some relatives in Perth; I'll have to go to them, even though we don't get on too well." Jennie shrugged her shoulders and added bitterly, "Carmody came to see me last week. He offered me less for the place than he did two years ago. He said the longer I held out, the lower the price I would eventually get." Her voice broke, and Lucy, appalled, tried to comfort her.

"Jennie, I don't know if I can help you, but someone has to stand up to him. Stay around and watch!"

"What are you going to do?"

"Take my woolclip to the railhead and sell it. I have the right to do that if I choose. If I can do it, think of the effect it will have. Carmody beaten by a woman! He'll never live it down, and it might break this awful hold he has on the town."

"It certainly would if you could do it." Jennie blew her nose vigorously. "Don't mind me Catherine, I'm not beaten yet. You know, you're probably right. If Carmody was taken down a peg it might stir up some of the men around here. They wouldn't like to think a woman had the guts to stand up to Carmody when they didn't. There's only one problem."

"What's that?"

"You might be dead."

They sat in silence for a moment. Then Lucy said slowly, "I think there is a way I could do it and stay alive, if you would help me."

"Anything Catherine."

Two heads, one rich chestnut and the other mousy brown, bent close over the table. By the time Lucy had finished her dessert, the plan was made.

At three in the morning the little settlement of Stannerton lay sleeping. Not a sound disturbed the tranquility of the main street, as the townspeople, exhausted by the toil of the day and the draining heat of the sun, dreamed out their hopes of a better tomorrow.

In the yard of the hotel, Lucy and Jennie Moore, armed with flour bags, old sheets, and string, quietly led out the surprised horses, and harnessed them swiftly to the wool waggon. Then they stuffed the flour bags with straw, and gently eased a horse foot into each bag, tying it securely above the fetlock. Then it was the turn of the waggon wheels. Working together, they swiftly twisted the sheets around the wheels, stuffing straw into the spaces where they could. After twenty minutes work all was ready.

The two women looked at each other, and smiled in silent agreement. Jennie, still clad in her dressing gown, bent forward impulsively and kissed Lucy on the cheek.

"Good luck, Catherine," she whispered. "Come straight here when you get back."

Lucy nodded, and climbed up onto the waggon. Jennie took the rein and led the horses out of the yard. The wheels made a low rumble on the uneven surface, but the noise was much reduced. As they reached the road Jennie whispered, "Not half past three yet, you'll have a good start."

"Yes," Lucy agreed, "And Jennie, thank you for everything."

The big wool waggon moved away, and within a minute the sound of its wheels was lost in the darkness. After listening to make sure all remained quiet, Jennie went back to bed.

A mile out of town Lucy stopped the waggon and removed the bags from the horses' feet and the padding from the wheels. Now the time had come to move quickly, to put as much distance as possible between herself and Carmody before dawn. She climbed back up on to the wagon and shouted to the horses. "Come on there boys, get up there!"

The horses pricked their ears and responded, and the wool waggon trundled on into the darkness.

It was after ten o'clock when George Carmody arrived at the stock and station office. The new baby was fretful and he had had a restless night. As he walked into the office his greasy haired clerk followed him with a pot of hot coffee, the standard routine no matter what time the boss arrived. George Carmody watched as the coffee splashed into the cup, and asked, "Anything interesting?"

"Nothing. Joe Miller wants to sell up. I asked for the details in case you're interested."

"Of course I am. Has the Marshall woman been around?"

"Haven't seen her. Mind you I haven't been out."

"Well, go out now and see what she's up to. I don't trust that one."

"Yes Mr. Carmody."

The clerk left the office, glad to be out of doors for a while. He made his way to the store, and accosted the storekeeper.

"Has Miss Marshall been in today?"

"No."

The clerk considered, and then realized the man was being deliberately uncooperative. He leaned on the counter and spoke as if to a child. "Then are you expecting her in today? Mr. Carmody would like to know," he added pointedly.

"No I'm not," said the storekeeper shortly. He looked at the clerk, who remained leaning on the counter, a picture of impudence. The storekeeper bridled.

"If you must know, Miss Marshall has ordered her stores and told me she will pick them up in a couple of days. I think she must be staying for a while."

The clerk smiled greasily, and left the store. He crossed to the hotel, and found Jennie Moore in the entrance hall polishing the counter.

"Good morning, Mrs. Moore."

Jennie stopped polishing and turned. "Oh it's you. Good morning."

"Miss Marshall around?"

"She's having a lie in, had her breakfast sent up. Don't expect she has much chance to rest up, making the most of it while she can."

"Oh yes, I expect so."

"Do you want me to fetch her?" Jennie offered.

The clerk backed off. "Oh no, that's all right. I can see her later, when she's rested."

He left. Jennie watched him make his way back to Carmody's office, and breathed a sigh of relief.

"That's it you sneaky little dog," she muttered. "Go on, back to your master to report." She snorted in disgust and resumed her polishing.

It was late in the afternoon before the tell tale signs of dust far ahead confirmed to Lucy that her plan was going to work. It was with immense relief that she recognized the tail end of a wool caravan, the last straggling waggons only able to be glimpsed briefly in the swirling clouds of dust. Pushing the tired horses for one last effort, she gradually made progress and an hour later she caught up with the tail waggon. She pulled alongside and slackened pace.

"Good evening!" she shouted across to the startled driver, "Mind if I join on for company?"

The driver was a lazy character and slightly drunk, and the sudden appearance of another waggon confused him.

"Where you come from?"

"From Stannerton."

"On yer own?"

"Yes. Who's in charge?"

"Tim Francis. He's up ahead, riding a big bay."

Lucy nodded and pulled ahead. The caravan was traveling at a fairly slow pace, and within a few minutes she saw a rider ahead. As she approached he turned his horse and rode back to meet her.

"Well, where did you spring from?" He was a big dark man, in stained work clothes and a greasy hat, but he had a huge smile.

"Stannerton. I'm taking my woolclip to the railhead to sell it, and would like to join up with you, if you're agreeable."

"Sure and welcome. I'm Tim Francis." He held out his hand and Lucy took it with relief.

Tim peered into the waggon. "You're not traveling alone?"

"Yes. I'm Catherine Marshall, there's only me and my Uncle Matthew, and he had to stay to look after the stock."

Tim Francis whistled through his teeth, whether in admiration or disapproval Lucy couldn't tell, but the big smile returned and he trotted alongside the waggon.

"I've been doing this trail a few years now, and I thought the folks around Stannerton always sent their wool along with George Carmody."

"Not quite. They sell their wool to George Carmody, and he re-sells at the railhead."

Tim looked puzzled, "Sounds like a good idea to me."

"It would be if he paid a fair price, but he doesn't."

Tim's eyes narrowed but he made no comment and rode on ahead. A few miles further on he came back and turned to ride alongside.

"Not far now until we camp for the night. When we're all set up, you can tell me about George Carmody."

With a quick smile he was gone, and the heavy waggons lumbered on into the gathering dusk.

Carmody's clerk was bored. It was hot and stuffy in the office and the flies were even more bothersome than usual. Having entered the monthly rent receipts into the big black ledger in front of him, he got up and approached Carmody's office door with his usual mixture of bravado and trepidation. He tried to cultivate an amiable air with the boss, even friendly, and most of the time he got away with it. However there was always a slight dread. Something might go wrong, the boss would be annoyed, and then it paid to show the utmost respect, even servility. He tapped on the door and opened it.

"George, just popping out to check on the Marshall woman."

Carmody grunted.

The clerk took this for assent and left. Five minutes later he burst into Carmody's office without knocking and stood there, his white face wearing a look of pathetic appeal. Carmody looked up, and his face changed.

"Well, what is it?"

"I think.... I think...."

"Well, out with it man!"

"I think," the clerk quavered, "Miss Marshall, she might be gone."

Carmody got up and walked around the desk to take the clerk by the lapels of his coat. He spoke very quietly, and with venom. "What do you mean, she might be gone? Is she, or isn't she?"

The clerk swallowed. "I think she must be. I just noticed her wool waggon wasn't in the yard. I asked at the hotel and Jennie Moore said she had left."

Carmody shook the clerk like a dog. "When? When did she leave?"

"I don't know, honest, I don't know." The clerk was gasping now, his breathing laboured. "That Jennie Moore, she says Miss Marshall paid her bill in advance."

"Jennie Moore," Carmody said slowly, realising the implications. He shook the clerk again. "You were supposed to check this morning."

"I did, I did. Mrs. Moore said she was still in bed."

"Was the waggon there then? Well was it?" Carmody's voice rose in fury.

"I...I don't know." The clerk crumbled into a snivelling heap. "I didn't look."

Carmody released the cowering bundle as if his hands had been soiled by contact with it. He went to the window and gazed out.

"Do you realise what you've done?" he said softly. "It's too late; we'll never catch her now." His mind raced through the implications, the possibilities.

"She's won, do you realize that?" He turned to the miserable clerk and his voice rose. "Do you realise that, you stupid fool?"

He turned back to the window, still thinking, searching for a way out, his knuckles clenched. "When the other farmers hear about this, what do you think will happen?"

The clerk was silent, knowing whatever he said would be wrong. Carmody remained at the window, swaying slightly back and forth. His anger was coming up to the boil. His face flushed, he trembled with frustration.

"Well, she may have won this battle, but she doesn't know what she's taken on. Who does she think she is anyway?" His voice was almost a shout. He turned back to the clerk. "Well, who is she?"

"Er.... well...Miss Marshall, that's all I know."

"You know nothing! Nothing, as usual. Well find out! There must be something in her background, something we can dig out. It's always struck me as funny a woman like that lives out in the wilds with that old man. How did they come here? Where are they from?"

"Er...Adelaide I think."

"Well get going and find out. Get a message to Bill Perks in Adelaide and tell him I want the complete story on her and her uncle. Tell him to get to the immigration office and find out exactly when they arrived in Australia and where from. There might be something nasty in England they were leaving behind. No matter how much trouble it takes, I'm going to get that cunning bitch! She thinks she's put one over on me but she'll soon find out she's taken on more than she can chew!"

He turned to the still trembling clerk, who was expecting to be sacked.

"Well get on with it! Move!"

The clerk hastened to obey; he too was filled with a seething antagonism towards Miss Catherine Marshall. She had got him into all this trouble, made a fool of him just when he had been thinking of asking Mr. Carmody for a rise in salary. He would get even. If there was any dirt to dig up on Miss Catherine Marshall and her precious uncle, he had a big spade.

It was with mixed feelings that Lucy waved goodbye to the wool drivers at the fork for Stannerton. She had been in their company for nearly two weeks and she had come to know them well. They were a good crowd, and had treated her with friendship and respect, especially after Tim Francis had told them how she had beaten George Carmody's monopoly.

Now they shouted and waved, a mixture of rowdy good humour and genuine regret that they wouldn't be seeing her again. It had been good to have a woman along, one of them said later to Tim, "It made you watch your language and comb your hair." As Lucy detached her waggon from the line, Tim rode alongside, and wished her good luck.

"And to you, Tim, and thank you for all your help, I couldn't have managed without you."

With a final wave she set off for Stannerton, pondering her own words. Maybe she could have managed without Tim Francis's help, but it would have been much more difficult. When she had told him the full story of Carmody's monopoly in the Stannerton area, Tim had been anxious to help her. Born of settler parents, he was a real New Australian, and a champion of the individual freedoms which had been so hard won in the developing country. The idea that one man could hold so many to ransom, and force them to accept his terms, was totally at odds with Tim's ideas of fair play. Out of earshot of Lucy, his comments on the character and lineage of the Stannerton area farmers were searing.

At the railhead he had been a pillar of strength. He showed Lucy where to leave the waggon and introduced her to the wool agent, a bald headed little man who seemed to be doing ten different things at once. However, after a quiet word from Tim, he gave Lucy his full attention and they agreed a price for her wool. It was the current Adelaide price less three per cent agent's fee and the cost of the freight, and after a quick calculation Lucy realised that she had made a good bargain, much better than the deal she had offered Carmody in his office. It was all very hectic and confusing, but Tim cleared the way, explaining the system, showing her how to see her wool graded, weighed and checked, and then taken away to be loaded into the rail waggons.

By the time Tim escorted Lucy back to the agent's office, the details of her sale had been worked out, and the agent gave her a docket for the transaction.

"There you are, Miss Marshall, and the money will be deposited by the Company into your bank account within the next few days, or rather into Mr. Matthew Marshall's bank account as you instructed." The agent smiled, it was a piddling little deal, but one he had enjoyed, it was rare to see a beautiful woman at the railhead. As they left the agent's office Lucy suddenly felt weakness run through her. For the last few days she had been keyed up to a high level of tension, and now she suddenly realised it was over. She had done it! Got her woolclip to the railhead and sold it! A wave of emotion swept over her, and trembling slightly, she caught at Tim Francis's arm.

"Where…what do I have to do now?"

Tim looked down at her. Her face was streaked with dirt and her hair was coming undone from the thick plait she normally wore. To his surprise he saw a small tear escape down the grubby cheek. He took her hand gently. "Come on, Miss Marshall, you're tired out, and no wonder. There's a hotel of sorts here, it's not much but you can get a bath and a clean bed. I'll show you, come on."

"But…"

"Nothing more to be said. We shan't be leaving till tomorrow; you can come back with us along the trail till we get to the Stannerton fork. I'll see to your waggon, you have a good night's rest and I'll see you at breakfast."

Lucy took his arm gratefully. "Are you sure?"

"Of course, and anyway," he smiled at her, "It will be good to get rid of you for a night."

"Will it?"

"Yes. Tonight we can all get drunk."

Ten minutes later Lucy sat on her small single bed and gazed at the wool receipt. She had sold the woolclip for almost a hundred and twenty pounds more than she would have got from George Carmody. *A hundred and twenty pounds! It was a small fortune. Even if Tomghin didn't return they might be able to employ a stockman to help Matthew.*

Danny was worried. It wasn't so much going to see Mr. Graham which unnerved him, but the request that his mother and Lela should be there too. Danny had developed a deep affection for Lela's employer, whom he regarded as something between a kindly guardian and God, but for his part, William Graham would have been surprised to know the role he played in Danny's daydreams. A frequent scene played out in Danny's imagination centred on William Graham as his father, seated behind a big desk as he congratulated Danny on his school report. This scene did not stray far from the truth, since Mr. Graham always expressed an interest in his progress, but in Danny's dream his imaginary father invariably shook him by the hand like a man and said he was proud of him.

Danny sighed, and wished the fingers on the big kitchen clock would move faster. The meeting must be about something important; it had thrown his mother Juminah into a state of nervous excitement. He looked to where she sat in the unfamiliar kitchen of Margot's house, and listened as she directed questions at Lela one after the other.

"What is this?" Juminah fingered the roller of the crimping iron with obvious fascination.

"It's an iron, but it puts little ruffles into the material..."

"But what for?" asked Juminah with genuine astonishment.

"For collars and cuffs mainly, European ladies like to be able to have their collars starched and then crimped...like little pleats," Lela explained.

"But what for?" Juminah repeated, as she had for the tenth time.

Lela sighed. "Because they are different to us and that's the way they like it. Anyway, it's four o'clock and time for us to go in. Tea is all ready, and remember mother, don't keep asking what the food is, just enjoy it." She poured water from the boiling kettle into the teapot and the hot water jug and then lifted the heavy tray. "Come along Danny, you can tap at the door and open it for me."

It was not at all as Juminah expected. Instead of Mr. Graham sitting behind a big desk as she had imagined, he was in an armchair, with Mrs. Graham sitting in a smaller one. They were all invited to sit down around the low table where Lela had placed the tray, and to her astonishment Mr. Graham got up and pulled forward a chair for her, asking her if she was quite comfortable, and thanking her for coming to see him.

Juminah relaxed a little, perhaps there was nothing wrong after all. She glanced at Danny, and her heart glowed with pride. He was becoming quite a handsome boy, she thought, and he looked so smart in the crisp white shirt and grey trousers he wore now the leg brace was gone.

"How nice this is for us all to have tea together," Margot said as she passed around tiny sandwiches.

"Yes," William agreed, "Thank you for coming on a Sunday. I have wanted to see you all together for some time, but during the week I am so busy, indeed we all are." He handed Juminah a cup of tea and then continued: "I want to discuss Danny's future with you. I realise it is perhaps none of my business, but as you know I administer Lady Howell's estate for her, and she was so fond of Lela and asked us to help in any way we could." He hesitated, and then continued: "Now, Lela has been with us for so long and we have come to know her, and of course Danny,"

He hesitated again, and Margot broke in, "We feel you are part of the family, so we hope you will not mind a little interference from friends."

Lela passed William his cup and saucer. "We shall be grateful for any advice you have," she said carefully, wondering what was coming.

"Danny has been doing very well at the mission school," William said.

"Although the school is excellent for younger boys, it is limited in the subjects it covers and the standard it sets. Boys of real potential like Danny need a challenging education."

"What do you have in mind?" Lela asked.

"I would like him to sit the entrance examination for the Academy," said William. "I am sure he will pass, and if he does so, and would like to attend there, we shall be happy to pay his fees and expenses until he leaves."

"The Academy? Is it a good school? I do not know it," said Juminah, a little apprehensively.

"It is a good school mother, it is the best there is, and costs a great deal of money," Lela answered slowly. "But my mother is right to question the idea Mr. Graham. The Academy is for Europeans."

"Not only Europeans, Lela. There are some Malay boys there now, and quite a few Chinese boys as well..."

"From very rich Malay and Chinese families," Lela broke in. "Danny comes from a poor home Mr. Graham, we cannot afford..."

"I have said we will pay for his education," William explained gently. "Of course, there will be other expenses, his clothes, books, sports equipment, all that kind of thing, and we shall see Danny has everything the other boys have. He will not be at a disadvantage."

There was silence. Lela was stunned by the offer, and Danny and Juminah were confused. At length Margot spoke.

"Perhaps we should ask Danny how he feels about it." She turned to the boy, who was wide eyed. "Now don't be nervous Danny, tell us whether you would like to go to another school. It is a very good school, and you would have to work very hard and learn lots of new things, but it would be interesting and would give you a good start in life."

"But I have a good start in life already," Danny said eagerly, "Now my leg is better, it is nearly the same as other boys, and is getting stronger and stronger all the time."

William looked perplexed, but Margot said gently, "Carry on Danny, tell us how your leg being better will give you a good start in life."

"I can do many jobs," Danny explained. "People will give you a job if you are healthy, but not if you are a cripple. The boys at the mission used to say I would be a beggar, but now I will have a job at the market or on the boats. I can run, perhaps I can have a rickshaw..."

There was a shocked silence, and then William said gently. "You are right Danny. Your leg being better means that these kind of jobs are open to you.

But they are all very hard work and the pay is poor. There are other jobs, where you use your brain, rather than your strength. You have a good brain Danny, and if you go to the Academy and do well there, you can do that kind of work. It will pay better and give you a good life."

"A shop assistant you mean?" Lela asked a little bitterly, "Or a clerk in one of the shipping houses?" She turned to William. "I know you mean well, Mr. Graham, and your offer is more than generous. Danny must decide for himself of course, but let us not delude ourselves as to the type of position he could expect after school. Malayan clerks are almost as poorly paid as manual workers." Lela stopped for a moment and gathered her courage before she continued, "At the Academy Danny would mix with young men whose expectations will be so much higher. I do not want him to be disappointed. I hope this does not sound ungrateful."

William was unruffled. "Of course not. You are quite right about the poor pay and conditions, and that is precisely why I want to continue my interest in Danny after he leaves school. I would like him to work with me, at the bank."

Lela's eyes opened wide in astonishment. "At the bank?" she repeated. "Your bank? But only Europeans work there."

"Not quite true," William interrupted. "I already have a Chinese clerk, and in the future we hope to employ more local people."

"A bank clerk!" Lela was obviously impressed, but William Graham shook his head.

"No Lela, not a bank clerk. If Danny does as well as I believe he can, I was thinking in terms of management. We have a scheme in the bank for promising young men, and I would try to get Danny a place on it."

He awaited Lela's reaction but she simply stared at him, so he continued, "Of course, at the moment our training places are almost always taken up by young men in London, and after they have proved their worth they are allocated to positions in Britain or an overseas posting. However, the bank is interested in taking local young men into the scheme provided they are of the right calibre. I shall still be here when Danny leaves school, God willing. I will help him all I can but he will have to work hard. But first he has to pass the examination."

He stopped in consternation, as he saw two huge tears run down Lela's face. She was unable to speak.

Juminah said "Does this mean you will help Danny to get an important job?"

"Yes, Juminah," William smiled. "Provided of course it is what Danny wants, and that you agree."

"But of course I agree, and Danny is too young to know what he wants so I will agree for him also."

"And you Lela, do you agree?" Margot asked softly. Lela said nothing, she just nodded briefly as she dabbed her eyes with her handkerchief, and Margot kissed her and laughed.

William laughed too, and turned to Juminah. "Now that the business is over, would you like to try the caraway cake?"

Half an hour later, as Danny walked home with his mother, he tried hard to remember every single thing that had been said during tea, but bits of the conversation kept slipping away from him. He knew he was going to take an examination to go to a new school, and that if he did well he would have a good job some day, and be able to support his mother and Lela in comfort. It was all very wonderful, as Lela had kept telling him as she saw them to the door. She was right; it was the fulfillment of a dream. For after tea, Mrs. Graham had kissed them all, and then Mr. Graham had come over to him and shaken him by the hand, as if he was already a man, and Danny knew that one day he would make William Graham proud of him.

Chapter Seventeen

Within minutes of arriving in Stannerton, Lucy realised she had become something of a celebrity. As the big waggon trundled along the main street, several people waved to her, and a man emerging from the general store called out, "Well done, Miss Marshall."

Lucy drove the waggon into the hotel yard and hurried in to see Jennie Moore, who gave her a rapturous welcome. Jennie despatched a young boy to see to the horses, then took Lucy's arm and led her into the sitting room.

"Well, you don't look any the worse for wear," she said, examining Lucy closely. "A bit dusty perhaps!" She laughed delightedly, and added; "Now you sit down and don't move a muscle. I'll go and get some tea, and we can catch up with all the news."

Lucy felt a small glow of satisfaction as she sat in the comfortable chair. Her pleasure derived not only from her success, but her welcome home by someone she could count on as a friend. Since she had left Singapore she had missed the company of other women, and had often thought how much she would have enjoyed a chat with Margot Graham or Lela, or even dear old Miss Collins, her headmistress at school.

When Jennie returned with the tray, it took Lucy almost half an hour to relate the story of her trip. Jennie listened with avid enjoyment, especially when she heard how much extra money Lucy had made from the wool sale. "That's marvellous," she said, "It will certainly settle it."

"Settle what?"

"The question of the Co-operative." In answer to Lucy's questioning look, Jennie hastened to explain.

"You're not the only one who's been having fun. On the day you left I managed to put Carmody off, and by the time he realised you had gone it was too late to catch you. He was furious, but I had got the word out by then. Everyone who came to the store got to know, and anyone who was going near any of the farms called in to spread the word. Several of the farmers who live fairly near came in to town to see if it was true, that you had taken your woolclip to the railhead. Then after Greg Lamont got here…"

"Greg Lamont?" Lucy felt her heart would fail her.

"Yes, he rode in the day after you went, with Bob Middleton and another half dozen or so of his men from the Lamont station. It seems Bob Middleton had told Greg he thought you might try to get the wool to the railhead yourself." Jennie giggled, "It seems they were worried about you, and were all ready to ride after you and rescue you from the jaws of death!"

Lucy felt a warm glow at the thought that Greg had come after her, and Bob and the others. *Of course Greg didn't know who she was, but even so....* She drew the thought close inside her.

"What happened?" she asked.

"I told them what we had done, and how Carmody had no chance of catching you."

"And what did Greg Lamont say?"

Jennie smiled. "He had a good laugh, and they all did. Greg said he reckoned you didn't need any help at all, and you were going to get to the railhead and do what you planned. Bob Middleton agreed with him, and they all had a good laugh again, at Carmody's expense." She looked carefully at Lucy. "I say Catherine, there isn't anything between you two is there?"

"Between who?"

"You and Gregory Lamont. If there is, I wouldn't blame you, he's very handsome isn't he?"

Lucy cut her short. "Of course not, I've never even met him."

"Oh, shame," said Jennie, "He's a good man you know, apart from his looks. Of course I've known him for years..."

Getting no response from Lucy, Jennie continued; "Anyway, everyone has been talking about your trip, and some of the farmers started to talk about a Wool Co-operative."

"A Co-operative, that sounds a good idea, how would it work?" asked Lucy, with a thrill of excitement.

"The proposal is that as the shearing is completed the woolclips will be brought in to Stannerton, and a group of men from the Co-operative will be elected to transport the wool to the railhead. There was no shortage of volunteers," said Jennie happily. "Once they agreed to stand together, everyone wanted to join in."

"And have you seen George Carmody?" Lucy asked anxiously.

"Not a sign of him," said Jennie. "I think he must be too embarrassed to show his face!"

The two women giggled, and after a while Lucy went up to her room, looking forward to a bath, followed by a pleasant dinner in Jennie's company. Jennie hurried to the kitchen, and as she helped prepare the evening meal, she wondered again why Catherine blushed so, when you talked about a man she had never even met.

The next day, George Carmody watched from his office window as Lucy's stores were loaded on to her waggon.

"There she goes, Miss Goody Two Shoes," he remarked to his clerk, "On her way back to that miserable plot with her profits."

"Are you going after her?" asked the clerk anxiously. "You could catch up with her tonight; she'll have to make camp."

Carmody turned on him. "You really are entirely without brains aren't you?" he said contemptuously. "No, I shall let Miss Marshall have her moment of triumph. If she met with an accident now the farmers would never wear it."

No, you would be lynched, the clerk thought to himself, but he said out loud, "What are you going to do then?"

"That depends," said Carmody, appraising Lucy's slim figure as she climbed up to the driver's seat. "It all depends on what she's hiding. What that nasty little skeleton in her cupboard is."

"But we haven't found any skeleton." The clerk was confused. "Bill Perks said he couldn't find any trace of her or her uncle in Adelaide."

Carmody turned to face him, and the clerk saw to his surprise that the boss was smiling. "Precisely." he said softly.

The clerk's confusion grew. "But I don't understand, if there isn't any trace of them in Adelaide..."

"Then we know they never were in Adelaide." Carmody spoke as if to a child. "So they lied, didn't they? Why did they lie? And if they weren't in Adelaide where were they? We know they arrived here from Perth, and they were supposed to have arrived in Perth by boat from Adelaide. If they were never in Adelaide where did they come from?"

A glimmer of light dawned in the clerk's vacant face.

"Of course," he said. "Would you like me to go to Perth and investigate? I'm sure I could..."

"Absolutely not. This investigation requires special handling; a certain finesse is needed to uncover the skeleton, whatever and wherever it is. I shall go myself."

He watched from the window as Lucy waved to the storekeeper, flicked the reins and started on her journey home.

"Farewell for now, Miss Marshall," he murmured. "When I have found your skeleton we shall meet again, and I shall strip those lovely white bones bare for all to see."

When Lucy arrived back at Kelly's place she was delighted to see Tomghin at the whip pole, pulling water for the stock.

"Hello Tomghin," she called, as he came running to greet her. "I am so glad to see you."

Tomghin gave his big smile. "Me along old fella do good things," he promised.

As he spoke Matthew appeared, and Lucy caught her breath. He looked so old, bent almost double under the weight of the bucket he was carrying. He staggered to the cabin and suddenly caught sight of Lucy. Immediately he straightened up, put down the bucket and walked across with a big smile.

"My dear, it's so good to have you back, come in, come in and I'll make tea." He kissed her gently, and Lucy made to walk to the cabin, but Matthew took her arm and redirected her.

"I'm sorry, you'll have to climb the hill," he said.

"But why?" Lucy wanted to seek the shade of the cabin.

"Because we've moved! When Tomghin turned up we decided to try and move house before you came back. We moved the range last week, so you can't have tea unless you come up to the house."

Lucy was torn between pleasure at the move, and distress about Matthew, who looked as if he would drop any moment.

"Uncle," she said, taking his arm, "You are going to have to stop working so hard. You should have waited till I was here to help, you're tired out."

Matthew shot her a glance. "Yes, I am a bit tired," he admitted, "But it was important to move as soon as we could. The range was the biggest problem, I had to take it apart and then rebuild the brickwork around it, but it's worked out fine. I've built in the wash boiler in the outhouse as well."

"And I've ordered the window glass," said Lucy happily.

She was entranced to see the house; it looked cosy now the furniture was in place. She went from room to room exclaiming with delight, while Matthew made tea. When she joined him in the kitchen he brought out his masterpiece.

"I've made a cake," he said, producing it like a rabbit out of a hat. "What do you think? It's the first I ever made."

"It's wonderful Uncle!" Lucy laughed, flinging herself into a chair. "It's so good to be home, especially with this sort of welcome."

"Well you deserve it," said Matthew. "Oh yes, I know all about it, or at least most of it. I know you went to the railhead to sell our woolclip when you had promised me you wouldn't, and I know you hoodwinked Carmody. All I don't know is the price you got."

"It was well worth it, believe me," said Lucy. "We have made an additional hundred and twenty pounds, so I went ahead and ordered the glass. Uncle, I'm sorry I went without telling you, but really, I had no option. How did you get to know?"

"Bob called here with Greg Lamont and some of his men. They had been in to Stannerton to see if you needed help, but it seemed you didn't, you had already gone."

Lucy felt the familiar lurch in her heart. "Greg Lamont was here?" she said faintly.

"Yes, and Bob. They helped me finish the connections on the pipes and put the pump in the kitchen. When it worked, we all jumped around, shouting and laughing, what a commotion! It seemed silly not to move once we had the water, so they stayed overnight and helped me carry up most of the furniture. The range was still in the cabin of course, so their cook made a big stew down there and we all had a get-together and a sing-song, like last time, it was great fun."

"Did Mr. Lamont say much?"

"Oh yes, quite a lot."

Lucy cut herself another slice of Matthew's cake. "This is quite good, Uncle," she said, trying to appear unconcerned. When Matthew remained silent however, she burst out, "Oh come on, Uncle! Don't be so exasperating! What did he say?"

Matthew smiled. "Oh, we talked about lots of things; he's a very interesting man."

"About me?"

"Not particularly." Matthew noticed the crestfallen look on Lucy's face and continued kindly, "He did say one thing you may find interesting. After the wet he is going on a trip to the gold mining area north of Kalgoorlie, he's going to try and trace Jack Lamont's footsteps, to find out if he ever found gold."

"But how does he know where to start?"

"He didn't at first. But when he received the map you sent him he began to investigate. He told me the whole story and I had to pretend it was all new to me. Greg said that although the map only showed local details, he had looked at it in conjunction with some old letters."

"Letters?"

"Yes. Letters sent home by Jack Lamont from the goldfields. There were only a few, but had been kept by the family for sentimental reasons and were still in his father's desk. Greg sorted them out, and he thinks the final letter, sent from a place called Shimmer Creek, may help to pinpoint where Jack was digging just before he decided to come home. The 'Town' Jack marked may have been Shimmer Creek. If it is, it could be a fairly simple matter to follow the map, and hopefully find something interesting."

"Does he believe Jack really found gold?"

"He doesn't know, but he seems impelled to investigate. I think perhaps it's a matter of laying old ghosts. He says his brother is an excellent manager and can easily spare him from the farm, so he's decided to go."

"Just like Jarvis said," Lucy whispered.

"What do you mean?"

"Don't you see? It's the same all over again. Two brothers, one stays at the station house, and the other goes away looking for gold. It's all happening over again."

Matthew looked sharply at his niece. "Now don't get any silly ideas," he said. "Brighten up; I want to hear all about your trip."

It was a month after Lucy's return from Stannerton before they had another visitor, and during this time the weather was drier and hotter than Lucy could remember. The window glass still had not arrived, but Lucy had received a note from the store informing her that the glass would be brought out to Kelly's place by the glazier, who would also install it if they wished. In the meantime, Lucy had tacked muslin at the windows in an attempt to defeat the flies, but it was a losing battle. She was doubly grateful for Will Kelly's forethought in including a cool cellar in the house plans, as at least they were able to keep the cheeses at the right temperature. Each day they waited for the rain to come, and each day they were disappointed. Lucy was exhausted from pulling water for the vegetable garden, and speculated that their well might go dry if she continued to use so much. She tried hard to ensure that Matthew rested for at least part of the day, but Tomghin had gone on his way again, and his help was sorely missed.

At long last the weather broke. In a rumble of thunder the first rain fell like huge teardrops on the sun bleached verandah where Lucy sat, mending a shirt for Matthew.

"Uncle, come and see, I think it's here at last."

They stood together on the verandah watching anxiously, for sometimes there was only a spatter of drops and then it stopped again. This time however, after a couple of minutes the drops came faster, and then suddenly the heavens opened and the deluge was upon them. Lucy inwardly blessed the terraces, as without them the vegetables would certainly have been washed out of the ground and down to the bottom of the slope.

She turned to Matthew: "I think I'll stay out here for a while, it's good to feel the moisture in the air at last, and the flies were becoming unbearable."

Matthew agreed, and went inside to check the walls and roof in case of leaks. It was their first wet in the new house, and he wanted to make sure everything was rain proof.

The rain continued for three days without stopping. Heavy torrents of water cascaded down the terraces and the creek quickly filled and threatened to flood. Normal work was stopped, and Lucy and Matthew only left the house to attend to the stock and the milking, returning soaked to the skin from each trip. Lucy took the opportunity to ensure that Matthew rested, as he had developed a hacking cough which troubled him greatly.

One evening as they sat near the fire, listening to the rain drumming on the roof, there was a loud knock at the door. They both started up, such a thing had never happened before. They went to the door together and Matthew opened it slowly. A man stood there, the most miserably wet and abject scrap of humanity it was possible to imagine. The sodden work clothes which clung to him were little more than muddy rags, and his thin body was hunched against the rain. As he lifted up his head to look at them a stream of water ran out of his hat brim and on to his shoulders.

"Mister Marshall?"

"Yes," Matthew said, amazed. "Come in man; come in out of the wet."

He came into the house, dripping uncomfortably onto the wood floor. Lucy fetched a towel and handed it to him.

"Thank you Miss." He took off his hat and they got a better look at him, a thin man, dark haired and blue eyed, with a sad looking moustache. He rubbed his face and hair with the towel and looked from one to the other.

"My name's Tom Nicholls," he said, holding out his hand. "And I'm mighty pleased to get here at last, I can tell you."

"Well Tom, you're something of a surprise," said Matthew, gesturing him to come near the fire. "We don't get many visitors, especially in the wet, how did you manage to get here?"

"Took me a couple of days from Stannerton," said Tom. "I hope you don't mind, but I put my horse and cart in your barn. I see you've got some nice cows there too."

"Yes, we keep them for milk, we make cheese," said Lucy unnecessarily, having hardly recovered from her surprise.

"I'm so sorry, this is my niece Catherine," said Matthew. "Now I'm sure you could do with something to eat and a hot drink. Would you see to that Catherine? I'll try to find Tom some dry clothes."

Matthew departed in the direction of his bedroom and Lucy smiled at Tom as she prepared some bread and cheese and a slice of custard pie.

"What are you doing here Mr. Nicholls?" she enquired easily. "Are you on your way somewhere else?"

"Oh no Miss, I came expressly to see you and Mr. Marshall. I was hoping you could give me some work. I've been looking for some time and when I got to Stannerton Mrs. Moore at the hotel said she thought you may have use for a stockman."

"Mrs. Moore, how is she?" said Lucy with pleasure as Matthew rejoined them. "Uncle, Mr. Nicholls is looking for work as a stockman, Jennie Moore sent him here."

"Well Mr. Nicholls, we certainly are looking for someone, although we can't pay a great deal. Anyway, come through to my bedroom and get into some dry things, they are rather old but I think they'll fit."

Tom Nicholls looked from one to the other, and Lucy had an odd impression that he was about to burst into tears. He blurted, "Very kind of you," and followed Matthew out.

An hour later, as Lucy cleared the table, she and Matthew discussed their strange visitor. After he had eaten, Tom had insisted on going back down to the barn to check on his horse, saying he would check the other stock at the same time. Although Matthew had assured him this was not necessary, Tom had been adamant, and said he would sleep in the cabin.

"If I'm going to work for you, I might as well start now," he said. "I always like to check the stock before I go to bed, and not be too far away from them. Can't sleep otherwise." And off he had gone into the rain.

"Do you think he's a good stockman?" Lucy pondered.

"I've no idea. He seems to know what he's talking about, and we are lucky to get anyone out here. We'll have to see."

"He certainly can eat," said Lucy, regarding the empty bread basket on the table. "I've never seen anyone put so much away. You know Uncle; I think Tom was famished when he got here."

"Perhaps he was," agreed Matthew, "He certainly looked a sorry sight. Let's hope he's stronger than he looks."

There was no real chance to test Tom's strength for the next couple of days, as the rain continued. From the earlier deluge it had now reduced to a steady downpour, and was beginning to ease off further by the end of the second day. Lucy was glad to have the opportunity to attend to some of the things she wanted to do in the house, and Tom proved a handy carpenter, putting up shelves, and making an enclosed cupboard under the sink.

"That looks really professional Tom," said Matthew when he saw it. "You didn't tell us you were a joiner as well as a stockman."

"Oh," said Tom, blushing a little. "I can turn my hand to most things you know."

He could indeed. The next day the rain stopped, and Matthew reported that Tom had made short work of everything he had been given to do, in spite of the mud.

"Let's hope we can keep him here," he said to Lucy as they met for their afternoon cup of tea. "Life will be so much easier, but whether he will stay for such a small wage I don't know."

"Where is he now? Doesn't he want some tea?" Lucy asked. "He still seems to be eating like a horse; I've more than doubled the baking since he came."

"He's gone off to look at the sheep," replied Matthew, "And as for eating like a horse I'm not surprised, he works like one."

Lucy laughed, pleased that things were working out so well. Matthew was already looking better, and Tom's arrival had taken some of the strain from both of them.

"Do you know Uncle, I haven't seen the cows for a week," she said. "since Tom came he's done the milking and everything else. I'll go down now, and take a look at the horses too, they will be forgetting me."

Matthew exhorted her to be careful not to slip in the mud, and Lucy made her way to the barn. As she stroked the horses, talking to them in a low voice, her mind roamed over the things she still wanted to do in the house. *The big curtains were up now, but she would really like some new muslins.*

The sound caught her ears suddenly and she was instantly alert. A rustling sound, in the corner, where the hay was stacked. Her eyes narrowed. *Rat?*

Rabbit? Snake? There it was again. This time she saw something, a small flash of darkness, a navy blue colour. Seizing a pitchfork she advanced to the corner and tossed out a forkful of hay, and then started back in consternation. There, cowering and huge eyed, were two very dirty small children. As Lucy stared at them open mouthed, they began to whimper, and a young woman, as filthy and unkempt as the children, emerged from the hay and stood up shakily to face her.

Lucy regarded her uncle with affection. One thing you had to say for Matthew, he was adaptable. Within ten minutes of Lucy's arrival back at the house with the young woman and two children in tow, he had them all organised.

Now, on his knees in the wash house beside the big tin bath, he smiled happily at the two serious faced children who sat, one at each end, regarding him gravely. He scooped dollops of green soft soap out of a big round tin and handed them out, talking gently all the time.

"For your hair, rub it in your hair,"

Two pairs of large eyes looked from Matthew to the soap, and from the soap to Matthew.

"Like this! Look, like this!" Matthew rubbed his bony fingers through his own grey hair and started to laugh. The girl responded first, lifting her arm up over her head, still eyeing Matthew with suspicion.

"Yes, that's it. Go on," said Matthew, rubbing his head vigorously. Gently at first, the girl rubbed her head with the soap. Suddenly she gave a mischievous smile, and started to lather her hair, and this was the cue for the boy, who joined in with gusto. Within a few minutes they were splashing and squealing, holding out their hands to Matthew for more soap to make the lovely bubbles.

"Come on Lizzie," said Lucy, taking the young woman's arm and leading her to the chair by the kitchen range, "Sit there while I get you all some food. When the children are clean you can have your bath in comfort, I've filled the copper again, it will be hot enough in an hour."

Lizzie sank into a chair. "You don't know how grateful I am ma'am," she said, "your being so kind to us and all."

"Nonsense, and don't call me ma'am," said Lucy a little briskly. "I don't know what Tom was thinking of, to let you stay out there in the barn all that time. Why were you hiding? Are you in some sort of trouble?"

"Oh yes ma'am, I mean Miss Catherine. Worst sort of trouble we've got and no mistake." The sudden bitterness in Lizzie's voice surprised Lucy, and she crossed the room to face her. "What is it Lizzie? Whatever it is you're safe here." She hesitated. "Is it the police? That sort of trouble?"

Lizzie lifted her head and Lucy saw that she was surprised by the question. "Wanted by the police? Us? Oh, no, not wanted by the police, not wanted by anyone, that's the trouble."

"I don't understand..."

"Poverty Miss Catherine, poverty. That's our trouble and our crime. Oh yes it is!" she added as Lucy made a soothing gesture, "Poverty is the crime they don't hunt you down for, but it's a crime all the same. When you're poor you suddenly become invisible, nobody wants to know you, and now you've found us! I don't know what Tom will say..." she broke down in tears, and Lucy hastened to comfort her.

"I still don't understand why you were hiding," said Lucy when Lizzie had calmed a little.

"You were our last chance, and we couldn't risk you seeing us," said Lizzie. She obviously needed to talk, and Lucy sat opposite to listen. After a moment Lizzie continued: "When we arrived from England we were all right for a while. We found a place with a family just outside Perth, Tom did the heavy work and I helped in the house. Then they decided to move on, and could not take us with them. We thought there would be no problem finding work, but although Tom could be hired quite easily there was no room for us. People kept advising us that Tom should go and work at the sugar cane, or the mines, leaving us in Perth, but he wouldn't do that. We didn't want to be parted see? Do you think that was so wrong of us Miss Catherine? To want to stay together?"

"No, of course not," said Lucy gently.

"Then, we thought if we moved further out we would be sure to find something," Lizzie went on. "We've been on the road ever since, and it was the same story everywhere, work for Tom but no room for us. By the time we got to Stannerton we were on our last few coppers, and had sold everything we possessed to buy food."

"But you saw Jennie Moore didn't you? Couldn't she help?"

"Tom saw her, she didn't know about us. By this time we realised the only way Tom could get a few days pay was to keep us well out of sight. We stayed outside the town while Tom went in. Jennie Moore gave him food to last him until he got here. It was plenty for one, but not much shared between us all."

Lucy suddenly realised why Tom had such a big appetite.

"And that's why you hid in the barn when you got here?" she said, "You thought you would be sent away?"

"It's the children, see," said Lizzie. "People are kind on the whole but we are a lot to feed…"

Yes, Lucy thought, *and how am I going to feed you?* Aloud she said, "Don't worry about anything, you're all right now."

"But what will Tom say when he knows we've been found?"

Lucy smiled. "He'll probably be relieved. After all, you couldn't have stayed in the barn forever could you? Now come into my bedroom and we'll find you some clean clothes. I have an old dimity dress which may fit…"

Late that night Lucy lay awake, wondering how they were going to manage. She had done so well, or so she thought. *All that effort to face up to Carmody, and the thrill of getting the extra hundred and twenty pounds, and now look what had happened. By the most economical reckoning the extra money would not keep them all.* She sighed as she thought of the things she had planned to buy for the house, the little extras she had promised herself. These were now out of the question if Tom and Lizzie stayed. *Yet how could she turn them away?* Anyway she liked them, little Beth was a sweet child, named Elizabeth after her mother, but called Beth by her doting father. The boy was a quiet, sturdy lad, and had been named for his grandfather Michael, but Tom insisted on calling him Mitch. After the initial shock of finding his family was discovered, Tom had been immensely relieved, especially when he saw his two well-scrubbed children sitting up at the kitchen table devouring their supper of bread and milk. As far as he and Lizzie were concerned, Lucy knew they would work hard, and that would be a real bonus to Kelly's place, and a great help to Matthew. Lucy suddenly knew that of course she had no option. The family would stay; Matthew would not have it otherwise. Lucy turned over in bed and tried to settle. Another few years of pinching and scraping would not hurt them, she reasoned with a sigh, and they really were lovely children.

George Carmody gritted his teeth, and drummed his fingers on the desk. He glared out of the window at the panorama of Fremantle harbour, but the bustle and excitement of the sunny scene did nothing to ease his frustration. *Where the devil had the man gone?*

As if in answer to his unspoken thought, the door opened and the harbour master came in. At first he seemed a little surprised to find someone in his office, but quickly assumed an air of busy efficiency.

"Ah, of course! Sorry to keep you waiting Mr…"

"Carmody. George Carmody." He could hardly keep the venom from his voice.

"Of course, of course. You must excuse me Mr. Carmody, but I have so many demands on my time…"

"Then please answer my query quickly and I'll be out of your way," Carmody snapped. "I've been here an hour already."

He quickly realised his mistake. The harbour master sat down at his desk and regarded him with a supercilious smile.

"You must remember, Mr…er…Carmody, that His Majesty's harbour master is not employed primarily to answer the questions of private individuals…even if they are wealthy individuals," he added pointedly.

Carmody swallowed. "Of course not," he replied smoothly. "It is because I am sure you can help me that I have not minded waiting, not minded at all."

The harbour master sniffed. "Well let's try again. You were trying to trace…what was the name again?"

"Marshall. Matthew Marshall and his niece Catherine. They would have arrived here about four years ago."

"I can't possibly recall everyone who embarks here."

"But surely you have records?"

The harbour master sniffed again. "The records are private business sir, not to be looked at by any Tom, Dick or Harry who wishes it."

Carmody adopted his most pleasant smile. "That is entirely proper sir, and I commend your punctilious attention to your duty. However sir, in recompense for your valuable time, I shall be delighted to make a substantial donation, which you may pass on to a deserving charity of your choice."

The harbour master appeared mollified. "Well of course, if charity is to benefit, it may just be possible…"

Carmody smiled again and leaned across the table. "And of course sir, I am not any Tom, Dick or Harry. My name is George."

The harbour master responded by reaching down a large volume. "About four years ago you say?" He scanned a few pages. "No, nothing. I told you there wasn't a Marshall. I would have remembered, I have a very good memory. Wait a minute, yes, of course…"

"Have you found something?"

The harbour master regarded him sternly. "You gave me the wrong name," he accused. "The boat was in the name of Mottram, Jarvis Mottram.

I remember now."

"What do you remember?" Carmody tried to keep the eagerness out of his voice. He took out his wallet and fingered it pointedly.

"Jarvis Mottram was the owner of the boat, and he had died. Snake bite. He had left the boat to Catherine Marshall, there was a will made out in a Testament. I registered the boat in her name."

"What happened to them?"

"She went on to Perth, and her uncle sold the boat to a couple of Englishmen, father and son I think."

Carmody frowned. "But where did they come from?"

The harbour master perused the record. "Says here they came from Adelaide, but the boat's papers were registered in Singapore. Look..." He traced the entry with his finger. "The *Selangor Lady*, one hundred tons, Jarvis Mottram, registered Singapore."

"Hold still Catherine, I'll never get it fastened!" Lizzie tugged once more at the waistband. "It's no use, take it off and I'll move the hook. It only needs half an inch but if I don't let it out you'll be uncomfortable all evening."

"Are you sure? I didn't realise I was any fatter," said Lucy, unbuttoning the neck of the soft green dress. "Mind you, it is nearly five years since I wore this dress; it was one of my mothers."

"It's lovely," said Lizzie, examining the seams, "It's so beautifully made. Look how even the wrist loop is embroidered."

Lucy giggled. "It's years since I wore a dress with a train at the back," she said. "I hope I don't forget to pick it up and fall over!"

They both giggled again as Lizzie threaded a needle. "You never talked about your mother before," she remarked. "She must have been quite wealthy to have a dress like this."

Lucy blenched; it was so easy to let something slip, especially when you became close friends with someone, as she had with Lizzie.

"Mother certainly wasn't wealthy," she denied, making light of it, "but this was her very best dress, worn for special occasions, that's why I kept it when she died. It used to fit perfectly, but I'm obviously better fed now than I used to be, it's your cooking that's to blame."

It was true, Lizzie was a marvellous cook. Given the simplest of ingredients she could make them into something very special. She had persuaded Lucy to send for a selection of herb seeds by mail order, and already the little herb garden she had made was making a flavoursome difference to their meals. Lucy still made the bread however; as Lizzie said she had never tasted anything as good as 'Miss Catherine's batch' and sang it's praises whenever she had an audience.

Now Lizzie sat down and reached for the sewing box. She smiled up at Lucy.

"I'm nearly finished Book Two," she said. "Will you check at the store and see if Book Three has come?"

"Of course I will," Lucy promised, "You are making really good progress. Soon you'll be catching up on me, and be able to teach Beth and Mitch yourself."

"I'm afraid that's a long way off," said Lizzie. "Mind you, it is getting easier. I don't suppose…" She hesitated. "There wouldn't be a fairly easy book I could read? I mean a proper book, with a story, not just a reader?"

Lucy groaned. "Lizzie Nicholls you are dreadful, you've just spoiled my surprise!" She laughed and patted Lizzie's arm. "I've ordered one for you. I'm sure you will be able to manage it," she said, "You'll be reading Mr. Dickens before very long."

To her surprise Lizzie's eyes filled with tears. "Lizzie, my dear, what is it? You're upset?"

"I'm not Catherine, I'm just so happy."

"Well if buying you a little book can make you so happy, I'll order a dozen."

Lizzie laughed a little, but then said hesitantly: "I don't think you realise how grateful Tom and I are, to you and Matthew."

"Grateful? What nonsense. You and Tom are worth your weight in gold for all the work you do…"

"I didn't mean that."

Lucy was puzzled. "Then what?"

"I don't think you realise how much it means to us to have you teach the children. We didn't know when we came here that you were such an educated person. Our children would never have been taught so well, even if we had stayed in Perth."

"It's the one thing England gave me," said Lucy. "A good education. I've been happy to use it, and the children are so bright and interested it's a pleasure to teach them."

"I knew you wouldn't understand," said Lizzie, in a matter of fact tone, "You see Catherine, no one like you can ever understand what it means not to be able to read and write. I didn't have the chance to learn when I was a child, and I've always felt at such odds, felt so stupid. I wanted to learn, but since I grew up there's been no opportunity, I've always seemed to be working. I suppose there have been people who might have taken the trouble to teach me, but I couldn't admit how desperately I wanted to learn. I used to pretend I didn't care. Here we have been made so welcome, and I have finally learned to read and write a little, and I'll get better with time and practice. Tom can write his name, but that's about all, and it doesn't seem to bother him so much, I suppose it's because a man can make his way by his work. He wants better for the children though, and he's really grateful to you both, same as me."

It was a long speech for Lizzie, and Lucy hardly knew how to respond, so she smiled and replied gently, "You know, you and Tom and the children have made a great difference to us too."

"Yes, we've nearly eaten you out of house and home."

Lucy laughed, "Well, yes, that too. But life is easier, even if we are no richer, and the children are a delight to us." She paused, considering. "I think we laugh a lot more since you came."

They sat in companionable silence for a few minutes, and then Lizzie said, "You're glad you're going now aren't you? I mean, you're looking forward to it?"

"The dance? I'm still not sure, but I'm certainly looking forward to seeing Jennie Moore again. It does seem to be rather extravagant, going all the way to Stannerton just for a dance."

"Not just any old dance," protested Lizzie. "Why, it's practically in your honour."

"Oh Lizzie, it's no such thing. If I thought that I shouldn't go, only Matthew seems so keen that I should."

"The first get-together of the Stannerton Wool Co-operative? It's a very important occasion; everyone for miles around will be there. If it hadn't been for you there wouldn't even be a Wool Co-operative, and when they see you in this dress they won't believe their eyes!"

"You think everyone will be there?" Lucy asked, her heart giving a lurch. She hesitated. "The Lamonts for example?"

"Probably not the Lamonts," said Lizzie, biting off a piece of thread and surveying her handiwork. "I mean they're graziers aren't they? Not interested in wool or a Wool Co-operative. But everyone else will be there I should think. There, that's better. Try it on again, and then I'll show you how you can plait the green ribbon into your hair at the back, it matches the dress

213

beautifully."

Lucy sighed and put the dress on again, Lizzie was making such a fuss, anyone would think she was going to the dance herself. The waist now fitted perfectly, and Lizzie nodded her approval.

"You're still wonderfully slim," she said, "Now sit still and I'll plait this ribbon through your hair."

Lucy rebelled. "I won't need the ribbon," she said flatly. "For one thing I can't do it myself, and if you do it here it will be undone by the time I get there. I have to camp out tomorrow night you know."

"Of course," said Lizzie sweetly, "I'm just going to show you how it's done, and then Jennie can do it for you when you get to the hotel."

Lucy gave up and allowed Lizzie to dress her hair. She smiled to herself, in a way it was pleasurable to contemplate the dance, she had never imagined she would ever attend a dance again. Her mind drifted along under Lizzie's soothing hands...*and once again she was at the Governor's ball in Singapore, in honour of the old Queen's birthday. She closed her eyes and was being waltzed around by a handsome stranger with intense grey eyes, eyes which seemed to penetrate the very core of her being. Then they were walking in the garden and he suddenly lifted her to sit on a stone mushroom, all the while talking nonsense about a princess and a frog prince, and the grey eyes were looking into hers with obvious enjoyment.*

"I'm sorry Lizzie, what did you say?" Lucy started, a faint blush colouring her cheeks.

Lizzie looked at her with concern. "Catherine, where were you?" she said.

"Oh, I was just dreaming," said Lucy. "I was nearly asleep."

"Come and look in the mirror," said Lizzie. Lucy sat at the dressing table, and Lizzie stood behind her and held up the hand mirror. Lucy gasped. The long chestnut tresses were folded and twisted behind her head into a thick pattern, with the soft green ribbon making a lattice trellis work through it.

"It's lovely! Lizzie, I didn't know you were a hairdresser."

"I'm not," said Lizzie, "but I always liked to dress hair. Before I was married I was a lady's maid and used to dress the mistress's hair for parties and dances. Mind you, her hair was not like yours, you have the sort of hair that pays for doing."

"It's really lovely," said Lucy, "but I doubt that Jennie will be able to manage it..."

"Yes, she will," said Lizzie confidently, "I'm going to make her a sketch to follow. I can draw even if I can't write too well."

Two days later at the Stannerton hotel, Lizzie's sketch proved readable. After a couple of practice attempts, Jennie pronounced herself satisfied and handed Lucy the hand mirror.

"You know Catherine," she said in her frank manner, "I knew you were a good looker, but I never knew you could look like that. That dress is just your colour, I don't think we've ever had such a good looker in Stannerton."

Lucy laughed. "You look pretty good yourself Jennie," she remarked dryly, "I thought you were hard up."

It was true, Jennie was resplendent in black velvet, embroidered with jet, and looked every inch the wealthy widow. She giggled. "Did push the boat out a bit," she admitted. "When I got this big booking from the Wool Co-operative, I thought I'd try and do it right, and perhaps if they have a good time they'll book the room again next year." She giggled again. "Have to really, won't they? Nowhere else to go." She turned in front of the mirror admiring her silhouette, much improved by a good corset and the black velvet. "Got this mail order from Perth," she said, "Not a bad fit is it?" She turned again, and at last seemed satisfied.

"Well Catherine, shall we join the party?"

And together they walked down into the crowded room.

"Some punch, Miss Marshall?" Lucy turned to see Clancy Bright, one of the local farmers, holding out a glass. She took it gratefully.

"Thank you Clancy."

He smiled at her. "You shouldn't be embarrassed Cath," he said. "I could tell you were though. When you came down the stairs and everybody clapped and cheered, you looked real put out."

Lucy laughed. "Well you're right Clancy, I was real put out, but I've got over it now."

He smiled and asked if she would like to meet his family. They were a cheerful lot, a chubby wife and two lanky sons, and in no time Lucy was chatting comfortably, and feeling thoroughly at home. The band struck up, and couples began to take the floor. Lucy found Jennie at her elbow.

"Oh Jennie, it's going so well, the punch is delicious."

"Not now Catherine, come on, there's someone I want you to meet."

Lucy followed her, and as she pressed through the crowd she was accosted on all sides by well wishers, the farmers wanting to meet the woman who had stood up to George Carmody. Lucy had difficulty in disengaging her hand from one man, who insisted on shaking it repeatedly, but eventually he released her and she caught up with Jennie, who turned with a smile.

"Oh there you are Catherine; I thought I'd lost you. I want you to meet Mr. Lamont, Gregory Lamont. Greg, this is Catherine Marshall."

And suddenly he had her hand, holding it in both his own as if to steady her, to stop her from fainting away. And there were the grey eyes, older, perhaps even a darker grey, but their effect was overwhelming, and they bored into her very soul.

Chapter Eighteen

In the moments that followed her introduction to Gregory Lamont, Lucy's brain reeled into panic. She was aware he was murmuring platitudes, "Very happy to meet you at last Miss Marshall," and "Of course I have met Matthew on two occasions," but she seemed frozen into immobility, and completely unable to respond.

Jennie continued to chat happily, and then moved away to attend to some crisis in the kitchens. Lucy still hadn't uttered a word, and Greg put his hand under her arm.

"We should dance I think," he muttered. "stop looking so dazed or people will notice."

Lucy allowed herself to be steered towards the dance floor. She felt as if she was made of wood, no feeling and no reaction was allowed, *she must simply keep quiet and it would all go away.* But the moment she was in Greg's arms the feeling flooded back. It was a torrent, a welter of emotions welling up as if to choke her, a tumultuous mixture of pleasure and panic, relief and anguish, which left her trembling and afraid.

"It's all right Miss Marshall, nothing to worry about," Greg murmured in her ear. "No need to panic, nothing dreadful is going to happen." He held her tighter as if to quell her trembling, and Lucy gradually relaxed under the hypnotic spell of the music and the feeling of security his nearness seemed to give her. After a few moments the grey eyes met her own.

"We seem destined to meet at dances. Better now?"

Lucy nodded dumbly.

"Then perhaps we could talk? It's been a long time."

"Yes."

Greg walked with her to one of the small tables set out at the edge of the room. "Sit there and don't move. I'll fetch some food and wine, and then it will look quite natural for us to be talking together for a while."

Lucy nodded, and he turned away, but seconds later he was back.

"You won't run away will you?" he asked. "It's taken me so long to find you, I don't want to lose you again." This was said with a reassuring grin, and

Lucy managed a faint smile in return. *Run away? She didn't have the strength to walk.* One thought penetrated the chaotic emotions which still engulfed her, it seemed he did not intend to give her away. He had not turned a hair when she was introduced to him, it was almost as if he knew that Miss Catherine Marshall would be the girl he had met in Singapore, the girl he had called "fairy princess" and "gypsy", the girl for whom he had sought and found a precious brooch. By the time he returned with a tray, Lucy had recovered somewhat.

"Here, drink this," he poured some red wine, and filled his own glass. "To our reunion," he toasted, smiling.

Lucy put the glass to her lips and sipped it.

"You didn't seem surprised to see me," she said after a moment. "How long have you known?"

"I had been watching you for ten minutes," Greg admitted, "so I had time to get over the shock. I must admit when you came down the stairs with Jennie and everyone started to clap and cheer, I was a bit overcome myself."

"Overcome by the fuss, or who I was?"

He looked surprised, "Oh, neither of those. Just overcome."

Lucy looked up and once again met the grey eyes, which regarded her with unashamed admiration. His meaning was so plain she felt the colour rise in her face, and turned her attention to her plate.

"But you knew who I was? I mean before tonight?"

"Not for certain, but I had a suspicion. You don't know this, but after you left Singapore I looked for you for ages. I knew you were in trouble, and thought I might be able to help. How you got away I'll never know, you seemed to vanish into thin air."

Lucy sighed. "It's a long story, and not a particularly happy one."

"You can tell me in your own time. Of course, I knew you were with Jarvis Mottram, he had disappeared too. The odd thing was that he disappeared before you, a week before Sir Gilbert…" His voice tailed off, and he looked at her anxiously. "I'm sorry, this is not the time or the place."

"You meant to say a week before I killed my husband." Lucy's voice was sharp, and Greg looked around before he murmured, "Of course not, and keep your voice down. I don't know what happened, but Sir Gilbert deserved what he got. If you had come to me for help I would have killed him myself."

Lucy looked at him in surprise, and in answer to her unspoken question he said, "I talked to Lela."

It was a statement, quiet and flat, but in his eyes Lucy read the truth behind the simple words. She looked around in confusion. *He knew, Greg Lamont, this man she had thought of so often, who seemed to affect her in such a strange way, he knew. He had talked to Lela, and she had told him of the depths of her degradation, her humiliation at Gilbert's hands.* She thanked God that Lela had not known everything, all the torments of that unspeakable time.

Aware of her distress, Greg said softly; "As I said, this is not the time or place Lucy. You mustn't worry, no one else knows your identity. I can help you. For now, just relax and enjoy your supper."

Lucy was glad of the respite, but after a moment Greg continued, "Just one question, and I promise I won't ask anything else. The map…it was you who sent it wasn't it?"

"Yes," Lucy admitted. "And according to Matthew you are going on a trip to try and find the location, I thought you would be gone by now."

He smiled. "That's what you were meant to think, and it worked didn't it?"

"You mean it was not true?"

"Oh yes, it's true all right. As a matter of fact I leave the day after tomorrow. I have everything prepared for the trip."

Lucy felt slightly deflated. *After all these years Greg Lamont had re-entered her life only to disappear again.* He seemed unaware of her reaction, and explained; "I became suspicious when Bob Middleton came to us having just met you. He had this wonderful story about a young lady and her uncle, who had taken him aboard their boat . When he described the young lady it was just possible it could be you." He hesitated a moment as if choosing his words, and then continued: "You had been on my mind quite a bit, and I imagined that Bob's lady was you and the uncle was Jarvis, and you had escaped on the *Selangor Lady*. It seemed to make sense, as Jarvis had lived in this area and it was likely he would make for a place he knew. It also explained the fact that neither the police nor myself had found any clues. You had escaped east, rather than back to England as everyone expected. The problem with my theory was that Bob's description of the uncle was nothing like Jarvis, and he couldn't remember the name of the boat. I decided I must be wrong, and told myself I was imagining things. Then out of the blue, I received the map."

Lucy watched as Greg refilled her glass. Then she asked, "Why did you think it was from me?"

"I kept asking myself who cared enough about Jarvis Mottram and his last wishes to make sure I got the map. The name Bill Jones was suspicious too, no one had ever heard of him."

"But you did nothing about it. When we first moved to Kelly's place you didn't try to contact us."

Greg gave a bitter laugh. "Remember, I wasn't sure, and I felt I was deluding myself again. I had looked for you a long time."

At that moment the band played a loud introduction, and Clancy Bright, standing on a chair, announced: "Quiet please everyone, this is the time for speeches!"

There was a chorus of groans and laughter, and Clancy went on, "Now, we're not grand folks around here, but we know how to enjoy ourselves, and I hope you are doing just that." More cheers greeted this statement, and Clancy, flushed and happy, warmed to his theme. "I want to thank our hostess, Jennie Moore, for the lovely spread, and of course for playing her part in the events of last year. You all know it took a bit of a jolt to make us stand together as men in this town, and that jolt was given by a lady we are proud to have with us tonight, Miss Catherine Marshall."

The room erupted with cheering, and as Clancy fought again to make himself heard, Lucy felt Greg take her hand. He remained holding it as Clancy continued, "We don't see much of you Catherine, but you're here tonight, and we shan't let you get away easy. As the newly elected president of the Stannerton Wool Cooperative..." A storm of jeering broke out at this, with cries of "show off!" and "Only for a year mind!" followed by much laughter, and Clancy had difficulty in restoring order, but eventually he ploughed on, "As your new president, I have much pleasure in proposing a toast, ladies and gentlemen, to a real fine lady, Miss Catherine Marshall."

A resounding echo of "Miss Catherine Marshall" went through the room, together with shouts of "Bottoms up Cath!" and noisy clapping. Then several of the farmers shouted 'speech!' and this was taken up until the noise became deafening. Lucy trembled, she could not believe this was happening. Greg squeezed her hand and said, "Come on," and suddenly she was being propelled to the front.

"Don't worry, just smile and say what you feel," Greg whispered in her ear. Then he pushed her gently forward and retired to the back of the hall.

Lucy turned and shot Greg a pleading look, but he only grinned and nodded. *You're enjoying this, Greg Lamont,* she thought, trying to collect her wits. As she reached Clancy's side the room fell silent, and Lucy, tentatively at first, began to speak.

"My friends, I am quite overcome by your kindness. I suppose I should not be surprised, because my uncle and I have been met with nothing but kindness since we came here. We are still newcomers, and there is not a man here who hasn't forgotten more than we shall ever know about sheep farming. I think the Co-operative is a wonderful idea, and I wish you all success." Lucy hesitated, and then raised her glass. "So I give you another toast, my friends. To the future, and the Stannerton Wool Cooperative!"

"The Stannerton Wool Cooperative!" was the deafening reply, followed by a burst of clapping, and as it died down a loud voice came from the doorway.

"For a so called business enterprise, this is a merry gathering!"

It was George Carmody, and he swaggered through the crowd towards Lucy.

"Get out Carmody, you're not invited," said Clancy, moving forward to face him as he reached the front of the hall.

Carmody turned to face the audience. "I'll go, in just a few moments," he said loudly, "But it's a poor kind of Cooperative that drinks a toast to criminals."

He was met by blank stares, and a man at the back shouted out, "We want no trouble Carmody, why don't you leave?"

"I've told you I will," answered Carmody. "When I've said what I have to say and what you ought to hear." He threw a sneering look at Clancy. "I know your new President doesn't have many brains," he said derisively, "But I thought even he would baulk at sucking up to a murderess!"

There was a sudden silence. A voice from the back shouted "What are you on about?" and a few boos and catcalls made Carmody raise his voice. "The woman you have just toasted so merrily is wanted for murder!"

Again the room fell silent, followed by a rumble of surprise, and cries of 'Nonsense,' and 'Get out!' Lucy was frozen to the spot, and Greg, trying to reach her, found his way blocked as the crowd surged forward.

"It's true, your precious Catherine Marshall is wanted for murder," shouted Carmody, relishing the moment. "Her real name is Lady Lucy Howell, and she murdered her husband Sir Gilbert Howell in Singapore. The police have been hunting her for nearly five years, and I'm pleased to tell you they are on their way here now." He turned to Lucy and grabbed her arm viciously. "Well deny it madam! Deny it if you can!"

At that moment Greg Lamont reached the front. He hit straight out, a great round armed blow which caught Carmody at the side of the jaw and knocked him senseless. Greg took Lucy's arm and bundled her up the stairs and along the corridor.

"Where is your room? Quickly now, get your things together." He turned to meet Jennie, who had raced up the stairs behind them. "Jennie, I need to get her out of here. Can you get my trap ready?"

"Yes, of course." Jennie was already on her way down the stairs. She turned and met Lucy's eyes, and Lucy read the question.

"Jennie, my real name is Lucy Howell," she whispered, "Carmody was right about that. But I didn't kill my husband."

Jennie gave a swift nod. "I'll get the trap hitched," she said, and hurried downstairs.

As Lucy scrambled her things together, she caught the bemused look on Greg Lamont's face, and quick realisation flashed through her brain. *Until her admission to Jennie, he had believed she was guilty, believed she really had murdered Gilbert.*

The journey back to Kelly's place seemed interminable. Greg hardly spoke, and Lucy's thoughts were dark and chaotic. As she climbed into the trap she had asked "Where are we going?" and Greg had answered briefly, "Back to Kelly's place to tell Matthew what's happened. Then you must get away."

"But Matthew is not well, he can't travel."

"He won't have to, they aren't looking for him."

It was true, she was the person wanted for murder, and Carmody had said the police were already on their way. Lucy had difficulty in adapting to the turn of events, hardly able to believe she had been discovered after all this time.

As the trap careered out of town and along the trail Lucy began to realise the extent to which she had adapted to her new life in Australia. She had come to love the simple pleasures of life at Kelly's place, and had become lulled into a false sense of security, believing that she and Matthew had at last escaped the past. Everything had been going so well recently in spite of the shortage of money, especially since Lizzie and Tom had joined them. Lucy felt slightly sick at the prospect of being on the run again, doubting she could survive it a second time. *How could she leave the farm, and Matthew? How could she live without Matthew, and where could she go?* She glanced at Greg's grim face but found no comfort there.

As dawn rose they stopped briefly, making a quick camp. They had left the hotel yard at eight thirty in the evening and had travelled all night, and now Greg said they must stop for breakfast.

"I don't want any breakfast," Lucy protested, feeling that food would choke her.

"It is the horses who need rest and breakfast," said Greg sharply. "They have been doing all the work."

His tone splintered her mood. *During the journey she had perhaps been indulging in self pity, but did he have to be so unpleasant?* With sudden insight she realised that Greg had put himself in serious trouble by helping her. *Several people must have seen them leave town in his trap, and now he was an accessory.* She mulled this over as she gathered wood for the fire and quickly lighted it. Having hitched the horses Greg had disappeared, obviously to attend a call of nature. When he reappeared, Lucy offered him coffee.

"I'm sorry Greg," she said, holding out the mug.

He looked puzzled.

"I mean for getting you involved. I could sign a statement to say you knew nothing about all this, and were just trying to help me."

"But that wouldn't be true would it? I did know all about it, right from the beginning."

Oh no, Lucy thought, *not from the beginning. How can you understand why I even married Gilbert?* Aloud, she said, "Why did you help me?"

Greg gave a quick grin, but he only said "Why indeed?" and started to make breakfast.

Thoroughly chastened, Lucy kept silent during the simple meal until Greg spoke again. "I think I have it."

Lucy looked at him, not understanding. "Have what?"

"The way out. For you I mean. You come with me on my trip to the goldfields, to look for Uncle Jack's mine."

"I can't do that," Lucy answered.

"Why not? Do you have a better idea?" he asked dryly.

Lucy fell silent again. She had no ideas at all.

Greg poured the coffee dregs on the fire, and then smothered it with earth, kicking roughly at the soil with his boot.

"I've thought it through now," he said, "And it's much the best option. I have had the journey planned for some time, everything is ready, and everyone knows I'm going, although only Sam and Mary know the true purpose of the trip. All we shall need is extra food and water, and your personal things. We can pick those up when we call at Kelly's place."

"But everyone will know where I've gone. Plenty of people know I left Stannerton with you."

"We will arrange for Matthew to tell the police that I brought you home and then went on to the Lamont station. He can say I was anxious to get back as I was starting my trip in a couple of days. Then you left, by yourself, and Matthew doesn't know where, as you made a point of not telling him."

"But the police may not believe that," Lucy remonstrated.

"Yes, they will." Greg answered firmly. "Remember they do not know we met before tonight, so what reason would I have for taking you on my trip? They will think I was just playing the gentleman, or being neighbourly, in getting you out of a tricky situation."

He began to pack up their things, and continued; "After we leave Kelly's place we shall go to the Lamont station. When we get near home I will leave you hidden, and go on to the house alone. I shall have to leave you all tomorrow night," he added apologetically, "but it would look odd if I arrived from Stannerton and then left immediately. Better to leave next morning as planned, which gives me a chance to explain to Sam and Mary what happened at the dance, and that I took you home to Kelly's place, just in case you're right and the police come nosing around."

"Do you think they will?"

"Probably not. You have many friends in Stannerton. People may be upset by what Carmody said, but they will give you the benefit of the doubt, and will not be anxious to help the police."

Lucy hesitated. "It is very kind of you to offer to help me Greg," she faltered, "But I think you misunderstand my objection. I cannot allow you to put yourself at such risk, and to lie to your family. You would become an accessory."

Greg came to her and took her firmly by the shoulders.

"There will be no risk," he said, and the grey eyes held her in a penetrating gaze. "No risk," he repeated, "Because Matthew will tell the police the truth."

"What truth?" His gaze was making her feel slightly weak.

"The truth about Sir Gilbert's death," Greg said gently. "I can understand the panic which made you run away, and your feelings of loyalty, but when the police finally arrive, Matthew can tell them the truth. By the time we return from our trip your name will have been cleared, and you will have missed all the unpleasantness. We shall be away five or six weeks at least, and that will give the police time to complete everything."

"But what about Matthew?" Lucy was aghast.

Greg looked puzzled. "Oh, he'll be all right, especially now you have this new couple to help with the farm, I'm sure they'll keep an eye on him. You know Lucy, you are perhaps a bit over-protective towards Matthew, and he's the same with you."

"Oh, do you think so?" Lucy said faintly, trying to fathom what was going on in Greg's mind. She had her answer within seconds, as Greg began to hitch the horses to the trap. Turning the grey glance towards her with a smile he announced; "No, there will be little for either of you to worry about. Once the police know it was Jarvis Mottram who shot Sir Gilbert, and that Jarvis is dead, that will be the end of the matter."

During the remainder of the journey to Kelly's place, Lucy's mind was in turmoil. She was surprised at her own reactions. *Why hadn't she challenged Greg right away, and why did she continue to allow him to believe his wrong assumption?* The more she thought about it, the more she came to understand Greg's reasoning. For over twenty years he had thought of Jarvis as a murderer, and it would take only a small leap of imagination to cast Jarvis in the role once more. Lucy realised it was only after the commotion at the dance that Greg had reached this conclusion, prior to that, she was sure he had believed her guilty.

Then why had he been so keen to help her, as indeed he had always helped her? There was the business of him finding her mother's brooch in Singapore, that could not have been easy. And when she had taken her woolclip to the railhead Greg had arrived in Stannerton with Bob and some of the other men, to help if needed. When he saw her at the dance he had not given away her identity, why had he done all these things? Surely not just because of those silly moments in the garden at the Governor's residence, when the frog prince met the princess? She recalled with a rush of pleasure the look in Greg's eyes at the Stannerton dance when he had said he was "Just overcome."

Lucy glanced sideways at Greg. His profile was stony, but he appeared to feel her gaze, because he turned and said affably enough, "Well, have you thought about it? Are you coming with me?"

"Yes," replied Lucy after a moment. "Yes, I'm coming with you."

Now why had she said that? There were a thousand reasons, she told herself. *She had to get away, that was certain, and where else could she go? To travel alone would be dangerous, whereas with Greg and all his experience of bush life she would be safe, at least as safe as was possible in this inhospitable country. Was there another reason she had agreed to go, a deeper reason, something she would not admit?* She blushed slightly as she acknowledged that she wanted to be with Greg, wanted to know and understand him, and how better to do that than embark on this trip? She felt a strange apprehension as she imagined this, and attempted to pull her thoughts together. *She was evading the issue. The issue was that Greg believed Jarvis had killed Gilbert, and she could not allow him to continue in that belief. Jarvis was her loyal and loving friend, who had lost his life because he helped her. She could not, and would not, allow his name to be blackened. Yet how could she tell Greg the truth? Matthew must be protected at all cost. If Greg knew that Matthew was responsible his attitude might well be that the truth must come out. Yet Greg had heard her tell Jennie that she had not killed Gilbert, and it was plain he believed her.* As they neared Kelly's place Lucy found no answer to her problems, and finally decided to confide in Matthew and seek his advice as to the best course of action.

It was near midday as they drove up to the cabin, and Lizzie came running out to meet them.

"Oh, Catherine, you're home early, we did not expect you for a few days yet."

"This is Mr. Lamont," said Lucy, giving no explanation for her early return. "Greg, this is Lizzie Nicholls, and here are Mitch and Beth," she laughed, as the two children came flying down the path from the house.

The children flung themselves at Lucy, shouting "we saw you, we saw you come." They suddenly became quiet as they looked at Greg with round eyes. To Lucy's surprise he held out his hands to them and said, "I'm Greg, will you help me see to the horses? Then you can take me up the hill to see Matthew." After a momentary shyness, the children accompanied Greg to the barn. Lucy and Lizzie followed, and soon Greg, with a child holding each hand, started off up the hill. Lucy and Lizzie followed, but made slow progress because Beth and Mitch were playing a silly game with Greg on the way.

Matthew had come out onto the verandah. Lucy was perturbed by his appearance, and intuitively understood why he had not come down to meet them. He looked thinner than ever, and very frail. Nevertheless he welcomed them warmly.

"You interrupted our Geography lesson. The children were delighted at the opportunity to play truant. Catherine my dear, you're home early, and Greg, how good to see you again."

As he took Greg's hand Lucy saw a quick glance pass between Matthew and Greg. It was a half nod, a look of complicity, as if they had some kind of tacit agreement. Then it was gone, and Lucy wondered if she had imagined it.

They went into the house, and Lizzie put the kettle on, as Matthew dismissed the children for the day. They departed with whoops of delight, and he turned to Lucy, smiling.

"I don't know who is more pleased to be free," he said. "They are so bright they are already asking questions I can't answer." Lucy watched as he lowered himself into a chair, rather painfully, she thought.

"Uncle, are you all right?" she asked. "You don't look too well."

"Had a bit of a cough, that's all." Matthew replied, and then as Lucy rose, "No need to fuss dear, I'm perfectly well, and Lizzie has been treating me like eggshell."

"Quite right too," said Lizzie, entering with a tray. "Catherine, will you take over? I must get back to the cheese."

Lucy smiled as Lizzie left the room. "How we ever managed without Lizzie and Tom I don't know," she said to Greg. "By the way Uncle, where is Tom?"

"Out with the sheep," Matthew replied. "And you're right, what a worker the man is, and we get on so well."

There was silence as Lucy began to pour the tea, no one quite knowing what to say. Eventually Matthew came to the rescue.

"Well Lucy, I expect you were surprised to meet up with Greg again, and I take it he didn't give you away?"

Lucy was bewildered at the lighthearted tone used by her uncle, expecting he would be upset at their discovery. Matthew regarded the two grave faces before him, and realised something was wrong.

"What is it?" he said, glancing from one to the other.

"You are right in surmising Greg didn't give me away," Lucy began. "But someone did. Carmody."

"Carmody? But how did he know anything? What happened?"

Greg took up the story, relating how the wool farmers had toasted Lucy, and how Carmody had interrupted with his revelation. Greg described their escape, and then added, "He must have investigated you after you stood up to him over the woolclip. So of course Lucy has to get away, until everything is cleared up. You will recall that I told you I am going on a trip to the goldfields, to try and find out if Jack Lamont ever found gold. Lucy can come with me, and you can rest assured I will take good care of her."

"That's a good idea," said Matthew, looking relieved. "Come to think of it, a very good idea."

"And so," continued Greg, "When the police come here, as I am sure they will, you can explain to them what happened, that Jarvis Mottram killed Sir Gilbert, and how Jarvis died." He looked at Lucy. "How did he die, by the way? The note you sent didn't tell me."

"Snake bite," said Lucy briefly, trying to avoid Matthew's shocked gaze. To give him time to adjust she added, "We buried Jarvis at sea. It was not easy to arrange but he wanted that. It was a nice service, only us, but it was all right."

From the corner of her eye she could see Matthew's still stricken face. "We hoisted the flag, and then half masted it," she said unnecessarily. Seeing that the dumbstruck Matthew was about to recover his voice, she rose quickly and said, "Greg, would you do me a great favour and go down to the cabin and ask Lizzie for some cheese? We may as well have some food before we go, and we can take some with us." She shot Matthew a warning glance.

"Of course." Greg rose immediately with the easy grace of his long limbs. "Is that all you need?"

"Yes, thank you."

Lucy watched Greg striding down the path to the cabin and then turned to her uncle. "I'm sorry Uncle. He just jumped to the conclusion that it was Jarvis. He heard me tell Jennic Moore that I didn't kill Gilbert, and he assumed Jarvis did."

"But, I can't allow it." Matthew was distressed, and Lucy noticed again how frail he was.

"Just for a while Uncle, perhaps we could let the police think it was Jarvis." Lucy was becoming a little distracted. "I'm sure Jarvis wouldn't mind."

"Of course." Matthew's voice was calm, weighing up the possibilities. "Perhaps for a while." He seemed to come to a decision, and smiled his big happy smile, much to Lucy's relief.

"Now, you go with Greg on this trip my dear, and I hope you have an exciting time, and find something worthwhile. If there is no gold, there may well be something else worth having, or worth seeing, or knowing about."

"But what about the police?"

"Just leave them to me." This was said with great determination.

Lucy was not impressed. "Uncle, I shall not go unless you promise me that you will not admit anything. You probably think it would be the right thing to do to own up to the shooting, but it is not the right thing, it is not!"

Lucy's voice became vehement, and tears started to her eyes. She took Matthew's hands and pressed them.

"Please Uncle, please," she begged.

Matthew patted her hands. "Calm yourself my dear, this is all most unnecessary. You are right, at one time I may have thought and acted as you predict, but I have changed. In a new country like this one learns self preservation. I promise you no police officers will take me for trial."

"You promise?"

Matthew smiled broadly. "I promise."

When Greg returned with the cheese he found Matthew alone in the kitchen.

"Where's Lucy?" Greg asked. "Lizzie sent some cheese, but she said there was already some here in the cellar."

"Never mind that," Matthew interjected. "Lucy is in her bedroom, packing for the journey. I must talk to you, it's important, and she mustn't hear." He beckoned to Greg. "Come here man, quickly!"

Greg crossed the kitchen, and as he reached the armchair Matthew grabbed his sleeve.

"Now, Greg," he commanded, "Don't talk, just listen!"

Lucy snuggled down and pulled her blanket closer about her. The night was becoming very cold, as it often did around this time of year. Greg had prepared a hot meal for dinner, but the effects of it were wearing off, and she knew that by dawn she would be both lacking in sleep and chilled through.

She wondered vaguely what Greg was doing. Probably tucked into a warm bed snoring his head off. He had been adamant that she must not accompany him to the ranch, and he was probably right. Apart from the danger of discovery, she could understand Greg not wanting his family to know she would be accompanying him on his trip.

As she rearranged the bracken pillow she had piled on her saddle, Lucy pondered on Greg's reasons for the trip to the goldfields, wondering whether he really expected to find something, or was simply trying to rehabilitate Jack Lamont into his family history. During their journey Greg had explained why he had kept his plans secret from everyone except Sam and Mary. "In case of another gold rush!" he had said flippantly.

The letter Greg had found in his father's desk had been sent from a small mining town called Shimmer Creek, north of Kalgoorlie. It was the last letter

229

ever received from Jack, and Greg was hoping that by searching the claims records at Shimmer Creek, he could find out where Jack had been working when he decided to pull up stakes and return home. His theory was that Jack may have found gold, but wanted to keep it quiet until he could come home and raise the cash needed for mining extraction equipment. Greg emphasised that this was only a theory, but after many hours of deliberation it seemed the only conclusion which fitted the known facts. It also might explain the quarrel between his father and Jack.

"Just imagine how my father would have felt Lucy," Greg had said as he explained his reasoning. "From what I know from people at home and from Jarvis Mottram, my father felt Jack had left him with all the work and responsibility, to go off on a wild-goose-chase looking for gold. For that reason alone he had a real grudge smouldering against Jack. My father loved Mother very deeply, and when she died, father added his grief to this grudge, almost as if her death was Jack's fault. Imagine his feelings when Jack suddenly turned up from nowhere asking for more cash. It's easy to see how a quarrel could have developed."

These events, almost thirty years old now, played through Lucy's mind as she shivered in her blanket. She tried to reconstruct the scene of the quarrel and its aftermath, using the shadowy figures of Greg's father, Jack Lamont, and a much younger Jarvis than she had known. It was possible Greg's theory was correct, she concluded.

Lucy stiffened as a sudden sound caught her ears. Alert in an instant, she sat up as she heard it again, nearer and louder. Whatever it was, it was big. Hairs stood up on the back of her neck.

"Lucy, are you awake?"

Greg's large form appeared against the dim light, and Lucy sighed with relief.

"Greg, thank goodness, I thought it was at least a big Roo!"

"Sorry to frighten you. Are you all right?"

"Yes of course, a bit cold that's all."

"That's what I thought. I've brought you some extra blankets, those I had ready for the trip."

"Wonderful! Thank you," Lucy took the blankets and put one underneath and an extra one on top of her makeshift bed, as Greg watched. "That's much better, I'll be able to sleep now."

"Good. And I thought this might warm you a little." He handed her a small flask, "Brandy. I know it's not usual for a lady to…"

He need not have worried. With a quick, "Oh yes, excellent!" Lucy had removed the stopper and taken a swig. Greg chuckled.

Lucy regarded him gravely, "Something is amusing?"

"Not at all." He smiled broadly. "Good night Lucy, see you at dawn."

"Good night Greg, thanks for the blankets. Oh, and Greg,"

He turned back.

"It's possible Jack didn't find gold. He could have come home to ask for more money to continue looking."

Greg considered. "It's possible certainly," he agreed. "But in that case why did he make the map, and why did he throw it to Jarvis?"

"I'll think about it," Lucy replied, snuggling down again. "Good night."

"Good night Lucy."

Greg went back to his horse and mounted slowly. He was still smiling. He could not get the image of Lucy out of his mind. *She was so different today, dressed in cotton shirt and loose riding drawers which looked as if they were made for hard wear rather than fashion. And now, sleeping out alone, she had not seemed perturbed or afraid, except when he had gone blundering in, and noises at night were enough to spook anyone. She had guts all right. How different from the young girl he had met in Singapore, that lovely creature in pale blue satin, beautiful beyond belief and slender as a wraith. She had woven a spell around him which had never let him go, not through all the years of doubt and conjecture about her. When he had seen her coming down the stairs at the Stannerton dance, a vision of loveliness dressed to perfection, the same feelings which had overwhelmed him in Singapore had rushed back like a torrent, and he had been seized with such happiness that he had difficulty not rushing to take her in his arms. On the long journey back to Kelly's place, with Lucy still dressed in her evening clothes, he had been unable to talk to her, unable to form the questions which had tortured him for so long.*

Suddenly today, he had seen a new Lucy, a woman of strong character, but perhaps a little more approachable, dressed for the outback as if its privations were of little consequence. It was almost as if Lucy Rowlands and Catherine Marshall really were two different people. He imagined her snuggled down in her blankets, and smiled as he recalled her taking a swig from the brandy flask. This was a different Lucy, but the confident woman she had become still seemed to exert the same influence on him. As he had bent over to hand her the flask, he had felt an almost incontrollable desire to kiss her, and he wondered idly what her reaction would have been if he had.

She certainly wouldn't have agreed to accompany him on his trip, he told himself. *He would need to be careful during the next few weeks, and remember his promise to Matthew.* He had been surprised that she had agreed to the trip, but of course that was because of her predicament, and because of the possibility of gold.

His face clouded as he dismounted and led his horse quietly back to the stable to avoid being heard. *Yes,* he thought, *the gold was what really fascinated her, even tonight it had been on her mind. How would he feel if they did find gold, and he suddenly became attractive to her? Would he accept her on those terms, knowing that her interest in him was only because he was rich? Just as she had married Sir Gilbert Howell for his money, would she marry him if he found gold?*

Greg and Lucy were well on their way to Shimmer Creek before the subject of events in Singapore was broached again. During that first week, as the horses plodded purposefully through a terrain of sparse bush and sandstone ridges, Greg seemed unwilling to mention Gilbert's death, and Lucy was more than happy to let the matter drop.

They saw no one except for a group of Aborigines, driving a herd of brumby horses. They stopped briefly and exchanged some of their flour for fresh kangaroo meat, and then pressed on. They had settled into a simple but disciplined daily routine, and Lucy soon adapted to the demands of life in the saddle. She had realised very quickly that Greg's experience of the outback was vastly superior to her own, and on the few occasions she had been tempted to disagree with him, she had soon realised her mistake.

I expect he doesn't know how to hoist a sail or plot a course at sea, she told herself, and with this thought in mind she set about learning all she could as they made their slow progress towards Shimmer Creek.

Their personal relationship was warm but formal. Greg was always kind and solicitous for her welfare, making sure she had every comfort he could provide on the journey, although these were necessarily few. However, apart from the daily discussion of routine matters, he spoke little, and Lucy relaxed into acceptance of this easygoing friendship. Not once did she see any evidence of the warm admiration she had seen in his eyes at the Stannerton dance, and she began to think she had imagined it. She tried to recall that look of overt sexuality, a look so open and natural that she blushed instinctively when she thought of it. Now she glanced across at Greg as they made their preparations for another night, their tenth in the outback, but he was intent on what he was doing and did not respond.

Their evening routine was simple but well organised. When Greg had selected their camp site, he would attend to the horses and the little pack donkey which also accompanied them, and Lucy would gather wood and get the fire going for their evening meal. Greg would set up what he called the wash tent, which consisted of four poles set in a square and covered by two lengths of mosquito net. Inside this he would put a stand which held an enamel wash bowl, and soap and towels. When Lucy had first seen this little enclave of civilisation erected in the middle of nowhere she had been both amazed and touched.

"How kind of you Greg," she had said, her pleasure evident in her voice, "And how thoughtful."

Greg had looked at her sharply. "It was not done simply for you Lucy," he said. "Everyone on a journey needs to wash, and I need to shave. Our family have used this system for years when we travel."

Lucy felt herself corrected. "Oh, I think you have misunderstood," she replied. "It's just that whenever I have camped overnight I have never been this well organised."

"Overnight is one thing," said Greg shortly. "If you are going to be traveling for weeks you have to plan properly."

Now, as Lucy deftly skinned and cleaned a rabbit Greg had shot an hour earlier, she watched out of the corner of her eye as he erected the wash tent. Satisfied, he came striding towards her.

"Wash tent ready, Lucy." He looked at the rabbit and frowned. "I've told you, I'll do that," he said crossly.

Lucy laughed. "You really must get over your idea of me as the English lady who mustn't soil her hands," she said. "If you could see some of the things I've had to do at sea, including cleaning fish much bigger than this…"

"That's as may be," said Greg, taking the knife and beginning to joint the rabbit. "But you had to do it then. Now you don't, and that's the difference."

Lucy laughed. "All right, Sir Galahad," she teased. "I'll go and wash my lily white hands, and transform myself back into the fair English damsel, then you'll be happy." She started for the wash tent.

"Lucy."

She turned back.

"I know you can look after yourself. It's been evident since we started out, and I admire it." He looked up and she saw the clouded grey eyes clear. "It's just that I like to do things for you," he said simply.

Lucy's heart gave a lurch. It was the first time a personal note had entered his voice since they began their journey. She came back to the fire.

"Greg," she said, stooping down to face him as he skewered the rabbit piece by piece. "You have done more for me than I can ever repay. It started with my mothers brooch. Yes, it did," she added quickly as she saw the surprise on his face. "You may have forgotten that, but I never shall. You have also helped me escape from the police, and as for our situation now, if it wasn't for you I'd certainly be lost." She gave him a quick smile and grasped the billycan. "The reason I skinned the rabbit is that Jarvis taught me that those who don't work don't eat. Can I have this water? I'll put more on for you to shave."

"Of course," he answered. "We're well off for water at present, but in a few days time we shall only have what we can carry, we may not find any more between here and Shimmer Creek."

"In that case I'll make the most of it."

When she returned Lucy found that Greg had set out what looked like a picnic, spread on a blanket on the ground. He was opening a bottle of wine, and laughed at her expression.

"I've been nursing this since we left," he explained. "I was sure it would get broken but it seems to have survived. It's by way of celebration, I'll explain over dinner," he promised.

Less than an hour later they began their dinner of rabbit and boiled potatoes. Greg, freshly shaved and wearing a clean shirt, poured the wine into their enamel mugs.

"You will have to tell me now," Lucy said, holding up her mug. "I can't drink if I don't know what we're celebrating."

"Nothing specific," said Greg, "But we're unlikely to have another decent overnight stop until we reach Shimmer Creek. We take all the water we can carry from here, because we are coming to the dry country. We shan't find a billabong or even a soak between here and Shimmer Creek, so we have to move fast and conserve everything we can."

"How long till we reach Shimmer Creek?"

"About ten days I imagine. I've never come this far before, but others have told me it's real killer country, so I thought we'd have a good last meal tonight."

"It was a good thought," Lucy said approvingly, as she sipped her wine.

"There is one other thing." Greg sounded hesitant.

234

"Yes?"

"It's about Matthew. Before we left Kelly's place he told me the truth about Sir Gilbert's death. Now don't look like that Lucy, Matthew is all right."

"He won't tell anyone else will he? I mean if the police come for me, he might."

"No, no. Don't worry. If the police come for you we agreed he would say it was Jarvis who fired the shot. They will probably believe that, after all, it was Jarvis's gun."

"You don't know Matthew. He's so honest, he wanted to own up ages ago, and he's not well."

"I know, and he promised me he will not do anything foolish. He only told me because we were going to be together for a long time, and he thought we should be able to talk without misunderstanding. He's hoping that by the time we return all the fuss will be over."

"Do you think it will?"

"Yes, I think so. You have made friends in Stannerton. They aren't going to hold you responsible for something that wasn't your fault, even if you did run away." Greg smiled, and the grey eyes lightened as he added, "You're in Australia now. Many people have backgrounds they would rather forget. They're a forgiving lot, you'll be all right."

Lucy felt a little better. "I'm glad you know the truth," she said. "I never intended to lie to you."

"I know," said Greg. "You were just protecting Matthew. But there is one thing Matthew didn't tell me Lucy, something which always puzzled me, and which only you can answer." He stopped, a little embarrassed.

"What is it? We may as well clear the air completely," Lucy offered.

Greg twisted the enamel mug around in his hands, and kept his eyes on it as he replied after some hesitation, "I could never understand why you married Sir Gilbert in the first place. It seems you only knew him a short time."

Lucy felt as if she had been slapped, as all the old feelings of guilt and remorse welled up, threatening to rob her of speech. Making a supreme effort, she swallowed and murmured, "Why indeed?"

There was silence for a few moments, before Greg broke out almost angrily, "Well, is there an answer?"

Lucy blenched. *How could she ever hope to make Greg understand?* "I don't know..." she stammered, defensively.

Greg reached into his breast pocket and pulled out a tattered old newspaper cutting. "Here," he said almost viciously. "This is what was said at the time." He handed the grubby scrap to Lucy. "Read it."

As she bent to decipher the creased newsprint, suddenly Lucy was back amid the events of that terrible year. Winchester Station, and the neglect and the poverty, her father's abject pleading, and Gilbert's offer of help on a grand scale. The journalist had drawn his own conclusions, and quoted telling examples to show that the penniless Lucy Rowlands had needed to cast her net for a rich husband, and had caught and married Sir Gilbert Howell, one of the richest men in Singapore.

"Well?"

Greg's sharp voice brought Lucy back to the present, and she heard him continue more gently, "It suggests you married Sir Gilbert for his money. That isn't true, is it?"

He watched her reaction closely. *Why didn't she lift her head? Why couldn't she meet his eyes?* Greg felt numbed and his mind raced as he waited for her answer. She whispered something but he could not hear. He leaned towards her.

"What did you say?"

At last Lucy raised a distraught face. "Yes, it's true," she said wonderingly. "I've often tried to pretend it isn't, but I think I did marry him for his money."

There, she had said it aloud, had admitted at last to the agony of self doubt and guilt which had tortured her for so long.

Greg said nothing, and when Lucy looked towards him she saw he had turned his head away. A few moments later he said, almost conversationally, "Well that's honest at least."

He reached across and poured more wine into Lucy's mug, and then his own. "Let's drink to honesty," he said, "And to Matthew. May he always shoot as straight!"

"Greg!" Lucy had recovered a little. "I don't think that's a very proper toast."

"Certainly is! If it hadn't been for Matthew you would be dead! Here's to Matthew!"

And Lucy couldn't help but raise her mug and agree, "To Matthew!"

Chapter Nineteen

Matthew stood up slowly and shaded his eyes from the sun. Yes, this must be him, the waiting was over at last. Matthew was glad, and watched carefully as the distant moving speck became recognisable as a horse and rider. It was a few minutes before the visitor rounded the bend of the creek and quickened pace as he rode towards the cabin. Matthew watched him dismount, and saw Lizzie come out and speak to him, wiping her floury hands on her apron. Then she started up the steep slope to the house, the visitor following behind her. He was a dark man, stocky, with a clean, healthy look which was at variance with his dusty riding clothes. Matthew moved with some difficulty to the edge of the verandah, his bones ached, and he had to move carefully or the coughing would start again. He managed a papery smile.

"Good morning."

The visitor reached the verandah and mopped his brow.

"Good morning. Is it Mr. Marshall?"

"Yes, that's right."

"My name is Thurlestone. John Thurlestone. I'm the constable for this area."

"Yes. I thought you might be. Come and sit down, I've been expecting you. Would you like some tea, or would you prefer a cold drink?" Matthew led the way slowly to the coolest part of the verandah; the spot where Lucy liked to sit and read aloud in the evenings. He gestured John Thurlestone to a seat, and turned to Lizzie.

"Would you mind Lizzie? I'm a bit slow this morning."

"Bless you Matthew, it's no trouble." She looked enquiringly at John Thurlestone, who seemed nonplussed.

"Er, a cold drink would go down very well, and perhaps I could draw water for my horse?"

"Of course, don't worry sir, I'll see to him." Lizzie bustled into the house, and John Thurlestone turned to Matthew with an air of apology.

"It wasn't you I came to see, Mr. Marshall, but the young lady who lives here as your niece, and is known as Catherine Marshall."

"The young lady you speak of is indeed my niece, and she is not here."

"Where is she?"

"A very long way away, I don't know exactly where. She will be back in a few weeks, and if you wish to see her then you can do so quite easily. However, I have a great deal to tell you, and when I have done I doubt if you will need to trouble my niece."

"John Thurlestone looked doubtful. "I believe your niece to be Lady Lucy Howell..."

"I know, I know." Matthew put up his hand to silence him, as Lizzie arrived with a jug of her homemade ginger beer. Matthew picked up the jug but his hand shook so much that Lizzie took it from him and poured the drinks.

"Mr. Thurlestone will be staying overnight," said Matthew. "Can we manage one extra for dinner?"

"Of course," said Lizzie, handing John Thurlestone his glass with a smile.

"That's good. And Lizzie, I'd like you and Tom to stay after dinner tonight, perhaps Beth and Mitch could go to bed a little earlier than usual? I have a long story to tell Mr. Thurlestone, and I'd like you and Tom to be witnesses to our conversation."

Lizzie shot him a guarded look. "Is it anything to do with all that writing you've been doing?" she asked.

"Yes, something to do with that."

Lizzie bent and kissed Matthew's cheek. "You're an old softy with all your writing and secrets and all." She smiled at the constable. "I'll see to your horse now, Mr. Thurlestone," she said. "Tom will be that pleased to find we have company tonight. It's a bit lonely sometimes, shepherding."

She drained her glass and then left them, and they watched her walk down the path to the cabin.

"She seems a good soul," said Thurlestone.

Matthew nodded. "The best." He got up slowly, holding on to the table to steady himself.

"Come on John, I'll show you where you can wash, and you can have Lucy's room tonight."

The constable rose and followed him, thinking he had come upon a queer kettle of fish. *Not often you went to arrest someone for murder and they made you welcome and offered you a bed for the night and a bedtime story too.* Not that he was experienced in these matters. He'd never tried to arrest anyone for murder before.

The warning Greg had given about hostile country ahead was more than justified. The sparse bush gave way to a desert-like plain, and they saw little wildlife apart from the occasional dingo. They pressed on day after day, starting at dawn and continuing until the heat became unbearable. Then they would rest for a few hours, attempting to hide from the blistering noonday sun wherever they could find a scrap of shade for themselves and the animals. Then, as the shadows grew longer they would travel on again, covering as much distance as possible before it became dark. The intense heat sapped Lucy's strength, and she was greatly tempted to drink more water than her daily allowance.

During the day Greg's mood was quiet and determined. He doled out the water ration carefully, and each evening he constructed hammock type beds, made from a piece of canvas held off the floor by four poles, to guard against insects and scorpions. All of this Lucy bore with fortitude and even humour, but her endurance was stretched to the limit by the flies. She was accustomed to flies being a nuisance, but here they sometimes arrived in such numbers that her shirt appeared to be black, and one morning she could stand it no longer. They were coming to the end of their morning trek, and the flies had been worse than usual. Lucy's hat was swathed in a piece of muslin to protect her from bites, and as she climbed thankfully down from her horse into a patch of shade she pulled off the muslin, only to find it heaving with black flies and mites. Overcome with revulsion, she flung it to the ground with a screech.

"Oh, how vile! I can't stand these flies any longer!"

Greg dismounted and led the horses to an area of shade under a black trunked ironbark tree. He came back to where Lucy stood, still trembling visibly. He attempted to lead her to a rock to sit down, but Lucy shook herself away, crying, "No! I daren't sit down, there's probably a snake under the rocks. As soon as I sit still the flies will come again, and I'm thirsty and…Oh God! Greg, this is a terrible place, truly God forsaken…" As she dissolved into tears, Greg put his arms round her and soothed her like a child.

"There, my darling," he murmured, stroking her hair. "I'll make sure there aren't any snakes, and then you can sit down. It will be cooler soon." Having inspected the rocks carefully, he chose one well off the ground and lifted her up onto it, exhorting her to stay there quietly while he "sorted it all out." Picking up the muslin from the ground, he walked about twenty yards away and shook it out thoroughly. Lucy watched him as he picked over the material, trying to get rid of every last insect. Watching his care, she felt a warm glow enfold her. *He had called her "my darling", and was so kind and loving. She wanted him to take her in his arms again, where she felt safe, protected from the horrors of this terrible country, so remote and empty you could hear your own heartbeat.*

Satisfied at last with the muslin, Greg walked over to Lucy's pack and found her hairbrush. He came back, and said quietly, "I should take your hair down and brush it out, then you'll know there are no insects."

Lucy took the hairbrush and looked at him guiltily.

"I'm sorry Greg, for being such a fool."

"You've been wonderful," he smiled. "I must admit the flies are getting me down too." He stood back and watched as Lucy let down her hair and began to brush it. After a moment she met his eyes, and blushed at what she saw there.

Greg looked away, and said quickly, "I'm sorry if I was staring, but you reminded me…"

"Of what?"

"You may not remember, but once before you were sitting on a rock; well, a mushroom actually."

"I don't feel much like a princess at this moment," Lucy said. Then she added dryly, "And to be honest you don't look much like the frog prince either."

Greg laughed, and regarded his sweat stained shirt and dusty trousers with disgust. "We could certainly both do with a bath," he said.

"I wouldn't mind just a wash," Lucy opined hopefully.

Greg shook his head.

"Sorry, perhaps in another three days or so. But in the meantime, you've forgotten something."

"Oh?"

"Yes. The frog prince is magic, and though he can't produce a bath, he does have a surprise."

Lucy watched as he walked over to his pack, returning with a can. "I've been saving this for just such a moment," he said, taking out his penknife. Lucy watched as he carefully opened the can, sawing around the edge with the knife. She could not imagine what it could contain, as they had brought only canned meat with them. At last the can was open, and Greg bent back the lid. He dipped in his penknife, and held out to Lucy a large glistening slice of peach. Lucy felt the saliva run in her mouth at the sight of it. She opened her mouth, afraid that the beautiful juicy segment really was magic, and would disappear as quickly as it had appeared. The next moment she tasted the bliss of the fragrant juicy flesh. Her eyes met Greg's and he held her look as he offered the next piece. She had not realised he was so close, close enough to raise his hand and stroke her cheek. The sensation was electric, and the yearning she saw in the grey eyes sparked the attraction that had always been there from the first, until she felt it flare as hot and bright as the burning sun. Then his mouth was on hers, demanding, exploring, savouring the kisses which she returned to his own, all reason lost.

Suddenly he pushed her away. "Sorry, I didn't mean to do that."

Lucy was unable to reply. She had been totally unprepared for the violent feelings which had swept over her, feelings she had never experienced before. She stared blankly as Greg apologised again.

"It's…it's all right…" she stammered at last.

Greg handed her the can of peaches. "We almost spilt them," he said shakily. "You'd better have the rest."

He strode off towards the horses, and as she watched him it was suddenly clear to Lucy what was meant by the 'loving relationship' which Margot had talked of, and which she knew Lizzie and Tom enjoyed. If Greg had not stopped their lovemaking, she would have wanted it to go on and on.

A few moments later Greg came back to join her in the shade, to wait out the next few hours until they could continue. He looked at her ruefully, and sat down. Lucy handed him what remained of the peaches.

"I left you some," she said. "But I'm afraid I had more than my share."

He speared the last few peach slices and ate them with relish. "Here," he said, "You can have the last drop of juice, but mind you don't cut your mouth."

Lucy tipped up the can and allowed the dregs of juice to flow.

"That was wonderful," she said. "Does the frog prince have any more surprises?"

"I wish he did," said Greg earnestly, and Lucy was not sure whether he yearned for more kisses or peaches. There was an awkward silence for a few moments before he spoke again.

"Look here, Lucy," he began and then began to laugh as he saw Lucy's intent eyes upon him. "Don't look at me like that!"

"Like what?"

"Like a little waif, an urchin, that's what you are." His finger traced a dirty mark on her cheek. "A grubby little urchin," he said softly.

"You're hardly clean yourself," Lucy retorted. "Anyway, what were you going to say?"

"Only that I think we should talk, get things straight between us."

"All right," answered Lucy expectantly. She waited, but Greg took his time, twisting his broad brimmed hat round and round in his fingers before he said quietly, "I'm sorry about before. I suppose it was bound to happen with us being out here alone."

"I didn't mind," Lucy volunteered candidly, and Greg gave a shout of laughter. "No, you didn't, I could tell that!" His eyes held her own in teasing affection before he added, "In fact I think you really enjoyed it."

Lucy felt herself blush and turned away, but Greg took her face in his hands and turned her to face him.

"No Lucy, don't turn away, there must be no false modesty, no secrets between us now. You wanted me, I know it, just as I have wanted you for so long...so long."

Lucy thought she would drown in the mesmerising grey eyes, but Greg released her and moved away a little. He made an obvious attempt to resume his normal tone. "One day, Lucy, one day soon, it will be time for us, but not today. I promised Matthew I would take care of you and I will. I hardly think he would approve of my taking advantage of this situation. When we return from this trip we shall talk together of the future, but all I can do now is make sure we both get home in one piece." He grinned and added, "Preferably with a gold mine."

Lucy felt a sharp disappointment. She wanted him close to her always, to feel safe behind the barrier his presence formed between herself and the pain and hurt of the world. She bit her lip and said, "Nevertheless, a little while ago you said you had wanted me for a long time. Did you mean since Singapore? We hardly knew each other after all."

"I am aware how silly it was." Greg hesitated. "After the night of the Governor's ball I couldn't get you out of my mind, in spite of your engagement." He grinned sheepishly. "Like a lovesick calf!"

Lucy smiled. "Was that why you found the brooch for me?"

"I suppose so. Jarvis told me you were upset at having had to sell, so I determined to get it back. Unfortunately it had already been sold on, and tracking it down became something of a treasure hunt. The man who had bought it for his wife had already left for Kuala Lumpur." Greg chuckled at the memory. "When I caught up with him on the road he could hardly believe I had ridden so far after him just for the brooch. It was about sixty miles," he

242

explained, still smiling.

"But he agreed to sell it back to you?"

"After a while. He said if it was as important as all that I had better have it." Greg tapped his leather boot with a stick. "Yes, quite a treasure hunt. And now I'm on another, and I don't even know what I'm looking for."

Lucy hesitated. "You know Greg, you've never explained to me why this trip is so important to you. Why this urge to follow in your uncle Jack's footsteps? He may never have found anything."

"I know, but it's possible, and that is why the map is so interesting, but you're right, it's more than that. Although I was so young, I can remember Jack. My brother Sam and I adored him, he was always so much fun. Dad wasn't fun, he was always too busy, and so was my mother. She died when my sister Mary was born."

"Yes, I know," Lucy said, fascinated to hear Jarvis's old story retold from a different point of view.

"When Jack went away, we really missed him," Greg continued, "And we never doubted for a moment that he would come back. After my Dad was killed there was some attempt to trace Jack, but I think it was a bit half hearted. Our farm manager was a wonderful man who had been with Dad for many years, and he continued to run everything until Sam was old enough to take over."

Greg smiled ruefully. "You know Lucy, all those years I was growing up, I was still waiting for Uncle Jack to come home. We had seen him off to the goldfields with such excitement, you can't imagine. My parents may have been full of doubt, but Sam and I were quite sure he would soon be back with his pockets full of gold nuggets! Of course we had letters for a while, but after Dad's death we heard nothing, ever again. I felt I had been rejected, and I know Sam felt the same."

"Of course, any child would have reacted that way."

"After a while if I mentioned Jack's name people started to change the subject," Greg continued. "It was understandable. We had a housekeeper, Mrs Jenkins. She was a real mother to us children after Dad died, but she had more bad names for Jack Lamont than you could count. The farm manager was the same. They both saw Jack as a real black sheep, and that was how we were encouraged to think of him. Somehow I never could, I never quite believed them." Greg's tone changed, and Lucy saw that he was still affected by the events which had changed his childhood so profoundly.

"When I finally traced Jarvis Mottram, that day on the boat, it was a revelation. When I heard Jarvis telling you his story…yes…I was there for some time before you realised it…I knew without a shadow of doubt that it was the truth, because everything suddenly made sense. Uncle Jack had returned home to us, he was not the black sheep who had left us without another thought. It also explained why the letters suddenly stopped. Of course, I was upset to find that Jack and Dad had fought, but at last I knew Dad's death was an accident."

Greg began to swipe at a small cloud of flies which had suddenly discovered them. "Pesky things!" he grumbled as he swept them away. "It should be better soon," he reassured Lucy. "When we get through to Shimmer Creek."

"And when we get there?" Lucy asked. "What will you do?"

"Try and trace what Jack Lamont did there," Greg answered simply. "His last letter was sent from Shimmer Creek, so presumably he was digging nearby. All claims had to be registered, and you had to have a licence, so I'm hoping that by looking back in the records I can find out where he was digging, and if we go there, I hope to find the map makes sense."

"Will the authorities allow you to see the records?"

"I should think so, why not? I have brought Jack's birth certificate with me, it was in Dad's desk with the family papers. I have my own as well, and if I can prove who I am and what my interest is, that should be enough." He stopped, and then went on quietly. "I just want to prove that Uncle Jack was not the wastrel he's been made out to be all these years. I know that whatever he was doing out here he was doing it for us. If he was successful I want everyone to know it."

Lucy clapped her hands. "Oh Greg, I do hope we can prove it," she said vehemently. "I hope Jack did find gold, and we can come home loaded with it!"

Lucy's words echoed through Greg's mind later, as he saddled the horses and led them out. "Time to trek again, Lucy."

She got up slowly and came across to her horse, mounting a little painfully. He felt her tiredness, and a well of pity almost choked him. He swung himself into the saddle and they set off again, the horses picking their way carefully through the scrubby terrain. He glanced across at Lucy and despite her tiredness she seemed to feel his look and answered with a dazzling smile. *He would have to watch himself,* Greg thought again. *He must keep his mind on the object of the trip. He was going to look for gold, Jack Lamont's gold*. He reflected sadly that for this venture he had chosen the right partner, Lucy had already proved in Singapore that she was an accomplished gold digger.

Shimmer Creek had never been a hospitable town, but to Greg and Lucy the sight of the sparse wooden buildings with their corrugated tin roofs was the most welcome sight imaginable. About two miles before they reached the settlement they had at last discovered its namesake, the thin straggling line of the creek bed, bone dry at this, its furthest extremity. As they followed the edge of the creek, the horses scented the water ahead and took heart, and a mile further on there was sufficient water for them to drink their fill, and half an hour later they entered the town.

Shimmer Creek had been masquerading under the name of town ever since the large mining extraction companies moved out, having ravaged the remains of the diggings with large dredges, which extracted every last mite of gold from the 'tailings' left by the hand diggers. With the departure of these companies, Shimmer Creek saw the last of the gold fever which had been its reason for existence.

There appeared to be no hotel, no bank and no guest house. There was however a dusty store, and Greg and Lucy entered it gratefully. The store keeper recognised the signs immediately, and had answers ready before they asked the questions.

"Yep, this is Shimmer Creek, no, there ain't no hotel, but you can get a room and a meal at the pub down the street, bloke name of McShane."

Greg thanked him and they went in search of McShane's pub, which proved to be as dingy and unkempt as the rest of the town. The bar was empty, and as they entered they were met with an overpowering smell of stale beer and tobacco. McShane himself was a heavily bearded Irishman with a huge belly, which bulged painfully at the buttons on his beer stained shirt. However, after he had got over his surprise at being introduced to what he called a 'female person', he confirmed he had rooms, but looked askance at Greg's request for two.

"Two?" he said, as if slightly baffled.

"Yes, two," Greg said pleasantly enough, and then because McShane appeared to need an explanation, "We are not married, the lady would like her own room."

The look on McShane's face said everything. His eyes traveled to Lucy with some amusement, and he spoke with a slow burr.

"You just come across the never-never, been out there alone together, probably for weeks, but you want two rooms?"

"Yes!" said Greg fiercely.

McShane put up his hands as if in defeat. "If you say so," he said with a smile. "If you're daft enough to pay for two rooms," he added meaningly.

Greg fished in his money belt. "Have this on account," he said, slamming the money down on the bar. "And make sure the lady's room is clean. We shall want baths, as soon as possible."

McShane gathered up the coins from the bar, and sized up the newcomers afresh, the money had obviously impressed him.

"Can be arranged," he said in his slow drawling tone, "But it's extra, take about an hour to hot the water."

"Then please do it right away," said Greg. He turned to Lucy. "You go to your room and I'll bring your things as soon as I've stabled the horses somewhere."

McShane led Lucy up the narrow stairs, remarking with a trace of sarcasm, "Masterful type isn't he, your friend Mr. Lamont?"

Lucy hid a smile. "Oh, he's just hot and tired," she said. "Like me."

McShane led the way along a stifling passage, and then opened the door to a narrow room. It was little more than a dingy boxroom, but the small bed and the tiny chest of drawers seemed like luxury personified.

"This will do fine Mr. McShane," she said happily. "Does the window open?"

"Sure it does, but you'll be bothered with the flies. Better to keep the blind drawn to keep out the sun."

"Of course." Lucy turned on her dazzling smile. "We should like a meal this evening if you could manage it."

McShane examined her closely, she looked as if she might scrub up a looker.

"Never had a female person stay here before," he said. He made it sound as if the entire female population of the world was to blame for this omission. "Never mind miss, you shall get your dinner. I'll try and rustle up something special, seeing as you are the first ever female person," he explained, as he shut the door behind him.

Lucy sat on the narrow bed and giggled. She felt a bit like Eve, and giggled again. She was going to have a bath.

Greg was bitterly disappointed. It showed in his pensive mood over dinner that evening, a meal which Lucy had hoped might be something of a celebration. McShane pronounced the dinner as "the best ever served in this establishment, seeing as we have a female person with us." Greg had been free with his thanks, but now he stared dejectedly at the tablecloth, twirling his glass round in his fingers, a picture of despondency.

Lucy watched him sadly, her own disappointment stemming from a different reason. Having travelled through some of the most inhospitable country in Australia and arrived in one piece, she felt they had something to celebrate. Free of the clogging dust of the bush at last, they were newly bathed and freshly clad, but Greg seemed hardly to have noticed, and having made a special effort with her hair, Lucy was a little resentful. She tried again, for the third time.

"Greg, please don't be so upset. You knew it was a remote chance that we should find anything."

"I know." Greg put down his glass and smiled briefly. "I'm not so disappointed that Jack found nothing, more that this is not the place on the map. We've come all this way for nothing."

"Are you quite sure?"

"Oh yes. The man at the assay office, or what's left of it, said there is definitely no river north east of here, so Shimmer Creek can't possibly be the town Jack drew on the map."

"Then it's somewhere else, nearby."

"There is nowhere else," Greg said savagely. "It's no use Lucy; we have come to a dead end." He raised his eyes and was immediately contrite.

"I'm sorry, I didn't mean to snap. It's just that you are asking me all the same questions that I asked at the assay office." He pursed his mouth thoughtfully. "I didn't like the answers I got then, and I don't like repeating them to you now."

"Well, humour me while I review things," said Lucy in her determined way. "You found Jack's claim registered at the assay office, so at least we know he was here. From the records it seems he worked a claim for some time with a partner, what did you say his name was?"

"Dan Drummond. The man at the office remembers him, he saw him about three years ago."

"Right. Jack and Dan Drummond worked the claim together, but according to the office they never found anything, or at least nothing was ever brought in for assay. Jack eventually left, and Dan Drummond took over the claim by himself?"

"Yes." Greg seemed a little more willing to talk now he had started. "Apparently Dan Drummond still lives on the claim. Still works it, or at least he was working it a couple of years ago, which is the last anyone heard of him. It's a fairly large area, and apparently he says he's not going to give up until he's dug the whole lot down to the bedrock. They seem to think he's a bit potty."

"He certainly sounds it," Lucy admitted. "He must have been there over twenty years."

"More like thirty I think," Greg responded gloomily. "so you see Lucy, it seems hopeless."

"Well, perhaps not," said Lucy. "Perhaps Jack went on somewhere else from here, after he split up with Dan Drummond, and then found gold."

"It's a possibility, but that's something we'll never know."

"Dan Drummond might," said Lucy quickly. "He might know where Jack was heading when they split up."

Greg regarded her gravely. "He might," he admitted at last, "If he's still alive of course, and if we could find him, and if he was prepared to tell us…even if he knew…that's a lot of 'if's' Lucy."

"Yes it is, but it's worth a try at least, now we've come so far. Where exactly is this claim?"

"About twenty miles east of here. Apparently at one time this whole area was full of miners, hundreds of them, all digging like mad almost anywhere and hoping to make a fortune. A few of them did of course, but only a few. The chap at the assay office told me that was how Shimmer Creek got its name. Rumour had it that all around this creek the ground shimmered with gold, it was just lying around waiting to be picked up or prised out of the ground. People actually believed that and came in their hundreds. When they got here of course they found no such thing, only lots of very hard work in the most awful conditions, and for very little return."

"But was no gold found at all then?" asked Lucy, disappointed.

"Oh yes, there was gold here, but it had to be worked for, and most of the miners only found enough to keep them working for a little longer. Just occasionally someone would find a decent nugget, and the news of the find would be enough to start another rumour, and to keep the miners digging. A vicious circle really."

Greg became thoughtful, "I suppose that's what happened to Jack," he said slowly. "He wanted to find a fortune, so he kept looking, and moving on, thinking that at the next place he tried it would be bound to happen."

"Like us," said Lucy, trying to lighten his mood. "We've come here to look for Jack's claim, and there's no gold here, so we'll look for Dan Drummond, and if we find him he will send us somewhere else."

"Yes," said Greg. "It's probably a wild-goose-chase, but as you say we may as well follow it, we have come so far already." He smiled at her. "Sorry if I've been poor company this evening. I'm tired I suppose, and I'm sure you are. Time for bed I think. Just imagine, a real bed and clean sheets, what luxury! And tomorrow we shall give it all up to go on the trail again, looking for a potty old gold digger, who may not even be alive…that is if you want to come," he added hastily.

"Of course I do," Lucy was eager.

"Wouldn't you rather stay here and wait for me?"

"Certainly not! If this is a wild-goose-chase, I want to be there when we find the goose!"

Yes, the one that lays the golden eggs, Greg thought as they mounted the narrow staircase. He wished Lucy good night and they went to their small separate rooms. Although the bed was comfortable and he revelled in the feel of the sheets, Greg did not find sleep easily. He lay on his back, thinking of Lucy on the other side of the thin dividing wall, and reflected on her eagerness to pursue the gold. *It would be wonderful if Dan Drummond was still alive, and they could find him. Greg would persuade him to talk about Jack, fill in the gaps. He would get to know his uncle all over again. And if by any chance there should be some gold, well, Lucy would like that.*

Their journey east from Shimmer Creek covered the same type of inhospitable bush that they had traversed on their way in. The big difference was that they had plenty of water and stores, and did not plan to be away for long. They had a precise location for the claim, which was part of a much larger diggings which had long since been worked out and abandoned.

As they drew near the site, man's desecration of the earth was plain to see. A huge area had been laid waste, initially by the hundreds of diggers who had poured in with the first rumours that 'color' had been sighted. Long after these men had departed, a colony of Chinese workers had descended. They were painstaking and meticulous, and made a good living from re-working the mullock heaps left by the earlier diggers, who could not be bothered to pan carefully enough to trap every last grain of gold. Then had come the blasting equipment and the big dredges, and these had cleaned out every last mite of value, leaving devastation behind them when they left. Time and nature had begun to reclaim some part of the ravaged land, but the evidence of man's greed was still visible everywhere.

Greg and Lucy dismounted and picked their way through the diggings, leading the horses with care, as the ground levels altered yard by yard.

"What's this?" asked Lucy, turning over a large wooden structure which looked fairly sound.

Greg came over to where she stood and examined it.

"Cradle," he said shortly. "Not the sort of cradle you're imagining," he added, laughing. "Look, I'll show you." He turned the cradle over. "You've heard of panning for gold, washing the dirt in a flat pan so the gold is washed to the bottom?"

"Yes."

"Well this is the same principle, but it enabled more to be washed at a time. You filled it with soil, and then poured in water and rocked it gently, so the gold went to the bottom, that's why it's called a cradle. This is broken..."

"Knows all about it do yer?" The raucous shout came from their right, and they both wheeled in its direction. Nothing was visible at first, and then Lucy discerned the edge of a bush hat just showing from behind a large rock. "Look—" she whispered to Greg.

"I've just spotted him," muttered Greg. "It must be Drummond, who else would be here?" He raised his voice.

"Is that Dan Drummond?"

"Who wants 'im?" was the suspicious reply.

"I do, Mr. Drummond. Could we have a chat?"

"Got nothin' to say." The edge of the hat disappeared behind the rock.

Greg tried again. "Mr. Drummond, I'd like to talk to you. My name is Greg Lamont. I think you knew my uncle many years ago. His name was Jack Lamont."

There was no reply, but after a moment the edge of the hat reappeared, and a gravelly voice said, "Who did you say?"

Greg repeated his name and that of Jack Lamont. Slowly the whole hat emerged from behind the rock, worn by its extraordinary owner.

Dan Drummond was the most severely bent and wizened old man Lucy had ever seen. Small, but seeming even smaller because of his bent back, he made his way towards them like a crusty old crab, his thin bandy legs weaving from side to side as he walked. As he neared them Lucy discerned a pair of alert blue eyes peering from a face almost entirely covered with bristly grey hair. He stopped, and Greg held out his hand.

"Very glad to meet you Mr. Drummond."

The hand was ignored, and the old man stood looking at them, as if unsure of what to do next. Suddenly he burst out explosively, "Dan. Me name's Dan. Me friends call me Sharky. Anybody ever called me mister, brought trouble."

"I haven't brought trouble Dan," said Greg gently. "My name is Greg, and this is Lucy."

The old man did not reply, but he looked at Lucy briefly and quickly away again. Then the gravelly voice rasped, "You said Lamont?"

"Yes, Jack Lamont was my uncle. Did you know him?"

The wary blue eyes darted left and right, he seemed upset.

"Did I know 'im? Did I know 'im? Knew 'im better nor nobody. An' 'e knew me. Oh yes, 'e knew me."

"I'd like to ask you about Jack," said Greg in the same soft tone. "Shall we make camp and have a talk together about the old times?"

The wary eyes flickered again, and then the old man walked away a few paces, beckoning Greg to follow. He put a cupped hand to his mouth and spoke quietly, Greg bending over to catch the old man's words. Greg smiled, shaking the old man's hand and nodding his head. Dan Drummond hurried away with his ungainly rocking motion, and Greg came across to Lucy shaking with laughter.

"I'm afraid it's you Lucy, you're causing all the trouble."

"What do you mean?"

"It appears Dan hasn't seen a lady for more than three years, which was the last time he went in to Shimmer Creek. He's ashamed of the way he looks, and won't talk to us until I've given him a haircut and a shave."

"But that's silly, I don't mind."

"I know, I told him. But he wants to wash and put on his one clean shirt, so let's humour him. We've found him, that's the main thing."

"But where does he live?"

"Here, apparently. He has a humpy over there behind those rocks."

They led their horses to the shade and then made their way to Dan's humpy. It was quite large, constructed securely of long poles bent over and covered with brush and bark. Lucy was surprised how spacious it was inside, with a hammock type bed and a chair. Lucy sat down, and Greg whispered, "Enjoy the rest, I'll go and help Dan make himself presentable."

An hour later they returned, Dan now sporting a well washed and trimmed beard and moustache. He wore a clean flannel shirt many sizes too large for him, as were the dark corduroy trousers secured around his middle with thick string. He looked Lucy in the eye, drew himself up to his full height, almost five feet, and gave a slight bow.

"Much honoured miss. Much honoured," he repeated as he took Lucy's outstretched hand.

As they made a camp fire and began to prepare a meal, Greg told Lucy what she had been aching to hear. As he had cut the old man's hair, Dan had confirmed that he had been Jack Lamont's partner all those years ago. He also knew where Jack worked after he left the diggings. It was, he told Greg, "Only about ten miles away, over a mountain towards the river."

It was a jovial meal. Dan seemed released from his inhibitions now he was clean and presentable, and his stories of good times with Jack Lamont kept them well entertained into the evening.

Greg was fascinated, and could not get enough of the old man's reminiscences. Occasionally Dan would veer wildly off the point, and Greg watched with enjoyment as Greg gently steered the conversation, trying to find out what he really wanted to know. One thing was clear, Dan Drummond and Jack Lamont had been great friends.

"Many's the time we shared our last bit o' damper, or our last bit o' stew," Dan said happily. "We was real mates, yes, real mates…" His gravelly voice tailed off sadly. "I'm sorry to 'ear 'e's dead, but I knew it, some'ow. 'E would'n a left me all that time, not if 'e could a come back. I knew that see? That's why I waited all this time…that's why I waited…" He became visibly upset, and decided to fill up his mug from the billy, spilling coffee in the attempt to cover his embarrassment.

"Is that why you stayed here all this time?" asked Greg. He was both concerned and amazed that this might be the case. Dan shrugged and replied stubbornly, "Might as well didn' I? 'Ad nothin' better to do. Got a good 'umpy, good water an' some diggin's 'ere. Jack said wait 'ere for me, 'e said 'e'd be back in a few months. Said…" he broke off in some distress.

"What did he say Dan?" Greg prompted him gently.

" 'E said, when 'e come back 'e'd 'ave money for blastin' an' suchlike. Said we'd need the big stuff for where 'e was goin' to dig. 'E says to me 'e says: Wait 'ere Dan, an' when I come back we'll be rich, you an' me. 'E never let me down, not never, not Jack Lamont. But 'e didn' come back, an' I waited an' waited, an' did a bit o' diggin'. It was real busy 'ere then. 'Undreds o' men, some of 'em did all right. I didn' like it when the big stuff came in, all them dredgers, it weren't the same. Most o' the old diggers 'ad gone then. All gone now."

"Did Jack say where he was going to dig, where he was going to use the blasting equipment?" Greg asked.

Dan's eyes twinkled. "Yer after it ain't yer?" He began to chuckle, and then continued seriously, "Yer think I ain't thought o' that? All these years I've thought of it. Me and Jack split up because 'e wanted to go further north and try somewhere else, 'e said it was finished 'ere, too many diggers. I didn' want to go, so I stayed 'ere an' 'e went off on 'is own. 'E come back after three months, an' that's when 'e told me to stay 'ere. An' e'd be back with the money. When 'e didn' come back after a year I went up north meself, an' I tried to find what 'e found. But I couldn't. Believe me Greg, I've searched every scrap o' ground between 'ere an' the river, an' I ain't found a brass yazoo…not a brass yazoo." His mind seemed to drift for a moment, and then he leaned forward confidentially.

"Did 'e tell yer? Tell yer where 'e found it? Is that why yer come?" His face changed. "It's took yer long enough!" he complained.

Greg smiled. "No Dan, he didn't tell us anything about it." Lucy thought for a moment Greg was going to mention the map, but he continued, "Jack only said that he'd come home for some money for equipment, so that he could carry on looking. He did mention Shimmer Creek, and the diggings, so that's how we knew where to come."

"Did 'e talk about me? Did 'e tell yer about 'is best mate?" asked Dan eagerly.

Lucy shot a pleading look at Greg, but she need not have worried.

"I was a small boy, so I don't remember much," said Greg carefully. "But I do recall folks at the Lamont station always told me that Jack had found a real good mate out here." The grey eyes met Lucy's but he hesitated for a second only. "The best mate a man could ever wish for, that's what he said," Greg lied evenly.

Dan Drummond said nothing but made an anguished attack on the fire, throwing on new sticks and making a scene of poking the embers. Lucy watched a tear glisten on his furrowed cheek and run into his grizzled beard. Then he said in his grating, explosive manner, "Talked about yer, Jack did. Yes, always on about 'is folks."

It was Greg's turn to hold his breath. The look on his face was agonised.

"Yes. Two boys, that's what 'e talked about, two boys, Sam an' Greg. Told me 'ow 'e used to take yer fishin', when it was 'olidays. 'An 'ow 'e got into trouble with yer Dad for lettin' yer bunk off yer lessons to see a calf bein' born. 'Ad me laughin' fit ter bust 'e did."

Greg got up and walked away towards the horses. Lucy watched as he checked their water bucket, and then she said, "Have you always been a miner Dan?"

The old man growled. "I ain't a miner," he stated flatly. "I'm a digger."

"Oh," said Lucy, duly chastened.

Greg came back to the fire. "Dan means that miners have to tunnel underground," he explained, "Whereas most of the men who came here had to dig, but not so deep."

"That's right," said Dan. "Mind Lucy, sometimes I've dug down as much as fifteen feet or more, dependin'."

"Depending on what?"

"On what yer find o' course. See Lucy, this is what yer does. Yer gets the overburden off, that's all the top stuff, grass and sand and gravel and suchlike, then yer digs down, a prospect 'ole we calls it. When yer get down a few feet yer see what yer can find. If yer finds some gold in the clay an' gravel, even a little bit, yer can be pretty sure there's more lower down see? If yer finds black sand yer know's there's rich pickin's for sure."

"And did you ever find rich pickings?" Lucy asked.

"On'y once, when I was a lad. It was in the first lot, the strikes at Ballarat. My that was a gold fever that was! 'Undreds of folks, 'undreds! I found a nugget an' got two 'undred pound for it. I should 'ave gone away then, an' made meself a good life, but I thought I could do it again see? I did get two others a bit later, about the size of a pea, but mostly it was dust. I seen the 'Welcome Stranger' though, that was found at Black Lead, I'd moved there by then."

"Tell us," said Greg, watching Lucy's mystified face.

"Well the blokes what found it, knew it might be stole, it was that big see? They dug a big 'ole an' buried it, an' put their cook fire on top, till they could get the military to move it to the bank in Ballarat." Dan chuckled. "What a commotion, yer never saw the like! Was over two thousand two 'undred ounces, I forget exactly, but it was over two thousand two 'undred I do know."

"What a find," Lucy enthused. "It must have been worth a fortune. It must have been very exciting, to find rich pickings, a big nugget or something."

She was so enthusiastic that Dan chuckled wildly and cried wheezily, "Got a fine one 'ere Greg, she's the dead finish our Lucy, the dead finish!"

Still chuckling, he settled back and took out a clay pipe, putting it in his

254

mouth and sucking on it noisily.

"Don't suppose yer got any baccy?" he asked Greg hopefully.

"Sorry," said Greg.

"Never mind, I ain't 'ad none fer two years," said Dan. "But I likes me pipe at sundown." He dragged noisily on the empty pipe, and Lucy suppressed a smile as Greg said carefully, "I did remember one thing Jack said about where he was digging. He said there was a town, and a river northeast of it. You mentioned a place like that as well, but I don't think it can be the place Jack meant because there isn't a town anywhere. We thought the town might be Shimmer Creek, but there's no river north east of it."

"There is a town," Dan said immediately.

"Where?"

" 'Ere!" said Dan defiantly.

"Here?…but…"

" 'Course it's 'ere! There ain't much town now, I 'as to agree with yer there, but there was! Gillstown it was called, after Jim Gill what found the first gold. The stream we got 'ere comes from the river Jack told yer about. When Jack was 'ere there was a fine town. Lot of folks, a store an' a office, an' lots o' buildin's an' 'uts an' 'umpies, tents an' waggons…"

"Of course," Greg said softly. "Of course."

"But what happened to it?" asked Lucy. "Where is everything gone?"

"Took it with 'em mostly," said Dan. Took the tents and waggons and suchlike."

"But the buildings, the huts and the humpies?"

"Made good kindlin' " said Dan mischievously. "started to fall down after a few years, so I used 'em all up a bit at a time. I been cookin' me dinner on 'em these twenty years past."

Greg and Lucy had little difficulty in dissuading Dan from accompanying them on their journey north. He said he would not come because of his 'blamed rheumatics' and told them he had not been on a horse for years. He was also quite convinced they would find nothing.

"Looked all over, looked all over I 'ave," he kept repeating. "Not a brass yazoo."

According to Dan the journey was not as simple as Greg had anticipated. To travel north meant crossing a mountain, not particularly high but of difficult terrain. Dan gave them explicit instructions, which entailed going round the mountain, not over it.

"Can't take a lady that way," he reiterated. "Nor the 'orses neither. Go round, that's the way. Mind you Greg, when I was your age I could climb that mountain easy. "It's pretty steep this side, a real 'ard climb, but when yer gets over the top it's not so bad the other side, more gradual like. Yer Uncle Jack, 'e went straight over. Saved a lot o' time, see?"

"How much time?" Greg queried, thinking of the stores and water.

"If yer goes round, it's p'raps fifty mile," said Dan, tugging his beard and loving every minute of being the expert. "If yer goes over, yer can do it in a day or so. Not Lucy though," he added hastily. "Not a lady."

Lucy decided she would reserve her judgment rather than argue with him. They packed stores and water with care, and took the small pack donkey with them, telling Dan to expect them back within two weeks.

As they left Greg commented to Lucy, "We may be back within days, if we are able to go over the mountain rather than round it. It would save a great deal of time."

Within half a mile of leaving Dan they were in scrubby grass country which undulated in a series of shallow gorges, forming the foothills of the mountain ahead. A few hours later they came to the start of a steep ascent, and it was plain that the easy route around the mountain tracked away to the east. Ahead a rocky peninsula high above them travelled across to a deep cleft on the far right, and as there was a small billabong nearby Greg suggested Lucy should make camp while he went up part of the way to take a closer look. He climbed up as far as the start of the stony ridge, and when he returned he was adamant that Lucy should not attempt it.

"I am pretty sure I can make it," he explained, "But I can't take the horses or supplies. You will be quite safe here near the billabong."

"But I want to go with you."

Greg laughed. "Lucy, is there nothing at all you are afraid of?"

Lucy dished out the evening meal and handed Greg an enamel plate. "Of course there is. I'm afraid of lots of things."

"Like what?"

"Perhaps not physical things, I'm not afraid of climbing that mountain. I'm afraid of other things, things you can't control, like when Jarvis died." She sat down and balanced her plate in her lap. "I sometimes think about Matthew. He's not young any longer and I know that one day something will happen to him. That's the thing I'm afraid of, more than anything else."

Greg did not reply. He seemed disconcerted, and Lucy continued:

"Don't you ever feel like that Greg?"

"I can understand your feelings certainly. But everyone is afraid of that kind of thing, and after all it is part of life. But most people are afraid of other things as well, like attempting that mountain."

"Well I'm not," said Lucy with determination. "I'm not certain I can manage it but I'll have a good try."

Greg sighed. "Lucy, we must be realistic. Dan reckons I can make it over the mountain in a day. We are only going to test the map, see if there is anything at the point Jack marked. We can't take the horses and supplies over the mountain, and someone has to stay with them."

"Oh." Lucy felt her hopes dashed, but she tried to hide it and poured out the coffee.

"What do you think?" Greg tried to see her face. "Are you annoyed?"

"Of course not. Anyway you're right. I'll stay with the horses."

Later that night as he lay on the slung canvas they always used now, Greg mused on Lucy's reaction to being left behind. In spite of her attempts to hide it he knew she was bitterly disappointed. She desperately wanted to be 'in at the kill,' to see if there really was gold.

For her part Lucy shed a few tears as she lay twenty yards away, snuggled into her blanket in the canvas hammock. Greg had not wanted her with him, and in spite of understanding his reasons, which were quite valid, she could not bear it. She could not bear him to be away from her, not even for a minute.

The atmosphere was slightly strained as Greg set out next morning. He took with him food and water for only two days, saying he would be back on the third.

"If I'm not," he said, "Wait one more day and then go back to Shimmer Creek as quickly as you can for help. It will mean I've found trouble, but I'm not planning to do that." He smiled and picked up his pack. As well as food, it also contained a spade, an axe, a pan and a lantern. "My gold finding equipment," he bragged, with an even broader smile.

Lucy felt slightly sick as she watched him go. She wanted to run after him, to kiss him goodbye, but it seemed such a thing did not enter his mind. All that morning, as the sun rose and became a fiery ball overhead, she watched as Greg climbed slowly and carefully, his red shirt becoming an ever smaller speck on the mountainside. Twice he stopped and looked back, and she thought she saw him wave, but couldn't be sure. Finally the small red speck disappeared over a ledge near the top, and she could see him no more.

Lucy sat for an hour and watched the ripples in the billabong made by the shadow of the trees against the darkening sky. She felt very alone, but after a while she collected her thoughts, checked the horses and the small pack donkey, and settled down to wait.

Greg clambered to the safety of a flat rock at the top of the stony ridge. The last part of the climb had been difficult, and he was glad to reach the top. He paused for a breather and to take his bearings. From here there was a view which stretched away to distant red and purple mountains, with a desert of scrubby bush between. To his right, the scrub became more dense and green as it bordered the river, which meandered along sluggishly at the base of the mountain. It was hardly a river at the moment, Greg thought, but a small stream edged by wide flat sand on either side, which marked its margins when the rains came.

"I'll bet it's a torrent in the wet," Greg murmured to himself, deciding to rest and eat before continuing down the other side of the mountain. He had taken a swig from his water bottle and was replacing the cork when he saw it. At first he couldn't believe his eyes, and stood up, squinting against the sun, trying to make sure.

Yes, it was certainly there. A big rock formation in the shape of a letter M, with one point of the letter, the right hand one, much higher than the other. From Greg's vantage point on the mountain the rock looked small and compact, but he realised that at ground level it was probably some forty feet high on its lowest side, and perhaps fifty five on the other. Greg's fingers trembled slightly as he fished out Jack Lamont's map and unfolded it carefully. He looked around him, checking the locations. *The town behind him, the big circle...of course, it was to identify the mountain! And away to his right the river, and the big rock like a letter M...*

He sat down again with a jolt, and his first thought was to wish that Lucy was with him to share this moment. *The map did mean something, that at least was certain. After all these years Jack Lamont's dream of a gold strike could become reality.*

Greg tried to calm himself. Finding the location of the map did not necessarily mean there was gold there. It may have just been a place Jack had decided was worth investigating. Nevertheless, Greg ate quickly and was soon on his way down the far side of the mountain, his tiredness forgotten. Dan had been right, as he had been about most things, this side of the mountain was not so difficult. He glanced ahead and frowned. The most straightforward route would bring him out far to the west of the M shaped rock. He decided to head straight for it to save time. The terrain was not too bad even here, although he had to force his way through some thick scrub…

It happened in a second. One moment he was plunging through a thicket of brush and the next he was hurtling down, his feet seeking the ground which was not there. The heavy brush had obscured a deep cleft in the mountainside, and he clutched wildly at the smooth rock as he fell, searing the skin from his hands, and catching at a small bush which sprouted out about half way down. The check in his fall was momentary. He hung suspended from the bush for a few seconds only, before it gave way, its roots torn from the dry stone. As Greg fell a further twenty feet his head caught a rocky outcrop, and when he hit the bottom he was unconscious.

Chapter Twenty

By the third day Lucy was bored and irritable. She was desperate to know what Greg had found, and because of his comments about saving time, had expected him back earlier. When he had not arrived by sunset on the third day she began to worry. His instructions had been to wait one extra day and then return to Shimmer Creek for help, and she knew he would not have extended his trip.

That night Lucy slept little, and at dawn she anxiously scanned the mountainside for the moving speck which would allay her fears. It was not there, and as the fourth day progressed she concocted ever more varied reasons for his delay. The day dragged by in an interminable routine of small chores and periods of staring at the mountainside, and by late afternoon Lucy forced herself to do some hard thinking. She was certain now that something was wrong, that Greg needed help. He had left instructions, but if she obeyed them it would take another three or four days for help to reach him. If she attempted the climb herself she could perhaps reach him in a day, although she would be unable to carry much with her. At least she was well rested and fit, and if Greg was short of food and water surely it was important to get that to him first? The reverse of the argument terrified her. What if she couldn't find him? Or found him but was unable to help? She would have wasted valuable time in the race for assistance from Shimmer Creek, and after all, that was what Greg had told her to do.

At last the answer forced itself into her confused reasoning, and when it came it was simple. She would go up the mountain, following the route she had watched Greg take. She decided this not for any logical reason, but because no power on earth could have made her turn her horse and head back to Shimmer Creek, knowing Greg was in trouble. During early evening she thought carefully about what she would take with her, trying to anticipate what could be useful but knowing she must carry as little as possible. A hideous image kept recurring, as she relived the torment of pulling Jarvis's body on the stretcher Matthew had made, and she was forced to concede that alive or dead, she could never manhandle Greg down the mountain by herself.

Just before she was ready to turn in an idea struck her. *The horses could never keep their footing on the mountain, but what about the donkey? He was a stalwart little animal and was well rested, and if he could make the climb he could very well be useful, especially if...but she did not want to think about that.* She realised she would not be able to ride the donkey or pull him behind her. She would be too busy trying to keep her footing to help him in any way. At length she decided to take the donkey and let him fend for himself. *The worst that could happen would be that she would have to let him free, when he would no doubt return to water and the horses, with whom he seemed to have made friends. The horses were not a problem, as she could leave them on a long tether near the billabong and the rest would do them good.* Having made her decision she went to bed and dozed fitfully till dawn, as myriad conflicting thoughts denied her sleep.

Greg braced his back hard against the rock, knowing that if he fell now he could easily break a leg. His feet were firmly planted on the opposite wall of the crevasse, as if he was sitting thirty feet up in mid air. He had found his way along the floor of the crevasse to its narrowest point, so narrow that he had hoped to climb up with his back braced on one side and his feet on the other, inching his way up and trying desperately to sustain himself in mid air by the tension between his back and legs. This was the second time he had tried it, and he could already see that the attempt was doomed to the same failure as the first. The problem was that the crevasse widened here to the point where he could no longer keep himself braced. He had altered the position of his second attempt slightly, to try to take advantage of a tree, which against all reason was growing out of the rock about twenty feet from the top. He could just reach the base of the tree, but could now see that it rapidly became very slender, and would never support his weight if he tried to climb to the surface. His eyes raked the walls of his prison, searching for handholds, footholds, anything to sustain what must be his last effort to escape, but the seismic apocalypse which had created the mountain in the dawn of time had split the rock as cleanly as a cracked plate, and the fissure had cooled to a smooth glassy surface, only lightly eroded by the centuries of wind and weather. There was no time left. The pressure on Greg's back and legs was excruciating, and he knew if he did not start down again he would surely fall.

Slowly and carefully he worked his way downwards, moving his feet a little, and then his back, aware of the rock scraping the skin from his bones through his shirt, already in shreds from his first attempt. Ten feet from the bottom, gasping with exertion, he looked briefly down, wanting desperately to jump the last bit, but knowing he could be badly injured if he did. Having chosen the narrowest point for his climb, there was no clear spot below him to land, just a ragged jumble of rock which would have broken an ankle, if not a leg. His breath came in jagged, shuddering gasps as he lowered himself gradually the last few feet and found the bottom.

Greg perched for a few moments recovering his breath, and then carefully made his way along the crevasse floor to the flat area which had been his home for the past three days. All he wanted was to stretch out, to lie flat and relieve the strain the climb had put on his back. He ached in every limb, and knew he did not have the strength to attempt another climb. So that was it, nothing to do but wait, and hope that Lucy could get help to him in time. He wondered for the hundredth time how long a man could survive without water. He recalled tales of the outback told to him by bushmen who loved to talk of the hardships they had endured in the old days. *Of course it depended on the conditions. At least his prison was shady and cool, but the last attempt to climb out had probably robbed him of much of his remaining body fluid. Had he been wrong to attempt it? He felt there was not a drop of moisture left in him, but he had felt that for two days now.* He ran his leathery tongue over his cracked lips and thought of Lucy, who of course imagined he had water for several days. His mind returned to his water bottle, lying with his pack at the top of the crevasse where he had dropped it as he fell, and he wondered again how long it would take Lucy to get to Shimmer Creek and back again. By that time he would be unable to shout, and they might not find him.

About half way up the mountain Lucy stopped to rest. She had attained a grassy slope where there was room to sit comfortably, and she took advantage of it, gently guiding the donkey to an area to the right of her, where he immediately began to graze at the end of his long tether. *So far so good,* she thought, *the donkey was doing much better than she expected.* Lucy had loaded him lightly but securely with blankets, ropes and stores, attempting to balance his load to make his task easier. In her own pack she had only some food and water wrapped in her blanket, in case she and the donkey became separated. She carried this pack slung across her back, together with the old shotgun, which Matthew had insisted she take with her on the trip, and which she now realised could be used to attract Greg's attention. Looking up, she could see this was where the real climb began. She searched the rocky outcrop ahead, *it was daunting certainly, but there were some handholds, it was a question of a bit at a time. Greg had done it, she had watched him, and she could do the same, the secret was not to become too tired.*

Having decided to rest for at least a quarter of an hour, Lucy took a swig from her water bottle. Every few minutes her eyes raked the mountainside, expecting to see the red speck she sought, but always finding only disappointment.

There was a point ahead where the rockface was sheer for about thirty feet, and Lucy had never climbed anything like it before. Even as she stood at the bottom looking up, she knew it could be done, she could see the little ledges and crevices in the surface which would assist her, and it was a matter of whether she had the nerve. Lucy started the climb, and once started there was no going back. She made her way up carefully, a foot at a time, not daring to look down. A few minutes later she had no thought in her mind but survival. It was not that it was difficult to find a foothold, but she was aware that one slip would spell disaster.

About half way up she was seized by sheer terror, she was in a precarious position and could not find her next handhold. Her heart thumped wildly and she laid her face flat on the rock, clinging on with fright and unable to move. Then an extraordinary thing happened. Quite clearly she heard Jarvis's voice, and in his reassuring Devon drawl he said "Look alive Miss Lucy, you'll have it dinner time." For some reason it seemed quite natural that Jarvis should be there, and Lucy giggled weakly and felt again for a handhold. By stretching as far as possible her fingers found a crevice to her right, and she continued on the climb, concentrating minutely on the task in hand.

When Lucy reached the top she sat down and wept a little. *Thank God she would never have to do such a thing again.* Her tears were a mixture of relief and reaction to her strange experience. *Had Jarvis really spoken to her? Or had she imagined it just when she needed him?* Looking ahead she saw she had covered the worst part of the climb, the route to the top looked relatively easy and was only about fifteen feet. Her immediate problem was the donkey. He certainly could not climb the route she had just taken, and there was no other way. She called to him and the donkey looked up. He gazed at her impassively as if to ask what she expected him to do, and then continued to graze. Lucy realised she would have to leave him there, and continued on to the top.

Reaching the top of the mountain was a bitter disappointment. She had been sure she would be able to see Greg, but there was nothing. A beautiful view, but no sign of him, not a thing to show he had ever been here, that he even existed. Her eyes raced along the edge of the sluggish river below hoping he was there, staying near water until help came, but there was nothing. Suddenly she felt terribly alone, and began to doubt her decision to follow him. It occurred to her that he could be injured, perhaps not badly, but enough to stop him attempting the climb back over the mountain. *Perhaps he had started back along the easy route?* She could only see part of the trail, as most of it was obscured by dense brush and a rocky promontory, *perhaps he was down there out of sight of her, making his way back to camp.*

Lucy sat down to eat while she thought of what to do next. Had she known it, she was sitting in exactly the same spot Greg had chosen a few days before. She ate some food and drank a little water, watching the scene below her all the time. She took the shotgun and loosed off a shot, wanting to see a movement somewhere in response, but there was nothing.

Then she heard it, or thought she did. *Was it her imagination?* She loosed off another shot, and unmistakeably she heard Greg's voice, so faintly she could hardly hear it, but she was sure it called "Lucy". She shouted out in joy, calling his name again and again, but then had to stop and listen, straining her ears to ascertain where the voice came from. She cursed the tinkling sound of the bellbirds, which she had always loved, but then she heard it again, over to her right and further down the mountain. She dashed forward, stopping now and then to shout, "Greg, shout again, I can't see you."

He was saying something, but it was inaudible. Where on earth was he? She stood still and shouted again, "Greg...where are you?" as loudly as she could, and at last made out the faint response.

"Don't move Lucy...crevasse...I fell...be careful Lucy...be careful."

So that was it! "Right Greg, I'll be careful," she answered, hoping he could hear, and made her way slowly forward in the direction of his voice.

She had been almost on top of it. The mouth of the crevasse was entirely obscured by thick brush which grew out over it, and she saw Greg's pack before she saw the opening, and as she retrieved it the water bottle fell out.

She tore at the brush to remove enough to see what she was doing, and then lay down flat to peer down into the crevasse. Greg was there, craning up to look at her, and at least he was standing. No wonder she couldn't hear him shouting, he must be about fifty feet down. Lucy wasted no words.

"Greg, I'll throw down your water bottle, try to catch it."

He didn't catch it but broke its fall, and Lucy saw him uncork it and swallow again and again.

"Don't drink too much at once," she shouted. "We don't have much."

Greg sat down and she saw him put his head in his hands. Then he looked up and shouted. "It's fortunate you didn't follow instructions."

Lucy laughed; her mood was almost frivolous with relief. She leaned over the edge and shouted "Are you all right?"

"Only cuts and bruises," Greg returned, "But very hungry."

Lucy took the food from her pack and wrapped it in her neck scarf, then threw it down. "Last night's damper and cold rabbit," she shouted, and Greg replied, "Wonderful," and began to eat.

Slowly the euphoria evaporated as Lucy began to comprehend just how difficult it would be to get Greg out. Greg explained his thinking, and showed Lucy where he had tried to climb up. "I can climb as far as that tree," he said, "But it won't stand my weight." He sighed, and added: "I don't suppose you thought to bring the rope."

Lucy sank down on the ground at the top of the crevasse. She cursed her stupidity in not wrapping the rope around herself before she set off to climb that steep bluff. *The rope was there, packed carefully on the donkey's back, at the bottom of the bluff.* She knew the answer, she would have to go down and fetch it. A low moan escaped her. *To get down the bluff would be a nightmare, then she would have to climb back up again, and she could not do it. There must be an alternative.* Her mind roved anxiously over the options. She could go down to the river and bring back all the water she could carry to leave with Greg, and then walk round the long trail back to the horses, and then fetch help from Shimmer Creek. She knew it would not work even as she considered it. *She only had the two water bottles as containers, and she would need some water herself to walk the fifty miles or so of the trail. But she could not do that climb again, she would fall and then where would they be? Even if she managed to get back with the rope, she might not be strong enough to pull Greg up those last twenty feet, and what if she let him fall?*

Lucy found her cheeks were wet with tears. She rubbed them away quickly and went back to the top of the crevasse.

"I'm not quite as disorganised as you think," she shouted to Greg. "I did bring the rope but it's a little way back, with the donkey."

"The donkey?" Greg said incredulously. "How..."

"Don't worry, I'm going to fetch the rope, I'll be an hour or so."

Then she was gone, and Greg was left to wonder what she was doing. *Surely the donkey couldn't have got up the mountain, especially that part where...*Suddenly Greg understood exactly where the donkey was and what

265

Lucy was intending to do. *She must not! She would kill herself!* Greg shouted repeatedly, but there was no reply. Trembling with frustration he settled to wait, marvelling at the courage of this woman he had found, and pondering on the contradictions in her nature.

After a few minutes he took a slim wallet from his shirt pocket and extracted the cutting from the *Straits Times* which he had kept so carefully. He read again the barely veiled references to the young girl from England who had set her cap at one of the richest men in Singapore, and had married him within weeks. He thought of Lela, who had told him of a kind and generous mistress who hated the man she married, and of Margot, who had told him that no matter what anyone said she would never believe the wee bairn had killed her husband. Margot had been right of course, but when he had asked her about it, Lucy had admitted that the story in the *Straits Times* was true, that she had married Gilbert for his money. *What kind of girl would do that?* Greg could not forget his conversation with Liam, who had explained; "We got no money here, and then Sir Gilbert he comes calling with plenty money."

"But did Miss Lucy love Sir Gilbert?" Greg had asked.

Liam had grinned happily. "Oh no, Miss Lucy say no marry at first. I hear it even if I'm not listening. Then Mr. James he tell her Sir Gilbert got plenty money, and she say yes all right, after she make a bit of fuss of course. Miss Lucy get plenty money from Sir Gilbert to fix Winchester Station, she very clever no doubt."

Greg sat and thought on these things, and on the strange nature of the woman he loved and knew he would always love. Since he had come to know her better she had not acted like a person driven by love of money. He thought of her concern for Jarvis and Matthew, and how she had taken in the destitute Tom and Lizzie Nicholls and their children; that must certainly have been a financial sacrifice. Then again there was that desperate ride to take her woolclip to the railhead, he could not think of another woman who would have dared to do that, except perhaps Jennie Moore. *Did Lucy do it as a matter of principle, to stand up to Carmody, or was it simply for the extra money she would clear? When she had talked to Dan about finding gold she had been as excited as a child. And now, when she could have headed back to Shimmer Creek she had risked her life to save him, and was about to do it again. It was a conundrum, and Greg had the feeling he would never really have the answer, but of one thing he was certain. If he did get out of this thing alive, he would never let Lucy out of his sight again.*

What was it Matthew had said to him? *"The only moments which really matter in life are the moments of love. "* Greg resolved that he and Lucy would have their moments of love in plenty. *He would marry her and take her to the Lamont station. Or perhaps she would prefer to stay at Kelly's place. Wherever it was, he would see that she stayed there, and he would never let her travel alone again, in this inhospitable country where you could die of thirst and the ground opened up under your feet. Why had he behaved like an idiot when she had kissed him so passionately? If he didn't get out of this hole he might never have the chance to kiss her again, might never have his arms around her...*His mind was running riot, and he cursed himself again for having made that promise to Matthew.

Lucy had almost reached the bottom of the bluff. The toes of her shoes were almost scraped away by the constant tentative search for footholds on the way down. She had tried to cheer herself by holding on to the thought that every foot further down was a foot less to fall. As she reached the small plateau with relief, the donkey gazed at her with unblinking eyes, indifferent to her problems, or indeed her presence. Lucy removed the ropes and he turned away and began to graze at the sparse vegetation. She released his tether, and after a short rest wound the rope around herself bandolier style.

"I can do it," she muttered to herself. "I've done it already, so I know I can do it." The difference was that she was now so desperately tired. Slowly and carefully she began to climb.

It had been years since William Graham had run really fast, and by the time he had gone a hundred yards he was out of breath. He stopped for a moment, gasping, and leaned against a shop doorway to catch his breath. As he stood there, a lady acquaintance approached the shop, and William, despite his discomfiture, raised his hat politely. The woman stared at him and then smiled.

"Mr. Graham, it is you after all! I thought my eyes were deceiving me, you were running were you not? Is something wrong?"

William laughed. He was still breathing heavily but it was a joyous laugh, and he almost shouted, "Wrong? Of course there's nothing wrong Mrs. Ritchie. On the contrary, everything is as right as can be."

He pushed open the heavy glass door to the shop and bowed slightly. Mrs Ritchie swept past him, wondering if the bank manager could be drunk at this time in the morning. She watched as he ran off again in the direction of the bank. "In this heat too," she murmured, "He'll give himself a heart attack."

When William reached his office he sent immediately for the assistant manager. He was still panting when the man arrived.

"Mr. Graham, is there something wrong?"

William laughed. "Why does everyone think something is wrong just because I take a little exercise? No, nothing is wrong, but I am going home right away, urgent personal business. I shall be back in a couple of hours, hold the fort for me will you?"

"Of course Mr. Graham. I'll have your carriage brought round."

By the time he arrived home, William had recovered his breath. He let himself in at the front door and had just removed his hat when Lela appeared.

"Mr. Graham! I thought I heard something...is..."

"If you ask me if something is wrong I'll brain you!" William retorted. "Where is Margot?"

"Still upstairs, I think she is dressing to go out."

"Go and ask her to come down to the study right away, and you are to come as well."

Lela was mystified. "But what...?"

"Right away Lela!" William commanded sternly, but Lela could see the smile behind his words, and as she mounted the stairs she looked back at him. *He was going into the kitchen, and he was never home at this time of day. Something was up for sure.*

A couple of minutes later Margot, still in her dressing gown, entered the study followed closely by Lela.

"William, what is it?" she asked a little anxiously. William turned from the desk and handed her a glass. "For you my dear, champagne." Margot took the glass in surprise, and William handed a second glass to Lela. "One for you too Lela, and one for me!"

Margot was nonplussed. "At this time in the morning?" Her face suddenly changed. "William! It's not...?"

"Yes my dearest," he whispered softly. "Yes it is, it's Lucy's bottle!"

Margot could not speak. She sat down heavily and stared at William, the glass of champagne trembling in her hand.

"Lucy's bottle?" Lela queried. "You mean you've heard something from Lady Howell?" ·

"Not from Lady Howell personally, but we have news at last." William explained. He took his wife's hand. "It's good news my dear. Lucy is alive and well in Australia."

"Australia?" Margot and Lela chorused together.

"Yes, she's been there all this time. But there is more good news, she has been completely cleared of Sir Gilbert's death!"

Tears were running down Margot's face. "Tell me," she pleaded eagerly.

"When I got to the bank this morning there was a message asking me to go to see the Police Commissioner on a matter of business. I did not connect it with Lucy at all, especially after all this time. The Commissioner told me he had received a long telegraph message from the police in Australia. Apparently someone has confessed to shooting Sir Gilbert, and Lucy is completely exonerated."

"That's wonderful, oh! wonderful!"

Margot and Lela kissed each other, and then William kissed them both, and they raised their glasses and drank a toast to Lucy.

"But why has it taken all this time?" Margot asked, wiping her eyes. "Why couldn't this person have confessed before?"

"Yes," Lela agreed, "and who is it anyway? Who did kill Sir Gilbert?"

"I don't know," William responded. "But the Commissioner said a full report is on the way."

"Why did the Commissioner send for you?" Margot asked.

"I know that at least," William answered. "Apparently the last sentence of the telegraph message read "Inform William Graham letter follows.""

"A letter!" Margot cried. "A letter from Lucy! Oh, I can hardly wait!"

William fetched the champagne bottle and as he refilled her glass Lela asked; "What did you mean when you called this Lucy's bottle?"

William smiled. "Do you remember that evening my dear?" he said as he replenished Margot's glass.

"Oh yes, so well," she responded happily. "It was a few months after the tragedy, Lela; and I was feeling very depressed. I told William I did not believe we should ever hear of Lucy again. He tried to reassure me, and said that sooner or later all would be resolved. He went to the cellar and brought up a bottle of champagne, and said it was to be kept in the ice box, ready for the day we had news of Lucy. I have often looked at it, wondering if it would ever be opened, and now…" she looked up happily, "here we are, drinking it!"

They clinked glasses again, and Lela said, "May I go over to Winchester Station to tell Liam?"

"But of course," said Margot, "we'll tell everybody!"

"Yes," William agreed, and then added grimly; "And the moment we know all the details I shall make sure the newspapers give as much space to clearing Lucy as they did five years ago to damning her!"

The sun was unbearably hot. Beads of sweat stood out on Lucy's brow as she rested herself, trying to press her body close against the rock, in an attempt to relieve the pressure on her legs. She realised now that it had been a mistake to wear the rope around her body. It was not so much the weight of it as the thickness of the coil. It got in the way and prevented her from keeping her body close to the rockface, but there was nothing she could do about it now. She glanced upwards, and was slightly heartened to see how far she had come already. The hardest part was still to come of course, and she scanned the smooth rock face ahead with care. It was about thirty feet to the top and there were few crevices and footholds. This was where she had heard Jarvis's voice but this time she heard nothing, and began to climb again.

Finding the crevices was not after all her major problem. As her sore and bleeding fingers searched painfully for a handhold, memory came to her rescue and she found her way more easily than before. The problem was that her strength was giving out. When her scrabbling toes had eventually found their next foothold, her strength seemed insufficient to push her body upwards, as her legs refused to take the strain. The encumbrance of the rope made it worse, forcing her body away from the rockface and increasing the strain on her arms and legs. Although her position was precarious, she dared not stop, as if she relaxed for even a second her limbs began to tremble, threatening to collapse and send her hurtling backwards. Gasping with exertion, she inched her way upwards, only dimly aware of what she was doing, knowing only that she had to find the next handhold, and then the next foothold. She had a moment of pure terror when her foot slipped suddenly, but she found a new foothold and struggled to the next position, willing on her aching limbs a foot at a time. Suddenly her fingers were groping for air, and she realised with a gasp of relief that she had reached the top. Her strength was now gone however, her searching fingers were unable to find a handhold on the smooth grass, and her legs simply refused to push her up the last few feet. After a few moments she managed to manoeuvre herself to a position where her feet were firm and one hand was secure, and with some difficulty she contrived to take off the coil of rope and push it up on to the firm ground above her. As the dragging weight was released from her body she felt a great deliverance, and with a last desperate struggle she hauled herself to safety and lay there gasping, crying with relief and exhaustion.

It was almost an hour later that Greg heard his name called softly, and he jumped up quickly, startled from his black reverie.

"Lucy, thank God! Are you all right?"

"Yes, I'm fine, and my name is Catherine. Remember?"

"Whatever you say. Did you have to climb down for the rope? Did you get it?"

"Yes of course. It's here. Greg, I'm sorry, but I won't be able to take the strain. There isn't a tree, or anything I can secure the rope to. I'm just a bit tired, so it will be safer to leave it until tomorrow. After a night's sleep we shall both make a better job of it."

Greg was stricken. *How could he have been so thoughtless? He had spent hours imagining what she must be going through, and then in his joy at her return was thinking of her as fresh as a daisy.* He chose his words carefully.

"You're quite right of course, being shut in down here has made me lose my judgement. Are you injured at all?"

"No, not injured. Just rather tired."

"Tomorrow it is then, or when you feel right about it."

"Good, I think that will be best. I'll get some supper and then make coffee." She left the top of the crevasse and Greg was left to his thoughts for half an hour. He was deeply worried. He realised that with Lucy's gift for understatement she was probably completely exhausted, and tomorrow he had to trust his life to her strength. He racked his brain for an alternative solution but found none. When Lucy returned he made his tone deliberately light.

"Thank you," he called as the billycan swayed down towards him at the end of the rope. He untied it in a moment. "Good heavens, hot soup! What a feast!"

"There's no damper I'm afraid, no flour. And the soup is the last tin. I'll send down a pack of biscuits, I brought plenty of them."

The biscuits duly arrived and Greg suggested that Lucy leave the rope in place. "It makes me feel I have a lifeline," he explained. "Now have your supper and make sure you make up a good fire for the night. Then sleep well my darling, this is the last night we shall be apart."

"Yes. Good night, Greg."

"Good night, Lucy."

If Greg had been able to see her crawl away from the top of the opening his misgivings about his ultimate rescue would have become a certainty. Lucy's considerable strength had completely deserted her, and she ached in every limb. Her legs were so weak it was easier not to try to stand, so she made her way back to the fire on her hands and knees. A mouthful of hot coffee revived her spirits a little, and she swallowed some soup and a few biscuits.

"Got to keep my strength up," she muttered to herself, and looked around her carefully. Greg had said to make a good fire, but it had been so difficult to make one at all. There was plenty of wood, but the sparse clump of trees was about a hundred yards away. *Too far, much too far.* She finished the coffee and then wrapped the blanket around herself and snuggled down, sucking her raw finger ends in an attempt to ease the pain. But as her fevered brain and aching limbs eased into heavy sleep she was quite happy. *Greg had called her "my darling."*

Greg's assertion that they would not be apart the following night proved to be wishful thinking. When Lucy awoke to the screaming of the butcher birds, she was so stiff she could hardly move. However, sleep had worked its healing magic, and after she had breakfast she felt much better, although hardly in any condition to haul Greg to safety. To her relief the decision was taken from her. As she let down the billycan Greg made it clear he did not expect to be rescued that day.

"I've been thinking about it," he called up, "we should leave it until tomorrow."

A huge wave of relief swept over Lucy, but she answered calmly, "If you like. Why do you want to delay it?"

"We can't allow it to go wrong, so we must plan as well as possible, and another day with food and water will help me regain my strength. I didn't tell you, but I exhausted myself trying to climb out before you found me. I expect you could do with more rest too, after your climb."

"Yes, I think it would help," Lucy admitted, overjoyed that she had a brief respite before another ordeal.

"Right, that's settled then. Spend the day resting as much as you can. Mind you, if you see a rabbit, I wouldn't mind a change from these biscuits." He grinned up at her. "Later today we'll talk about it, but in the meantime look around and see if there is a tree close enough for you to attach the rope."

"There isn't," Lucy answered immediately. "I've already looked, the nearest tree is over a hundred yards away."

"A rock then?"

Lucy glanced around. "It's possible."

"No hurry Lucy, we have all day, and tomorrow too if we need it."

"Right." Lucy went back to the camp fire relieved and hopeful, and made more coffee.

Greg was bitterly disappointed. His suggestion that the rescue be delayed had been a tentative inquiry, and he knew that Lucy's normal reaction would have been an immediate insistence on getting him out without delay. Her quiet acceptance of the delay confirmed his worst fears, it was plain she was still exhausted from the climb. His frustration was intense, not so much because of his privations but his helplessness. He finished the biscuits and began his routine of exercises, determined that his own strength should take as much of the strain as possible when the time came, whenever that proved to be.

The rope dangled invitingly, tempting Greg to catch at it, to relieve the pressure on his back and legs. He resisted the temptation, inching his way slowly up the narrow chimney of the crevasse, his back already grazed and sore from the rough pressure of the rock. He was determined to delay his reliance on the rope until the last possible moment, at this stage it would be enough to get it around his body. As he came level with the rope he braced his back and feet hard against the rock and called "Lucy, I'm tying myself on now!"

"Yes." Lucy's head was framed against the light above him as she watched him knot the rope around his chest, and once again begin his slow inching progress. After a few feet he gasped, "I'm almost at the tree...I'm going to climb it as far as I can."

"No! It won't hold you Greg!"

"It will for perhaps ten feet...that's ten feet you won't have to haul me." Greg eased his way a little further. "When it won't hold me, you'll have to take the strain. Are you ready?"

"Yes."

"Are your feet well braced? We don't want you down here as well." As he spoke Greg could see Lucy's features more clearly, and he caught the look of determination he had seen so often.

"Yes, and the rope is secured around me and then around the rock."

"One last thing then. If it goes wrong and you can't hold me, you must let me go. The worst that can happen is that I'll be left suspended, and I can always climb down again somehow. What mustn't happen is that we both end up down here."

"Understood." Lucy replied quickly, not daring to think of it.

"Right. Here goes then."

As Greg reached for the base of the tree, his feet, braced against the opposite wall of the crevasse, were unable to maintain the tension, and in seconds he was suspended over the crevasse, both hands grasped firmly around the slim trunk of the tree. Moving quickly hand over hand his feet found a foothold and he pushed upwards, wrapping his legs around the tree and working his way up quickly, like a sailor climbing a rope. As he climbed the slender trunk began to bend and he stopped momentarily.

"Now Lucy! Have the rope taut and try to take my weight. Now!"

As the tree finally gave way Greg flung himself at the rockface, attempting to gain a hand or foothold, but he slithered several feet before he was jolted to a stop by the rope, which cut into his flesh like a knife. Lucy, her feet braced against a huge rock and leaning back against the rope, felt she had been cut in two. The strain of taking Greg's weight was so sudden it flung her against the rock and she lay there, spread- eagled, bound tightly by the dreadful cutting rope. She held the weight for only about ten seconds, but it seemed like an eternity. Then, as Greg found a foothold on the rockface and took his weight on his legs, the strain eased.

"I'm starting to climb again Lucy," she heard him shout. "Try to keep the rope taut as I come up, and be ready to take the strain in case I slip."

Lucy eased in the rope, trying to keep the tension steady, knowing that every foot of rope through her hands meant Greg was a foot nearer the top. Five minutes later it was still going well, if slowly, and she was beginning to anticipate Greg's appearance at the top of the crevasse, when the rope became taut again. Greg had stopped climbing.

"Lucy, just a moment. I can't find a handhold." His voice sounded reassuringly near.

"How far are you from the top?" Lucy called, trying to keep the tension on the rope without restricting Greg's freedom of movement.

"About fifteen feet or so, we're nearly there, but the last bit is like glass. Keep the tension."

Lucy waited for what seemed an age before Greg's voice came again.

"I'm sorry Lucy, but it's no go. There isn't a handhold or a foothold at all. I can't even move sideways, and if I could it wouldn't help. It's a different kind of strata, smooth, not a crack in it."

Lucy groaned inwardly. "You mean I'll have to pull you up?"

"If you can. If you can't, I'll have to go down again. What do you think? If you can't do it, better to say so now."

"Of course I can do it," Lucy replied brightly.

No I can't, she thought, *I'm not strong enough. It will jerk like it did before and I won't be able to hold him and we'll both hurtle down to the bottom.* She took a deep breath.

"Greg, I think I can manage it if there isn't a sudden jerk. If I can gradually take the strain and pull steadily that's our best chance. Do you think you can keep as still as possible?"

"Yes. I'll keep flat and try to help with my hands and feet. Tell me when you're ready."

Lucy braced her feet against the rock in front of her and checked the rope. The piece of her shirt she had wound around her hands for protection was already in tatters, and she adjusted it carefully, trying to make sure her grip on the rope would not slip. "Ready," she called, and began to pull steadily.

Nothing happened. An immoveable dead weight was at the end of the rope and it did not move an inch. Lucy pushed her feet against the rock in front of her and tried harder, and pulled in an inch of rope. The next few minutes were a torment of concentrated exertion. Lucy's mind alternated between hope and black despair, as there was some sudden movement followed by periods when the rope refused to move an inch. She was managing to hold Greg's weight, but had moved him only a couple of feet, and she knew she could not hold him much longer. Her arms felt as if they would be torn from their sockets, and her fingers seemed unable to keep a firm grip on the rope. Dimly she recognised this as the major problem, and realised that unless she could make use of her whole body weight she would never pull Greg to safety.

Knowing her strength was giving out, she made a desperate heave and allowed her feet to leave the safety of the rock, digging in her heels in an attempt to move slowly backwards. In the recesses of her mind was a long lost vision of a tug-of-war she had seen at a village fete in England, and she now attempted something of the kind, leaning far back on her heels and trying to force her feet slowly backwards, a step at a time.

An urgent rhythm imposed itself, and she gasped out "ONE, two, three...ONE, two, three," digging in her heels further back on every count of ONE.

It was working. She had already moved a few feet backwards...she had to keep it up...keep it up...ONE, two, three...ONE, two, three...ONE, two, three...Not moving now...ONE, two, three...One, two, three...Got to stop...ONE, two, three...

Suddenly she was lying on her back, thoroughly winded by the force with which she hit the ground. Gasping for breath she looked up in desperation, and saw Greg bounding towards her. Then the grey eyes enveloped her in a look of love so deep that it seemed her heart stopped, before she found the incomparable sanctuary of his arms.

It was three days before Lucy was fit enough to enable them to resume their journey. Each morning Greg walked down the grassy slopes of the mountainside to the river below, and brought back their water supply. As they had with them only two water bottles, the billycan and one other container, there was never really enough, but they managed. The daily journey took Greg about an hour, and he was constantly visible from Lucy's vantage point near the top of the mountain. She would sit near the fire and keep him in sight as he made his way down, waving when he turned to look back, and watching as he filled the water bottles at a small spring which fed a tributary running down to the river. Each day she watched as he undressed and swam in the river, refreshing himself before the long climb back to camp, and she longed to be fit enough to accompany him. In the afternoon Greg hunted, and although he found nothing other than rabbit, at least they had meat for dinner each evening, although the supplies they had brought with them were almost gone.

Greg had been astonished and upset when he discovered the extent of Lucy's problems. He had tended her bruises and cuts with great care, bathing her raw fingers and going to great lengths to make her as comfortable as possible. He collected dry brushwood and made Lucy a day couch in the shade where she could rest in relative comfort. At these times Lucy had plenty of time to reflect, and she contemplated on the nature of this man, the man she now knew she loved with all her heart, who had helped her escape from the problems of her past, and had led her through this strange and hazardous land. She was aware that during the terrible ordeal of Greg's rescue she had held his life in her hands, and that, mercifully, she had been equal to the task, and this thought comforted and restored her.

She knew beyond a shadow of doubt that she was loved in return, and with a passion as deep as her own. At the moment of Greg's escape from the crevasse, she had been aware of the intensity of the love smouldering in the grey eyes, and this had since been matched by a hundred small acts of kindness. She had wondered at his care for her on the long journey to Shimmer Creek, but she now understood its source, a much deeper and genuine affection. It was as if the underlying attraction which had always been there between them had suddenly become of age. It was acknowledged now, not openly or in words, but by the trust and care which each showed for the other, a tacit understanding that from now on their destinies were inextricably entwined.

Lucy watched Greg now, as he bent down near the river's edge, but he was too far away for her to make out what he was doing. She poured the last of their current water supply into the billycan and put it on the fire, so that coffee would be ready when Greg returned. When she looked back again, Greg was already on his way back, and she watched his slow progress until he arrived, twenty minutes later.

"All right?" He strode across to the fire. "I do enjoy this coffee when I get back but it's something of an indulgence. We must be getting short."

Lucy smiled. "We have enough for three more days." She waited until Greg was settled with his coffee and then said happily, "you'll be glad to know I am fit enough to travel again."

"Are you sure?"

"Quite sure. It hardly hurts to move now, and I think some exercise will help."

"In that case we'll go on tomorrow." Greg unloaded the water bottles from his pack and held out some wet clothing.

"It's your spare shirt and…things…and your other skirt. I washed them," he explained, slightly embarrassed.

Lucy took the clothing with gratitude. "Thank you."

She began to spread it out to dry on the big rock which shaded their camp. "About moving," she said. "I thought we could break camp today."

"If you're sure, but we don't need to rush."

"I do," Lucy responded firmly. "For days I've been watching you swim in that river, and you don't know how much I want to bathe too, and wash my hair."

Greg laughed. "Of course. We'll take it gently and camp by the river tonight."

"Wonderful!" Lucy agreed, delighting in the thought of a swim and clean clothes to put on afterwards. Greg offered Lucy the last of the coffee, and when she declined he poured it into his mug, and then said briskly, "As you've been lying there watching me toil up and down have you noticed anything else?"

"What sort of thing?"

"The reason we came here," Greg said pointedly. "Think of the map, and look."

Bemused, Lucy thought of the map, and looked, but could see nothing. "I don't know what I'm looking for."

"Keep looking. I don't want to show you, I want you to see it for yourself."

Greg watched Lucy's face as she scanned the mountainside carefully. "I can only see the same as I've always seen. The mountain going down, and those hillocks at the bottom, and the river. I suppose the river could be the river Jack drew on the map, it's roughly the same shape, but I'm not sure. Then there's that big rock, a funny shape, like an 'M'..."

Lucy jerked bolt upright. "Like an 'M'," she repeated with wonder, "and in the right place in relation to the river..."

"Exactly!" Greg was jubilant.

Lucy leapt up and began to dance with delight, her aches and pains forgotten. "We've found it! Greg, we've found it!" Her enthusiasm was infectious and Greg laughed as she took his hands and pulled him to his feet, still dancing with excitement.

"But how can you be so calm?" she bubbled, "When did you see it? Why didn't you tell me before?"

"Calm down," he said, still laughing. "The reason I didn't tell you before was exactly this. You would have refused to rest. You would have wanted to go straight down there no matter how you felt."

His words touched her deeply. Knowing how important Jack's map was to Greg, she was chastened to think that he had waited quietly each day for her to recover, when he must have been itching to investigate further.

"Come and look." Greg took her hand and they sat down together and traced the landmarks on the map. "It was seeing it suddenly that made me fall down that blasted hole," Greg said. "I'd stopped to rest and suddenly I saw it. I was so excited I just raced down the mountain and crashed down the crevasse. I stopped thinking for a moment, and so brought on all our troubles."

"But our troubles are over now and we've found it, found what we came for."

"We have found nothing actually, except the site of Jack's map," Greg said carefully. "We don't know that he really found gold, he only told Dan he was going to raise money for mining equipment."

"Do you think that's why Jack and your father quarrelled? Because Jack came home and immediately asked your father for money?"

"It's possible. Jack turned up late at night, very much the worse for wear according to Jarvis, with talk of a gold mine and a demand for money. While he was away my father had been struggling to run the farm alone and had lost his wife. I can understand Dad losing his temper; he would have seen it all as a cock and bull story."

"And was it, do you think? A cock and bull story?"

"Who knows? There are two things that make me hopeful. One, is that according to Jarvis, Jack was insistent on secrecy, and didn't want anyone to know he was home. In those days even the smell of a possible gold strike would send hundreds of people racing to the area. If Jack did find something he would have wanted to keep it secret, even from Dan, who he obviously trusted completely. He may have thought it was better for Dan not to know in order to protect him. He intended to come back here, that's certain, which is why he made the map. One other thing makes me hopeful, and that is the map itself. When he was drowning it was the one thing Jack wanted to save, and he threw it to Jarvis."

Greg stopped suddenly and then smiled briefly. "We'll soon know," he promised. "We'll camp by the river tonight and look for the gold tomorrow." He held up the map again. "From the 'M' rock there's a sort of dotted line, it's rather indistinct because it's on the line where the paper was creased, but look closely and you'll see it. It's marked 20N and then the cross."

Lucy took the map and studied it carefully. "Yes, I can just about see the dotted line, but I think the 20 might be 26. I suppose the N means north," she volunteered, handing back the map.

"I imagine so." Greg peered at the map again. "Yes, you could be right, it could be 26. But twenty-six what? Yards perhaps? Or paces?"

"Or feet," Lucy suggested.

Greg smiled. "Well, certainly the cross marks the gold. It always did in the stories Jack used to tell us when we were children." He got to his feet. "Come on then Lucy. If we're going to break camp we might as well do it now."

It was well they started down the mountainside early, as Lucy found it quite tiring and had to stop twice to rest on the way. Nevertheless they were at the river bank in an hour, and after Greg had struck camp Lucy demanded she be allowed to swim.

"I suppose that's a hint for me to go hunting," Greg responded. "Although I could stay here, to make sure you don't drown or anything," he added innocently.

Lucy blushed, and Greg was immediately penitent. "All right, I'm going." He picked up his pack and opened it. "There," he said proudly. "The only tin of soft soap for fifty miles."

He threw the tin across and laughed as Lucy purred with delight. Greg picked up his gun and left, and minutes later Lucy was in the water, soaping herself all over and washing her hair thoroughly before she began to swim. Her enjoyment was intense after the dust and heat of the last few days, and when she finally left the water she was tired but refreshed. Drying herself as well as she could on the only small towel she had, she brushed out her hair and put on her clean clothes. Then she went back to the water and washed the clothes she had just taken off, spreading them to dry on the river bank. The luxury of easy access to water delighted her, and she wandered downstream a little way, wondering if she could make a fishing rod. A single shot rang out not far away, and she smiled to herself. "Rabbit for dinner again," she thought, but not without some pleasure, as she was hungry after her swim.

By the time she had collected wood and got the fire going Greg was back, bursting with pride.

"Look Lucy," he yelled. "Look what I got!"

It was beyond the dreams of avarice. A wild turkey.

Later that evening, after they had dined on delicious turkey and their last tin of pineapple, they sat and talked, watching the red and purple shadows deepen, the rich colours reflected in the river as the sun slowly sank on the horizon. Lucy, feeling clean, refreshed and well fed, told Greg she felt wonderful.

"This may well be the happiest evening of my life," she told him, a little drunk with the beauty of it all.

Greg laughed. "And tomorrow we find a gold mine," he said.

It wasn't twenty yards, or twenty six, or paces or feet either. Having determined north from the compass, Greg measured carefully and double checked everything. He spent the whole morning digging in the most likely spots, and they found nothing. He dug down only to a depth of about two feet, reasoning that Jack would have left some indication that the correct place had been found. There was nothing. It was hard work, as the area was covered with brush and scrubby grass, and there was no indication it had ever been dug before.

Just before noon they called a halt, as it was impossible to work in the midday heat, and Greg went away to bathe away the dust and sweat of the morning's work. Duly refreshed, he collected the tin containing the left over turkey, which Lucy had suspended in the water to keep cool overnight, and made his way back to camp, a picture of despondency.

Lucy took the tin from him and regarded him gravely.

"Cheer up, all is not lost."

"I'm afraid it probably is." He watched Lucy prepare their meal, noticing the deft movements he had come to love.

"Well perhaps not…"

"No Lucy. The fact that we want to believe there is gold here doesn't mean it is here. Perhaps Jack just *thought* it was here."

"Well, I don't think we should give up yet," said Lucy, handing him a plate. "We haven't found the right place that's all."

"I don't see where else we can look," Greg burst out. His exasperation was showing, and he smiled apologetically.

Lucy pondered, picking at a turkey bone. "When you were digging I was thinking. I thought of two things which might help. It might be nothing but…how tall was Jack?"

"How tall? I don't really know. I only remember him as a child, and all grown ups are big to a child. Why?"

"When you were striding out the twenty paces it occurred to me that if I was doing it, my twenty paces would be about half the distance…"

"Yes!" Greg shot to his feet. "Of course! Jack's paces might not be the same as mine. Now let me think." He paced a little and turned, his face alight.

"That's it Lucy, I'm sure you're right. At home there is an old photograph of Dad and Jack together. They are standing side by side, hands in waistcoat pockets; you know the kind of thing. Jack was certainly shorter than my father, it's difficult to know how much, but perhaps four inches, and Dad was only five feet ten, whereas I'm over six feet."

"Which would make Jack only a little taller than I am," said Lucy, and his paces much shorter than yours."

"Well, we know the number doesn't refer to yards or feet" said Greg, "and I didn't expect it to be, because Jack probably didn't have proper measuring equipment with him. This will mean the place marked with a cross is much closer to the rock."

Lucy agreed. "The problem is to decide how long or short Jack's paces were. He was probably only slightly taller than me, but being a man he will have had a longer stride."

She got to her feet and positioned herself at the corner of the rock and then strode forward, counting out twenty paces loudly. When she got to twenty she was about four yards short of Greg's nearest dig. She turned triumphantly, to see Greg shaking with laughter.

"What's so funny?" she asked. "It looks as if I might be right."

"I'm sure you are," said Greg, still laughing. "I'm just enjoying seeing you trying to walk like a man."

"This little bush marks the spot," said Lucy, pointing. "Keep your eye on it." She came back to the fire and poured coffee, deciding to ignore Greg's banter.

"The little green bush," she repeated. "That's if it's twenty paces, of course. It might be twenty six."

Greg's eyes twinkled. "Do you think you could go and pace out twenty six of Jack's paces for me?" he asked innocently. "Just so I can see where to dig."

He fell backwards as he tried to avoid the towel Lucy flung at his face. "Oops, I only meant...really Lucy..." He tried to fend her off. "You're sitting on my chest...I thought you were a lady..."

"No, a princess, don't you remember?"

The grey eyes misted. "Yes, and the frog prince wants his kiss."

Chapter Twenty-One

With the first spadeful dug near Lucy's small green bush Greg knew they had the right place. The turned spit of earth revealed a fine black sandy loam he had not found at the earlier digs. He looked up and met Lucy's eyes.

"Black sand, Lucy. You recall what Dan said about black sand?"

"Yes, but so near the surface?"

"It probably wasn't originally. My bet is that Jack put it back here when he filled in his prospect hole. Anyway, we'll see."

Greg dug down a few more feet and struck something hard.

"It's the edge of something," he said briefly, and got down to scrape away with both hands.

"A box perhaps?" Lucy began to scrape too. "Oh," she said, disappointed. It's only a piece of wood."

"It's a very big piece of wood," Greg responded, reaching again for his spade. He set to work and dug away the topsoil, following the line of what appeared to be a long plank.

"I think this is much more exciting than a box Lucy."

"Why? What is it?"

"I'm not certain, but if I'm not mistaken…" Greg dug fiercely along the plank, "this is shoring timber, and it just might be part of the shoring Jack used for a really big prospect hole."

"But how do we get in?" asked Lucy, mystified.

"My guess is that your paces have led us near, but not to the exact spot. I think we've missed the entrance. If I follow this plank to the end perhaps…" Greg continued to dig as Lucy watched in silence. She experienced a strange feeling, almost of awe, gazing at the manmade plank of wood so far from any sign of civilisation. Stranger still was the thought that it was probably put there by Jack Lamont all those years before. As she watched Greg at work, the shadowy figure of Jack Lamont suddenly became very real, and she wondered about his real character. *There was Uncle Jack, adored by his two young nephews, taking them fishing and telling them stories. Then there was Jack the Black Sheep, so easy going and shallow that he had deserted his family to follow the lure of easy riches in the goldfields. For Dan Drummond there had been another Jack, the good mate who had inspired such confidence that the old man had waited twenty five years for him to return, and had never forgotten him.* Most of all, Lucy could not forget that it had been Jack's reappearance on that rain soaked night long ago, which had led to Jarvis running from the law, and ending up in Singapore. She would never have known Jarvis at all if...

"Here we are, this is it." Lucy's reverie was broken as Greg changed direction with his spade.

"What is it?"

Greg continued working as he answered, "I'm not sure, it looks like a trap door."

Within a few minutes he had uncovered what appeared to be a square door, which had obviously been made to cover the entrance to the prospect hole. It took Greg a few minutes to loosen it around the edges, and then he lifted it out almost reverentially, and held it for Lucy to see.

"Uncle Jack made that, Lucy," he whispered, obviously moved.

The door was edged with rough timber, which had been interfiled with thin sapling branches interwoven to make a firm cover. Lucy inspected it carefully as Greg brushed away the soil with his hands.

"Oh Greg, it must have taken him ages to make it."

"Yes. Just imagine Lucy. Jack sitting alone by his camp fire at night after a days hard digging, making this. I wonder what he thought about..."

Lucy saw that Greg's eyes were full of tears.

"He thought about you and Sam, all his family, and how he was going to make you all rich."

"Perhaps." Greg put the door down. "Perhaps he did. Anyway, we'd better see what he found."

The entrance to the prospect hole was about four feet square, and as they peered down they could see nothing.

"At last I know why I lugged the lantern all this way," said Greg. "Looks like I'm going down a hole again." He caught Lucy's look of apprehension. "Don't worry; I'll try not to get stuck down this one. Let's get the rope."

This time there was a tree sufficiently near to secure the rope, and within minutes Greg had affixed the lantern to his back pack and was letting himself into the gloom.

Lucy watched as the dim glow from the lantern illuminated the sides of the prospect hole, but she could see very little.

"It's all right," Greg shouted, "I'm at the bottom, it isn't very deep, perhaps fifteen feet or so."

"What can you see?"

"There's a tunnel, it's quite big, I can almost stand upright. It must have taken weeks to dig. I'm going along it now, I can see quite well. Hey! Look at this!"

Lucy could hear something scraping but could see nothing as the light had gone. "What is it?"

"Just a minute." The scraping continued and then the dim glow of the lantern reappeared and Greg shouted, "It's ladder! A homemade ladder, Jack must have made it for his own use and he left it just inside the tunnel."

"Is it useable?"

"Sound as a bell, but it's a bit difficult to manoeuvre, not much space down here…that's it." Lucy saw the ends of the roughhewn ladder come towards her.

"Jack was certainly a good handyman," Greg called. "Lucy, do you think you can manage…"

But Lucy was already half way down.

The tunnel was only about five yards long. Even so, it was quite a feat of engineering for one man to have accomplished. Jack had installed props made from the trunks of trees, and had obviously used larger trees to fashion the roughhewn planks which shored up the roof, and it was one of these which Greg had exposed earlier. There was no shoring at the sides of the tunnel, and Greg inspected them carefully.

"It seems quite sound," he said. "The first thing we have to do is make sure it won't all fall in on us. It's been here twenty-five years after all."

"Greg! Look here!"

In the far corner of the tunnel was a pile of equipment. Greg put down the lantern and they investigated. There were two worn shovels, and several tin dishes, pans, ropes and a sledge hammer, and a small panning cradle. There was also a waterproof tent, some worn gloves and boots, and an opossum skin rug. The find gave them an eerie feeling of Jack's presence, and they became quiet and thoughtful as they sorted through the belongings. As she pulled out the big folded tent Lucy suddenly gave a cry.

"Greg, look! Bring the lantern nearer."

Her urgent tone broke Greg's mood of reverie, and then as he lifted the lantern towards the corner his heart missed a beat. Along the bottom of the wall, where Jack had dug down to the solid bedrock, there was a seam of pure yellow colour about a foot wide, which continued to the end of the tunnel. Greg bent down and ran his fingers along the seam.

"Is it gold? Is it Greg?"

"I don't know, it certainly looks like it doesn't it? And it goes further." He continued to examine the seam and then turned to Lucy in exasperation.

"I don't know enough about gold mining Lucy. When I planned this trip I read up all I could find, which wasn't that much, and I thought I'd recognise gold if I saw it, but now I'm not sure."

"Well I'm sure," said Lucy vehemently. "Greg, we've found it, don't you understand? We've found Jack's gold mine! This is why you came all this way!"

Greg smiled at her excitement. "We've certainly found what Jack intended us to find," he agreed. "Whether it can be called a gold mine, I'm not so sure."

"Of course it is! Of course it's a gold mine!"

"We can't be certain. There's something called 'fool's gold' you know, it looks like gold but it isn't."

"It is gold, I know it is!" Lucy pranced around with excitement and then planted a kiss on Greg's cheek, and in spite of himself he began to laugh.

"Now be sensible," he said. "How can you possibly be sure it's gold?"

Lucy turned her radiant face to him. "Faith, Greg," she said simply. "Jack was sure it was gold, that's why he made the map, and he knew a lot more about it than either of us." She kissed Greg's cheek again. "And I have faith in Jack," she added.

Her simple words caught a sensitive spot, and for a moment Greg could not speak. He took Lucy's arm and led her to the ladder, and when they surfaced he made an excuse and strode away to the river to swim. Intense feelings welled up within him so that he felt he would choke. *Why did he hide the depth of his love from her? Was it because she had told him she had married Sir Gilbert Howell for his money? Since he had come to know her well it seemed so out of character, and yet she had admitted it. All through their journey together he had deliberately kept matters light between them. Even when they kissed he held himself back, exerting an iron control over his emotions. He told himself that this was because of the promise he had made to Matthew, the promise to care for Lucy and protect her with his life while she was in his care; but was that entirely true?*

Greg reached the river bank and took off his clothes. As he felt the cool water on his body he considered Lucy again, and tried to take a rational approach, the thing he found most difficult when thinking about Lucy. *Why had it upset him when she said she had faith in Jack Lamont?* He saw again Lucy's radiant face turned towards him, and the answer was obvious. *He was upset because she had faith and he didn't. She had shown him in a flash of instinct how paltry and sordid were his doubts.* Greg turned on to his back and swam lazily. *After all these years,* he thought, *all these years of wondering what happened to Jack, and wanting to disprove the bad things that were said about him, the moment I get the chance to show my faith in him I start to doubt. Lucy is right, Jack knew what he was doing, of course it is gold.*

Greg climbed out of the water and retrieved his clothes from a bush. *I wonder if I'm just a doubting Thomas,* he mused as he dressed. *Is that why I doubt Lucy, why I can't believe she is what she seems, why I can't let go and tell her all I feel?* He reminded himself again of his promise to Matthew, but knew he was deceiving himself. He could never face losing her again, and the misery of those months when he had looked for her so desperately still haunted him. *He had found her at last, and in the most unexpected place, close to home. But it was as if he held her only by a fine silken thread, which could be broken in an instant.*

As he approached their camp, Lucy was bending over the fire. When she turned and saw him she smiled and ran towards him and he felt his heart lurch.

"Coffee's made," she said. "There's only enough for breakfast tomorrow but I thought we should celebrate."

"Good idea." He smiled guardedly. "You are right of course. I think we have found a gold mine."

She laughed delightedly, and Greg reflected that Matthew had been right when he talked about her zest for life, her joy in all she found. He put his arm around her and they walked back to the fire. Greg sensed her eyes on him, and glanced down at her.

"All right now?" she asked softly. She put out her hand and stroked his cheek, her eyes full of love and concern.

"I'm fine," he answered, and thought his heart would burst.

The morning after they found Jack's gold mine they began their journey home. Now Greg had proved the mine's existence, there was no reason to stay and their food was running low. Greg put back the cover of the prospect hole and filled in all the holes he had dug, aware that within weeks little trace of their visit would remain.

Their journey back to Dan's camp was much easier than the outward trip. As they now had the rope to assist them, the steep bluff of the mountainside presented few problems, and they found the little pack donkey and the horses well rested and content.

By early evening they were only half a mile from Dan's camp, and although they could have reached it quite easily Greg insisted they make camp for the night. As they sat near the fire and roasted their rabbit, he explained his reasons.

"I brought this," he said, fishing something from his shirt pocket and handing it to Lucy. It was a small piece of the yellow rock from Jack's tunnel. "I prized it from the wall before we came away. I thought it best to have it checked at the assay office in Shimmer Creek."

"You still think it might not be gold?"

"I'm sure it is, but I still need to have it officially confirmed if I'm going to invest in all the equipment needed to extract it. It will be a big operation, but the very first thing to do is to stake our claim to the land, buy it if necessary. I am sure Jack will have staked a claim and obtained a licence when he found the gold twenty-five years ago, but both have probably lapsed."

"I see," said Lucy, considering this. "Do you think there will be a problem?"

"I shouldn't think so, but I wanted to talk to you about our plans before we see Dan again."

Lucy smiled as she eased the rabbit from the skewer. She liked the way Greg had said 'our plans,' as if she was included in them. She jointed the rabbit on to their plates as Greg continued; "The way I see it, is this. The situation hasn't changed so much since Jack's day. If news of this got out the area would be swamped with prospectors in weeks, so we must keep it secret until we are sure we have a proper claim to the land and rights to dig. The one person we can trust is Dan Drummond, and if anyone can tell us if this is real gold, he can."

"Yes, of course," Lucy agreed.

"I think our best plan is to tell Dan everything, and leave him here until I can get back with an expert to advise on the extraction, I'm sure the bank will recommend someone. When we get to Shimmer Creek I'll go into the assay office and ensure we have the land, if possible I'll buy it."

"But won't that give the game away?"

"Not if I handle it properly. The man at the office knows I came up here looking for Dan Drummond, and the area where my uncle worked his claim, so it's only natural I should be interested in it. I thought I could say I wanted to buy it for sentimental reasons."

"Do you think he will believe that?" said Lucy. "After all, you're hardly the sentimental type."

Greg smiled. "You don't think so? Just wait till I've finished my dinner."

Although they had started out at dawn, they could see Dan Drummond was up and had his fire going as they approached his camp at Gillstown very early next day. Greg hailed him, and the old man immediately appeared from his humpy and ran to meet them, his bandy legs weaving a crab-like progress towards them at an amazingly fast pace.

"Where yer been?" he gasped out when he reached them. "Been ages, you 'ave."

"We had a few adventures Dan, and we have a lot to tell you," Greg explained. "But first, let's have some coffee, we've run out."

Over their coffee Greg told Dan first about the map they had brought with them.

"I didn't want to mention it when we arrived in case it led to nothing," he said. "I didn't want you to be disappointed."

"Bless yer lad, 'ow could I be disappointed now? Disappointment is fer youngsters, them as still 'as 'opes. I ain't got no 'opes now, so no disappointments neither. Anyway, you comin' was a real tonic. I'm real 'appy, now I knows what 'appened to Jack."

Greg smiled and then told his story. He told it all, about his fall into the crevasse and how Lucy had rescued him, and then about the big 'M' rock and the river beyond the mountain. Dan's face was a picture as the story unfolded, and when Greg fished out the small gold nugget and held it out to him he was ashen.

"Strike me down!" he said, and then as he turned the nugget over in his hands he seemed unable to speak. After a few moments he said 'strike me down!' again, and raised his head. "You ain't 'avin' me on Greg?" he asked. "Yer Uncle Jack was a terror fer pranks…"

"No, I'm not having you on. I found this where I told you. What I want to know is if you think it's gold."

"Pretty sure it is Greg, but it's a different colour to most o' what was dug 'ere. You'll 'ave to 'ave it assayed, there's a bloke in Shimmer Creek will do it, name o' Jim Dalton."

"Yes, I've met him…"

"Second thoughts, better not Greg. Might start a rush! Yer must make sure yer got a proper claim, that's the first thing."

"I agree Dan. What we thought we would do, is this. Lucy and I will go back to Shimmer Creek and I'll tell them that I found you, and we had a long talk about Jack and the old days, and that we had a look around. I'll say that you are running short of stores and that I agreed to buy some for you and have them sent out. For payment I'll sell this nugget at the assay office." Greg held up his hand. "Hear me out. I'll say that you gave me the nugget to pay for the stores, I'll say it's one you have saved for years, that when you found it at Ballarat you put it by for a rainy day."

Dan chuckled. "That's the idea Greg! An' when they comes with the stores I'll say 'is there any change from me nugget?" He chuckled again.

"Then, I'll see if I can put in a claim for the land, or buy it," said Greg. "I'll say it's for you in your old age, to build a little place here. So you'll have to go along with that."

Dan chuckled with glee. "Sure will Greg, and they'll believe it too. Every bloke in Shimmer Creek knows I'll never leave this place. Never! 'specially now." He turned to Lucy and chuckled again. " 'Ow do you like it Lucy? Bein' rich?"

"I'm not rich Dan, it's Greg's family…"

"But you an' Greg is sweet'arts aren't yer? Yer'll be gettin' wed?"

There was a sudden silence, and Lucy felt the colour suffuse her cheeks, but before she could protest Greg said, "Give me time Dan; I'm still working on her. But, in any case you're wrong; it's you who will be rich. The mine belonged to Jack and you were his partner. One thing I'm certain of is that Jack still intended you to be his partner when he mined the gold. That's why he left you in charge. As Jack is dead, the mine is half yours and half ours."

Dan's mouth dropped open. "Oh no! yer don't mean it Greg?"

"I do indeed, it's only fair. After all, you have guarded the mine all these years."

"Yes, but I didn' know I was guardin' it, or where it was! I don't think I'm entitled, not legal like. I think Greg…" the old man became tearful, "It's p'raps better I don't 'ave any of it, I'm getting' on a bit, too old now."

"Nonsense. Anyway, while we are away you can think about it. If you really want to stay here for the rest of your life you could at least have a nice house and someone to take care of you. Half the mine is yours so you might as well enjoy it. When we have arranged everything at Shimmer Creek I will write to you and send the letter with the stores." Greg stopped. "Can you read Dan?"

The old man was still snuffling. 'some…if it ain't too many long words."

"I'll make it easy," Greg promised. "Then Lucy and I have to go home. When we get there I'll arrange for a team to come out here and start work, but it may be about three months before they get here. Will you stay and look after things till then Dan?"

"Course I will, where else would I be? Will you come back Greg?" There was an unspoken plea in the old man's voice, and Greg took his hand.

"I'll be back old friend. It won't be twenty five years this time."

Half an hour later they mounted the horses and set off for Shimmer Creek, Dan watching them out of sight. Greg waited for the comment Lucy would surely make about Dan having half of the mine. He expected her to be angry, but he was determined to carry out what he felt would have been Jack's wishes. When she had said nothing after an hour he could not contain his curiosity, and remarked, "Dan seemed quite reticent about having half the mine."

Lucy turned her dazzling smile towards him. "Yes, didn't he? But he will feel different when he's had a chance to get used to the idea."

"You agree then?" Greg could hardly keep the surprise out of his voice, "You think it's a good idea?"

"But of course. The only thing that worries me is whether he will be able to find someone to live with him out there, to look after him. It's very remote."

"It won't be once the mining starts," Greg responded grimly. "Of course we don't know how much gold is there, but if it's a good strike he could be as rich as Croesus, and in that case someone will probably marry him."

If he expected Lucy to take the point he was disappointed. She simply giggled.

"What fun!" she said.

The arrangement at Shimmer Creek went without a hitch, and Lucy, installed in her stuffy room at the pub, was still waiting for her bath water to be heated when Greg returned from the assay office.

"Guess what?" he said as soon as she opened the door. "It is gold, and very high quality. I should think the gold which was visible is worth a small fortune, apart from any more we may find. Jim Dalton believed the story about it being Dan's nugget, he actually said there had never been any gold of that colour found in this area."

Lucy laughed; she loved to see Greg so happy.

"And guess what Lucy? I didn't need to stake any claim. Jim Dalton told me that after I left the office last time he delved into the records to see if he could find out anything more for when we returned. Nice chap really, he went to a lot of trouble. He apologised, because apparently Jack did stake another claim, but he couldn't find it at first. It is a large tract of land about ten miles north of the Gillstown workings, just over a mountain, and bordering a river on the east side. He actually showed me the plan, and it's our site, no doubt at all."

"And did you manage to renew the claim?"

"Didn't need to. That's why Jim couldn't find it at first. Jack bought the land before he came home. We already own it."

Lucy patted her mare's neck and muttered a few consoling words. Like herself, the mare was tired, and anxious to stop for rest and water. Lucy looked ahead to where Greg's broad back swayed rhythmically, and wondered again why he had been so insistent they press on and reach Stannerton tonight. For her part, Lucy could not bear the thought of returning to the scene of the Wool Co-operative dance. In spite of the heat she shivered slightly as she recalled that night. Strange to think that almost three months had elapsed since she had fled from the horrified gaze of her neighbours and friends, with the shouted taunts of George Carmody ringing in her ears.

She still could not quite believe Greg's assurances.

"We must reach Stannerton in the dark, and go straight to the hotel," he had explained. "Jennie Moore will take us in and will know what the situation is. There is nothing to worry about, there won't be a constable waiting for you."

Lucy had given in gracefully, but was still nervous. She would have much preferred to skirt the town and camp overnight, in spite of the lure of a bath and a comfortable bed at the hotel. She was now desperate to get back to Kelly's place and find out how things were with Matthew. Her trip with Greg had been so crowded with incident that it had not been difficult to put her personal worries behind her, but as they neared home a mental chaos of formless fears added to her physical exhaustion. She wondered how Matthew had dealt with the constable, if Lizzie had coped with the cheese, and whether the children had kept up with their lessons, not to mention her precious vegetables.

The mare suddenly stopped, and Lucy was roused from her reverie. Greg had dismounted and was walking back towards her.

"Get down Lucy, we'll walk from here," he said. "It will be quieter if we lead the horses."

"It's not so late, someone will be bound to see us," Lucy grumbled as she dismounted.

"No, they won't, and if they do it doesn't matter," said Greg.

"That's illogical," Lucy responded tiredly. "If it doesn't matter, why are we being quiet?" Nevertheless she took the mare's rein and followed Greg, who led his worn horse and the little pack donkey, and they made their way as quietly as possible along the main street and towards the hotel.

Lucy wondered briefly about Greg's mood. It had changed in the last few days. When they had left Shimmer Creek he had been cheerful and optimistic, supporting and comforting her all the way across the barren and arid country which had almost broken her spirit on the way out. True, conditions had been better on the homeward journey, as they were freshly supplied and well organised for what was the most difficult terrain of the trip. Although the flies were still troublesome and the heat intense, they had been able to use the water they carried, sure now of the location of soaks and billabongs which awaited when they emerged from the thirsty plains. Greg had been lighthearted, and as solicitous and caring as ever, and Lucy's one regret was that he did not seem inclined to discuss serious matters, or to look ahead to what awaited their return. On the few occasions when Lucy had attempted to discuss the future, Greg had changed the subject with a joke or some general banter, and Lucy was sure this was deliberate. She recalled his remark to Dan Drummond that he was 'working on her' and reflected that if this was so, he was not making it obvious.

As they reached the hotel, Greg led the horses around to the yard at the rear, and Lucy followed. There appeared to be no one around, and Greg turned to Lucy with a whisper, "Take the horses into the stable and see to them if you will. I'll go in by the back door and see if I can find Jennie. I won't be long."

"But Greg…"

"Please Lucy; just for once do as I ask without arguing."

He went towards the dim light which glowed dully from the kitchens. Lucy attended to the horses, and then, tired beyond belief, she sat down in the straw to await events. *Greg was tetchy*, she thought, *but she was too tired to complain.*

It seemed only seconds before she was woken suddenly, and in that moment she caught again a fleeting glimpse of love in Greg's eyes. It was gone immediately however, and he said quietly, "It's all right, you can go in. Jennie's waiting for you. I'll bring our things."

He helped her to her feet and within second Jennie Moore was embracing her and leading her upstairs.

"Thank God you're safe Catherine, but what a fright you look! I knew you were safe with Greg, but that is killer country, I couldn't help being worried."

"Jennie, what has happened about…"

"Never mind all that now, Catherine," Jennie interrupted, opening the bathroom door. "Have your bath and then get into bed, your room is next door on the right, it's all ready. I'll go and get you some supper and bring you a tray."

"But Jennie, I must know…"

"All you need to know for tonight is that everything at Kelly's place is fine. Tomorrow you can have all the news."

"Are you sure?"

"Yes, of course. Now get undressed, you ragamuffin!"

In spite of her tiredness, Lucy revelled in the scented luxury of the water, washing her hair, and wrapping a towel around her head turban style. After she had finished, she put on a robe she found behind the bathroom door, and went to her room. The big comfortable bed awaited, its crisp white sheets and pink coverlet already turned down, and a nightgown of Jennie's put out for her. Lucy slipped it over her head, and then climbed into the bed, her tired bones responding to the soft comfort with a feeling of pure ecstasy. *Jennie had said Matthew was all right, everything was fine at Kelly's place, and that was all that mattered.*

When Jennie arrived with the tray, she found Lucy fast asleep. She returned to the kitchen where Greg sat at the scrubbed wooden table. Fresh from his bath, and wearing a clean shirt and trousers, he presented a very different picture to the grimy stockman who had entered her kitchen an hour earlier. Jennie fetched a warm plate from the range and ladled out a big helping of stew.

"Catherine's dead to the world," she said. "I think it will be better to let her sleep until she wakes naturally, she'll need all her strength to cope with tomorrow."

Greg looked at her sharply. "There wasn't any problem with the police?"

"No, none at all, they sent John Thurlestone to investigate, and he's a decent chap. No, I meant Matthew, he has deteriorated quite fast. Bob

Middleton took me over to Kelly's place for a visit. I wanted to go in case they needed help, but they're fine."

Jennie sawed at a thick slice of bread and handed it to Greg. "Tuck in," she said. "Tom and Lizzie Nicholls are fine folks Greg, they've looked after the old man really well."

"I was sure they would. I suppose Matthew told you everything?"

"Yes, and he made a full confession to the constable. Before John even arrived at Kelly's place Matthew had it all written out, and he signed it in front of John, and it was witnessed by Tom and Lizzie."

"So Lucy is completely cleared?"

"Yes, Matthew thought he might be arrested and taken to Perth, but thank God John Thurlestone has more sense than that. Lizzie told him about Matthew's condition, and of course he could see it for himself, the old man would never have survived the trip. So John told them he had been sent out to arrest someone called Catherine Marshall, and that was all he had orders to do. He thought it best to return to Perth with Matthew's confession, and have it forwarded to the police in Singapore. It will be up to them to decide if Matthew is to be arrested. John envisages all this will take considerable time, perhaps even months."

"Longer than Matthew has left," Greg nodded. "Yes, I see. It seems to me John Thurlestone is a very sensible man."

Jennie leaned across the table and spoke softly, "Now Greg, what of your news?"

She listened intently as Greg recounted the details of their trip. It took over an hour but he told her everything, including the finding of Jack's gold mine, swearing her to secrecy until he could get a team out there.

Jennie agreed, but then said quietly, "This is all very exciting news Greg, but you haven't told me the one thing I want to know. You and Catherine...I mean Lucy. Are you...? Well, did you...?"

"Heavens," said Greg, a little sheepishly, "Is it so obvious?"

"No, it isn't, that's why I have to ask!" Jennie opined. "When I saw you together on the night of the dance I could have sworn there was something between you."

"You don't understand Jennie. We had met before, in Singapore."

Jennie's eyes widened. "Then Catherine told me a fib, although I can understand why. Then you have even more to tell me Greg, and before you tell me to mind my own business, let me remind you I watched you grow up."

"She's the one for me, Jennie. I'm certain about that, but you know what

I have to do tomorrow, and I don't know how she will take it."

By the time he went to bed Greg felt a little better. He was still worried about what he had to do, but Jennie had helped him to see how the blow could perhaps be softened. *He hoped to Heaven she was right, but even if she wasn't, tomorrow he must keep his promise to Matthew.*

It was almost noon next day before Lucy awoke with a start. For a moment she did not know where she was, then memory dawned, and she got out of bed and crossed to the window. Drawing the heavy curtains the sudden light startled her, and she quickly put on the robe and hurried downstairs. In the kitchen she found Jennie packing a basket.

"Catherine, at last…I mean Lucy. I shall never get used to calling you Lucy. Have some coffee." Jennie poured out a cup as Lucy sat down at the big scrubbed table.

"What time is it?"

"Nearly twelve, we thought it best to let you have your sleep out."

"Twelve! But we have to be at Kelly's place."

"Not today, we don't." Greg was standing in the doorway. He was dressed formally, in a black jacket and cream silk cravat, and momentarily Lucy saw the same Greg Lamont she had met at the ball in Singapore. His good looks and affectionate smile made her heart pound, and she became thoroughly disconcerted.

"Oh dear, I'm not dressed. It's so late, I must go home, Matthew will be…"

"Yes, I'll take you home, but tomorrow." Greg crossed and gave her a quick kiss on the cheek. "Go and get dressed now, Jennie has found you some clothes. Hurry up now, we are going down to the Creek for a picnic. Jennie has it all packed."

Lucy cast a despairing glance at Jennie. "Do you know what this is all about?" she asked. "We have had a picnic every day for the last three months."

"This one is different," said Jennie, smiling. "I've packed a special basket, so just enjoy it."

"But I don't want a picnic, I want to go home."

"Tomorrow, Lucy." Jennie's tone brooked no nonsense, and then she added gently, "Greg wants to talk to you before you go home."

Lucy looked from one to the other uncertainly, sensing some sort of conspiracy. She sighed and rose from the table.

"All right, I'm used to obeying orders," she grumbled, and went upstairs to dress.

The lunch Jennie had provided was very special, and as she unpacked the basket Lucy made little sounds of delight.

"Oh Greg, it's cold chicken, and some fruit and some cheese," she called. "Do come and sit down, there are glasses but nothing to drink."

She looked up and watched as he walked towards her from the tree where he had tethered the pony and cart. He looked elegant and polished, every inch the frog prince again. She felt a little shy, and tried to remind herself that this was still Greg, the bushman she had travelled with for the last three months, and who knew her almost better than she knew herself. He was carrying a bottle of wine, and Lucy voiced her approval as he reached her.

Greg opened the bottle and Lucy held out her glass. "It seems to me there's some sort of conspiracy here," she said. "Between you and Jennie. I must admit it's rather nice." She sipped her wine. "Very civilised, an improvement on the last few weeks." She giggled. "It was lovely being driven in the pony and trap, how did you manage to get hold of it?"

"Don't laugh," said Greg, pouring wine for himself. "I borrowed it from George Carmody."

"You what?" Lucy sat bolt upright.

"Yes, I just went across and asked him for it. Said I wanted to take a lady on a picnic, and he agreed. Of course, he didn't know who the lady was."

Lucy giggled again. "What fun!"

"Yes, we didn't even mention the fact that last time we met I knocked him down! George Carmody is attempting to make himself a little more agreeable to his neighbours these days, so Jennie tells me."

"What else did she tell you?"

Greg looked up and met her frank gaze, and his mouth went suddenly dry. Lucy leaned forward.

"Jennie said you want to talk to me." Her voice was intense. "It's obviously important and you've been trying to soften the blow. All this..." Lucy gestured to the picnic spread out on the rug. "I'm not a fool Greg, it's bad news isn't it? Is this my last good meal before being carted off to prison?"

"Oh Lucy, no! It's nothing like that, please believe me." Greg was penitent.

"Then why all this? Why are you dressed up like a peacock and driving me to a picnic with wine?"

"Oh Lucy, please. It was only that I thought asking you to marry me should be special, and Jennie agreed."

Lucy heard no more. After the first shock of his words a crescendo of feeling overwhelmed her, and she found herself trembling violently. She gazed at Greg unable to speak, and when he looked up and she met the uncertainty in the grey eyes she thought her heart would burst.

"I got it wrong again," he said lamely.

"Oh Greg you didn't! It was me, spoiling your lovely surprise, I didn't think."

"Then will you? Will you have me?"

Her heart was beating like a drum. "Oh Greg, of course, of course my darling."

His eyes filled with pure delight, and he kissed her then, a kiss that rekindled the strange passion she had felt in the desert, so that it now burst upon her like an all-consuming fire. When he released her, she was shaking, overcome by the tumultuous emotions, which she had been holding back for so long. Then she lunged at him and pushed him on to his back, and he succumbed, laughing and making a mock struggle. Lucy sat on him, and planted dozens of kisses on his brow, eyes, nose, cheeks and mouth until he begged for mercy.

"Stop, you brazen wretch!" he gasped. "I give in."

Lucy planted three more kisses. "Why?"

"Why what?"

More kisses rained down. "Why did it take you so long? I've been waiting for you to ask me for ages."

"If you let me up, I'll explain!"

Reluctantly Lucy allowed him to sit upright. He bent over and kissed her soundly, and then poured more wine. They clinked glasses and Greg said "To us!"

"To us," Lucy responded.

Greg took her hand and his tone became serious. "There's much I have to tell you, dearest," he said. "Some of what I have to say will be hard for you to accept. I hardly know where to begin."

His troubled look caught at Lucy's heart and she had a portent of danger as she felt his sudden change of mood. In her mind's eye a fleeting glimpse of herself five years ago appeared, as she sat in the drawing room at Winchester Station, trying to find the courage to tell her father about Gilbert's cruelty. She took Greg's face in her hands and turned it to her, forcing him to meet her gaze.

"Start at the beginning, leave nothing out, and go on to the end," she said softly, echoing her father's words. "All the best explanations are thus."

Chapter Twenty-Two

Greg smiled hesitantly. "I suppose for me, the beginning was when I met you at the Governor's ball in Singapore. Do you believe in love at first sight?"

"I'm not sure," she said, holding her breath.

"Well I don't," said Greg firmly. "Except that it happened to me. I couldn't believe it, but I had to get to know you. When I think of how I cut in and forced my company on you I feel ashamed."

"It's called sweeping a girl off her feet," Lucy laughed. "Literally," she added, remembering how she had enjoyed it.

"The next thing I knew Sir Gilbert was announcing your engagement, and I felt such a fool. There were lots of comments about how good a catch Sir Gilbert was, and I felt like some backward clod who had just stumbled out of the bush. The Governor's ball was a very sophisticated event for me, Lucy. It was obvious you and Sir Gilbert attended affairs like that all the time."

"Hardly," Lucy murmured.

"I felt out of my depth and tried to put you out of my mind, but after I saw you again at Jarvis's boat, it was as bad as ever. I decided the best way to forget you was to attend the wedding."

"And you found Mother's brooch."

"Yes. After the wedding I went to India but my plan didn't work. I found myself back in Singapore again."

"I've always wondered what it was like," Lucy whispered. "What happened after we left."

"It was dreadful," Greg replied. "The papers were full of it, and implied you had killed your rich husband and run away, probably with a great deal of cash and jewellery." He gave a hollow laugh. "It's amazing how much dirt can be dragged up if people put their minds to it."

"And you? What did you think?" Lucy asked softly.

"I just wanted to find you. You were in trouble and I could have helped you get away. Of course I had in mind Australia," he added a little sheepishly. "Australia is a place to break free of the past, and you obviously had the same idea."

It wasn't as simple as that, Lucy thought, *and some day I'll tell you how it was.* She took a sip of wine and said "Go on."

"I talked to everyone I could. The police were convinced you had shot Sir Gilbert and so were the servants. Lela refused to speak against you, and when she told me about Gilbert's cruelty towards you, I was even more determined to find you. Margot and William Graham leapt to your defence. Margot gave a statement to the *Straits Times* saying it was not possible for you to be guilty of murder, and I think she lost most of her friends as a result."

"Margot was always a true friend to me," Lucy whispered, as she felt hot tears spring to her eyes.

"And to me," said Greg. "They showed me the letter you had sent, and we speculated for hours as to where you could have gone. We decided it had to be England."

"That's what you were meant to think."

"Margot knew your Uncle's name and that he lived in Maida Vale and had worked in a bank. The problem was there was no trace of your having left on a ship for England. When Jarvis Mottram did not return from his trip in the *Selangor Lady,* all the rumours started again. People decided it had not been a killing done on the spur of the moment, but that you and Jarvis had planned it all in advance. I was desperate to find you, and took ship for England right away."

"England?" Lucy's mouth dropped open, and she repeated, "England? You went to England?"

"Yes, I was there four months. I had intended to visit England at some time to buy some pedigree stock. I did that before I returned, but most of the time I was looking for you."

"I can't believe it," Lucy breathed. "And all the time I was sailing for Australia."

"I drew a blank in Maida Vale; I was told Matthew had moved out before Gilbert's death. The bank had no idea where he was, and said his account was closed."

"That was on Matthew's instructions," said Lucy. "He took care to cover his tracks, in case Gilbert ever came looking for me."

"He succeeded," said Greg grimly. "Miss Collins was helpful…"

"Miss Collins! You went to my old school?"

"I went everywhere, but there was no information. I even went to Devon, in case you had gone to Jarvis Mottram's old home."

"Oh Greg." Lucy hardly knew how to respond. "You tried so hard to find me."

"I also visited Sir Gilbert's family home."

Lucy was horror struck. "Why?"

"I was getting desperate I suppose. Gilbert's younger brother had been to Singapore to settle his affairs, and I hoped he had brought back some news."

"And had he?"

"No. At least no news of you."

"Oh Greg, how his family must hate me!" Lucy whispered.

"On the contrary," Greg responded. "Sir Gilbert's parents are both dead, and when I mentioned you to his brother he simply said, "Poor young woman, no wonder she tried to run away."

"Really?" Lucy said, mystified.

"Yes, apparently as a young man Gilbert got himself into trouble at home, and was sent to Singapore as punishment. The family wanted to be rid of him."

"What had he done?"

"His brother didn't elaborate, and it seemed indelicate to ask; but later that evening in the local pub I was introduced to someone who had worked for the family for many years. He told me Sir Gilbert was sent away because he attacked his mother."

"Good Heavens!"

"Yes. He beat her about the head so badly that she never really recovered. It was all hushed up at the time, and the story was put out that she had fallen down some steps in the garden."

"Did they say why he did it?"

"Apparently he had already beaten up a local girl, a...." Greg sought for a word.

"I understand," said Lucy swiftly.

Greg shot her a look, Lucy still surprised him sometimes.

"The girl was injured quite badly," Greg continued, "and her family came to see Gilbert's father asking for recompense, which was paid. That evening, Gilbert's mother, who was a very strict disciplinarian, by the way, began to berate Gilbert about it, and he lost his temper, with dire results."

"Yes, he would," Lucy said, remembering with a shudder.

"So you see, none of it was ever your fault, and no one hates you, not even Gilbert's family. But visiting them was not helpful, I still found no clue as to where you were."

Greg's face was a study. "It was a very depressing process," he murmured. "You seemed to have vanished into thin air. I went home to Australia and you know the rest."

Lucy tried to digest this new aspect of Greg, which he had now revealed so openly. She felt deep humility as she realised how much effort he had put into looking for her, and she wanted him to know how much it meant to her. Words seemed inadequate, and she leaned forward and kissed him gently. The troubled look cleared the grey eyes, and he commented quite airily, "And when I was looking for you in England I suppose you never gave me a thought?"

Lucy smiled. "You're wrong. When we were sailing on the *Selangor Lady* I used to find myself thinking of you for no apparent reason, but I always felt guilty about those thoughts. Guilt was a very heavy burden for me at that time." Tears misted her eyes. "Try to understand Greg," she said softly. "I hadn't forgotten you, but I was trying to."

Greg stroked her hand and raised it to his lips, kissing each finger in turn. "Of course I understand," he said, "And you had more immediate priorities, like staying alive."

A few moments passed, and they enjoyed Jennie's delicious picnic, each of them reflecting on what they had discovered of the other. At length Greg broke the silence.

"Now, to the most difficult part, Lucy. When you left Stannerton with your woolclip after your run-in with George Carmody, Bob and I and some others went to Stannerton to see if we could help. I talked to Jennie about Catherine Marshall and from our conversation I became convinced that we were talking about my lost love. I told Jennie I would be interested to meet you, and during the next few days some of the men started to talk about forming a Wool Co-operative. Jennie said she would organise a dance for the inauguration, and I asked her to make sure you came, so that I could meet you."

"So there has been a conspiracy after all. I was right."

"Yes, and Matthew was part of it. When I left Stannerton, I went home by way of Kelly's place, I wanted to tell Matthew what had happened and that you were all right. He was relieved, and asked me to stay the night. During that evening over our meal, I took the opportunity to tell Matthew about the young lady I had met in Singapore. I told him everything, just as I have told you. I said I wanted to find this young woman more than anything in the world, and that if she had assumed a new identity her secret was safe with me."

"But Matthew didn't tell me this."

"No. We talked it over thoroughly and Matthew didn't want you to know you had been found. He thought you would want to run, in spite of the fact that he was sure you felt as I did."

"But I never said so! How could he know that?"

"Matthew knows you, dearest. I told him about the plan for the dance, and begged him to persuade you to attend, so that we could meet as it were by chance."

"So that's why he was so keen on my going! The old romantic!" In spite of her annoyance Lucy began to laugh. "Do you know Greg, that's the first time in my life I have ever known Matthew keep something from me."

Greg's eyes were troubled. "There's something else he has been keeping from you Lucy, something important, but he only kept it from you to relieve you of worry."

Lucy's heart missed a beat. "He hasn't confessed while I've been away? He promised me…"

"Well yes, Lucy, but that is not the problem."

"Not the problem?" Lucy was on her feet. "Has he been arrested?"

"Please listen, Lucy. Matthew hasn't been arrested, he is safe at Kelly's place waiting for us, and we shall see him tomorrow."

"How do you know that?" Lucy said slowly. Keeping her eyes on Greg's face she sat down again on the rug, a formless black fear rising in the back of her mind.

"Tell me," she said.

Greg took her hand. "You remember that Matthew told me about the shooting? That it was he who did it, not Jarvis, as I thought?"

"Yes." Lucy's eyes did not leave his face.

"He also told me that once you and I had left he would make sure your name was cleared. Matthew intended to make a full written confession and sign it."

Lucy recoiled in horror. "You agreed to let him do that? I could have got him away." She snatched her hand away, but Greg caught it and turned her to face him again.

"I'm sorry Lucy, let me finish and you'll understand. Trust me, Lucy."

She looked into the intense grey eyes and suddenly knew she could trust completely. She waited; his eyes were full of compassion.

"Matthew," he said softly, "Matthew is very ill Lucy; he has known it for a long time. Tuberculosis. He doesn't have much time left."

Her mind dismissed it. Greg was talking about someone else, not Matthew. Aloud, she said firmly; "Matthew's not ill. He's old of course, and becoming rather frail, but he's not ill, he hasn't even seen a doctor since we came to Australia."

"No dear, he didn't need to see a doctor, he knew what was wrong. He was told in London, over five years ago. He was going to sell up and come and live with you in Singapore, because the doctors said the climate would be better for him. Then he received your letter asking for help, so he came anyway. He didn't tell you because you had enough to worry about."

Lucy was visibly shrinking before his gaze, and Greg took her in his arms and rocked her gently. "Matthew told me that as soon as he got out of the London air he felt so much better. The doctors there only gave him about eighteen months to live, and because he came here he has had five years."

Lucy's eyes were full of horror. "Yes, five years of hard work, heavy work he wasn't fit for! It's all my fault…"

"No my dear, it's noone's fault, it's just life that's all. Matthew has had a good life, and he is not unhappy. He told me that he wouldn't have missed these last five years for anything."

Lucy gave a strange cry. "But why didn't he tell me? We have always told each other everything. And if he told you about it so long ago why did you keep it from me? How could you?"

"Because Matthew made me swear I would not tell you until now. He made me promise Lucy. He made me swear on my love for you, that I would care for you and protect you on the trip to the goldfields, and would keep secret his intention to confess to the shooting, and his condition. He knew it would be a difficult trip, and did not want you to be worried".

Lucy's tragic face tore at Greg's heartstrings, but he knew he had to complete his task.

"Matthew knows you love him, Lucy, and he understood what this news would mean to you. That's why he could not tell you this himself, he cannot bear to see your grief. I am to tell you that he wants things to be just the same as usual, and doesn't want any fuss. He has been so happy at Kelly's place, and he wants life to go on as normal as long as possible. He does not want to see you cry."

She broke down then and sobbed, great racking sounds as if her heart would break. Greg held her closely, rocking her like a child, murmuring his love while he caressed her hair, but she would not be comforted.

"Are you all right?"

Lucy, lost in deep thought, looked up uncertainly as if she had forgotten where she was. "Oh yes, Greg. Thank you. I'm quite all right."

She's not, Greg thought, as they pushed the horses on towards the creek which bordered Kelly's place. He tried again.

"You won't be too upset when you see Matthew? Jennie said he has become very frail."

"Of course not. I just can't wait to get there."

As if to prove her point Lucy dug in her heels, urging her mare to a canter for the last few hundred yards. Suddenly Beth and Mitch appeared, and Greg smiled as he saw them run back inside the cabin for their mother.

As Lucy dismounted, Lizzie came running out, and the two women embraced. Lizzie wiped tears of joy from her eyes with the edge of her apron, as she kept up a stream of disconnected chatter.

"Oh my Lord! Miss Catherine, well of course I know it's Lucy really, but still…Beth, leave Miss Lucy alone do, and of course you'll have heard…We have missed you so, but it's all fine here. Mr. Lamont do come in."

They entered the cabin and Lucy said "Where's Matthew?"

"He's at Maida Beach. He's been so poorly, and hasn't been out for a few days, but today he felt so much better he wanted to do some fishing."

"Fishing? Is he alone?" Lucy asked, a little alarmed.

"Bless you, no, Tomghin is with him. He never lets Matthew go anywhere without him, waits on him hand and foot he does." Lizzie put her arm round Lucy. "Don't worry, he's well looked after."

"I know Lizzie, but…oh Lizzie…"

"Can't wrap him in cotton wool Miss Catherine, er…Lucy. Drat it, I'll never remember."

Lucy smiled. "Thank you Lizzie, you and Tom, for all your help to us. We have lots to talk about, but first I must go and see Matthew."

They watched her go, remounting her horse and cantering away west. Lizzie turned to Greg.

"I expect she's very upset."

Greg nodded. "She took it badly yesterday when I told her, but she's better today, and is going to be brave for Matthew's sake."

"Poor lass. Thank goodness he's having one of his better days, although they are becoming few and far between. Come and sit down Mr. Lamont and I'll put the kettle on."

"If I'm to call you Lizzie, you are to call me Greg," he said. "As for Lucy, she'll feel better when she's seen Matthew and talked to him. I'll let them have half an hour and then I'll join them."

As Lizzie bustled around the tiny cabin, Greg talked briefly about their trip, and then, as they sipped their tea, confided that he and Lucy were to be married.

Lizzie squealed with delight, shouting to the children and repeating over and over, "Oh Catherine...Lucy...she'll make a beautiful bride...do you hear Mitch, Beth...Oh Mr. Lamont...Greg I mean...."

Her excitement had only subsided a little before it took off again as Tom entered. "Oh Tom, you must have guessed, Miss Catherine's back, I mean Lucy of course, and she's going to marry Mr. Lamont."

Tom pumped Greg's hand up and down as if he would never stop. "Well, I never," he kept repeating. "Well, I never."

Lizzie suddenly remembered the cheese. "Oh my Lord the cheese! Come on children, help me paddle the cheese, come on Mitch, you as well, then we can be done for when Miss Catherine comes back...I mean Lucy..."

Greg and Tom settled back at the kitchen table and Tom helped himself to tea from the pot, and refilled Greg's cup.

"It's real good news this is, Mr. Lamont," he said. "Our Miss Catherine can do with a bit o' luck; after all she's been through." He stopped, and his face changed.

"What is it Tom? And my name is Greg, by the way."

"I was only thinking, well, it just occurred to me..."

"If you're bothered what might happen to Kelly's place, don't worry Tom. Lucy really loves this place; I know she won't want to leave it".

Tom looked disconcerted. "But what about you, sir? This is only a very small spread; it wouldn't suit you after the Lamont station, not enough land for cattle."

"I've already been thinking about it Tom, and if Lucy agrees I think I have the answer. A third of the Lamont station is mine, and as we adjoin Kelly's place, I think my brother and sister will agree to me taking some land on this side and adding it to Kelly's place. Then I'll be out of their hair," he added, smiling.

"You mean Kelly's place will be bigger?" Tom said.

"Yes. Think of it Tom, we can build up a prize herd, that's always been my ambition, and you will be head stockman. Of course I have to discuss it with Lucy, but I think she will agree, I doubt she would want to move to the Lamont station."

"But your brother and sister, surely they will not want to lose a third of their land?"

"I think they will. We have far too much anyway, and it will still be in the family. My sister Mary is getting married soon to one of our stockmen, and they will need room at the house to expand. I think they'll be happy about my moving out."

"Well Greg, if it works out that way it will be wonderful," said Tom, "And I wish you both luck. It's time our Catherine had a bit of luck."

"I'll try hard to make her happy, Tom."

"You can't fail to make her happier than that last cruel pig she was married to…begging your pardon, Greg."

"Don't worry Tom, I know all about it. As you say, he was a cruel pig. I met her in Singapore you know Tom, the same night she got engaged to Sir Gilbert."

"Ah yes, poor girl…"

"Well, it was her choice, of course," Greg said, voicing the thought over which he had agonised so long. "But she was young, and of course didn't know the kind of man he was. It's so easy for a young girl to have her head turned by someone as rich and powerful as Sir Gilbert Howell."

"I beg your pardon sir!" Tom's tone was so fierce that Greg looked up in surprise. "I hope you aren't implying that our Miss Catherine married that cruel pig for his money!"

Greg was startled. "Well…er…"

"I hope you're not!" Tom exploded. "Because if you are, you and me had better go out to the yard and I'll knock your block off!"

"Of course not Tom, please don't be offended. I should not have said what I did. I have no idea why Lucy married Sir Gilbert, it has just always struck me as odd that she did."

"Odd? Odd?" Tom was still angry. "Odd to try and keep her father out of prison and provide for his old age? I wouldn't call it odd, I'd call it self-sacrifice, that's what I'd call it."

"Prison? What do you mean? Are you sure?"

"Of course I'm sure. Matthew told me and Lizzie everything, when the constable was here. We were that upset for our Miss Catherine…"

"Tom, you must believe that I know nothing of this. Please tell me what happened."

When Lizzie returned to the kitchen Tom had gone back to his work and she found Greg sitting alone, staring out of the window. As she entered, he rose to his feet and gave her a shaky smile.

"I'll go and find Lucy and Matthew at this famous Maida Beach, if you'll direct me, Lizzie."

She accompanied him to the door and pointed out the way. As he turned to go, she told him again how pleased she was about the wedding. He smiled briefly.

"I'll do my best for her Lizzie," he said.

"I know that Greg, and she'll do her best for you. Always does her best for everyone she meets, does our Catherine…Lucy."

"Yes, I realise that now," Greg said slowly. "You know Lizzie, men are stupid creatures sometimes, can't see what is under their noses, and when they see it they don't believe it."

"Bless you Greg; I know how daft men can be. That's what I'm always telling Tom!"

"Oh well, we can learn Lizzie. We get it right in the end."

He mounted his horse and rode off in the direction she indicated. Lizzie went back to the cheese smiling but perplexed. "Now what was all that about?" she murmured as she began to stir.

Matthew and Lucy were sitting on a rock near the water's edge, and Greg was relieved to see they seemed to be chatting happily. Matthew hailed him as he dismounted, and voiced his congratulations.

"I shall be glad to get this young lady off my hands at last," he said. "She has always been a trial to me, ever since she was at school."

"Now don't start telling tales about my school days, Matthew," Lucy retorted. "I want to get him to the altar before he finds out my bad points, time enough for that after we're married."

She giggled, and Matthew said, "Have some lemonade."

Greg took the proffered water bottle. It was plain there was to be no dolorous sadness here. He took a swig of lemonade and gazed out to sea.

"Guess what Greg?" Lucy said happily. "Matthew has had a long letter from Margot and William Graham. He wrote to them with all our news and had a reply yesterday." She smiled. "I can't wait to read it."

"Lucy's been telling me about your gold mine," Matthew remarked, as if finding a gold mine was something one did every day.

"Yes, and I'm looking forward to telling the family," Greg said cheerfully. "But Lucy, I've been thinking. If you've no objection, and if there's enough, I'd like my share of the gold to found a school in Stannerton. What do you think?"

"It sounds a wonderful idea. What made you think of it?"

"I want to do something as a memorial to Uncle Jack. It will mean children like Beth and Mitch, and Clancy Bright's tribe won't have to go away to Perth when they are older, as Sam and I did." He hesitated. "You're sure you don't mind? Losing the gold I mean? It's going to be a lot of money."

Lucy smiled. "I've had gold all my life Greg, and plenty of it," she answered. "Perhaps not the kind of gold that will found the school, but a more precious kind."

"What other kind is there?"

"Friendship, Greg, Matthew and I were talking about it a while ago. I've always found it, lovely strands of golden friendship which have always been there when I needed them. There was everyone in England, and dear Miss Collins, then in Singapore there was Margot and William, and Lela, and of course my dear Jarvis." She bit her lip, but continued. "Then when we came here there was Bob Middleton, and the men who helped with the house, and Tom and Lizzie and Jennie Moore, and of course, you Greg." She smiled shyly, and Greg took her hand and found a space to sit beside her.

"I'm glad you feel as I do, about the school." He looked out to sea and took a deep breath. "So this is Maida Beach? It's certainly a beautiful spot."

"More beautiful in a few minutes as the sun goes down," said Lucy. "We'll watch a bit longer and then we'll have to move."

She looked across at Greg, and noticed again the way the thick brown hair curled at the nape of his neck. *He looked every inch the bushman today, but she knew that he could become the frog prince again in an instant, and she was in love with both of them.* The bushman was the one who broke the silence.

"You don't seem to have caught any fish," he said.

"That's all you know," Matthew retorted. "Tomghin has taken them back to the house; you'll be having them for supper."

They sat and watched the huge red orb of the sun drop slowly towards the sea. Suddenly Lucy gave a start, and jumped to her feet.

"Look Uncle! I can't believe it! It's the *Selangor Lady!*"

Matthew and Greg got to their feet, Matthew shading his eyes against the sun. It was indeed the *Selangor Lady* in her new role as a trader, passing them in full sail as she made her way down the coast.

A sense of quiet peace enveloped them as they stood together and watched her canvas billowing strongly with the shoreward wind, and for a few moments it was as if Jarvis was with them, as they watched the *Selangor Lady* slowly disappear in the rosy gleam of the setting sun.